Anne snuggled closer to Michael,

aware of the impropriety of her behavior as she did so. Still, he'd seen her shamed, he'd held her as she'd cried and eased her broken pride; what difference would it make if she rested against him, particularly when he'd helped her forget her embarrassment?

"Ah, lass, you'd better stop doing that." He shifted against the grass and ran his fingers through her hair, lightly tugging the knots out. "I'll take you back inside."

But he made no effort to move.

Neither did she.

Time passed, seconds in which a lazy heat curled through her. The heavens were a velvety black, filling the land with shadows; but the moon tinged Michael's hair with a pale silver glow, and suddenly Anne saw the light amidst the dark, the soothing quality of pleasure especially when surrounded by pain. In that moment she made a decision.

Tonight, she would live, and love.

Tomorrow she'd deal with the consequences.

"Whatever you do, don't miss *Heart of the Dove* for some heart-pounding romance, electrifying magic, and first-class writing from the extremely talented Tracy Fobes, whose novels are so fresh, innovative and different in scope that you can't help wondering what she will come up with next." —*Belles and Beaux of Romance*

"Gifted with an ability to spin yarns of incomparable splendor, Tracy Fobes casts a spell on her readers from page one." —*Under the Covers Book Reviews*

TOUCH NOT THE CAT

"Tracy Fobes' debut is a stunning novel, beautifully blending the haunting magic of the Highlands with a sensual romance and a love that has the power to confront an ancient curse. . . . You'll be lured into the magical and highly romantic world Tracy Fobes creates in this dazzling debut. . . . She crafts memorable characters and a spellbinding paranormal romance that will appeal to readers seeking something very special."

—*Romantic Times*

"Pulled into a world where mythical creatures, magical transformations, and a legendary love exist, the reader is taken on a delightful journey into the unbelievable, made believable by Ms. Fobes' extraordinary skill as a storyteller." —*Rendezvous*

"*Touch Not the Cat* is an intriguing and passionate story. The fairy magic of the Scots is woven throughout the tale and gives a mystical atmosphere that will appeal to lovers of romance and fantasy alike. An excellent debut." —*Writers Write*

Books by Tracy Fobes

Forbidden Garden
Touch Not the Cat
Heart of the Dove

Published by POCKET BOOKS

TRACY FOBES

FORBIDDEN GARDEN

SONNET BOOKS

New York   London   Toronto   Sydney   Singapore

This book is a work of fiction. Names, characters, places and incidents are products of the author's imagination or are used ficti-
tiously. Any resemblance to actual events or locales or persons, living or dead, is entirely coincidental.

An *Original* Publication of POCKET BOOKS

 A Sonnet Book published by
POCKET BOOKS, a division of Simon & Schuster Inc.
1230 Avenue of the Americas, New York, NY 10020

ISBN: 0-671-04173-8

First Sonnet Books printing March 2000

10 9 8 7 6 5 4 3 2 1

SONNET BOOKS and colophon are trademarks of
Simon & Schuster Inc.

Front cover illustration by Gregg Gulbronson

Printed in the U.S.A.

*This book is for my husband, Dan,
with love*

FORBIDDEN GARDEN

1

London, England,
1860

When Anne Sherwood heard footsteps crunching down the gravel drive toward her, she clenched her pencil and groaned aloud. She was in a black mood and wanted only to be left alone, to wrestle with her sketchbook. The curves and lines in her illustration of *Violaceae* looked all wrong, the flower head too large, the leaves too pointed.

A child, she thought, could do better.

She'd spent most of the morning on that drawing, trying to duplicate the winsome beauty of spring's first violets peeping out from beneath brown, moldy leaves. She'd wanted to capture that excitement of new beginnings in her sketch. And yet she seemed fated to draw only rubbish today. Perhaps her sketch looked dull because she felt dull.

The sound of boots striding along the gravel path grew louder. She looked up and recognized the man coming toward her. Sir Richard Hooker, her cousin, had given her a post as botanical illustrator at Kew Gardens. He'd raved about the beauty of the violets in this spot, but she couldn't drag her attention from the cracked fountain, clogged with debris and abandoned, which squatted among the dead leaves like a rotting mushroom. Rather than smell promise in the moist earth, she smelled decay. Even the sunlight that fought its way through the canopy of leaves above her shone a sickly yellow.

If there was beauty to be found here, she couldn't see it. Indeed, beauty held no interest for her. She felt unlovely and severe, far older than her five-and-twenty years, and for good reason. Her brief marriage had aged her a lifetime. Henry, Baron Sherwood, had been her husband for five long years before dying of apoplexy. He had touched her but left her untouched.

Still, that severity didn't show in the lustrous sheen of her dark blond hair or in her full lower lip. It certainly didn't show in the more-than-generous breasts and hips that mocked the loneliness she'd deliberately immersed herself in. Only the small lines above her delicate nose hinted of cynicism and broken dreams.

Frowning, Anne pressed her pencil firmly against the paper, creating her first truly smooth line in hours . . . until the black core slid out of the top of the pencil. Suddenly bereft of lead, the wood casing created a tiny rip on the paper. She glared at the pencil for a moment, then crumpled the paper she'd been sketching on. She had no patience for failure, particularly her own.

Sir Richard stopped by her side. "How does it go, Anne?"

He stood nearly a head taller than she, his eyes a faded blue in his thin, bewhiskered face. Dressed in a tweed frock coat and fawn trousers, both impeccably tailored and pressed, he appeared both a scholar and a man who knew his way around the drawing rooms of London. He laced his hands behind his back and studied her, his expression kind.

"Fairly well." She placed her pencil and sketchbook in her lap and disciplined her features into a pleasant expression.

His gaze slid to the crumpled piece of paper. He must have known she was lying, but he nodded anyway. "Isn't this a beautiful spot?"

Unwilling to answer, she shrugged. She didn't want to tell him how she couldn't see anything but the crumbling fountain. She didn't want to admit how she loathed these gardens but accepted them, too. The tentative unfurling of color around her reminded her how lifeless she'd become, but at the same time, Kew Gardens represented her salvation. Her post as botanical illustrator was her one good chance of emerging in the world as a respected scholar in her own right.

He shifted from one foot to the other. "Eliza and I missed you at breakfast."

"I've been here since dawn." She did that sometimes—left the house before anyone knew she had gone. Her time with Henry had left her with more than black moods. She'd also learned to treasure her freedom. She was an artist, one who saw past the frills to the simple lines beneath, and her marriage had taught her a glaring truth about herself. She required independence. She would never again live by anyone's dictates but her own.

" 'Tis nearly noon. Come back to Kew Cottage with me," he coaxed. "Eliza has asked Cook to prepare us a small repast."

Sir Richard held out a hand. She accepted it and rose from her wooden folding chair, noticing how moist his skin felt. He gripped her hand slightly harder than necessary before letting her go.

She eyed him carefully. "A repast? Why?"

"We have a visitor."

"I didn't know you and Eliza were expecting anyone today."

He grimaced wryly. "Lord Connock, an Irish nobleman, has been in London visiting with the Royal Botanic Society in Regent's Park. He's decided to pay us a call."

Nonplussed, Anne searched her memory. The name sounded familiar, but she couldn't remember the context in which she'd heard it before. Regardless, she wasn't in the mood to entertain anyone. "Have I met him before?"

"I don't think so."

"His name sounds familiar."

"You've probably heard Eliza and me grumbling about him," he admitted. "Lord Connock's gardens in Ireland are the only ones that have more rare species of plants than Kew Gardens. Her Majesty is highly annoyed with the man for threatening the superiority of the royal gardens."

"He is a collector, then?"

"An obsessive one. Nearly bankrupted himself cultivating his glasshouses. He regained his fortune by selling rare plants. Oddly enough, a few of his rare plants were thought exclusively Kew's."

"Are you suggesting he bribed someone within Kew to smuggle out plants?"

"No, no, not at all. I'm simply saying that his resources for procuring rare plants are equal to if not better than ours. Lord Connock and I have corresponded about our methods, and if I remember correctly, he has a naturalist working for him, a Michael McEvoy, whose skills in the wild have no equal."

Anne raised an eyebrow, unimpressed. She'd met her share of adventurers who searched foreign lands for new species of plants. They were hard men who had grown used to living alone, in the wild, with only natives to talk to and gourds to drink from. Long spells in the jungle left them without manners and totally unfit for polite society.

Three years ago she'd spoken with Charles Barter just before he'd joined Baikie's Niger expedition. She'd found him a loud-mouthed bore. After Barter had succumbed to dysentery and died somewhere in Africa, Sir Richard had commissioned Richard Oldham, a young gardener, to explore the Japanese islands and China seas. The youth had cornered her and kissed her the night before he'd sailed. She'd felt nothing but a sense of invasion and had left the youth with a decided limp.

She supposed men who lived so close to death took advantage of every chance to live life to its fullest; nevertheless, she shuddered at the thought of Lord Connock's naturalist, an adventurer who knew no equal. "Has Lord Connock brought Mr. McEvoy with him?"

"I don't believe so."

"Thank God."

"Anne?" Sir Richard's gaze on her was complex, censuring and sympathetic all at once.

In a flat voice she said, "Michael McEvoy sounds like an adventurer, and a talented one at that. I have no time for adventurers."

Her cousin winced. She knew he'd caught the deeper meaning beneath what she'd said. Baron Sherwood, in his own wizened little way, had been an adventurer, a man who used women. He'd married her because he had recognized her talent. For five years she had acted as his secretary, copyist, and illustrator, and when they had finished *Encyclopedia of Flowering Plants*, he had taken full credit for the work. But he'd never loved her. The woman who had shown up at his graveside—Henry's mistress—was more than adequate proof of that.

"I've corresponded with Lord Connock for more than a year," Sir Richard said more gently. "His naturalist is often abroad. I doubt you'll even meet him. Why not come and talk to Lord Connock? He has some interesting news for us, or so he claims."

She hesitated, hearing the odd inflection to his voice, and tried to fight off an answering spark of curiosity. She didn't want to involve herself in Lord Connock's intrigues in the plant world. She simply wished to sketch.

In the end, however, the excitement in Sir Richard's eyes snared her. "Interesting in what way?"

"Come with me and find out."

She glanced down at her gown. A navy day dress of severe cut and without a single gewgaw, it was hardly fit for entertaining but perfect in Anne's opinion. Her wardrobe stood full of such gowns, uniforms that downplayed her femininity in exchange for competence and trustworthiness. She wanted the men who denied her access to their scholarly circles to see her as a fellow scholar, not a woman. God willing, no one would ever discover her one feminine weakness.

Sir Richard drew her toward the pony cart and

helped her climb in. As he joined her and they began to plod back toward Kew Cottage, she imagined the meeting ahead. Anticipations of awkward conversation and embarrassing silences filled her. She had never been good at idle chatter and now refused to indulge in it, while many believed small talk was all a woman could manage. Still, she felt a curious glow within her and realized that Sir Richard's excitement had infected her.

Perhaps this time the awkward conversation and embarrassing silences would prove worthwhile.

In less than ten minutes the pony cart rattled to a halt outside Kew Cottage, a rustic villa Anne had called home for the past two years. Built of red brick, with decorative timber framing and a thatched roof, the cottage sported a tangled mantle of brown vines that would soon bloom into fragrant honeysuckle and scarlet climbing roses. For now, ivy provided the only green foil to the browns of winter, and a tendril of the stuff brushed her hand as she climbed out of the cart and walked with Sir Richard to the front door.

Eliza met them in the foyer, the wrinkles near the corners of her eyes hardly noticeable next to her pretty smile and soft brown waves of hair. She grasped Anne's hands, pausing long enough to level a significant stare at Sir Richard. "Lord Connock has paid us a call. He has exciting news."

"Yes, I've heard."

Anne hardly had time to say anything else, for suddenly Eliza was patting her on the cheeks, drawing color into them, then smoothing her curls with one hand. When she'd finished, the older woman stood back a pace from Anne and considered her for a moment before nodding briskly. "That'll have to do."

Anne grew cold at her pronouncement. Sir Richard and his wife acted as though they considered this mysterious Lord Connock a potential beau. She felt weary and bitter, in no mood to fend off some unexpected and confounding matchmaking attempt. Her mind searched for a way to escape. She cast an involuntary glance at the front door.

Sir Richard stepped to her side and took her arm. Eliza grabbed the other one.

Outflanked, Anne thought. She examined the pair with a narrowed stare. "I find it very odd that you two have left our distinguished visitor alone in the salon in your effort to find me and make me presentable. Why is it so important that I meet him? What can I possibly add to the conversation? You both know I have no interest in entertaining male suitors—"

Eliza's step faltered. Guilt flickered behind her brown eyes. "Why, Anne, Lord Connock has not come courting. He reviewed your orchid plates, the ones we donated to the Royal Botanic Society, and was so dazzled that he came here to meet you. He has an exciting proposition for you."

"Tell me Lord Connock's exciting proposition, now, before I meet him. I don't like surprises."

"Neither do I, Mrs. Sherwood," a male voice said from the doorway to the salon.

Anne looked up and met the gaze of an older man, his hair a distinguished-looking brown shot with gray. At least twice her age, he studied her, the pouches beneath his blue eyes making him look weary. His full lips seemed far too pink, surrounded as they were by grayish-brown whiskers and a small mustache.

"Lord Connock, a pleasure to meet you." Anne sank into a curtsey, a rueful smile on her lips.

Connock bowed briefly at the waist, and in that quick moment she scanned him, realizing he didn't stand much taller than she, his body stocky and muscular despite his advancing years.

Eliza, her attitude full of hopeful satisfaction, ushered them into the salon and poured a round of tea for all.

Lord Connock's attention rested briefly on the painted clematis and nasturtium climbing the walls before he focused on Anne. "Did you paint these?" he asked, his voice cultured, mellifluous.

Anne nodded unwillingly. "During the winter months, I often paint flower garlands in rooms that could use a bit of brightening."

Eliza handed out the tea, bringing temporary quiet to the salon. Anne selected a comfortable damask chair and sat, the slight rattle of her cup in its saucer the only evidence of her nervousness.

Sir Richard sank onto a settee and sipped his tea. "Our Anne has talent, does she not?"

"Indeed." Lord Connock, the only one left standing, finally chose a seat. Still, when he sat down, he seemed tense, as if he might spring up from the cushion at any moment. The ruddy glow to his cheeks, his intense gaze, the suppressed energy in his frame, all spoke of a high-strung disposition. "And she doesn't like surprises."

Anne forced a smile to her lips. "Thank you, sir, for your compliment on my talent. I understand you reviewed my orchid plates."

"I did, and I found them marvelous," he enthused. "Tell me about your training. Whom did you study with?"

"Training?"

The enthusiasm drained from his face. "Surely you didn't learn to draw like that on your own."

Startled by the accusation, she said nothing.

Head tilted, Lord Connock leaned forward in his chair. "How much experience have you had in dissection?"

"None."

Eyebrows raised, he shot Sir Richard a frown. The other man simply shrugged. Lord Connock returned his attention to Anne. "I find it nearly impossible to imagine anyone could portray orchids in such fine detail without formal training and firsthand experience."

His verbal attack forced her from her chair. She stood and walked to the bay window, where a group of the very orchids she'd drawn sat drooping in the sun. All of the critics who had reviewed her drawings had said the same thing as Lord Connock. Impossible for a woman to have such a fine, detailed hand. Unthinkable for a woman to understand the intricacies of floral structure. The conclusion? She was copying her late husband's work, perhaps even putting her name to drawings he'd never published. They would never believe her if she told them that she, not Henry, had sketched every one of the plates in his *Encyclopedia of Flowering Plants*. Henry had stolen from her, not the other way around.

"Lord Connock," she began, her voice tight, "I began drawing plants and landscapes just after I started to walk. Through the years I've honed my skills. I have no formal training. Instead I rely upon many years of experience and a determination to improve myself. If you are suggesting that the orchid plates are not my own, I'm afraid I'll have to excuse myself."

"No, no." Lord Connock rose from his chair and stepped quickly to her side. " 'Tis obvious your ability is God-given, an inborn talent so few of us possess."

Some of the stiffness left her limbs. "Thank you for allowing that much."

"Your parents must be very proud of you."

"My parents own a large horse farm in Cambridge that consumes all of their free time. I'm afraid I disappointed them with my drawings. They would rather I had learned to ride."

Anne said this without the slightest hint of bitterness. Her parents had never understood her. When her mother had married her off to Baron Sherwood at the tender age of eighteen, the ties between them had broken completely, much to everyone's satisfaction.

"But *we* are proud of her," Sir Richard insisted, touching her arm in a fatherly gesture.

Eliza, her face composed but her eyes alight, refilled their cups with tea.

"With good reason." Lord Connock moved closer to her side. "In our correspondence, Sir Richard has often mentioned you. He said you have a remarkable way with the plants themselves. Plants that expire under the supervision of hired gardeners seem to thrive when you tend them."

Warmth crept into Anne's cheeks. "Sir Richard tries to turn commonsense plant care into something magical."

"There is a bit of magic in you, Anne," Sir Richard insisted.

Frowning, she fell silent. She had no desire to explain to Lord Connock the strange connection she felt to plants. He would never understand how the petals and leaves of a flower seemed to speak to her, creating colors in her mind that she translated into simple needs. He would think her mad.

Instead, she touched an orchid's ivory petal with a gentle finger, its exotic, almost waxen beauty at odds with its delicate coloring. She focused on its long, swordlike leaves and saw brownish-red. This flower was thirsty. It was dying, despite the moist soil in which it rooted. As always, the contradiction confused her.

"Orchids are my favorite," she said, distracted. "But they don't seem to like England. They die quickly, as though longing for home."

Lord Connock nodded toward the plant on the sill before her. "And this one? It seems healthy enough."

"It will die soon. It's thirsty."

"Thirsty?" He pressed a finger against the mulch at the orchid's base. "The soil feels moist enough."

Anne shrugged. "Kew's orchid losses have always been high, even though we nurse them carefully in our glasshouses. Orchids have needs we don't understand, and until we discover what they are, the orchids will die."

The Irish nobleman nodded thoughtfully. "I have a naturalist working for me who has brought back many species of orchids from foreign locations. Since orchids are your favorites, Mrs. Sherwood, I will ask him what sort of conditions the orchids grow naturally in. Perhaps there is something the English growers have missed. Indeed, you could even ask him yourself."

"He is here?"

"No, Mr. McEvoy is abroad. I expect him to return to Ireland in the next few weeks. I'm hoping you'll accompany me home, Mrs. Sherwood, and discuss orchids with him then."

She stilled, not certain what had prompted his offer. Common sense suggested that when a man asked a woman to his home, he had more than polite conversation in mind. And yet, regardless of Eliza's rather obvious hopes, Lord Connock's expression had remained utterly devoid of physical interest in her. "Why do you wish to bring me to Ireland?"

"I'd like you to return to Glendale Hall with me for a brief stay as a botanical illustrator."

"You want to hire me?"

"Sir Richard has explained to me your difficulty. You're a fine artist who receives no recognition for her work. I had planned to employ Mr. Townsend of the Royal Botanic Society, but when I saw your sketches, I changed my mind. I propose you return to Glendale Hall with me and illustrate the species I have collected, many of them new and rare.

"Indeed, there is a tree you must see, an odd-looking specimen growing on my estate that has no match. If you document this tree for me, Mrs. Sherwood, no one will accuse you of copying your husband's work, because he died before this species was discovered. You will finally be accorded the acclaim you deserve."

"What does this tree look like, and where did it come from?" Anne asked. Doubt gave her voice an inflection that Lord Connock didn't appear to notice.

"My naturalist brought it back from the far reaches of the Himalayas. I've made a sketch of it myself. It's not very good." He reached into his jacket and withdrew a piece of rolled vellum, which he then unfurled before her. "I've tried to make sketches of my collection, but I can't. I haven't the talent. And I demand only the best." He admitted his inadequacy without the slightest degree of shame, his calm dignity swaying her determination to have nothing to do with him.

She took the vellum and examined his sketch near the window, in full light of the afternoon sun. Thick, bold lines and disproportionate shapes cut across the vellum. She had to agree with him. He hadn't much talent as an illustrator. The tree might just as easily have been a new species of primate.

"I need you, Mrs. Sherwood. Just for a few months. I can't pay you much. A stipend, at most. My finances aren't what they used to be. Nevertheless, you won't regret helping me, I assure you." He spoke quietly yet passionately, his hands spread open in a supplicating gesture she couldn't ignore.

His plea struck at the core of her own need. She wanted nothing more than to have her work credited to her name. She rolled the vellum up carefully and handed it back to him. Inside, her stomach knotted in a tight coil.

If she stayed on at Kew Gardens, she might never convince scholarly circles of her expertise as a botanical illustrator. She had submitted sketch after sketch, plate after plate, with little success. Even Sir Richard couldn't convince the critics otherwise. He was family, they said, which rendered his defense of her suspect.

But Lord Connock was not a relative. Indeed, he was a respected peer and a well-known collector. His word would have more weight in scholarly circles. If he promoted her work, she might finally gain what she'd been seeking the past several years.

Breath coming quicker, she realized she couldn't refuse him. His offer came too close to satisfying the compulsions that had ruled her life for the last seven years. With Lord Connock's help, she would realize success. And all she had to do was draw.

"I'll come to Glendale Hall," she said, and felt a spark of excitement she hadn't known in ages.

2

*A*nne closed her eyes and tried to sleep, but she couldn't even relax. Squeezed between a matron holding a toddler and a gent whose snores could wake the dead, she glanced out the window at wild and desolate hills. As the stagecoach rocked over a nasty pothole, she wondered how much longer she'd find herself confined to its interior.

Lord Connock had left for Ireland within a week of their meeting in Kew Gardens. She'd taken a bit more time, finishing a few sketches before arranging passage to Ireland. Her widowed status freed her from the need of a chaperone, and so she'd traveled alone to Liverpool, in a first-class compartment aboard a passenger train. A steamer packet had taken her across the gray Irish seas and deposited her in Dublin that morning.

Dublin. She'd heard much of the city from a young scullery maid they'd hired at Kew Gardens. The girl had talked of sweet Irish soil and potatoes with cabbage and emerald hills and quaint thatched cottages until Anne could almost see the leprechauns dancing at the end of the rainbow. She'd expected the city to dazzle her. Instead she'd discovered filthy alleys and streets, gaunt Irish faces, babbling Irish voices, and the reek of freshly caught fish.

As in most cities, many of Dublin's plants looked warped, their stems too long or their growth stunted for lack of sunshine and water. They grew between cracks in stone and in ditches filled with sewage, and in some of them Anne had sensed madness. The knowledge had depressed her. She'd decided to buy a seat on the first stagecoach heading into the Wicklow Mountains, rather than wait for Lord Connock's carriage.

They'd rattled down Military Road for several hours. Now, as dusk slowly gave way to the velvety black of night, their driver shouted out, "Sally Gap!" Anne looked out the window, craning her neck to see the passage carved out of the mountains. Black shapes and an unsettling perception of sheer stone walls filled her vision.

Without warning, the conveyance suffered a huge bump that sent her bouncing off her seat before settling back into the same, uncomfortable rhythm. The old man woke up abruptly and uttered a few choice curses, while the matron crossed herself and her toddler wailed.

Minutes later they slowed to a halt. The old man grabbed the matron's hand, and together they got off the stagecoach at a station whose sign proclaimed Glencree. Anne also disembarked to stretch her legs and looked at the mountains which created a gray shadow against purplish skies. A forest of oak stretched up the slopes about halfway before surrendering to rocks and heath.

"The mountain's called Kippure," the driver slurred, evidently following her gaze. "Those to the south are Mullaghcleevaun, Tonelagee, and Lugnaquilla. Balkilly's not five miles away."

Anne refocused on the driver. "How long are we stopping here?"

"Ten minutes, ma'am."

Grateful for every second, she walked away and stretched, her palms pressed against the small of her back. About halfway through their respite, the sound of thumping hooves filled the yard, accompanied by the squeaks and groans of an ill-used carriage. Seconds later, an elderly man in a pony cart raced past the station. A cap covered his gray hair and his face had a ruddy flush, while the pony frothed at the mouth.

Anne watched them disappear down the road, then wandered back over to the driver, whose raised eyebrows expressed a good measure of curiosity.

"The way old Paddy's driving," the driver muttered, "you'd think he found a crock full of gold. Wonder what he has in that cart of his."

She didn't feel the same spark of curiosity. She simply wanted a warm bed that didn't rock back and forth. "I suppose we'll never know."

He grunted and gestured toward the carriage. "Hop back in, ma'am, and we'll be at Balkilly within half an hour."

For the first time, she noticed an earthenware jug propped up against the driver's bench. His partner, a bearded man who wore a tattered cap, sprawled on the bench. He snored at the sky.

The driver nudged his head toward the stagecoach door. "Are you coming with us, or will you be staying here at Glencree?"

With a sigh, Anne boarded the stagecoach and leaned against the cracked leather seat. The driver closed the door behind her and climbed back onto his bench. Moments later the carriage was swaying and bumping in the tiresome manner she had grown less and less able to tolerate. If she had to remain inside the compartment for more than half an hour, she just might be tempted to scream.

The smell of strong Irish whiskey—poteen maybe— drifted into the compartment. A sudden pain in her temples made her wince. She hoped those two fools hadn't been dipping too hard into that jug of theirs. She didn't relish the thought of running off the road and breaking her neck.

The stagecoach picked up speed.

Laughter from the driver's seat accosted her ears. The carriage started shimmying in an odd manner, back and forth as though the driver were following the twisting path of a snake.

She frowned. Whatever were they doing up there?

The shimmying motion continued sporadically for a minute or so, each instance followed by a spate of laughter. Anne stared at the roof above her with narrowed eyes. She wished she could force some common sense into the pair on the driver's bench through sheer willpower.

Without warning, a horrendous screeching noise filled the carriage. The wheels hit something hard. She cried out. The conveyance bounced into the air and down again. She flew off her seat, her hat squashed against the roof, and bumped her shoulder against the side wall. Before her backside resettled on the bench, the stagecoach jumped for a second time. Up in the air she went, and down again, her spine miserably jolted.

Her shawl flew through the air and draped itself across the doorknob on the third bump, and then, mercifully, the stagecoach ground to a halt and settled on an uneven keel.

She pressed her hand against her chest. Her heart gave one mighty thump before settling down into a rapid pace. She checked her limbs to make sure nothing had broken and then clasped the doorknob, prepared to give the driver the worst tongue lashing he'd ever experienced. Lips pressed together, she pushed the latch, snapped the door open, and stepped out.

Woods cloaked in impenetrable blackness surrounded her. Shaking, she assessed the stagecoach's condition. An old drag that some enterprising soul had purchased used from an aristocratic family and hitched up to a team of ill-matched hacks, the stagecoach hadn't borne the rough driving well. Three wheels looked fine, but a fourth had split in two different places. They'd come to rest in a ditch, she saw. The carriage listed toward its damaged wheel like a horse favoring a broken leg.

The driver had fallen to the road and lay near the horses, which snorted and danced in agitation. Still clutching the reins, he mumbled to himself. She raced over to him, certain she'd find his neck broken.

Poteen fumes nearly made her eyes water.

She poked him in the arm. "Driver, are you all right?"

He gave a drunken snort, swatted at her with his hand, and smiled before settling into a peaceful stupor.

Eyes narrowed, she assessed him thoroughly before moving on to his companion, still perched on the driver's bench. That hearty didn't appear much more sober. Although he sat at a crazy angle, fully awake, his gaze drifted in and out of focus. Whiskey fumes clung to him like bad perfume.

Her heart began to beat harder, this time with anger. "And you . . . are you drunk, too?"

He mumbled something, put his hand around a jug, and took a swig. The fool was drinking more. The louts hadn't an ounce of responsibility. She grabbed the jug from him and threw it into the woods. He peered at her owlishly before collapsing back against the bench.

No help there, she thought. She climbed down from the driver's seat and considered her options. She could either wait for rescue or walk the rest of the way to Balkilly. Since the thought of sleeping in the stagecoach's mildewed interior for an entire night almost made her ill, she decided to walk to the village and have a few hours' rest on a proper mattress. She was made of sturdy stuff. She could do it.

She returned to the driver and poked him on the arm again. "How far are we from the village of Balkilly? Five miles, you said?"

He opened one bleary eye and squinted into the black night.

"Only about two miles, ma'am."

"I'm going to walk to the village. If I arrive in a good mood, I'll send someone to rescue you."

"No, lassie, you have to stay in the stagecoach."

"I'm not staying. You're on your own."

"You have to stay."

"No, I don't. Good-bye."

The driver reached out and grasped the hem of her skirt. Brows drawn together, Anne frowned. "Let me go, sir." She tried to pull her skirts away from him, but he held on fast.

"Don't go alone. Not at night."

"I'll be perfectly fine," Anne insisted, irritation creeping into her tone. "I'd walk a lot farther than two miles for a warm, clean bed."

The man's face clenched into a mask of agitation. "You don't understand. You can't go. The woods are dangerous, especially at night. Stay here."

Anne paused. Something had flickered in the drunkard's eyes. "Why are the woods so dangerous?"

"Anything could be hiding in the undergrowth," he whispered. "The Cluricaun, the Far Darrig, the Pooka . . . or even the Dullahan."

"Dullahan? What is that? Some sort of badger?"

"Nay. 'Tis a hideous ghoul. He has no head and carries it under his arm as he rides the coach-a-bower. You can hear the coach-a-bower rumbling from miles away. And if the Dullahan sees you, he'll throw a basin of blood into your face."

Anne narrowed her eyes. Irish fairies! Or drunken hallucinations. She yanked her skirt from his hand. "I'll tell them in the village about our accident. Someone will come for you."

She walked away before he could protest further.

Around her, the night pressed in, smothering her in blackness. She slung a shawl around her shoulders and started off down the road, in the direction the stagecoach had been traveling. Ten minutes passed. Still, she saw nothing to indicate a nearby village.

Scanning the dark blanket of trees and thickets on either side of the lane, she quickened her pace. Soon her feet began to ache from stepping on stones in the road. She'd worn boots, but her frequent jaunts through Kew Gardens had abraded their soles, and now she chided herself for not buying a new pair before leaving

London. Hobbling a little, she moved to the grass strip that bordered the road.

A peculiar rustling noise to her left caught her attention. Even as her pace slowed, her heart began to beat just a little faster. The noise had a furtiveness about it, a purpose. She couldn't see anything; the edge of the woods hid all but the shadowy outline of tree trunks.

Anne was not a high-strung woman prone to fanciful imaginings. She did not fall prey to panic very easily. A woman on her own soon learned how to take care of herself. Even so, she felt an uncharacteristic stab of anxiety.

She held her breath and placed each foot carefully to avoid making any noise. Perhaps "it" didn't know she was nearby.

The rustling grew louder, as though someone had picked up a handful of dried leaves and crushed them in his palm.

Whatever it was, it had come closer.

Her chest grew tight. A primitive voice within her was saying a word over and over, but she refused to acknowledge it.

Wolves.

They knew she was near. She wasn't fooling them by walking quietly, making as little noise as possible. Still, if she ran, they might give up all pretense of secrecy and chase after her, jumping on her from behind and taking her down. Shivering, she continued to tiptoe along, but it was a fast tiptoe, she was almost gliding, and wildly she thought how proud Eliza would be of her, because ladies didn't walk, they glided across the floor with true aristocratic delicacy . . .

Suddenly, the rustling stopped. Whatever moved had grown still.

No, not wolves, she told herself. Wolves wouldn't paw around in the leaves, watching her. They would remain silent until they attacked. She must have heard branches blowing in the wind, or more likely a squirrel.

But her stomach still had a sour feeling to it.

She quickened her pace.

The road wound through the stand of oaks. After a few minutes she topped a small rise. Before her, in the valley, she could see the glow of several small buildings. A larger estate loomed higher up, in the distance.

Balkilly, she thought. *And Glendale Hall.*

The very sight of them eased some of the tension inside her. She pressed a hand against the burning stitch in her side and sniffed. An odd smell had joined the other night smells in the air. Beneath the mist and the pine and mulchy forest odors, she detected something honeyed, but with a rotten undertone.

Rustle-rustle.

There it was again. To her left. Nearer this time. Almost at her heels. A stealthy, dry sound. She looked over her shoulder, straining through the darkness to see what was chasing her, her heart pounding with hard, quick strokes. She saw nothing but the vague outline of a strand of ivy.

"Get away!" she cried, and broke into a run, the rustling noise stealthy no longer, becoming a scraping and hissing as it went after her. Her chest ached and she took great, heaving breaths and suddenly it was around her ankle, pulling her down, and she screamed, her fingers hooked into claws as she scrabbled at the delicate bones above her foot.

She was babbling, crying, trying to free herself from the long, dry fingers that had caught her. Moment by moment, the fingers peeled away, and one of them came off in her hand. She threw it aside with a yelp, her sense of touch telling her something her mind couldn't accept.

She'd tangled her ankle in a piece of ivy. Ivy so old and thick it had grown into a vine at least an inch in diameter. Small offshoots and leaves brushed against her skirts. Slowly, the panic left her and she began to feel like the biggest fool Ireland had ever seen. The driver's misplaced anxiety and the tension of the journey had left her susceptible to all sorts of idiocy.

Her cheeks flushed with warmth. Good God, she'd heard a few leaves rustling and gone running down the road as if a banshee howled at her heels. And screamed when she tangled her foot in a vine. It almost sounded like a scene from one of the farces she'd attended in London. She forced a laugh. And had an unsettling feeling that someone—or something—was peering at her from the oily blackness at the edge of the woods.

Suppressing a shiver, she pulled the last piece of ivy from her ankle and held it in her fingers. The leaves had an odd, leathery feel to them, not at all like the ivy that climbed stone walls and trees. She ran a finger along the edge of one leaf. Serrated, not smooth, the edges had a sandpaper texture.

As she touched it, her ability to sense a plant's emotions supplied an odd impression which made her heart beat fast all over again. The ivy radiated only one color: pitch black. The color of death. But it wasn't dead. She could feel the supple quality of its leaves against her skin. It had left some sort of sticky substance on her hands. Frowning, she threw the strand down and wiped her palms against her skirts.

The ivy felt wrong somehow.

She returned to the road and hurried toward the

lights of Balkilly, wondering all the while about the
strange perception her gift had supplied. Not a single
explanation came to her. In any case, she heard no
more of the stealthy rustling as she approached the village, and she managed to convince herself anew that
she'd made more of the ivy than necessary.

Just ahead, a well-lit building stood on the edge of
the road. Two lanterns flanked the front door. She
glanced at the sign above the door: Balkilly Arms. Muffled voices and low-pitched male laughter from the inn
helped to banish the shadows that fell beyond the
lantern's glow. Suddenly she didn't feel quite so alone.
She paused in the yard to catch her breath and leaned
against an oak tree of considerable girth.

Instantly she recoiled. Blackness emanated from the
tree. Still, this was blackness with a green cast to it, the
way a dying plant normally appeared to her. Her surprise melted away, replaced by reassurance. She understood these colors. Her fright must have affected her
interpretation of the ivy.

Feeling more confident, she pressed her palms
against the tree and tried to gauge what had happened
to it, to cause this slow death. Colors swirled in her
mind again, black coalescing to form tiny spots within
the green. Some sort of insect, she realized, had eaten
away the core of the tree. She brushed her fingers
along the base of the tree, then lifted her hand into the
light cast by a lantern. A carpenter ant clung to her little finger.

Frowning, she gauged the distance between the oak
and the Balkilly Arms and discovered they stood very
close indeed. In another month or so, the ants would
finish their work and the tree would topple directly
onto the inn's roof. She'd have to warn someone. Later.

Right now, thoughts of that warm, steady mattress called to her.

She brushed the grass off her traveling gown, smoothed a hand over her hair, and fought for calm. After a few deep breaths she felt ready. Squaring her shoulders, she lifted her chin and pushed the door open.

Conversation spilled out into the night. Swallowing, she stepped into the foyer and squinted through the whiskey fumes clogging the air. The door had opened on the inn's dining room. A rectangular pine table stretched nearly the length of the room. At the center of the table, a group of men clustered. They were a rough bunch, their frieze coats tattered and bespeaking lean times. She wondered what had drawn their attention so thoroughly. A game of cards, perhaps?

Wood burned in a open-hearth fireplace. The flames warmed her but didn't cast enough light to dispel the pocket of darkness near the door. Her entrance went unmarked. She navigated around a peasant whose drunken snores drowned out the men's conversation, then scanned the crowd for the innkeeper.

When she didn't find a likely candidate, she decided to pick out the least threatening man and ask for assistance. Nevertheless, as the seconds passed, she felt so completely out of her element, among men whose behavior she couldn't even begin to fathom after a lifetime of proper English gentlemen, that she couldn't find the nerve to push into the crowd and ask for the innkeeper. At least not yet.

The men continued to focus on something in the middle of the table. Between huddled bodies, she caught a glimpse of ivory and pink and white. *Fabric*, she suddenly realized. They had satins and silks, for

heaven's sake. Since when did a bunch of Irishmen find
fabric so interesting?

One of them sat apart from the others. He was a big
man, his legs stretched out casually, his shoulders broad
and powerful, easily spanning the captain's chair he had
folded his frame into. His hair was dark and shaggy, his
skin swarthy, and his nose looked lopsided near the bottom, as though someone had broken it for him—more
than once. A small gold loop sparkled in his left ear.

She found herself unable to look away.

Alone, he watched but didn't participate. He held a
slim cigar between two fingers, and lifted it to his lips.
A playful smile curving there, he puffed on it and blew
a smoke circle at the ceiling.

Her attention slid lower, to his mud-spotted trousers
and boots. His frieze coat appeared filthy, and she wrinkled her nose in distaste. It wasn't the dirt that bothered her. During her years at Kew Gardens she'd
learned to respect the gardeners who tended the plants,
and they usually wore a coating of earth on their
clothes. Rather, she disliked the way it looked on him.
The dirt lent him a dangerous air, conjuring images of
brawls on hard-packed earth. Clearly the man was one
of Wicklow County's rowdier peasants.

At that moment, as she stood there with her nose
scrunched and her aversion for him obvious, he glanced
up and saw her. She quickly tried to school her features
into a more pleasant expression, but it was too late. His
smile became a grin and she could tell he didn't give a
damn what she thought of him. He even seemed to
enjoy her look of distaste. Warmth crept into her
cheeks at the realization he'd caught her in such an ill-
mannered display.

He set his cigar on a pewter tray, scraped back his

chair, and stood. His gaze upon her was intense as he walked to her side, his eyes the color of a lough on a stormy day. Blue, flecked liberally with gray, fringed with dark lashes. A peculiar giddiness curled in her stomach. She shrank backward a few steps before pride took over and insisted she hold her ground.

"Good evening to you, my lady." He bent a full smile upon her, blasting her with Irish charm. " 'Tis certain the fairies have deposited you on the doorstep. Where else could you have come from?"

She cleared her throat once, twice, finding it difficult to speak. Most of the men she knew were scholarly types. Their fine breeding and preoccupation with cerebral matters sometimes made her forget they were men. Even her late husband had been quick with her, giving her carnal knowledge while teaching her nothing of pleasure. But this dark Irishman had a certain vitality, a primitive earthiness she'd never encountered before.

His smile grew broader. "From the fairies, then. They've been good to us tonight." He motioned to a weary-looking innkeeper, who had appeared behind the counter to serve up pints of ale. "Some water, Sean, for the lady. I'll not have her telling her tale with a dry throat. And an ale for me."

She frowned. "I'm Mrs. Sherwood. I've been traveling by stagecoach—"

"So, you're not from the fairies but from England. Michael McEvoy, at your service."

Her breath coming faster, she narrowed her eyes. Michael McEvoy. She remembered the name well. Lord Connock had employed him as a naturalist who traveled to foreign lands for rare plants. *The adventurer.*

He sketched her a bow, his gaze flickering across her breasts and lips, the shift so quick and practiced she might not have noticed it if she hadn't been watching him so carefully. "And Mr. Sherwood? Will he be coming along, too?"

"I'm a widow."

"My condolences."

"Mr. McEvoy," she said crisply, "I appreciate your fine Irish courtesy, but I'm afraid—"

A sudden burst of whistling cut her off. They both looked toward the clustered men. One of the Irishmen had a wispy piece of ivory silk in his hands.

Anne narrowed her eyes. That ivory silk looked familiar . . .

"The stagecoach was late tonight." Michael McEvoy grabbed the two tankards the innkeeper had pushed toward him. He handed one to her, somehow managing to brush his fingertips across her wrist. "I'm assuming your bags are outside. How did you enjoy your journey, and whom are you here to visit?"

"I didn't enjoy my journey at all." She raised the tankard to her lips and, expecting water, gulped warm Irish beer instead. Immediately she broke into a fit of coughing as the bitters assaulted her tongue.

He grinned and switched their drinks. "I beg your pardon. Wrong tankard."

Anne eyed him closely. She told herself his earthiness was no more fetching than a pig in a sty. "Mr. McEvoy," she said in her most forbidding tone, "I am from England. I'm also tired and hungry. If you'll be silent for a moment, and allow me to 'tell my tale,' as you put it, perhaps I might seek my bed before too much longer."

"My mouth is closed, ma'am."

"You're a man with sense, I see. A rare breed."

Her retort startled a grunt out of him. His eyes

glinted with male appreciation before his lids dropped to half-mast. It was a look designed to draw a response from her and respond she did, helplessly, her heart quickening in her chest. He was, quite simply, the most masculine male she'd ever met, and the woman in her could not dismiss him.

She clasped her hands together and took a few steps toward the men clustered around the pine table. She had to put some distance between herself and this dark Irishman. Words didn't come easily with him standing so nearby. "Obviously you didn't recognize my name, but I know yours. I've come from London to work for Lord Connock as a botanical illustrator. And you are Lord Connock's naturalist."

His dark eyebrows twitched upward. "By all that's holy, Lord Connock never told me he hired a woman. I was expecting a Mr. Townsend to arrive tomorrow."

"Lord Connock changed his mind. He hired me instead."

"A man with taste, Lord Connock. What brings you here a day early?"

"I didn't want to spend the night in Dublin, so I bought a seat on the next stagecoach bound for the Wicklow Mountains."

"Dublin didn't agree with you?"

"No, I didn't like the city," she confided, remembering the squalor and poverty and the green madness.

"I'm a Connaught man myself. 'Tis the fairest country in the land. Still, if you saw Dublin on a good day, with sunlight turning the mountains to an emerald green while a soft Irish rain misted down upon the avenues and the sailboats in Dublin Bay, you might change your mind."

Brow furrowed, Anne tilted her head. "I saw only the poor."

"No man's poor who lives in Ireland."

"I must have missed something."

"That you have, ma'am."

Her expression smoothed out and she fell silent, his words resonating within her. She'd known Michael McEvoy for no more than a few minutes, and yet how easily he'd pointed out the one thing that had been bothering her most these past years. She was missing something.

"Will you be wanting me to take you to Glendale Hall?" he asked, breaking into her thoughts.

"I wouldn't disturb Lord Connock at such an hour. A room in this inn will do fine for now."

"And your baggage—'tis outside?"

She began to tell him that her baggage was two miles away, strapped to a broken-down stagecoach. Hoots from the men around the table drowned her out. Abruptly she recognized a gray-haired man as the same person who'd raced a pony cart past the stagecoach while they'd rested the horses in Glencree. Seconds later, she caught a glimpse of sky-blue satin edged with ivory lace in a set of hammy fingers and froze. Her insides clenched into a knot.

By God, they had her underclothes.

How it had happened, she couldn't guess, but these papist heretics had her underclothes. Lord, the whole village would know her little secret, her weakness for fancy underclothes. The flush that had kept her cheeks warm while she'd talked to Michael McEvoy abruptly drained away.

"Mrs. Sherwood? Are you ill?" He placed a hand on her arm, his palm warm and gentle, and in a distracted way she recognized how very good it felt.

She gestured toward the men. "What, exactly, are they pawing through?"

"A small trunk. Paddy O'Shanley found it several miles away, just sitting in the middle of the road. Said his horse almost tripped over it."

She remembered that odd thump she'd experienced as the stagecoach had passed through Sally Gap and felt her inner temperature plummet several degrees. "What does the trunk contain?"

"Lady's underclothes." He grinned. "And not just any lady's underclothes. No stiff, starched bloomers for our lassie. All silks and satins in colors that this village has never seen the like of. Old Paddy thought he'd died and gone to heaven when he opened it."

"Mr. McEvoy—" She paused, searching for words, her cheeks filling with heat again, the heat spreading down to the tops of her breasts. "Those lady's unmentionables . . ."

His brow furrowed. "What about them?"

"Would you gather them from the men for me?"

"Why?"

Before she could answer, sudden comprehension widened his eyes. He stared down at her brown serge traveling gown, one even she thought of as pure ugliness. His look of shock would have been comical in any other circumstance. Then he eyed the silken underclothes draped across the pine table and swallowed.

She pressed a hand against her forehead. "Our driver was drinking poteen. The stagecoach shimmied from one side of the road to the other. When we passed through Sally Gap, I felt a bump, and now I realize one of my trunks must have fallen off—"

"Mother of God," he murmured. He left her side and pushed toward the men, his attention fastening on a rose-colored chemise embroidered with tiny flowers along the bodice. "Lads, I'm afraid you can't be looking at these anymore."

"Why not?" a grizzled man asked, his gray hair topped by a felt hat which had seen better days.

McEvoy slid a glance her way before facing his cronies again. "Because I'm going to buy them from you, that's why, and I don't want them damaged."

Anne took a deep breath and let it out slowly. Evidently Michael McEvoy was gentleman enough to spare her further embarrassment. Her estimation of him went up a notch or two.

"What if I don't want to sell 'em?" the old man asked.

"Come on, Paddy, who're you going to give them to? Your Moira? She'll give you the beating of your life for visiting a fancy woman."

Amid a chorus of guffaws, McEvoy touched the chemise, his fingers running reverently along the embroidery before he picked it up with gentle fingers and placed it back in the trunk. A pair of her ivory silk hose followed, the wisps of fabric draping across his arm as he set them next to the chemise.

Paddy grumbled good-naturedly. "I guess I can buy Moira something nice, maybe even earn myself a smile. What are you going to do with 'em, McEvoy?"

"Give them to the poor."

Hearty laughter broke out around the table.

Anne could hardly bear to watch; still, she knew if she didn't watch, her imagination would torture her even worse. She forced herself to keep her attention on the dark Irishman and squinted with embarrassment at the red flush that had risen in his cheeks.

He grasped her sky-blue drawers and slipped them

into the trunk, but rather than withdraw his hand, he paused, his eyes growing wider. "Holy mother of God," he murmured again.

The grizzled man's eyebrows climbed. "What did you find?"

"Come on, McEvoy, show us," a man with a brutally scarred face shouted.

He withdrew his hand, slowly, as if he couldn't help himself. She saw scarlet silk between his fingers and let out a low moan.

He had found the corset.

He didn't remove it entirely, just enough so he might examine it himself, fully, the red flush creeping down to his neck.

"A scarlet corset," one male voice whispered.

"With black lace and black ties," another said.

Anne closed her eyes. She wondered if a person could die from shame. She only wore the corset on days when she was feeling particularly dismal, and it never failed to brighten her mood. Surely that wasn't a crime?

When she opened her eyes, she found Michael McEvoy staring at her, his expression curious, his gaze very warm. She shivered. Somehow she managed to raise her chin.

He dropped the corset and closed the trunk. "I'll be by with a purse tomorrow, Paddy. Do you mind if I take the trunk tonight?"

Still grumbling, the old man nodded his assent.

Now that the trunk ceased to be the center of attention, the men dispersed, and one of them saw her. He jumped in surprise and pointed, and soon they'd all eyed her up.

Anne pressed a hand against her throat. She wondered if any of them suspected she owned the scandalous underclothes.

McEvoy returned to her side but angled himself so he stood partially in front of her, shielding her from the other Irishmen's eyes. "I want you all to meet Mrs. Sherwood, from London. She's here as Lord Connock's guest and will be staying at the inn for the night." He turned and indicated the innkeeper. "Mrs. Sherwood, this is Sean O'Sullivan. Mr. O'Sullivan, can you fix her a room?"

The innkeeper smiled. "We'll have you in a warm bed in no time, Mrs. Sherwood."

Tugging on his felt hat, Paddy nodded. "Pleased to meet you, ma'am."

For the first time, Anne noticed an odd growth on the side of Paddy's head. A deformity of some sort, on the skin beneath his ear. Her scientific curiosity piqued, she wondered at its origin.

A chorus of greetings followed Paddy's, and then the men dispersed, two of them sidling up to the bar, the others stomping out the door. Many of the older men, she noted, had deformities similar to Paddy's. Silently she decided that the people of Balkilly must have suffered greatly during the potato famine. Their poor nutrition had obviously produced visible effects.

"Good evening, ma'am," the last man said and closed the door behind him.

Anne sighed. She must have made quite an impression on everyone.

"Mrs. Sherwood, you still haven't finished telling me what happened on the way from Dublin," McEvoy said, guiding her over to a chair. "Sit down and finish your tale."

She collapsed into the chair, grateful to him for diverting her attention from her embarrassment. He settled into another chair by her side.

"The stagecoach driver grew so drunk," she revealed, her voice low, "that he steered the carriage into a ditch, and the wheel broke. He and his companion are lying on the side of the road, some two miles back. I can't say they're waiting for rescue, however. They probably won't even remember the accident."

He thumped his palm against his forehead. "Why didn't you tell me sooner that you'd been in an accident? Are you hurt?" He assessed her figure with another swift glance.

"No, I'm not hurt. I didn't mention the accident because you didn't give me a chance to."

"And you let me fold underclothes, knowing you'd just had a nasty shock." He shook his head in evident disgust. "What else haven't you told me?"

Anne frowned. First he made love to her with his gaze, then he badgered her with reprimands. What would he do next? Her patience, already stretched to a thread, suddenly snapped. "What haven't I told you? Well, I didn't tell you about my fright when we crashed, and my horrific walk down the road, and the peculiar rustling in the woods, and the ivy that tripped me—"

She broke off and drew a breath, her chest heaving. "—Nor about the oak tree in the yard, which is ready to topple upon this lovely little establishment!"

She could see his surprise in the way he stiffened, but he recovered quickly, and when he spoke, his voice was gentle. "Easy, easy. I can see you've had a bad time of it. We'll get you into bed."

"I'll get myself into bed," she informed him.

An unwilling smile twitched his lips. "Tomorrow, I'll

bring you to Glendale Hall. Once you're settled in, we'll start our work."

"Our work?"

The dark Irishman raised one eyebrow. "Lord Connock had asked me to assist Townsend in whatever manner necessary. As you're Townsend's replacement, you and I will be working together. Didn't Lord Connock mention that?"

"No, he most certainly didn't."

"Mrs. Sherwood, tomorrow we embark on what I'm certain will be a long and fruitful relationship." He winked at her. "But first, I'll bring your underclothes up."

3

Seated in a hard-backed little chair, Michael McEvoy rubbed his chin with two long fingers and waited for the Englishwoman to come down to breakfast. All around him, the Balkilly Arms hummed with life. Early-morning sunlight shone through the dining-room windows and settled a pink glow upon the scarred pine table and chairs. From behind the set of swinging doors that led to the kitchen, pots clanged, and the innkeeper's wife grumbled as she prepared breakfast for her guests. A gush of warm air that smelled like apples wafted past Michael.

Moments later, the innkeeper emerged from behind the swinging doors and slung a platter of oatmeal pancakes with fresh apple butter Michael's way.

"Breakfast, McEvoy," the innkeeper informed him, his brown hair sticking up at the back of his head. "Best my Mary could do, what with having to wait on that English lady."

"Thank her for me," Michael said.

"Who, the Englishwoman?"

"God, no. Thank your Mary for serving up the first pancakes I've had in a while that'll stick to my ribs."

The innkeeper smiled, his expression knowing. "I've heard about those soggy French things and the tough ones from America. There's no sweeter pancakes than Irish ones."

Michael nodded in agreement. He'd eaten breakfast in too many countries to count, none of them memorable events. In fact, if he was having something without grubs or maggots in it, he counted himself lucky. His last trip had taken him across the Atlantic and around Cape Fear to Fiji—Jesus, the food in Fiji!—before bringing him back to Ireland's emerald hills.

"Will you be taking that Mrs. Sherwood over to Glendale Hall this morning?" the innkeeper asked, his attention divided between Michael and his effort to put away last night's tankards.

"As soon as she makes herself ready," Michael confirmed between mouthfuls.

He had to admit the Englishwoman had him puzzled. Those fine manners of hers left her as stiff and reserved as every other tea-swilling noble he'd ever met, and judging by that look of affront when she'd sized him up, her standards were a wee bit higher than his own lowly person could ever aspire to. He might as well have been scum from the back alleys in Dublin.

And yet, beneath her dresses, which he hoped weren't all as ugly as that brown one from last night, she wore an eye-popping scarlet corset. Who would have thought it? And, once knowing, who could stop thinking of it?

" 'Tis a good thing she's going on to Glendale Hall," the innkeeper grumbled. "She has her airs, and I say the gentry should stay with the gentry and bother each other, not us poor folk."

Michael nodded, but he didn't agree completely with the other man's assessment. For all her smart tailoring, the high-and-mighty widow was a wanton little piece, and he silently vowed to see her model every silken scrap of underclothes she owned or crawl forever dishonored to his grave. Not that he made a habit of plundering widows. Mrs. Sherwood's contempt for him had piqued his interest. He admitted that his weakness lay in the direction of the unattainable. The harder he had to work for something, the more it satisfied his appetite.

Consider cigars, for example. He'd had his first cheroot on a trip to the West Indies, but after he'd smoked a well-aged Montecristo from Cuba he'd decided that only Havana cigars would touch his lips. Now, the Spanish made their Cuban cigars, especially those from Vuelta Abajo, difficult to obtain and very expensive, but in Michael's opinion that only made them more enjoyable. He never sailed past Cuba without making port in Havana. Likewise, the widow was forbidden territory, and that made her even more intriguing and desirable.

He leaned back in his chair and imagined the prim Mrs. Sherwood garbed in her scarlet corset . . . and nothing else. "What did she ask Mary to do last night, give her a bath and scrub her back?"

"Nothing so easy as that." The innkeeper picked up a mop and started mopping behind the counter. "She spent the night complaining about strange noises. Had me and my Mary beating the bushes beneath her window, trying to find the culprit that was keeping her awake."

"Did you find anything?"

"Not so much as a mouse. The trees harbor any number of wee beasties that would love to sneak into our larder. We keep the windows locked and stay out of the woods at night, and sleep as peaceful as babes."

Michael glanced out the window, at the oak that drooped lazily in the yard. He had no problem with the woods, even at night. Trees were his brothers. The woods had sheltered him. They'd been his home for years. In fact, he'd once been a "wee beastie," rattling at the windows, waiting to sneak into the larder.

He paused in his chewing, memories catching at him and throwing shadows on what had started out as a good day. His life hadn't been easy, God knew, but he liked to think he'd turned out the better for it. After all, the tree that grows on the stoniest ground has the strongest roots.

He'd been born in Connaught to a poor young couple who'd married the year before. They'd rented a seventy-five-acre farm from old Lord de Burghe, forty acres of it arable and another thirty-five of bog so treacherous it had sucked the shoes off their feet when they'd dared walk in it. His parents had worked that fickle ground until it damned near killed them, sometimes yielding a king's harvest, other times barely enough to feed themselves. Michael remembered the hard work, the months of privation; and yet he also recalled running through those neat, grassy fields and heather-clad hills with his dog.

For all their poverty, those times were good.

Even so, the early memories were ragged and hard to find. Pain and grief had almost obscured them. The potato famine had taken his parents when he was only ten years old, and Lord de Burghe, may Satan have mercy on his immortal soul, had put him in a workhouse in

Dublin. It hadn't been a shelter for boys but a work-house, a pest hole belonging to no one, a doorway to purgatory that de Burghe had forced him to walk through. He used to pray, *God Almighty, deliver me from evil, from the workhouse, from the whole city of Dublin, amen.*

God hadn't delivered him, however. Michael had delivered himself. At the tender age of fourteen, he'd run away from the workhouse and gone to live in the wilderness north of Dublin, alone, for the next five years.

Yes, he knew trees. They didn't frighten him.

Evidently Mrs. Sherwood understood trees too. He still couldn't figure out how she'd known about that diseased old oak in the yard. He recognized it hadn't long to live; his keen senses and experience with nature had told him so.

The innkeeper propped his mop up against a post and rested his arm against the counter. "For all her uppity ways, Mrs. Sherwood had an interesting story to tell."

Michael's interest perked up. "Oh?"

"She thinks she saw the Dullahan on her walk from the stagecoach to the Balkilly Arms," the other man said in low tones.

Unable to suppress a grunt of surprise, Michael raised both eyebrows. "Isn't the Dullahan a headless fairy who throws a bucket of blood in his victim's face?"

"The very same."

"And Mrs. Sherwood met up with him?"

"Well, according to the lady, he didn't actually throw blood in her face but grabbed her ankle."

Michael shook his head. "Come, man, that's just a story. We all know the Dullahan doesn't exist. She must have tripped over a root and frightened herself."

"I thought the same thing," the innkeeper agreed, his eyes wide, unconvinced. "Although lately, people have been coming back from the woods with some strange tales to tell. No one walks through the forest at night anymore."

"What sorts of tales?"

"Peculiar sounds, rustling, unseen hands reaching out to grab the unwary."

"And who's been telling them?"

"Well, old Paddy's had a few incidents—"

"Paddy?" Michael snorted. "Considering the way that laddie downs his poteen, I'm surprised he hasn't seen Brian Boru himself, returned to free Ireland from the Protestant devils across the sea."

"You've been away for a year on your collecting trip, McEvoy. Things are different."

Michael narrowed his eyes. He sensed an undercurrent in the innkeeper's voice, one that set his instinct on edge. He'd heard that tone before and knew it well.

Fear.

The innkeeper sighed. "Well, no matter. We've grown used to the noises, whatever they might be. Mrs. Sherwood will become used to them, too. She's from London, no?"

"From the queen's own royal gardens."

"She'll fit right in with Lord Connock. Never met a man such as he, fussing over those plants of his, squawking about this new variety or that. I say, if it can't feed a hungry mouth, it isn't worth the dirt it grows in."

The innkeeper paused and threw Michael a quick glance, his cheeks reddening a bit. "Well, maybe the right man could find some use for them. I didn't mean to suggest your collecting trips are worthless, McEvoy, nor disrespect for Lord Connock. He's a generous man and I owe him."

"No offense taken." Michael scraped his plate clean, stood, and placed the plate on the counter for the innkeeper to remove later. "Lord Connock's plants may not seem useful at the outset, but he's looking for ways to improve them, and in the end reduce Ireland's chance of suffering another famine to none."

The innkeeper busied himself with sweeping. "A fine goal for a fine man. I suppose his wife's dying in the famine has something to do with it."

Michael shrugged. He'd heard tales of Lord Connock watching his wife starve to death. The second son of a nobleman, Connock hadn't inherited his title until his brother had died. He'd lived like a pauper and suffered through the famine like the rest of them. When his brother had died and he'd inherited the lordship, Lord Connock had announced plans to breed and crossbreed plants. He'd vowed to created strains that could produce fruits and vegetables twice their normal size and withstand even the harshest weather.

Michael sympathized with his goal.

Outside, a carriage rattled up the lane and stopped behind the Balkilly Arms. Murmuring voices drifted into the dining room. The innkeeper propped up his broom against the wall. "That'll be this morning's delivery from Lord Connock. When you see him, McEvoy, give him my best."

"I will at that."

The innkeeper disappeared through the kitchen. Michael peered out the window that opened onto the yard behind the inn. A wagon loaded with cabbages, potatoes, carrots, scallions, onions, and assorted other vegetables created a splash of color against trees and

brush that had the slightest touch of green to them, signaling the arrival of spring.

From Connock's glasshouses, Michael mused.
Throughout the year, as part of his research, the aristocrat grew a variety of vegetables. While he stocked his
own kitchen with village-grown produce and livestock,
supporting the local economy, he routinely delivered
the vegetables from his experimentation to the village,
free of charge. The Balkilly Arms had come to depend
on Lord Connock's generosity, and as a result, Balkilly
was one of the most well-fed villages in the Wicklow
Mountains. A rush of affection for the man he thought
of as a second father surprised Michael with its intensity.

Behind him, the click of high-heeled slippers against
the stairs warned him that Lord Connock's newest em-
ployee was on her way down. Moments later she entered the dining room, her cheeks pink and
fresh-looking. When she saw him, she paused, her eyes
becoming shuttered. "Good morning, Mr. McEvoy."

"Good morning, ma'am," he said, taking a moment
to study her. A white chip hat trimmed with rows of
velvet around the crown sat atop her blond curls. It
gave her almost a military air, one matched by her lips,
which she'd firmly pressed together.

His attention dropped lower. Her dress was almost as
ugly as the previous evening's. Of a coarse gray fabric,
almost like nun's cloth, it sported a row of buttons from
neck to hem, each of them tightly fastened. A narrow
black cravat held the collar at her throat closed and a
shawl covered her shoulders. If he hadn't seen her underclothes, he would have thought her a dowd. Now, he
couldn't help wondering what she wore against her
skin. Soft, sky-blue pantaloons whose lace brushed

against her? Or even better, the scarlet corset? What a delightful present she made, ripe for the unwrapping.

He smiled. "Won't you sit down? I'll call the innkeeper and have him make you something to eat."

"I've already eaten breakfast." Gloves in hand, she slapped them lightly against her palm. "The innkeeper's wife delivered a tray to my room earlier this morning. Thank you for fetching my trunks. I received them along with breakfast."

"My pleasure." He wanted to ask her what she had on beneath that dress and bit his tongue before the words tumbled out.

"I've already settled with the innkeeper. Shall we be off to Glendale Hall, then?"

She was all business, he thought. No mention of the lovely morning, her delicious breakfast, or the innkeeper's kind hospitality. He wondered if this was the way she lived each day—with blinders on, like a high-strung carriage horse. "As you wish, ma'am."

"Please, stop calling me ma'am," she told him. "You make me feel a million years old."

"What would you prefer?"

"Mrs. Sherwood will do fine."

He nodded and gestured toward the door. "This way, Mrs. Sherwood. I've a gig waiting outside."

She followed his lead and walked out the front door and into a fine spring day. Looking neither left nor right, she made straight for the conveyance and waited by the door, presumably for his assistance in handing her in. She didn't see the cherry trees that rained fragrant white petals down on her hat, didn't pause to remark on the tulips and daffodils that poked their heads up from newly warmed earth.

Michael shook his head. He opened the gig's door,

took her hand, and stared at her stiff back as she entered. Her fingers held his with just the right amount of pressure, for just the right amount of time, before releasing them to settle herself against the leather squabs. He sat beside her and took up the reins. Soon they were trotting down the lane toward the outskirts of town and Glendale Hall.

The sun shone down upon his head and warmed his hair. He reveled in the way a breeze curled around his body and in the musty smell of earth in the air. He wondered if she realized how much she missed by ignoring these things. A sudden urge grabbed hold of him, to bring her one of his Montecristo cigars and ask her to smoke it with him. A tiny grin played about his mouth at the thought of her reaction.

"Mr. McEvoy, is something amusing?"

Michael raised an eyebrow. "Amusing? Why do you ask?"

"You're smiling."

"Am I now? Well, in these parts, folks smile. 'Tis the warm Irish breeze that does it."

She crossed her arms over her breasts and fixed her attention on the road ahead. Their lane, although graveled, was not much wider than a farmer's path as it wound through Glendale Forest. Ferns and violets unfurled themselves on either side of the path, and deep within the woods, sunlight fought through leaves to splash the forest floor with patterns of light.

"I'm curious, Mrs. Sherwood," he couldn't stop himself from asking.

She sat up straighter. "Curious about what?"

"How did you know that oak outside the Balkilly Arms was dying?"

"What do you mean?"

He had the notion that she'd deliberately misunderstood him. "You said the oak tree was about to topple upon 'our lovely little establishment.'"

"Oh, I suppose I did." Lip caught between her teeth, she examined the passing scenery for a moment before turning to face him. "I saw carpenter ants crawling around the oak's base. Anyone with botanical experience would recognize what that meant for the tree."

Michael felt another little jolt of surprise. She not only knew the tree was dying, but *why*. "You saw ants? I've never seen ants. Besides, it was dark. How could you have seen them?"

"The lanterns outside the inn provided enough light," she insisted.

Eyes narrowed, he regarded her closely. Why in heaven's name would a woman who had just endured a carriage accident squint through the darkness to stare at the base of a tree? "You're not telling me something."

She bristled. "Why should I tell you anything? Besides, how did *you* know the oak was dying?"

"I've had a lot of experience." Not wanting to elaborate further, he let the subject drop.

Silence fell between them. After a minute or two of being completely ignored, Michael tried another conversational gambit.

"Did you have a good rest at the inn last night?"

"I slept tolerably well."

"The Dullahan didn't visit you, I hope."

She turned toward him and observed him with narrowed eyes. "I see the innkeeper has been talking."

Michael shrugged. "Don't be ashamed. You're a city lass, not used to the sounds of the country. 'Twas probably a tree limb tapping against your window."

"I may be from London, but I know what a tree limb

tapping against a window sounds like. I heard a strange rustling noise, with a stealth to it that suggested intelligence."

"Like a raccoon?"

"No. More like a man." Her tone was faintly accusing.

"I sincerely doubt someone was trying to break into your room, Mrs. Sherwood. This is a small village. You're the only visitor here. None of the locals would dare try to burgle the Balkilly Arms."

"I know what I heard," she stubbornly insisted.

Michael raised an eyebrow. "Well, then, 'tis a good thing you survived the night."

She sent him a withering look that merely widened his smile. "I'm not certain I'm liking your Ireland, Mr. McEvoy."

"No one likes Ireland. You either love her or you hate her. She's that kind of lady." He slapped the reins against the horse's rump to keep him moving. "Tell me about the fright you had on your walk to the Arms last night. The innkeeper offered a garbled explanation of the Dullahan grabbing your ankle. What really happened?"

"Well, the stagecoach crashed, and the driver urged me to stay with the coach rather than walk for the Balkilly Arms. I, however, wanted to stretch out in a warm, comfortable bed for once, so I ignored his tales of this Dullahan, which was supposedly lying in wait for me, and began to walk toward Balkilly.

"As I walked, I began to hear an odd rustling noise. It had a stealthiness to it. When I stopped and listened, the rustling stopped. When I walked, it became louder. For almost a mile it grew closer and closer, until finally something grabbed my ankle. In a panic, I pulled at the thing touching my skin and discovered I had tripped on a vine of ivy. Even so, I am certain some sort of animal was stalking me through the woods. Wolves, maybe."

"Ireland hasn't seen any wolves for centuries. You probably stepped into a hedgehog's nest and woke it up."

Her lips parted, as though she wanted to protest this easy explanation, but then she shrugged. " 'Tis plain you'll never believe me. Why don't we talk about something else? If we are to work together over the next few weeks, perhaps you might tell me about yourself. You said you were a Connaught man. What are you doing here, in County Wicklow?"

Michael took a breath. The lass had asked him to lay out his entire life in less than ten minutes, the amount of time it would take them to reach Glendale Hall. A man simply couldn't do that. Besides, there were certain things he wasn't going to tell her. Things he didn't want her to know.

"Lord Connock and I met when I was just a lad of nineteen. He offered me employ as his naturalist, and for the last eleven years, I've been traveling on his behalf. I collect rare plant species from the jungles and mountains of foreign lands. Brazil, the Indies, the China Seas, and most recently Fiji—there aren't many places I've missed. When I'm not traveling I stay here, in Balkilly."

"Not in Glendale Hall?"

"No, I have my own cottage just south of the village."

"I see." She smiled faintly, those manners of hers under as tight a control as ever.

"What about you, Mrs. Sherwood? I'm assuming Mr. Sherwood passed some time ago, or you'd still be wearing widow's weeds." Privately he considered the two gowns he'd already seen pretty damned close to widow's weeds.

"My husband died two years ago. Of apoplexy. His name was Henry, Baron Sherwood. He wrote the *Encyclopedia of Flowering Plants*. Have you heard of it?"

Something in her voice, some buried twist of pain, warned him to tread carefully. "Can't say I have. I suppose I ought to be calling you *Lady Sherwood*."

"I was never Lady Sherwood. Mrs. Sherwood will do."

He noticed that her lips trembled. What did she mean, she was never Lady Sherwood? Had she married the man or hadn't she? "Mrs. Sherwood, I don't understand—"

"After my husband died," she cut in, her voice firm, "the barony passed to a nephew of his, leaving me in dire need of funds. My cousin, Sir Richard Hooker, offered me employ at Kew Gardens in London. I accepted and soon found myself busily sketching plants. I've done so for the last two years, bringing me to the present time. And to you."

Michael nodded, unsure of what to say. She'd described her past in calm tones, and yet he knew enough of life to understand things were never that easy. At the very least, the widow was not what she seemed. She'd buried her husband and felt the pain of it. His earlier vow to seduce her suddenly struck a sour note.

"So, Mr. McEvoy, is Connaught still your home, or have you adopted County Wicklow?" she asked, her profile turned toward him.

And a mighty fine profile it was, Michael thought. Her nose formed a delicate line before turning up at the end, while her chin showed just the right amount of firmness, suggesting a stubborn nature. He liked stubborn women. He enjoyed persuading them around to his way of thinking.

"Home? I don't have a home." He spoke quickly, without really thinking, his attention on her pert nose.

"But you said you have a cottage south of the village."

"I do, but it isn't a home. It's a place where I sleep."

"So Connaught is your home, then?"

"Connaught was my home." Suddenly uncomfortable, he shifted on his seat. "I travel a lot, Mrs. Sherwood. Men like me don't have homes. We have ports of call."

Unbidden, memories arose of his nights in the workhouse, twisting in the sheets, soaked in sweat, an endless longing for that little farm in Connaught gnawing at his insides. In all of his thirty years, he'd never seen a land so pretty as Connaught, with its scarlet fuchsia growing along the coast and the mountains whose green peaks nudged the clouds into a soft, misty rain. Gray rocks, scraggly sheep, and the silvery blue of a lough nestled between the mountains and teeming with trout worked on the heart and mind until no other land would ever satisfy.

He'd been to many lands but had never found one to take the place of that farm he'd grown up on, somewhere that made him feel safe, accepted, the way he'd felt when surrounded by his family. Even so, he went on searching, hoping against the odds that someday he'd find a place that eased the loneliness in his soul, a place where he could set down roots.

"I hope someday you return to Connaught," she abruptly said, turning to look at him directly in the eye, her own gaze intense, searching, like a lighthouse beam shined directly upon his puny and vulnerable carcass.

"Why?"

"Because you sound as if you miss it terribly."

Her intuitive assessment of his character couldn't have surprised him more. Before he could respond, however, she gestured toward the left with a nod of her head. "I suppose *that* is Glendale Hall."

4

❧

*M*ichael McEvoy's blue gaze settled upon her, impudent and full of mischief. " 'Tis a pleasant place in which to do business, no?"

Anne swallowed. Intensely aware of the man sitting next to her, she tried not to gape and amuse him with more ill-mannered behavior. She'd seen several imposing castles in her day, but none so magnificent as Glendale Hall. At first glance, the sight of it assaulted the senses, producing a series of images that couldn't fail to overwhelm. Enormous. Stately. Ancient. Proud. Surrounded by green, awash in sunlight.

The more sunlight, she thought, the better. Particularly after last evening in the Balkilly Arms. That odd rustling seemed to have followed her to the inn and had lurked outside her window all night long. The innkeeper and his wife hadn't believed her, and she could tell McEvoy considered her tale absurd. Even so, she felt certain something had decided to bedevil her here in Ireland, besides Connock's far-too-attractive naturalist.

"Have you ever seen another place as grand?" he asked.

"It's rather impressive."

He sent her a sharp glance. Instinct told her she'd disappointed him with her answer. Still, what did he expect her to do, sing the praises of Glendale Hall at full volume?

She sniffed and looked away. Even though they sat several inches apart, the vitality radiating from him touched her on some primal level. Like a flower yearning for the sun after days of clouds, she wanted to shift a little closer to him, to let go, although she wasn't quite certain what "letting go" meant.

She had no doubt that Michael McEvoy knew what it meant.

Sternly she reminded herself that Lord Connock had offered her an unparalleled opportunity by bringing her here. If she could keep her mind on her work and produce exemplary sketches, soon she would be moving in the scientific circles she'd been courting for years. She refused to squander this opportunity and disgrace herself by having a torrid affair with Connock's naturalist.

Still, she felt him watching her. She looked away, only to find herself staring at his powerful hands curled upon the reins. Without warning the most shocking thoughts came to her. Heat flooding her face, she pictured him running his palms across the smooth flesh of her bare breasts, his fingers trailing down her stomach to stroke the softest parts of her.

She caught her breath, then let it out slowly, thinking it strange that such lurid imaginings would invade her thoughts. Her experiences with Henry had taught her that she wasn't made for love. Even Henry had admitted as much and found a mistress. *Not a very pas-sionate person*, he'd said. *Useless. A failure*. With a deep breath she forced the images away. Instead she concen-trated on the brilliant blue sky and the sunlight, which spilled through the treetops to diffuse into soft green rays.

They rolled down the carriageway, toward an arched stone bridge spanning the river. As they crossed the bridge, the horse's hooves clip-clopping on the stone, a whole new vista opened up. Irish flags of green, orange, and white, raised atop several battlements, snapped briskly in the wind, while numerous windows reflected the sun, dazzling anyone who dared to stare too long. A river flowed on one side of the building, whose walls rose sheer from those lazy currents.

The gig rolled to a stop outside an immense oak door, arched at the top and girded with iron hasps. A footman standing by the door rushed over to help her alight, his face politely averted. She smiled at him any-way, feeling a bit more at home at the servant's refine-ment, and stepped down onto the gravel.

Michael McEvoy walked to her side. Shaking out her skirts, she forced herself to compare him to the servant. She knew he would compare unfavorably and wanted to chip away at the attraction he held for her.

Beneath her lashes, she studied them both. Where the servant wore an impeccably tailored coat, wrinkle-free trousers, and highly polished pumps, the Irishman looked like a furlong of bad road. He'd neglected a jacket for a simple linen shirt, open at the throat and revealing a V of curly black hair. As on the previous night, mud spotted his fawn-colored trousers and he'd rubbed his brown boots raw in places. His earring sparkled in the sunlight like pirate's gold. He was not, she told herself, a prime example of gentility.

And yet, the footman faded to a mere shadow in Michael McEvoy's presence.

Anne pressed her lips together and directed her attention exclusively at the footman. She didn't even glance in McEvoy's direction when he took her gloved fingers in his own and led her up a short flight of stairs to the oaken doors. The footman pulled one open, and together she and McEvoy walked into Glendale Hall.

"Well." Anne sucked in a breath. The place had the attitude of a cathedral with its high, vaulted ceilings and colored glass windows. Rich tapestries of burgundy and dark green covered the gray stone walls, and several suits of armor stood at attention at the back of the room. If not for the delicate intricacy and soft green color of the tables and chairs, which Anne recognized as pieces by Robert Adams, she might have guessed those who lived in Glendale Hall were throwbacks from an earlier age.

"Is that all you have to say?" he prodded with a half grin.

" 'Tis very nice," she added, earning a chuckle from him.

He squeezed her gloved fingers before releasing her hand. "Sure and you're a lass who's very sparing with her compliments."

"Michael, Mrs. Sherwood," a cultured voice said from a doorway to the left. "You've arrived."

Lord Connock walked toward them, a smile wreathing his broad face, the pouches beneath his eyes pulled tight. He took Anne's hand and bent over it in a courtly gesture. "When I heard you had suffered a stagecoach accident, I grew exceedingly worried. Michael assured me you hadn't been injured."

"Thank you, my Lord. I feel fine."

"I'll see those miscreant drivers punished, I promise you."

Anne nodded, her smile faltering. A thread of steel ran through Connock's voice. She wouldn't want to trade places with the two drivers.

The old nobleman turned to McEvoy and clapped him on the back. "I trust your journey was without mishap."

"I thought I'd never see Galway Bay again," the younger man said. "But you'll be pleased with the plants I've brought back."

"Good, good." Lord Connock smiled benignly at both of them. "Our Michael has been gone to Fiji and the China Seas for more than a year. He just returned yesterday. And how about you, Mrs. Sherwood? Why did you decide to brave a stagecoach, rather than wait for my carriage?"

"I arrived in Dublin a day early, and rather than linger in a city I didn't know and had no taste for, I decided to finish the journey with all possible haste," she explained.

"Dublin didn't inspire you?"

"No. I dislike cities in general. Even though Kew Gardens is in the heart of London, I usually confined myself to its grounds."

"Why do you dislike London?"

"I see too much black and gray. Not enough green." She didn't dare tell him she simply couldn't withstand the red aura around such plants that had the misfortune to grow in sewage ditches and near factories. Warped and sickly, they fought for life every day. She felt their suffering, their agony, too keenly.

"I see." Lord Connock's brow creased for a moment before giving way to another benign smile. "No matter, you're here and you're safe. Carlyle will take you to your room."

He paused to gesture toward a distinguished-looking gent wearing a coat and trousers similar to the footman's. "After you've had a chance to settle in, we'll have an early dinner, say, four o'clock. When we're finished, Michael will bring you to my sapling."

"What sapling?" McEvoy asked.

"One of the seeds you brought back from the Himalayas has produced a most remarkable tree, perhaps even an unclassified species. Mrs. Sherwood plans to illustrate the tree as well as the rest of my collection."

McEvoy raised an eyebrow. "I'm intrigued."

"As well you should be." Lord Connock glanced at Anne. "I trust you find these plans agreeable."

Anne nodded, a bit disappointed she'd have to wait so long before seeing the tree that had lured her to Ireland. Carlyle, presumably the butler, moved to her side.

Lord Connock began to turn away, then paused. "Oh, Mrs. Sherwood, I forgot to mention the small dinner party I've arranged for the end of the week. I wish to introduce you to some of my scholarly friends."

"That sounds lovely."

With a dismissive nod, the nobleman focused on McEvoy. "You must show me what you have found on your latest trip. I, too, have made some discoveries. Come to the library with me."

McEvoy paused, his gaze catching Anne's. "Mrs. Sherwood, until this evening, then."

She smiled, at first seeing naught but an easygoing, uncomplicated man. A moment later, something flickered within his eyes, and she sensed that hidden currents within him ran deep, that the man on the surface was as far from the real Michael McEvoy as the surface swells on a lough.

He knew far more than he allowed, she suddenly thought, not knowing where the perception had come from but trusting in it. He wasn't afraid, either. He was stronger than she, stronger than most. Warmth flooding her limbs, leaving her weak, she summed up that flicker in his eyes with a single word: *power.*

The pair moved off, deep in conversation. A smile curving his lips, McEvoy withdrew a cigar from his coat and handed it to Lord Connock. The elder man held the cigar to his nose, sniffed it, and slipped it into his jacket. Laughing, they disappeared into the library.

Carlyle cleared his throat and inclined his head toward a magnificent stone staircase near the end of the hall. "This way, ma'am."

Anne nodded. The butler led her across the hall and up the stone staircase. They paused in a comfortable little foyer filled with tables and sofas before he deposited her in her bedchamber, a Renaissance-style room with a curtained tester bed. Generously embroidered Persian carpets covered the wooden floor and an embroidered fire screen sat near the fireplace.

"Your trunks will be up in a few minutes, ma'am. Will there be anything else?"

"No, Carlyle. Thank you."

The butler bowed and left the bedchamber.

Anne moved to the windows and opened them wide. Warm spring air gushed past her and chased away the room's musty smell. She surveyed the grounds below, her attention drifting from one distant glasshouse to another. The largest looked about the size of a single-story cottage, while the smaller ones were no bigger than a shed. Painted a dazzling white, the glasshouses themselves were a work of art, with their curving wrought-iron arches and spiraling vines carved into the columns.

Between the glasshouses, manicured lawns covered gently rolling hills. In the distance, Glendale Forest formed an impenetrable line of trees that marched right up the slopes of the mountain. Everywhere she saw splashes of bright green as the trees and bushes prepared to unfurl their leaves. As though inviting her to join him on a fine spring walk, a magpie swooped past her window, chattering all the while.

An itch to explore grabbed hold of her. She wondered what sort of auras she might expect from the plants on Connock's estate. Surely Glendale Hall was as close to Eden as any living plant could expect to come. Anticipating a healthy white light, indicating an equal balance of all colors, she exchanged her brown traveling dress for an ivory gown and sturdy walking boots.

She found her way through Glendale Hall to the front door without encountering anyone, and emerged onto the lawn beneath her window. Those glasshouses she'd seen from her bedchamber drew her like a lodestone; she could hardly wait to examine the rare plants that had made Her Majesty jealous. Even better, she hoped to stumble upon Connock's strange sapling. Her opinion of the tree might prove more objective if she saw it alone for the first time, without Michael McEvoy's or Lord Connock's theories ringing in her ears.

To the left of the door, snowdrops surrounded a hedge that a gardener had clipped to look like a Grecian urn. She ran her fingers across the hedge and down to the snowdrops, expecting to see a brilliant white in her mind. Instead, she saw a hazy wash of red—not the sort of pain she sometimes experienced with flowers in London, but a strange low-key distress.

Brow furrowed, she decided her gift might continue to prove faulty until she'd settled herself into Glendale Hall. Her nerves needed a chance to calm and she had to learn more about this land before interpreting the colors properly.

Shrugging, she left the hedge and strode across the lawn, her booted heels sinking into moist earth, the sky pale blue where it met the mountains in the distance. Barely noticing the fragrant breeze that teased stray tendrils of her hair, or the wildflowers that bobbed on the edge of the forest, she made for the first glasshouse.

A rectangular structure with several open vents on the roof, the glasshouse wasn't on the scale of those in Kew Gardens but impressed her nevertheless. She couldn't see inside the building; all the windows from the ground to about three feet above eye level were frosted, no doubt to cut down on the sun's glare. None stood open, either, and this she found odd. In her experience, a vented roof alone didn't provide enough circulation to keep plants healthy, especially on a warm day like this one.

She walked over to the door, a wooden panel that looked out of place amidst all the glass, and tried the knob.

Locked.

Lord Connock, she thought, jealously guarded his plants. No matter, she would try another glasshouse. Anne walked on to the next building, a bit of moisture building on her brow and between her breasts. Fanning herself in the unexpected heat, she tried to peer through a crack in the window and had no success. When she twisted the latch, she found this glasshouse locked, too.

Disappointment crept through her. Whatever did Connock have in those glasshouses, that he felt it necessary to keep them under lock and key? Even at Kew Gardens, Her Majesty's own glasshouses remained open for public viewing.

She worked her way around the grounds, frustration lengthening her stride. She'd checked at least five glasshouses before she noticed the odd smell. Very ripe, honeyed . . . but not delicious. Beneath the sugary sweetness she detected a decomposing odor, similar to that of rotten meat. She thought she'd smelled it before but couldn't remember when or where.

Eyebrows drawn together, she followed the scent and discovered another two glasshouses directly behind those she'd already checked. The latest two were quite large, with frosted windows that reached all the way to the roofline. After a quick look, she mentally labeled the first extra-large glasshouse unremarkable.

The second one, however, captured her interest. The peculiar smell, she realized, emanated from the open vents on its roof, drifting down to offend her nose before vanishing on the breeze. The windows—all frosted—looked dirty. She took a step closer and realized the dirt was squirming.

No, not dirt. Flies.

Hordes of flies clung to the windows.

Nose crinkled, she moved closer to the second glasshouse, curiosity burning through her like a wildfire. She could understand why the flies hovered about; the smell had become quite potent. Almost revolting. Perhaps Connock composted waste materials in the second glasshouse. That would account for the smell. And yet, why would he bother to lock a composting glasshouse? Obviously he had something in there that he didn't want anyone to see.

She walked over to a tree that grew several feet beyond the glasshouse, found a dead branch, and returned to a fly-covered window. Grimacing, knowing the gesture would most likely prove futile, she brushed the flies away with the stick and tried to peer inside.

She saw nothing but cloudy glass.

Perhaps she could open the window. Her gorge rising, she brushed even more flies away and felt around the edges of the window to determine which way it opened. She discovered hinges and tried to push the window accordingly. It budged a little, giving her hope. She knew she was abusing Lord Connock's hospitality by prying into a glasshouse he had clearly delineated as off-limits, but curiosity had gotten the better of her.

Just a little peek, she thought. She wouldn't harm anything. She wouldn't even tell. Breathing more quickly, she shoved the edge of the stick into the small gap she'd created and tried to lever the window open.

The stick broke with a loud snapping noise.

"Ma'am!" a gruff voice chided.

She jumped, her cheeks flooding with heat, and dropped the stick. A grizzled old gardener rolled his wheelbarrow up to her and observed her with narrowed eyes. "These gardens are forbidden. That's why the doors are locked and the windows closed. I'll ask you to stay away from now on."

A few flies clung to her hand. She brushed them off, the insectile caress of their legs against her skin faintly disgusting. "I'm Mrs. Sherwood, the illustrator from

London. Lord Connock has employed me to sketch his plants—"

"I don't care if you're Saint Paddy himself. Stay away from these glasshouses," he barked. Scowling at her, he held his wheelbarrow by the handles and waited.

Taking the hint, Anne walked away, the feel of the old man's gaze hot on her back, aware that he didn't move until she'd gone several hundred feet from the glasshouses. If he reported her to Lord Connock, what would she say? That she had a penchant for snooping? She silently prayed that Lord Connock appreciated inquisitive minds. Then again, rather than waiting for her employer to confront her, perhaps she ought simply to tell him that the malodorous glasshouse had intrigued her and ask him to take her inside.

A glance at the sun, which had sunk significantly toward the horizon, convinced her she ought to hurry if she wished to appear at dinner on time. She strode briskly toward Glendale Hall, went directly to her room, and rang for a lady's maid. A young Irish girl arrived promptly and helped her remove the ivory gown. Anne blushed a little when the maid caught sight of her scarlet corset and began to stutter.

While dressing this morning, she'd eyed the scarlet corset and instantly decided to put it on. When she wore it, she flaunted the rules proper ladies obeyed, and that small freedom usually gave her enough confidence to stand tall throughout the day. And yet, as she and a maid from the Balkilly Arms had fought with the black laces, she'd felt the tiniest bit wicked, too. She kept remembering the red flush that had colored McEvoy's cheeks when he'd touched it.

The lady's maid helped Anne into an apricot silk dress that dripped ivory lace and fastened a cameo around her throat. She brushed Anne's hair until it shone like sun-drenched wheat and arranged it around a black velvet headband decorated with gauze and flowers. When the girl had finished, Anne stared at herself in the looking glass and knew a touch of fear; she was the same but different, her expression more lively in some subtle way, her eyes glinting with excitement that had long been absent.

Michael McEvoy, she thought.

He'd wrought this change in her, damn him. He'd cracked the armor she'd so carefully constructed to protect herself. The knowledge only increased her determination to resist his Irish charm.

Mouth pinched into a line, she left her bedchamber and made her way down toward the dining room. As she passed the library, she saw the muted glow of a pair of sconces and paused to see if Lord Connock and Michael McEvoy still lingered there. Other than books and ponderous mahogany furniture, the room was empty. She remembered the two men coming in here earlier to converse in private. What had they talked about? The malodorous glasshouse?

The library had a feeling of secrets. She could almost hear the whispers on the air. She stepped into the room and glanced around. Bookcases stretched toward the two-story ceiling, the books themselves well worn but clean and ordered, obviously maintained with a loving hand. A large, stiff-looking desk sat at an angle near windows covered with velvet drapes so heavy they blocked all outdoor light.

Squinting through the darkness, she moved closer to a few framed documents hanging above the desk. To her surprise, she discovered a diploma from the Royal College of Surgeons in Ireland, for an Owain

Connock. Evidently Lord Connock had a surgical background.

The candlelight from the sconces flickered unevenly and made reading difficult. Frowning, she moved to the next document. Lord Connock, she read, had also received a commendation from the Royal Botanic Society for "visionary research in botany."

What sort of research? According to Sir Richard, Lord Connock was naught more than an obsessive collector.

A letter from Charles Darwin occupied the last frame. In the letter, Darwin stated his appreciation for Connock's assistance in providing research for Darwin's most recent publication, *On the Origin of Species*.

Anne stepped back, her eyes wide.

A surgeon, a scholar, a visionary . . .

Here was a truly great man, not an obsessive collector but someone who had collaborated with Charles Darwin, the most forward-thinking scholar in all of history. She would give much to spend a few minutes conversing with Mr. Darwin. Abruptly she realized the true scale of the opportunity Lord Connock had given her. She couldn't think of a higher honor than to have her name associated with such a scholar, to document the rare new species he had cultivated.

"Mrs. Sherwood."

Anne spun around and faced the man in the doorway.

He stood several inches taller than she, his long legs encased in black trousers of super-fine wool. A tailored black jacket, white shirt, and black waistcoat without the least bit of embellishment hugged his shoulders and torso. The cravat at his throat, tied in a simple knot, looked like an afterthought.

Priest's clothes, Anne thought.

On McEvoy, they only served to emphasize the clean, powerful lines of his body and brought anything but religion to mind.

She drew in a quick breath.

An urbane smile on his lips, he moved to her side and took her hand, the warm pressure of his fingers against her skin unnerving her. "Ready for dinner?"

At a loss for words, she nodded.

His smile grew wider as he assessed her with those damnable blue-gray eyes. He knew exactly what he did to her and enjoyed every moment of it. "You look very pretty tonight, Mrs. Sherwood."

"And your tongue is very comfortable with flattery."

He squinted in mock-injury. "I thought English-women appreciated courtliness."

"Only when it is sincere."

"In my case, 'tis most sincere and no mistake." A glint of male appreciation warmed his eyes and she knew he'd spoken truthfully. "But don't be expecting any more praise out of me. I'm not good with words."

She raised an eyebrow. She'd never met a man better with words. "I don't place much weight in praise or censure, Mr. McEvoy. I don't need them. I prefer to make up my own mind."

"Is that so? What do you need, then?"

She lifted her chin. "Nothing that you can provide, I assure you."

"Have you ever tried smoking a pipe or a cigar?" he suddenly asked.

"No, of course not."

"Do you drink anything other than water?"

"Tea. Sometimes ratafia. And lemonade," she added, frowning, feeling inadequate.

He shook his head. "Do you sniff the honeysuckle that twines its way through a fence?"

"Not lately."

"Have you ever run through the grass in bare feet?"

She hesitated, a long-forgotten memory of just such a moment flashing into her mind. She'd been seven or eight at the most, and the fields around the barn were freshly mowed, leaving her feet green as she'd raced her father's prized yearling. A sudden longing for that lost freedom grabbed hold of her. "When I was a child, perhaps. Where are these questions leading?"

"I'm thinking you need a lot of things, Mrs. Sherwood," he said, his voice solemn.

An absurd desire to point out her weakness for fancy underclothes came over her, one she quickly smothered. Mr. McEvoy seemed to promote vice. She, for one, would not lower her standards and join in with him. The stakes were far too high. "I suppose all *your* needs are satisfied?"

His face grew still, and a shadow flickered deep within his eyes. Seconds passed. He offered no answer.

Anne swallowed. She wondered what old wounds he hid. "Will you show me to the dining room, Mr. McEvoy?"

"Consider me your guide," he said with a wink, his good humor restored.

He placed his arm beneath hers and led her from the library. Touching from wrist to elbow, they entered the hall and walked toward a room whose large double doors stood propped open.

As they walked, his gaze roved surreptitiously over her bodice and down to the hem of her apricot silk dress. His lips parted as though he wished to say something, or ask a question. The slight color in his cheeks gave her a pretty good idea what he wanted to ask, and she took perverse delight in his struggle.

Good manners. Curiosity. Which would win out?

As they reached the dining room and he still hadn't asked her about her underclothes, she realized good manners had won and suppressed a wave of regret.

"Ah, Mrs. Sherwood," Lord Connock exclaimed as they entered the dining room. The nobleman stepped up to her just as McEvoy relinquished her arm, and escorted her to one of three place settings clustered intimately near the end of the table.

The dining room, just like every other room on the first floor, had a vaulted ceiling and colored glass windows. Walnut burl furniture stained a soft brown lightened the ponderous atmosphere somewhat, and a multitude of candles burning in two chandeliers lent an orange glow to the crisp white table linens. The smell of roast duckling perfumed the air and clanging pots rang in the kitchen.

The two men seated themselves. A footman moved toward her wine glass with a bottle in hand. Quickly she covered the top of her glass with her palm. "No, thank you."

"Come now, Mrs. Sherwood, 'tis our first night together," McEvoy chided in a husky voice. "We've a lot of celebrating ahead of us. Do me the personal favor of allowing this good man to pour you wine, so you might join in a few toasts with Lord Connock and me."

She thought she detected a gleam in his eye and decided the blue-eyed devil was baiting her. Even so, she graciously inclined her head and beckoned the footman back. She wouldn't have Lord Connock thinking her churlish. "Mr. McEvoy has an irresistible gift of persuasion. I'll have a glass after all."

"A gift of blarney, I'd call it," Lord Connock offered. McEvoy chuckled.

"Blarney?"

"Insincere speech," the older man clarified.

"Hmm." Anne nodded in agreement. "Thank you for the warning."

The footman poured burgundy liquid into her glass, then attended to the gentlemen. Shortly afterward, maidservants began to serve the first course. Anne sipped her soup, noting in an abstract fashion that it tasted like marjoram. Lord Connock lifted his spoon with scholarly precision and frequently dabbed his lips with a napkin.

McEvoy ate with gusto, taking as much pleasure in the act of eating as she suspected he did with everything else.

"Lord Connock," Anne said, "I visited your library a moment before and noticed the framed documents hanging on the wall. I must say they quite impressed me."

"They keep my spirits up. I find them particularly useful when an experiment I'm working on produces a poor result . . . or no result at all."

"What sort of experimentation are you working on?" she asked.

"My theories are far too dry a topic for the dinner table." The nobleman smiled.

"Oddly enough, my cousin Sir Richard mentioned nothing of your scientific endeavors. He simply called you a collector, when obviously you are so much more. Indeed, those documents on your library wall indicate you're a scholar of substantial reputation."

"Most of those documents are eleven years old," Lord Connock explained. "Shortly after receiving them

I retired from the public eye to conduct my studies in private. Very few people remember my scientific background."

Anne nodded slowly. A long-forgotten memory was nagging at her. Something about the name *Connock*. It drifted in her head, sending her back at least fifteen years. She must have been just a girl. Where had she seen the name? In a newspaper? She simply couldn't recall. "I'm certain Sir Richard forgot as well."

McEvoy grabbed a loaf of bread and broke a chunk off, distracting her. "I, for one, am impressed by Cook's soup. 'Tis sorrel soup, no?"

Lord Connock nodded. "That it is. I'll tell her. You'll likely find a cooked chicken on your doorstep tomorrow."

McEvoy laughed, a deep, masculine rumble that resonated though the room. "Let's toast to Cook. May she live in pleasure and die out of debt."

Lord Connock took up his glass. "Hear, hear."

Anne followed suit, her uneasiness of a moment before evaporating. "To Cook."

The burgundy liquid slid easily down her throat, its fruity taste pleasant on her tongue. Warmth pooled in her stomach and suddenly, she found the courage to edge around the question nagging at her most. "Lord Connock, I took a walk on the grounds earlier."

The older man paused in sipping his soup and looked at her. "Oh?"

"I wanted to look inside your glasshouses but found them all locked."

A half-smile broke out on the nobleman's face. "And your curiosity is piqued?"

"Yes, it is," she admitted.

"Tomorrow we'll have a look inside." He returned to his soup.

"Wonderful. There was one glasshouse in particular—"

"Which one?"

"A large glasshouse, toward the back of the lawn. It smelled rather ripe."

Lord Connock's hand froze midway above his soup. "My composting glasshouse, you mean."

She nodded, his explanation precisely what she'd expected. But she couldn't help wondering why he locked it.

"I don't think you want to explore that one, Mrs. Sherwood," Lord Connock explained. "Even on the best days the smell is overpowering. The compost we produce in there is of extremely high quality, however, consisting not only of vegetable waste but also animal entrails and the like. We tolerate the smell for that reason."

"I'm surprised animal entrails don't spoil your compost. Usually they introduce all sorts of nasty elements into the mix."

"Nature provides no better fertilizer than blood and bone," Connock insisted.

Anne swallowed, a vague feeling of disgust stirring within her. "Of course."

They both went back to their soup. McEvoy, his eyebrow raised, didn't offer any comments. After their soup bowls had been removed and a potato pudding placed in front of them, the conversation inevitably drifted toward the subject of plants.

"I can hardly wait to taste your new fruit," Lord Connock said.

Anne looked up from her pudding. "New fruit?"

"A cherimoya," McEvoy supplied. "From the foothills of the Andes. On the journey back from Fiji, we stopped in Peru before sailing around Cape Horn. There I had the most delicious fruit imaginable."

"What did it taste like?"

"Custard. Its flesh literally melts on your tongue. 'Tis a cross between banana and pineapple."

The enthusiasm in his voice intrigued her. "Do you have one here?"

He grinned. "Sorry, Mrs. Sherwood. A cherimoya would spoil before arriving in England. I do have seeds, however. Lord Connock is planning to cultivate them. Perhaps in a few years . . ."

"I sincerely hope we are successful," Lord Connock added. "I'm afraid the cherimoya will prove a bit like your orchids, Mrs. Sherwood. Unwilling to grow anywhere but in the Andes."

"Orchids?" McEvoy asked.

"Our orchids at Kew Gardens rarely thrive," Anne admitted. "In fact, we work very hard to keep them from dying. Even though the mulch they're planted in is sopping wet, they become thirsty. How about you, Lord Connock? Do you cultivate orchids?"

"I haven't formed a taste for them." The nobleman leaned back in his chair. "Mrs. Sherwood and I speculated that you might be able to help, Michael. What sort of conditions do they naturally grow in?"

McEvoy fixed his attention on Anne. "First, tell me how you know the orchids are thirsty, especially when they're frequently watered."

"Well, ah . . ." Anne stuttered for a second, searching for a likely explanation, and found none.

Both men were looking at her now. Studying her.

He finally took pity on her. "What conditions do orchids grow in at Kew Gardens?"

She let out a little sigh. "We grow them in

glasshouses with plenty of sun and ventilation. In the winter, stoves keep the temperature an even seventy degrees."

"In my experience, orchids grow best when they're near water," he said. "They like to cling to the slopes on either side of waterfalls. Maybe they enjoy the mist."

The mist.

Instinctively Anne knew he had just hit upon the solution. Orchids needed sun, an even temperature, water, and humidity. She gave him a brilliant smile. "Mr. McEvoy, you are exceptional."

He blinked. Seconds later, a slow grin curved his lips. "Thank you, Mrs. Sherwood."

Lord Connock called for a toast. "To orchids."

"To orchids," she and McEvoy repeated, and both took a hearty sips of wine.

After that, the evening progressed more slowly, and Anne's stomach began to feel uncomfortably full. The two men discussed in great detail an island off the coast of Australia. Her attention began to wander and, lost in thoughts about the Irishman, she studied him surreptitiously whenever she found a chance. More than once their gazes met, and although she quickly looked away, she saw the speculation and warmth in his eyes. Lord Connock, deep in the telling of a tale about his experiences with the natives, didn't seem to notice her fascination with McEvoy.

After several sonorous minutes, the nobleman finally ended his story with a muttered, "They damned near killed me."

"A toast to your health," McEvoy immediately demanded, and lifted his wine glass.

Lord Connock followed suit.

Anne hesitated. She felt tipsy and more than a little

suspicious, too. Earlier McEvoy had asked her all those strange questions. And then said she needed something, and had proceeded to ply her with wine. What did the man have planned?

Her cheeks burned and a slow, lazy liquid—honey, perhaps—filled her limbs.

"Those damned natives almost killed Lord Connock. Come on, lass, won't you toast to his health?" he coaxed.

"Of course." Recklessly she lifted the glass to her lips and swallowed.

"We can't toast to my health without toasting the queen," Lord Connock said, his cheeks beginning to show a ruddy flush.

"You're right." McEvoy winked at her. "Here's to England and Her Majesty the queen."

"To the queen," she muttered, and more of the burgundy liquid slipped down her throat.

Lord Connock pulled out a watch fob from his waistcoat pocket and glanced at it as the final course left the dining room. " 'Tis six o'clock. There's still time before the sun sets to see the tree that brought you to Ireland, Mrs. Sherwood. Are you interested?"

Anne stood up so quickly her plate rattled. Not only did she want to see the tree, but she knew another glass of wine would confound any chance she had of having intelligent conversation with anyone. "I'd like to go right away."

The nobleman chuckled. "Michael, will you take her to see the tree?"

"Aren't you going to show me?" she asked Lord Connock, her voice rising.

"I'm afraid I must get back to my laboratory."

"I'd be more than happy to take you to the sapling,

Mrs. Sherwood," McEvoy offered in dark and velvety tones.

"I must leave." Lord Connock stood. "Tell me at breakfast what you thought of my tree, Mrs. Sherwood. Perhaps tomorrow you might try to sketch it." With a nod he left the dining room.

Anne stood also, on legs that suddenly felt shaky, and faced McEvoy. "Perhaps I ought to return to my bedchamber—"

"And miss studying this rare new species?" he teased, and before she knew it he had moved next to her and grasped her hand in his, his touch warm, persuasive. "Come with me, Mrs. Sherwood. I'm thinking you need nothing more than this little walk with me into the forest. The fresh air will clear your mind."

And his nearness, she thought, would leave her hopelessly befuddled.

5

*A*nne took his hand as he led her out of Glendale Hall and into the fading twilight. Her evening gown swayed and rustled around her, and her petticoat hems brushed against the lawn, becoming wet with dew. The substantial skirts kept him a distance away, despite their linked hands, and for that she was grateful. Practical thoughts fled when he stepped too close. "I'm not dressed for a tramp through the woods, Mr. McEvoy."

"We haven't enough light left to wait for you to change," he murmured, the grass beneath their feet beginning to show a few pink clover flowers. "I happen to like the dress you're wearing, anyway."

She cast an involuntary glance down at her apricot silk gown. The last time she'd worn this dress, she and Henry had been attending a fete in London, almost three years ago. The dress hadn't come out of her wardrobe since. It was far too frilly, too pretty, completely unsuitable for a woman of science. She frowned. "I don't like this gown at all."

"Why are you wearing it, then?"

She glanced toward the sun, which had dipped perilously close to the horizon. His was a question whose answer she didn't want to acknowledge, even to herself. " 'Tis almost night. Perhaps we should turn around."

He clasped her hand more tightly. "If you wish. We're only about a minute or so from the tree. And nights in Ireland are magical, if you need another reason. When you see Glendale Hall all lit up, you'll swear you've gone to Tir-na-n-Og."

"Tir-na-n-Og?"

"The country of the fairies."

Anne suppressed a sigh. She'd had enough of fairies. Still, she kept walking. The thought of the strange tree only a short distance away spurred her on. Her hand warm in his larger one, she left the lawn and started into the forest with him. A wide path cut through the trees. Beneath the canopy of leaves just beginning to unfurl, shadows reigned. Mist plumed from her mouth and the smell of pine and hemlock hung thick in the air. Absurdly large toadstools clung to fallen logs and blue-belled creepers twined around the lowest branches of the trees, most of them oaks. A large boulder, covered in patchy moss that made it look like a turtle, silently invited her to sit and contemplate.

Raspberry bushes and brambles, all seeking to rip her gown, grew thick around the path as they walked deeper into the woods. At last they arrived in a very small glen, not really a glen at all but a place where three very old trees had fallen, clearing some room. Twigs and dried flower stems snapped beneath their feet as they edged into the clearing. The fading light was brighter here, illuminating the sapling that stood in the center.

Anne stopped short. She sucked in a breath, her mind suddenly sharp despite all the wine.

Small, only about two feet tall, the sapling had a soft, golden bark and leathery green leaves similar in shape to cloven hooves. Two limbs sprouted from its tiny trunk, each limb amply protected by sharp, vicious-looking thorns. Several swallowtail butterflies sat between the thorns, their black wings glistening in the dying sunlight.

Anne moved closer. "Incredible."

They both studied the tree. Anne hardly noticed the insects humming around her head or the stealthy rustling coming from the woods.

After a while, he nodded. "Saw it myself for the first time this afternoon. I don't know what to make of it."

"Lord Connock said you'd brought the tree back from the Himalayas."

"I returned with several different types of seeds. Rose chestnut, bamboo, alder, pine, laurel . . . they all grow in India's tropical evergreen forests, up to about three thousand feet. I don't remember stumbling upon a tree like this one. I can only assume that the seed somehow slipped into my specimen pouch."

"Why are the butterflies sitting on its branch?"

"The sapling secretes a honeylike substance. I suspect they're eating."

Anne took another step toward the sapling and, evidently disturbed by her nearness, the butterflies took flight in a cloud of black. "Lord Connock grew the tree from seed, then?"

"Apparently he had expected a rose chestnut. This sapling grew instead."

"A happy surprise," she murmured, touching its bark with one finger. A familiar yet disturbing tingle stole over her. Faint red. Watercolor-red. As with the hedge outside Glendale Hall, the sapling emanated a low-key distress. She withdrew her finger, noticing the sticky coating on her skin.

Her eyebrows drew together. She glanced at the mulch in which it grew and found it rich-looking, very moist. The sapling also received a good deal of sunlight in this little clearing, so what could possibly be causing its difficulty?

"Is something wrong?" McEvoy asked.

"No," she lied, wondering if her gift for perceiving plants' emotions would prove untrustworthy in all of Ireland or just at Glendale Hall.

"You sense it, don't you?"

"Sense what?"

"Not all is well with this tree." Frowning, all traces of the carefree Irishman gone, he had the look of a man who had turned over a rock and discovered a nest of ugly white grubs.

"I don't know what you mean," she insisted.

"You know damned well what I mean, although I don't understand *how* you know or why you deny it. Stop pretending ignorance and give me your impression."

Anne raised an eyebrow but said nothing. She wasn't telling anyone about her gift, not even the fairy-obsessed Irishman. He might believe her, but then again, he might think her mad and tell Lord Connock so. Did Lord Connock want a crazed illustrator working for him? Anne thought not.

"All right, I'll give you *my* impression," he challenged. "There is no sense of harmony between its delicate golden limbs and the rough, leathery leaves that terminate them. The sharp thorns on its branches ward off man and beast, and yet it bears no real fruit worth protecting, just a honeylike substance insects favor."

She turned to look at the tree again.

He waved a hand toward its tiny golden trunk. "If you'll press a thumbnail into the wood, you'll notice 'tis rather soft. I even found marks from borer attacks near the roots. What sort of a tree secretes honey to attract the very insects that will riddle it with holes?"

Her eyes widened. "Good Lord, Mr. McEvoy, you are an inspired observer. I didn't see any of those things until you pointed them out, and I have trained myself to see the details of a plant on first inspection."

He directed his attention toward the sapling. "I'm a seasoned naturalist."

"I've known many seasoned naturalists, but none as perceptive as you." She looked at him with new respect. "You don't just see the details, you interpret them."

"And here I thought you were sparing of your praise."

"All that wine has loosened my tongue," she offered with a hesitant smile.

He eyed her as though suspicious of her sincerity.

To her left, a rustling noise disturbed the underbrush. She cocked her head and listened. Abruptly the rustling disappeared.

He took her hand again and nodded toward the west. "We should return to Glendale Hall. The sun's all but gone. We'll come back tomorrow."

She had the distinct impression he was trying to change the subject and wondered why. "How long have you been a naturalist, Mr. McEvoy?"

"Why do you ask?"

"Your insights are rather precocious, more suited to a botanist who's worked in the field for decades. What

did you do before Lord Connock employed you as a naturalist eleven years ago?"

"Mrs. Sherwood, you ask a lot of questions."

"Questions *you* aren't willing to answer."

He shrugged. "You have a few of those yourself."

A smile twitched her lips. "I suppose we are even."

"We are at that." He pulled her hand, urging her
back onto the path. The sun had set completely and
only the slightest bit of light remained.

Anne began to follow. Then that damnable rustling
started up in the bushes again and she froze. "Wait."

"What's wrong?"

"Listen. Do you hear it?"

Eyebrows drawn together, he looked at the ground
for a second or so before returning his attention to her.
"Hear what? That squirrel in the brush?"

"Squirrel? Are you certain?"

"Not really. Could be a wood mouse."

"Now it's stopped," she whispered. "As though it
knew we'd marked its presence." A chill crept over her.
She shivered. The gloom around them gained a feeling
of menace.

"Animals do that," he said. "They don't like to be
caught."

She examined the forest floor for a small furry body.
"I suppose any number of creatures could be hiding—"
Abruptly she broke off, her gaze fastened on his left
boot. "Mr. McEvoy, look down."

Eyes widening, he twisted his ankle. A muffled snort
emerged from him. "Damn. Must have tangled my foot
in this piece of ivy." A tendril of the stuff had curled
around his boot and refused to let go.

Anne's rational side wanted to believe him. Still, a
deeper, more primitive instinct suggested they should

leave the forest with all haste possible. She reached down and unfastened the ivy, her fingers becoming sticky. A black aura filled her mind. Black, not red. The color of death. She recoiled, the hairs at the back of her neck standing on end, and wiped her fingers on her skirts. "Let's go."

"Are you seeing bogeys, Mrs. Sherwood?"

"No, of course not."

"A scholar such as yourself knows better," he teased, then took her hand. Silently she followed him through the forest to Glendale Hall, every little rustling noise setting her nerves on edge.

As soon as they emerged onto the lawn, which stretched in a greenish-gray carpet before them, the sense of menace dissipated. Brow furrowed, wondering if the wine had gotten to her, she glanced up at the vista before her and paused.

Mist about a foot thick hovered directly above the grass and wafted down to the river that flowed past Glendale Hall. The hall itself was ablaze with lights, each one sparkling in a larger bank of fog rolling down from the mountains. Beyond the mountains, a spray of stars decorated the purplish sky. Frogs croaked and wildflowers whispered against her skirt and the clean scent of pine filled her nose.

"How beautiful," she breathed.

A strange, unexpected yearning grabbed hold of her. For all of her life, she'd understood the plant world with her mind. She'd seen its colors. Now, for one startling moment, she wanted to know it with her body. She wanted to absorb everything—the manicured lawn which seemed to stretch into forever, the mist blanketing the earth, the twinkling lights of Glendale Hall, the stars, everything. She wanted to draw them into her pores until she understood them better than she understood herself. She wanted to run, to laugh, to lie upon the earth and feel the grass wetting her back while looking at the stars . . .

She'd had *far* too much wine.

McEvoy glanced at her, his smile widening. "What do you see?"

"Why, the castle, the river, trees, stars—"

"Tell me what you *see*," he insisted.

"It's hard to *see* anything. 'Tis almost pitch black outside."

"At night, if you look closely, you'll see the true nature of the world."

Anne wrinkled her brow. "I don't understand."

"During the day, everything beneath the sun is exposed," he said, his voice deep, husky. "Old men pull in their bellies and women sit ramrod straight to cut a finer figure. But under the sheltering darkness of night, the old man relaxes and lets his belly drape over his waistband, and the woman, feeling an ache in her shoulders, finally slouches."

He encompassed the land around them with a sweep of his hand. "Darkness forgives. At night, the need for struggle is gone, and everything—the trees, the boulders, the sky—returns to its true nature. That's when the soul comes out to play."

Lips parted, Anne stared through the shadows at the trees and river. "I can't see any difference."

"You have to look with your heart."

"What do *you* see, when you look with your heart?"

"A woman who looks a bit like a fairy, with moonlight on her hair and a smile on her lips."

She giggled. "You have more than your fair share of charm, Michael McEvoy."

"As do you, Mrs. Sherwood."

"Mrs. Sherwood sounds so formal, does it not? Why don't you call me Anne?"

"My pleasure, Anne. Call me Michael."

"Well, Michael, I have to thank you for insisting we visit the sapling this evening. The view of Glendale Hall at night is splendid."

"Nothing matches it. Come on!"

He tugged on her hand, and suddenly they were both running across the lawn, toward the river. Her leg muscles, not accustomed to the violent spurt of exercise, contracted almost painfully, but soon they settled into a warm glow that felt surprisingly good.

Anne didn't care that her behavior was anything but that of a proper matron's. Who could possibly see her? Her heart working hard but oh so alive, she felt like a child. Too soon, they stopped near the steps leading to the front door and paused, laughing, breathing hard.

A lantern used by footmen to guide carriages up the drive hung on a nearby hook. In that dim light, he looked mysterious, compelling, his face full of angles and planes. Her artist's eye took in the firm shape of his chin, the slight ridge on his nose suggesting he'd broken it at least once, the way his powerful shoulders filled his jacket without the need of padding.

Silently she acknowledged that Michael McEvoy's face would prove much more interesting to draw than any plant. His wasn't a boy's countenance, unmarked by the passage of time and untested by strife. Boys didn't interest her. No, Michael's face had character. Those lines on his forehead were the lines of a man who spent some time thinking, while the grooves around his full lips suggested pain. Anne liked the wrinkles around his eyes the most. People who laughed often had them.

She pressed her hand against a stitch in her side. "Why did we run like that?"

"You need to acknowledge your true nature," he murmured, and without warning, put two strong arms around her waist. "I suspect you need this even more."

Excitement scorched through her. She pressed her hands against his chest, feeling the strength of the muscles beneath her palms. "Michael—"

He leaned forward and gathered her into his arms, his body blocking out the light as he pressed his mouth to hers and parted her lips with his own. When his tongue tangled with hers, she grew weak all over and clung to his shoulders for support, her face flushing with heat, blood shuddering through her limbs, her gaze fastened on the blue-gray eyes that suddenly seemed dark with secrets. How different this was from the empty, pain-filled nights with Henry, the fumbling, the cold dryness, the cursing, the shame.

He pulled her closer, one strong thigh nudging her legs apart until she felt completely off-balance, powerless, unable to do anything but lick his tongue with her own and allow him to take whatever he wished. He went on kissing her, sparing her nothing in his exploration, devouring her, plundering her, leaving her breathless and limp even as a scalding knot tightened mercilessly between her legs. Moisture slicked the uppermost skin of her thighs and her breasts felt heavy, and she knew she would find no peace until he soothed them with his touch.

From beneath half-mast lids he watched her as they kissed, his dark lashes an enviable fringe around eyes that glowed with male satisfaction. How easily he'd conquered her! The thought gave her pause. What was she doing? What about her scholarly goals? She shifted her mouth from his.

Michael smiled at her, a lazy grin that melted her insides and swept away her thoughts of scholarly pursuits. How could she think of anything but his mouth on hers when he looked at her like that? Her pulse pounding so hard she could hear it in her ears, she entwined her fingers through his silky black hair and pulled, wanting him to know how terribly she desired him, how tight the knot inside her had become.

He growled deep in his throat and began to trail kisses down her neck to the tops of her breasts, his fingers reaching inside her neckline to cup her flesh beneath her chemise, his palms hot and rough and utterly foreign. He released one of her breasts from its silken binding, exposing her skin to the evening air. At some point he must have undone some of the hooks at the back of her gown, but she hadn't even realized it, so focused was she on the feel of his lips against her—their warm pressure, their gentleness. She tingled everywhere he touched her, as if his hands commanded some magical power.

The shadow of his beard was dark on his chin as he nuzzled the breast he'd freed, running his tongue all around the fullness of it before he took her nipple into his mouth and played with it. The gentle yet relentless motion continued to rob her of any will to stop him, to end his seductive torture in favor of her long-sought-after goals. She stared at him, noting how tanned his face was against the creamy whiteness of her breast, how the sharp angles of his jaw contrasted with her full round flesh, how her nipple was soft and pink against his tongue as he licked it. Already hard, her nipple contracted even more and sharp pleasure stabbed through her.

She moaned, low in her throat. Her breath came in quick little gasps as the pleasure between her legs mounted. Suddenly she wanted her gown off, her corset thrown to the winds, and her chemise discarded on the grass. She wanted to be completely naked, a female given over to sensuality, quivering with anticipation for the moment when he would fill her with his hard length.

With a groan, he dragged his mouth from her breasts and buried his face in her neck. She felt his lips against her skin for a moment before he lifted his head to look at her. Limp in his arms, her breath coming in quick pants, she returned his gaze, feeling all over again the shock, the power of his kiss, that sense of rightness between them. She wondered if he'd felt the same.

"Mother of God," he murmured, his voice shaky. Frowning, he smoothed her hair away from her face.

They gazed at each other. A few moments passed, moments in which she thought about their lovemaking and how it would have ended if he hadn't shown enough sense to stop. Her passion drained away, replaced by the knowledge of what she'd almost lost and embarrassment over the fact that he'd shown more control than she.

"Anne, I shouldn't have—"

She silenced him with a quick finger to his lips. "Please, say no more." She knew they'd made a mistake. He obviously knew, too. It wouldn't happen again, no matter what she'd felt between them.

He released her, slowly, giving her enough time to regain her balance. After several wobbly seconds, she stood facing him, standing on her own.

"Can I escort you back into the hall?" He ran a hand

through his hair and shifted on his feet, clearly uncomfortable.

"No. I'll find my own way in." Trying for a casual smile and failing miserably, Anne fixed her bodice. "Good night."

"Anne . . ."

"Good night, Michael," she repeated.

He paused a moment, then nodded, as if he'd come to a decision. "I'll see you in the morning." He took the lantern hanging on the hook and turned toward the woods. His stride determined, he walked away across the lawn.

She touched her lips with her fingers, watching him go. A little pain formed somewhere near her heart and she knew that her life had just changed in some ineffable way.

Michael cut across the lawn and strode back into Glendale Forest. He had stopped whistling. He didn't want to alert whatever little beasties hid in the wood to his presence. Anne Sherwood was going to occupy his thoughts for a good deal of time tonight, if the ache in his loins was any indication, but for now, he had to find out what had created that uneasy feeling in him while they'd walked among the trees.

All around him, oaks and alders, aspen and rowans stretched their venerable old trunks toward the sky, while on the forest floor, lichens and wild primroses and anemones grew with primeval abandon. Their colors were a dim gray in the lantern's light, and yet he knew them well enough not to question their form or presence.

What he did question was the ivy that had tangled around his ankle. In old woods like these—God knew there weren't many of them left in Ireland—ivy and wood anemones didn't usually grow together. Wood anemones wanted to grow in the thick mulch of an old forest, while ivy liked the stone and dirt patches found in newer forests. In fact, in the stretch before his last trip he couldn't remember seeing any ivy in Glendale Forest at all. He didn't see any now, for that matter.

Each foot placed slowly and carefully, Michael crept through the forest. Every sense he possessed stood on alert as he retraced his path to Lord Connock's sapling. He scanned the trees, relying on the lantern and the moonlight that filtered through the leaves to light the way. He heard the angry chattering of a squirrel and the soft whisper of wind stirring the treetops. Mist settled on his skin and stems brushed against his boots. He took a deep breath. Pine, decaying leaves, the subtle perfume of newly awakened primroses . . . and beneath it, something sweet yet rotten. Like the smell of an animal that had died in the woods a month before.

Nostrils flaring, he stopped and spun around in a tight circle, searching for the odor's source. Not very strong, more a faint whiff, the honeyed scent disappeared as soon as he'd detected it. He stared into the darkness. A bat flapped erratically overhead, but otherwise nothing moved. All appeared normal.

That didn't stop the uneasiness from turning a slow flip in his gut. He tried to grasp the knife he normally wore in his belt when exploring jungles, and then realized he'd left it in his cottage. And why not? He wasn't walking through a jungle. He'd known Glendale Forest for eleven years now and hadn't any reason to fear it. Still, something definitely seemed off.

He reached the sapling minutes later and walked around it, studying it from all angles. The ugly little bastard had its roots deep into the forest floor, as if it knew it had roused his dislike and wouldn't go easily if he decided to pull it up. He would never pull it up, of course; the tree meant too much to Lord Connock.

Michael touched one of its limbs and sniffed the sap on his fingers. Sweet but almost odorless, certainly not the honeyed smell that had caught on the air minutes before, then faded and caught again. He wondered how long the sapling had before carpenter ants found it and reduced it to pulp.

He sat down on a nearby boulder and stared at the little tree. The more he looked at it, the less real it seemed. *Too many inconsistencies*, he thought. In fact, it looked like a combination of several different trees and plants he'd brought back on his various trips. A maple tree oozed sap that tasted like sugar. The sassafras tree on the island of Formosa had leaves the shape of cloven hooves. The black locust sported brutal thorns, and twigs on a cottonwood tree were the same ocher-yellow of the sapling's bark.

In short, the tree looked pieced together, and that perception had begun to worry him. Lord Connock's strange sapling didn't seem to him like a new species at all. Instead, it appeared a man-made invention. He wondered if the nobleman was pretending the tree had natural origins to raise its value and bring in funding for new research. A new species was worth more than a man-made one, just as a natural pearl was prized above its cultured cousin.

Michael rubbed his forehead. A headache was beginning to form behind his temples. He just couldn't believe where his logic was leading him. He'd always thought Lord Connock an honorable man. In fact, he preferred to think Connock an honorable man and find another explanation for the sapling.

In any case, he wouldn't admit his suspicions to anyone, not even Anne, though she appeared to possess very good instincts of her own. Lord Connock deserved at least that much from him. All those years ago, the nobleman had drawn him from the wild, treated him well, and renewed his faith in mankind when all others had left him to rot. Besides, he had no proof of misdeeds. His sense of fairness dictated he keep quiet and watch the situation carefully.

Michael skirted around the sapling and strode deeper into the woods, listening carefully, still very aware of the forest around him. After a few minutes of walking, he heard a strange rustling in the bushes, one that seemed to chase him down the path.

He stopped.

The rustling stopped.

He began walking again.

The rustling promptly resumed.

Eyes narrowed, he paused and studied the location where he'd last heard the noise. A vine of what looked like ivy—the first he'd seen since he left Anne— twined along the ground. In the darkness, he had difficulty seeing the details. A few of its leaves crackled, as if stirred by an errant breeze. Only Michael couldn't feel a breeze. An animal, perhaps?

He took a breath and let it out quietly. Wolves were the only animals he could think of that might stalk a human in these forests. And yet, wolves had become extinct centuries before. Each foot cautiously placed, he left the path and skulked into the bushes. He smelled the slightly rusty odor and hint of decay seconds before he stumbled upon it—a rabbit, long dead, almost desiccated. A dark, crusty substance caked its mouth and ears. Michael didn't need any more light to know what the substance was.

Blood.

Grimacing, he held the lantern close to the corpse and examined it. Its fur, a soft clean gray, just hung over its skeleton. He could find no evidence of tissue, fat, organs, anything. Even the eyes were gone. The thin film covering its sockets looked like scum upon a pond's surface.

His brow furrowed and he backed away, wondering what could have done such a thing. A moment's thought convinced him he wouldn't find an answer, not easily. Dead things often reached this state of decomposition after many weeks, but that fur—it looked so fresh. Nothing made sense. Disquieted, he waded out of the thicket and continued on to his cottage.

He discovered nothing untoward during the rest of his walk. Within half an hour he had reached his cottage, on the other side of the woods. The gardens he'd tilled last year had grown wild, the stems dry and broken, pointing at him like an accusing finger. If not for the mock orange which had begun to leaf out, he'd have thought he'd ruined the garden entirely.

Michael stepped up to his front door, threw it open, and entered his cottage. He put the lantern on a side table and looked around. With its whitewashed stone walls and plaster ceiling, the place was plenty luxurious—not a high-flying castle like Glendale Hall but no weather-beaten croft either. Nevertheless, it simply lacked the comfortable feeling he'd always yearned for and never achieved. It didn't feel like home.

Maybe the problem wasn't in the cottage but in *him*.

Frowning, Michael pushed the notion aside. He pre-

ferred not to acknowledge it. Instead, he scanned the
room, looking for evidence of intruders, a habit he'd
fallen into at the workhouse and never managed to
banish.

Carpets covered the limestone floor. A few pieces of
mismatched furniture—a pine bureau, a table made of
burled walnut, a wrought-iron rack—all looked exactly
as he'd left them earlier. The open hearth, which swallowed an entire wall, had a fine collection of copper
cooking pots, each hanging in the usual manner.
Michael let out a deep breath and wondered when he'd
have a chance to use all those pots. Why in hell had he
collected them? He wasn't sure. He hadn't any talent at
cooking and never used those fancy spices that smothered a dish's true taste. The scrubbed pine table in the
center of the room still bore the remains of his lunch,
the fanciest food he'd ever prepared: bolognese, salad,
bread, and Cabernet Sauvignon.

He shrugged out of his jacket and slung it over a pine
chair. The good-sized room, a combination of a salon,
library, and dining room, remained dim and unfriendly
despite the lantern's glow. In a short amount of time
he'd lit some candles and had a hearty fire crackling behind the fire grate. Sighing, he slouched onto a deacon's bench, the only chair in the room with cushions,
and contemplated the fire. Rather than see the orange
and yellow flames, however, he saw the face of Anne
Sherwood.

And a fine face it was, he admitted, a perfect oval
with delicate bones. Very beautiful, in a classic way.
There wasn't a man alive who could pass by her and not
stop to take a second look, once he saw past her iron
maiden disguise. Her eyebrows, a gentle arch of blond,
widened her gray eyes and gave her an air of innocence,

one that the blush staining her cheeks enhanced even more. Her lips, a soft pink, were full and luscious. She often kept them pressed together as if afraid she might appear too sensual.

But it was her body that had him intrigued. God knew she tried to hide those curves beneath her nun's clothes, but he'd known enough women to realize exactly what he might find if he undressed her. A jealous old crone might be vicious enough to call her plump. Michael preferred the term *voluptuous*. Full breasts, perhaps even a little heavy for her, a soft backside and well-rounded hips . . . she was made for sex, for pleasure. He'd nearly fallen into a frenzy of worship, kissing and stroking her creamy skin, cupping his hands around her fullness. He imagined burying his face between her legs and unleashing himself on her. Damn, just thinking about it left him unbelievably hard.

At the same time, he knew he'd moved too fast. He just couldn't help himself. She was too damned tempting. If he didn't show more control, she'd fly from him for good. Besides, he wasn't in the habit of ruining widows. In the future, they would have to be more careful, choose a more discreet place.

He shifted on the bench, the movement doing little to ease the painful fullness that had built between his legs. He muttered a few choice oaths, stood, and walked over to the wooden sideboard stacked with blue and white cups, saucers, mugs, and pewter pans. Moments like these called for smoky cigars.

Frowning, he opened a mahogany box and selected a cigar he'd purchased in the Philippine province of Isabella. He returned to his deacon's bench, cut the cigar tip with a knife, and lit up on a candle.

Fragrant gray tendrils wafted from the cigar. Michael

contemplated the lazy patterns it made and tried to lose himself in its fragrance. Cigars, he thought, had a lot in common with a fine bottle of wine. He wouldn't open an expensive French Cabernet in a two-bit whorehouse, and wouldn't light up a cigar in a place with a lot of wind and distraction. The sweet, spicy smoke deserved respect and was good for reflection. It often cleared his head. At the moment, however, the smoke did little to steady him.

Beautiful Anne, she was a puzzle. A combination of society and science, she seemed content to study nature rather than immerse herself in it. And yet her plant knowledge, while not the same as his, was just as impressive. How could a woman who didn't even notice the trees blooming around her know that carpenter ants had riddled the inside of an oak tree with holes? He had an itch in him, an itch to discover how she'd learned so much about plants, and he knew if he didn't scratch this particular itch he'd go to his grave wondering.

He wasn't the type of man who liked to remain baffled for long.

Still, if he were honest with himself, he'd admit it was more than their shared connection to nature that drew him to her. Something about her manner appealed to him, too. She tried so hard to appear tough, hiding her gentleness and vulnerability beneath a drab gray exterior. And yet, when her quiet joy in the little things he showed to her broke through, a lump formed in his throat and he thought, *God, she is lovely*.

He shifted on the bench and flicked cigar ashes into the fireplace, thinking about a lily he'd brought back from a jungle near the Amazon River. By the time he'd returned it to Ireland, a year had passed and the damned thing looked so shriveled and dead that even Lord Connock had wanted to throw it out. Still, Michael had stubbornly kept the lily, remembering how beautiful it had looked in the jungle and feeling unexpectedly guilty for killing such an exquisite thing.

Feeling like a fool, he'd put the flower, dried roots and all, into a little earthenware pot and watered it for several months. He'd even brought it with him on a short journey into Europe. The thing had remained brown and dried-up. Finally, when he returned to Ireland, he planted it in his garden, buried it, really, and let nature take its course.

Two days later, a green, spearlike leaf poked through the dirt. A week later, flower buds had formed on the tops of the leaves. Within two weeks, Michael had the most beautiful lily he'd ever seen growing in his garden, its petals pink and waxy-soft.

The sense of fulfillment he'd had in bringing that lily back to life had eclipsed anything else he'd ever known. Anne, in some strange way, reminded him of the lily: brown, dead on the outside, yet full of promise, ready to bloom given the right conditions. Just as he'd nursed the lily back to life, he knew an almost irresistible urge to bring Anne's true nature to the surface, and to delight in her beauty and sensuality. He suspected he'd gotten a glimpse of the real Anne tonight, and he could only imagine the pleasure and satisfaction that awakening her fully would bring him.

Michael kicked his boots up onto the bench and leaned his head against the backrest. Yesterday Lord Connock had asked him to plan a trip to India, to collect a certain species of alpine flower, possibly near the middle of May. Michael wondered if he might start out in June rather than May and still avoid the monsoon season. Another month in Ireland would give him another month with Anne. With a fair bit of dismay, he slowly realized that for the first time in his life he was considering postponing one of his trips.

For a *woman*.

6

*A*nne stretched in her curtained tester bed. Sunlight was intruding on some rather pleasant dreams, memories of a dark-eyed, laughing Irishman. He was kissing her, his mouth warm, his arms strong as he held her, his lips making her tremble, making her yearn in a way she'd never anticipated.

She tried to hold on to the dreams, but as she came to full wakefulness, her rational side reminded her how dangerous her relationship with Michael had become. She hadn't uttered the tiniest protest when he'd pressed his lips against hers, a fact that boded ill for her future and her scholarly goals.

She opened her eyes, swung her legs over the edge of the bed, and stood. Beyond the windows, the sun sparkled gently on lawns and trees that seemed greener than they did yesterday. Not by much, but noticeable nevertheless. Spring had come, she thought, and every day the land would awaken a little more. The perception brought an urgency with it; unlike that morning in

Kew Gardens, when she'd tried to sketch *Violaceae*, she felt more than capable of capturing the excitement of a new beginning. Silently she acknowledged a subtle change had come over her since she'd arrived at Glendale Hall. A tiny spark of hope had entered her life, and she feared she had Michael to thank for it.

Frowning, she rang for a lady's maid, ordered breakfast, and selected a pristine white chemise and cotton stockings to wear beneath her gown. Today, she thought, she needed to quell her unruly impulses on all fronts, rather than give them free rein as she had last night.

Quickly she pulled on the undergarments. Their virginal whiteness did little to make her feel innocent. Reluctantly she turned her thoughts to Michael once again. Had he felt the power of their kiss, the pure shock of her lips against his, as she had? Lord, she'd never expected such a fire to sweep through her. Henry had never made her heart pound like that. Henry had told her she wasn't a very passionate person. Useless, he'd called her. A failure. And then he'd gone and found some middle-aged widow and put her up in a town house.

But now, for the first time, she questioned Henry's assessment of her. She was beginning to understand that she and Henry, while they shared many interests, had never experienced any real attraction for each other. Her thoughts raced ahead. If she and Michael were to make love, fully, how different would it feel? How much more pleasure would she experience?

Heat began to coil deep inside her, bringing a blush of shame to her cheeks. God help her, she couldn't even think about him without feeling warm and languid and needy. If she and Michael became lovers and Lord Connock discovered the affair, she would at the very least lose credibility with him, if not her post as botanical illustrator. She ought to cut Michael off before he seduced her completely.

A knock at the door made her jump. She fanned her cheeks for a furious few seconds before admitting the maid, who bore a tray of tea and toast.

While Anne nibbled on toast that fairly dripped butter, the maid threw open the wardrobe doors and rifled through its contents. Her brown curls tucked neatly beneath a white cap, the girl studied each dress for a brief moment. When she'd reached the last one, she turned to regard Anne with a little frown curving her pink lips. "Where are your fancy gowns, ma'am? If you give me the one you're planning to wear to the dinner party this weekend, I'll see that it's pressed."

"Oh, blast it, I forgot all about the dinner party. Saturday night, is it?"

The maid nodded. "We've plenty of time. My name's Jane, ma'am, and while you're here I'm to see to your needs. Did I forget to unpack one of your trunks?"

"No, you unpacked them all, Jane, and did so with great skill."

Jane hesitated, her brows knit together. "Then where are the rest of your gowns?"

"I'm afraid you're going to have a rather boring time seeing to my needs. I have no fancy gowns."

"No fancy gowns?" Her brow furrowed, Jane looked toward the bureau holding all of Anne's lacy underclothes.

"None at all."

"Don't you want to look pretty?"

Anne studied the maid's slender, girlish figure, the freckles across her nose and the blemish on her chin.

She estimated Jane's age as just shy of fifteen. In short, Jane was a girl with a lot to learn. "I would rather be known for my intellect."

The maid's attention drifted toward the under-clothes bureau again. "Are you certain?"

"Very." Anne couldn't stop a smile from curving her lips. "I don't care which gown I wear to the party. Why don't you pick one for me?"

"Of course." Jane turned away, but not before Anne saw her little moue of displeasure.

Nevertheless, Anne felt good about herself. She was here to work, not to make love with a Irishman who looked at things in a way she might never understand. At least she'd shown enough sense to forsake those fancy underclothes.

She brushed toast crumbs off her fingers. "Jane, please fetch the ivory muslin for me, the one with small blue dots on it."

"The dress with the dirty hem?" the girl asked in dour tones.

"Yes, that's the one." Jane didn't yet understand that sketching in the woods and gardens wreaked havoc with a lady's wardrobe, but she'd soon learn.

While Jane retrieved the gown, Anne stepped over to her underclothes drawer, found a plain white petti-coat, and slipped it on.

Jane returned to her side with the ivory muslin gown in hand. She glanced at Anne's petticoat and her lips drooped. "Won't you be wearing a corset, ma'am?"

"Not today. I'm sketching."

"And a hoop petticoat?"

"No."

Shaking her head, Jane helped Anne into her muslin gown. Anne had the feeling she'd disappointed the girl mightily. No doubt she'd been looking forward to satins and silks, ribbons and bows, and fine French styles. Well, Anne simply didn't dress that way. Jane would have to content herself with the fancy underclothes, should Anne decide to risk them again.

In short order Anne finished dressing and slipped out of her bedchamber with her sketchbook case in hand. She saw few servants as she made her way through Glendale Hall. Of Lord Connock she saw nothing. She crossed through the great hall, noting the cleanliness of the floor and furniture. A footman seated near the entrance noticed her approach and opened the door for her. Soon she felt the sun's rays against her face. A weak yellow, the sunlight hardly seemed potent enough to draw seedlings up from the earth, but as Anne had discovered last night, the sun had coaxed seedlings to life and something much stranger. *Something* that might give her the respect and recognition she craved.

Anne hurried across the lawn and into Glendale Forest, her boots becoming soggy and chafing the tops of her ankles. She paid little attention to the discomfort, instead trying to remember the path Michael had taken to reach the sapling. Ahead, two giant trees stood on either side of a lane like sentinels. Shrugging, Anne decided to try the lane.

As she entered the forest, the air became cooler and dew-laden, full of the smells of decaying leaves and young plants. She sensed none of the menace that had dogged her the previous two nights. Trees towered over her, moss blanketed fallen logs that lurked in the underbrush, and tiny song birds twittered happily among the branches.

The greenness had a calming effect on her. She temporarily dismissed her battle to remain aloof from Michael, and pushed aside her burning ambition to achieve recognition for her work. Rather, she breathed deep of the forest loam and imagined the sapling in her mind.

After several minutes she recognized the turtle boulder and congratulated herself on finding the correct path on the first attempt. Smiling, she paused and ran her fingers over a fern's leaves. As before, a faint red wash of distress emanated from the plant.

Her smile faltered.

She walked more quickly down the path, which grew smaller with each step she took. She couldn't remember the path narrowing the previous night and speculated that she'd made a wrong turn somewhere. Well, she could still find her way back to Glendale Hall. All she had to do was turn around and retrace her steps.

You're lost, Anne, a little voice inside her announced.

She ignored it. She'd heard that little voice before. It liked to speak at the worst moments. It had talked a lot during her marriage to Henry, became quieter once she'd moved in with her cousin at Kew Gardens. In Ireland it had hardly spoken at all. Until now.

You're lost.

Loath to turn around and give in to the voice, she kept walking. There was something about turning around and backtracking that just didn't sit well with her. She would much rather go forward and hope the sapling lurked just around the corner, than tramp through the forest for endless minutes, only to end up exactly where she'd started.

Ten very long minutes later, she was reevaluating

her decision to go forward rather than backward. Just as the first strings of panic began to strum inside her, she espied a tiny cottage in the distance. Centered in the middle of a grass-covered clearing, with a stream running through the front yard, it had a welcoming aura.

She let out a breath that almost sounded like gasp, so relieved was she to see even a modicum of civilization. Her step became slower as she took in the details.

Smoke curled up from a little round chimney set at the peak of the cottage's thatch roof. *Woodsmoke*, she thought, the aroma curling pleasantly through the air. A combination of brown timber and gray stone, the cottage blended in so easily with the trees and boulders around it that Anne wondered if visitors ever arrived or strayed hopelessly in the forest.

Gardens surrounded the cottage and edged the small glen. Thick, luscious with flowers, they poised on the edge of blossoming like a girl on the edge of womanhood.

Like a girl with her first lover.

Anne's steps slowed.

She'd been a tightly furled flower once, quivering with excitement, waiting for the warmth of her lover's touch. That first night she'd gone to Henry in a white nightgown, her stomach trembling with nervous anticipation. He may have been several years older than she and rather ugly besides, but he was her husband. Surely he loved her. Surely he would treat her well.

She had trusted in her husband implicitly.

Anne slowed to a halt, her gaze unfocused. The bedchamber had smelled of lavender water. Henry had worn a red robe, his bald pate gleaming in the light of a few candles. By God, she would *never* forget that red robe. Nor the shriveled thing between his legs that he'd plunged into her a few minutes later.

He'd taken the nightgown off her with one practiced yank, put her on the bed gently enough, and pressed her down on her back. Then he'd doused the candles, leaving the gray light of twilight to illuminate the distasteful ceremony about to commence.

It didn't last long. He spread her legs, roughly almost, then thrust into her, making her bleed, making her cry. She tried to shrink away from him. He didn't seem to care, as long as she remained near enough for him to rear up over her before pressing forward and back again. After he'd dumped his fluid into her, she'd leaned over the bed and become violently sick.

That first night had set the tone between them. Although growing more tolerable with time, her wifely duties had always remained a vile task. And when she thought about those years now, she understood that Henry had taken the vulnerable flower that was Anne and crushed it between his fingers. He had killed her innocence, taken her joy, and left her with nothing but ambition. A few tears gathered in her eyes. Angrily she dashed them away. Only fools mourned for lost innocence.

Anne shook her head, forcing the memories aside. She could not allow herself to dwell upon them. Even today they had the power to hurt her deeply. Instead she reminded herself how close she had come to achieving her goal of scholarly recognition, by coming here to Ireland to sketch for Lord Connock. She *would* prove herself a worthwhile person.

As she crossed over the stream on an arched wooden bridge, she identified pennyroyal and parsley, bee balm and peony buds thrusting up from the earth, and a host of other plants that had come to England and Ireland from Europe. Often the gardeners "up at the big house" passed the hardier exotics into the hands of their cottage neighbors; likewise, this cottage's owner must have had some dealings with Lord Connock.

She passed through the gardens, admiring the skill of the gardener and imagining the lush beauty of the flowers in summer, and paused at the front door. She would knock and ask for directions back to Glendale Hall. Later, she'd find one of Lord Connock's gardeners to take her to the sapling.

Smoothing her skirts, she shifted her sketch case to her left hand and rapped sharply on the little wooden door with her right. Seconds passed, then a minute. The spicy fragrance of bee balm began to tease Anne. She glanced down at a garden near the front door and discovered the bright green leaves close to her feet. With a smile she plucked a leaf. White light exploded from the plant the moment she touched it, dazzling her with its expression of health and joy. Unlike the plants in Glendale Forest, the bee balm seemed quite content.

Brow furrowed, Anne twirled the leaf between her fingers before dropping it back into the garden.

The cottage door creaked open.

Anne looked up and stared into Michael's wide blue eyes. She stilled. The memory of his tongue flicking against hers came back in a rush and her breath caught in her throat. Thoughts of scholarly achievement fled before the much more primal memory of the way he had smelled, of earth and brandy and freshly washed linen.

"Anne?" Hair tousled, his chin and cheeks stubbly, he looked as if he'd been asleep.

She went on watching him, mute. A slow, budding

warmth curled through her, and along with it, panic at her body's helpless response to his nearness. She'd had Henry between her legs for five years and had felt nothing but revulsion. And now this, when she most needed to project a level-headed, scholarly image.

"Michael! Hello, ah, good morning . . ." She trailed off, her tale of getting lost in the woods stuck in her throat. She knew he'd think she'd come here on purpose, no matter what excuse she provided. After all, she'd kissed him with utter abandon a mere twelve hours before. And damn him to hell, she wanted to kiss him like that again. Now.

Michael dragged a hand through his hair and rubbed the back of his neck, eyeing her all the while. The thin lawn shirt he wore stretched tight with the movement, outlining his broad chest, and when he dropped his hand his shirt bagged where he'd hastily tucked it into his waistband. He looked casual, comfortable, and very male.

When he finally spoke, his voice was husky. "What are you doing here?"

"I was trying to find Lord Connock's sapling and . . . became lost."

A quick frown marred his features. "You wandered all this way from Glendale Hall? You're damned lucky you found anything at all. Glendale Forest is a large one, easy to wander in for days. Don't leave without an escort the next time."

Anne narrowed her eyes. "Your advice is so humbly offered, how could I ignore it?"

A beat of silence passed between them as he digested her response. Then a gleam drove the sleepiness from his gaze and the corners of his mouth began to twitch upward. "Come in and have some breakfast."

"I'm alone," she informed him with eyebrows raised. Surely he understood a woman could not visit a man in his quarters.

"What of it? Are you afraid I might attack your lovely person?"

"No, of course not. You're missing the point. Ladies don't visit gentlemen in their cottages alone."

"You aren't going to find a gaggle of biddies hiding out in the woods, watching us at this very moment and prepared to report that you entered my cottage un-chaperoned."

Cornered, Anne hesitated, unable to voice her most important reason for needing to stay out of his cottage. She didn't want to know him better, didn't want to draw any closer to him, didn't want to discover any other endearing qualities of his that would make her want him even more.

He watched her, waiting for her to speak. After a moment, he jumped into the silence. "Come in. You must be tired."

"I can't."

"Why?"

More silence. Michael gazed at her, waiting. He looked ready to wait forever. The pressure for Anne to give an answer built until she felt ready to explode.

"I'm afraid," she blurted, fresh out of excuses, and then promptly cursed herself for revealing so much.

His brow furrowed. "Of what?"

"Myself." She swallowed. The conversation had already gotten out of control, as it so often did with Michael. That insidious rapport was growing between them again.

He reached out and took her hand in his much larger, much warmer one. His eyes had darkened, no

doubt with speculation. "I'm not certain I'm understanding what you mean, but I do understand fear. If
you'll come inside, I'll tell you a story about it."

She wavered. She didn't want to hear his story. The
good Lord knew he had a way with words. He made
love with words.

"Come on." He gestured at her to follow.

Frowning, she scanned the thickets around the cottage, hoping she might find at least one old biddy
watching. Only the trees seemed interested, however,
and they wouldn't talk. Reluctantly she trailed inside.

He yawned as he led her to a spindle-backed chair
set near a pine table. "Have a seat, Anne. I'll see to
breakfast."

Her cheeks grew warm at his use of her first name.
She remembered inviting him last night to use it, but
now, in the cold light of day, her name on his tongue
sounded far too intimate. "Mr. McEvoy, I—"

"It's Michael."

"I didn't come here on purpose. I was trying to find
Lord Connock's sapling and became lost."

"Glendale Forest is a big place with many paths. It's
easy to get lost unless you're with someone who knows
the way. I'll take you to the sapling, *after* we've eaten
and I've told my story."

Anne contented herself with a nod and looked
around. She was curious about the place a man as complicated as Michael would call home. Then again, he
hadn't called this cottage home but a mere port of call.
She tended not to believe him. The cottage had a certain warmth that only a place well loved could gain.

Rag mats covered a limestone floor which sparkled
with cleanliness and patchwork cushions lay scattered
on a deacon's bench. Blue and white china cups, pewter

plates, and a brass sconce sat atop shelves placed near the rafters girding the low ceiling. A Yorkshire-pattern range filled the open hearth and provided shelving for copper pots, each one scrupulously polished, while a pine table, bearing the scars of many a knife, sprawled in the corner. Utilitarian, she thought, but arranged with a certain finesse, as if he were trying to keep the cottage impersonal but failing. Only the rocking chair in the corner of the room, its bow-backed seat draped with a crocheted shawl, betrayed any sense of frivolity.

To the left, a doorway opened to a scullery, judging by the sink she could see from her position, and near the back of the room, a tiny stone staircase, its limestone treads indented with use, led upward.

"Does my humble cottage pass inspection?" he asked, his tone faintly amused.

"It seems quite comfortable."

"Ah, such tact, particularly after the grandeur of Glendale Hall. What will you be having this morning? Will oatmeal do?"

"I'm not hungry. I'd prefer to skip breakfast."

"In Ireland, we're known for our hospitality. A visitor always receives a meal before any business is undertaken, especially a story."

"In that case, oatmeal sounds fine."

Michael nodded and walked over to the hearth. He removed a kettle from the open-fire portion of the range, put a copper pot on the boiler, and poured boiling water from the kettle into the pot. From the larder he selected an earthenware container, scooped out some oatmeal, and added it to the copper pot.

Anne sat quietly in her chair and watched him. He did these things with such confidence and ease that she knew he'd taken care of himself for a long time. That brought certain questions to mind. Why did he live in such a small, isolated cottage? Why hadn't he ever married? Were there any women in his life?

She glanced around the room and couldn't see the slightest trace of a feminine hand. No flowers, portraits, lace curtains, nothing. The observation brought her a measure of satisfaction she found wholly unsettling.

After stirring his concoction and covering it with a lid, he settled onto the deacon's bench. "While we're waiting for the oatmeal to boil, I'll tell you my story. 'Tis an old Irish tale about a boy who had been condemned to spend the night in a room with a sword hanging over his head. At the boy's slightest twitch, the sword would fall and strike him a mortal blow."

Anne felt her limbs relax at his easy tone. Smiling, she fell into the spirit of the story. "What crime did the boy commit?"

"He stole an apple from a fruit seller in the marketplace and, as you know, thievery is poorly tolerated, even in the youngest." Michael's gaze became unfocused as he stared into the open flames in the range. "They blindfolded him and placed him on his back in a small room. They hung the sword so the tip grazed the skin above his heart, and balanced its handle on a wooden board. The sword itself, they told him, was a heavy thing, not likely to be deterred from its target once it began to fall."

Anne tilted her head and studied him more closely. He didn't seem to be telling a story as much as . . . recollecting. "Who were *they?*"

"The local authorities."

"Their methods sound rather extreme."

He shrugged. "It's a story, Anne."

She nodded, her smile fading.

"A rope was tied from the boy's arms to the wooden board," he continued, his voice growing soft. "If he so much as moved a muscle, the board would twitch and the sword fall. All night long he lay there, sweating, his muscles cramping into knots, staring through the utter blackness, imagining the sword hanging above him, ready to slice his skinny carcass in two if he moved.

"When the first rays of dawn crept into the room, he stared at the long, skinny shadow above him and thanked the blessed Virgin herself that she'd given him the strength to remain still for so long, despite the agony and torment to his muscles. After a few minutes, however, the sun had lifted itself fully above the horizon and flooded the room with light, revealing the sword that was not a sword at all but the splayed stick of a butter churn. The boy twitched and the wooden stick smacked him in the head."

Anne couldn't prevent a smile. "I suppose the stick knocked some sense into him."

Blinking, Michael refocused on her. A pensive smile twitched his lips briefly before disappearing. "You might say that. It made him reconsider all of the swords in his life, swords that had kept him from doing the things he was meant to do. With time he realized those swords were just wooden sticks his anxious mind had falsely sharpened."

Something inside her softened. "Some fears aren't so easy to dismiss."

"As I said, it's just a story. The oatmeal's ready." With that infuriating disclaimer, he stood up and began to set the pine table.

Anne stood as well. She felt bad for the skinny boy who'd stolen an apple and been tormented for it. "May I help?"

"No, just sit."

He put bowls, spoons, a creamer, honey, and a cast-iron trivet on the pine table before depositing the pot of oatmeal on the trivet. A sticky, wholesome fragrance rose from the pot and to her chagrin, Anne heard her stomach growl.

Michael spooned some oatmeal into her bowl, then into his. Anne took her bowl from there, adding a dollop of cream to her oatmeal and an outrageous amount of honey before stirring it into a delicious mess.

"God save us, you have a liking for honey," he remarked, adding a restrained teaspoonful to his own bowl.

" 'Tis a weakness of mine," she admitted. "Sweets."

"I'm liking your weaknesses, lass. Every one of them."

About to raise the spoon to her lips, Anne paused. Her gaze locked with his. A flush of embarrassment made her cheeks hot. She had only one other weakness—for fancy underclothes. Rather than reply, she lifted the spoon to her lips and ate a mouthful of oatmeal. In her opinion, corsets were *not* an appropriate topic for discussion.

He went on watching her.

"Mmm, delicious, Michael. You have a way with oatmeal." She fixed her attention on her bowl and took a second bite, and a third, trying to appear so involved in eating oatmeal that she'd forgotten his remark. When he didn't even lift his spoon, however, she peeked at him through her lashes.

He smiled at her, that warm speculation in his gaze again.

"Are you going to eat?" she asked crisply.

At last he picked up his spoon and brought a mouthful of oatmeal to his lips, the smile never leaving his eyes.

Her cheeks burned even hotter.

They ate quietly, Anne shooting little glances in his direction. She noticed the way he'd folded his large frame into a spindle-backed chair, saw the strength in his hands as he held his spoon, and caught the faint scent of his soap, something masculine and musky and utterly exotic.

The cottage suddenly felt far too close.

"Tell me about Lord Connock," she said, seizing on the one subject guaranteed to turn her thoughts to more serious matters. "Have you ever been inside his glasshouses?"

"Several times. He keeps his rare plants under lock and key because they have a habit of disappearing."

"Kew Gardens has the same sort of problem. Our rarest—and most expensive—plants end up in competitors' glasshouses."

They fell into silence again, this one more companionable.

"Do you know what sort of experiments he conducts?" Anne eventually asked.

The blue eyes that had been so warm grew shuttered. "I know the rudiments behind them, but I'm no scholar. I have no desire to be."

"Tell me the rudiments, then."

Several seconds of silence followed as Michael apparently searched for words. "Lord Connock investigates ways to improve plants so they produce more. In the end, he hopes to reduce Ireland's chance of suffering another famine to none."

"A noble goal."

"He lost his wife in the famine. He's never forgiven himself for allowing her to starve."

"Lady Connock starved in the famine?" Anne couldn't keep the surprise from her voice. How could a nobleman's wife starve, with all that land and wealth in the family?

"She did at that. His snob of an older brother inherited the title and lands and treated Lord Connock like a shoddy little farmer. Lord Connock didn't receive so much as a loaf of bread from his brother; he lived like a pauper and suffered through the famine with the rest of us. After Lady Connock died and his brother passed on too, Lord Connock inherited everything and said that'd be the last famine Ireland ever suffered through."

Anne nodded slowly. Sympathy for the nobleman who had endured so much swept through her. "Poor Lord Connock. I see why he pursues his experiments to the point of bankruptcy. Still, I wonder why he's so secretive about it."

Eyes suddenly narrowed, Michael assessed her for a moment or two. "If I thought he was doing something wrong, I wouldn't be working for him."

"I didn't mean to suggest Lord Connock's need for privacy had anything furtive about it."

And yet, even as the words left her lips, that long-forgotten memory about the name *Connock* nagged at her again, although this time it was stronger, as though her subconscious had taken time to work on it. Black ink, bold headlines . . . CONNOCK'S WEEVILS? CONNOCK'S BORERS? Something silly like that. The black ink swam in her memory, and she almost gave up on it, when suddenly the ink formed comprehensible lines.

"Connock's Pestilence."

Michael stiffened. "You've heard the story, then?"

"Saw it in the newspaper. The *London Evening Star*," she added, recalling more of the story. It had become the talk of the dinner table at her parents' home, and now she remembered why. Lord Connock had used some sort of foreign beetle in his experiments and accidentally released it into the wild. Farmers feared the beetle would eat their grain products. Her father had worried for quite a time that they might have to import hay for their horses.

"You must have been very young," Michael observed.

"I'd just turned seventeen. My parents followed the story quite closely. They raised horses and were afraid their feed would be spoiled."

His lips thinned. "A journalist broke into Lord Connock's laboratory and pawed through an ongoing experiment. He warped the facts to suit the public taste for gruesome tales, and printed a sensational piece shortly afterward."

Anne nodded. She remembered the *pestilence* referred not so much to the beetles released as to the morbid conditions of his laboratory, involving galvanization and blood; her parents had kept the details from her. Perhaps Connock had deserved the public outcry, but Anne thought it more likely he hadn't. Too many scientists, Charles Darwin most recently, had suffered the effects of sensational press for her to believe any of it.

"Every one of Lord Connock's colleagues deserted him. The Royal Agricultural College howled him out of Dublin. No man deserves to be abandoned like that." He stood and took their bowls into the scullery.

When he returned, she stood as well and picked up her sketch case. "I don't believe Lord Connock is guilty of anything but an equal helping of generosity and genius, Michael. I'm thrilled to work for him."

He nodded, and his features seemed to relax.

Michael was a staunch ally of his employer, Anne thought. The ties between them ran deep. She wondered what Lord Connock had done for his naturalist to engender such loyalty. She remembered the story of the boy and the sword and knew there were depths to Michael she'd never touch.

"Thank you for breakfast," she said. "And for the story."

He smiled and took her sketch case from her, but it was a casual smile, one he might give a stranger, and his eyes held none of the teasing glint she'd come to expect. "I'll take you to the sapling."

They left the cottage and started off through the gardens. *His* gardens. She paused to touch the reddish-green leaves of a peony thrusting up from the earth. Again, she saw the white light of health and contentment.

"Your gardens are beautiful," she murmured.

"In a few months they'll be so. I've been gone a year now. I'm surprised they aren't all dead."

"Oh no, on the contrary, they're nearly bursting with life."

Forehead wrinkled, he studied her with that dark blue gaze. "How do you know that? They're hardly up from the earth yet."

She looked away. "I can tell."

"How?"

"Oh, I don't know. You could call it a gift of mine." She felt him staring at her and fought a compulsion to reveal all. "Did you plant them yourself?"

He nodded. "I found them on my travels. Most of them come from England."

Remembering the burst of glorious white from Michael's plants, as compared to the red haze of distress from Lord Connock's, she began to wonder if Lord

Connock himself were responsible for the plants' suffering. "Did you plant the flowers directly into your gardens, or give them to Lord Connock first?"

"I planted them directly into my gardens. Why are you asking?"

"No particular reason."

"You have a reason. You're just not willing to tell me."

"Michael, I have no idea what you're talking about."

Frowning, he took her hand. "This way, Mrs. Sherwood."

He led her through the woods, his steps quick but not enough to outpace her. Throughout their walk he remained silent, an obvious register of his displeasure with her. She didn't break the silence, for she had nothing she wanted to reveal to him, at least not yet. Rather, she puzzled over this newest piece of information she'd learned.

Michael's plants were happy, for lack of a better description. Lord Connock's plants seemed anxious. Why? Perhaps the distress she'd sensed in Lord Connock's plants had sinister origins, and Michael's plants thrived because they'd escaped Lord Connock's laboratory.

Then again, perhaps her gift was simply faulty when considering Irish plants. Several of Michael's plants had come from England, a place she knew quite well; that could be why they had seemed so happy to her.

She smiled. She was starting to sound like a sensational journalist.

His palm warm, Michael led her around a large gray boulder and through a stand of ferns. He noticed her smile and raised an eyebrow. "Have I said something to amuse you?"

"I'm just happy," she said, teasing him a bit and enjoying it, too. "Like your plants."

His eyes narrowed. "I'll leave you here to your smiling and your sketching, then. When would you like me to fetch you?"

Blinking, she realized they'd reached the sapling. Golden beneath the rays of sunlight that shone upon the small glen, the tree looked like a gangly youth with thin limbs and big, unwieldy leaves. "I'll need perhaps two hours. I can find my way back on my own, Michael. Thank you."

He snorted. "I'll return for you in two hours. Good day, Anne."

"Will you be attending Lord Connock's dinner party this weekend?" she called out to him, as he turned and started back down the path.

"I've been invited."

With that noncommittal answer, Michael disappeared among the trees and the underbrush, leaving Anne to her sapling and feeling rather lonely.

7

Anne spent the rest of the morning drawing a few practice sketches of the sapling. It was a small specimen but not so easy to depict, and her sketches left her far from satisfied. Most trees followed a certain form, the lines springing from one another at predictable angles. The sapling's inconsistent combination of qualities, however, confounded her attempts to make smooth, clean lines while still capturing its character.

After devoting ten pages of vellum and untold amounts of pencil to the attempt, she folded her sketchbook and waited for Michael. As the minutes passed, she began to anticipate the moment he'd come to fetch her and called herself a fool for doing so. Consequently, when the old, grizzled gardener who had chastised her the day before showed up at about noon, she felt such disappointment that she frowned at him without thinking.

The old man frowned back. Grimy wool trousers and a grayish cotton shirt garbed his bony frame. That, coupled with his fierce, deep-set eyes and flowing gray beard, gave him the appearance of an overgrown troll. "I'm here to bring you back to Glendale Hall, ma'am. Get your things together."

She immediately traded her frown for a more pleasant expression. The old gardener wouldn't frighten her no matter how hard he tried. The mere fact that he cared for plants gave him a humanity that his fiercest scowl could never erase. "Right away, Mr., ah . . . what may I call you?"

"Griswold," he barked, scowling.

"All right, Mr. Griswold. Please call me Mrs. Sherwood."

With an abrupt nod of his head he indicated for her to follow him. Hiding a smile, she put her sketchbook and pencil into her case, and followed him out of the woods. A short time later she had returned to her bedchamber at Glendale Hall.

The rest of the afternoon passed in slow, lazy hours. She enjoyed a light repast at around three in the afternoon, took a nap, and struggled some more with her sketch of the sapling. Not once did she leave her bedchamber. Around five o'clock she discovered that both Michael and Lord Connock were otherwise occupied, and decided to have dinner in her bedchamber as well.

During the next three days, events fell into a similar pattern. Michael would escort her to the sapling, his manner distant yet faintly teasing. While he nearly charmed her pantaloons off during their walk, he treated her with perfect respect and left her once they'd arrived, so she might concentrate on her sketching. Although many would find his gentlemanly behavior commendable, Anne knew a perverse desire to have him lingering at her side. His insouciance made him all the more attractive.

After she'd sketched for a few hours, Griswold would come and collect her around noon. He'd leave her off at Glendale Hall and to her own devices. She'd spend the night working with her sketches and often elected to have dinner in her bedchamber.

The nights, she discovered, quickly grew lonely, and her bed felt doubly so. Consequently, when Jane, her lady's maid, appeared at precisely five forty-five on the evening of Lord Connock's dinner party, Anne was looking forward to a good meal and scholarly conversation.

The girl appeared a bit more wilted than she had in the morning. Her mobcap sat askew on her brown curls and her cheeks bloomed a bright pink, evidence of considerable industry. She poured the bucket of hot water she carried into a porcelain basin. "I've pressed your gown for this evening. A housemaid will bring it up shortly. By the time we're done tonight, they'll be taking a long look at you."

"But I don't want them to take a long look, Jane. I've already explained this to you."

Jane's eyes darkened. "I remember. You want to be known as figuresome."

"Figuresome?"

"Good at sums."

"Well then, you're quite correct on that score. Figuresome I am."

The maid nodded meekly and began tidying Anne's bed.

With that battle won, Anne freshened up with the hot water Jane had brought. A knock at the door interrupted them both. Jane answered the summons and accepted Anne's newly pressed gown from a housemaid. Before leaving, the housemaid pressed a notecard into Anne's hand. "From the master," she said.

Brow furrowed, Anne opened the little ivory card and read, in scrawling ink, an appeal from Lord Connock:

My dear Mrs. Sherwood,
    Please refrain from mentioning the sapling in the woods to my esteemed colleagues who are joining us for dinner. I am not ready to share this particular discovery with them. Of course you understand, having watched too many of Kew Gardens' valuable species appear at auctions sponsored by houses other than Kew!

                                Dutifully yours,
                                Owain, Lord Connock

Anne smiled. So, Lord Connock didn't trust his scientific associates. She couldn't blame him. As he'd mentioned, Kew Gardens had lost thousands of pounds when exclusive flowers were stolen, propagated, and auctioned elsewhere.

Jane shook out the gown, recapturing Anne's attention. Lower lip caught between her teeth, Anne carefully examined the deep green silk with its full cap sleeves. It was serviceable rather than attractive.

"I hope this gown meets with your approval," Jane remarked. "I took the liberty of resewing a seam that had begun to pull apart along the bodice. My sewing is fairly good, but a little lace at the bodice to hide the new stitches wouldn't be amiss."

Anne shrugged. "The gown is fine. I don't think it needs lace."

"The color of the thread I used doesn't match the dress exactly." Her steps brisk, Jane walked over to the bureau that held Anne's underclothes, opened a drawer, and selected a chemise made of fine lawn and edged with Brussels lace along the bodice. "If you wear this chemise, we could pull the lace out to drape over the edge of the gown's bodice and hide my clumsy sewing."

Jane's voice held almost a pleading note to it. Anne frowned at Jane's insistence, but then it occurred to her that her appearance this eve would reflect directly on Jane's skill as a lady's maid. Her frown smoothed out. "All right, Jane, you've talked me into it. I'll wear the chemise."

A smile brightened Jane's face. "Thank you, ma'am."

Without any further argument Anne began to dress. Jane slipped the chemise over Anne's head, the soft fabric whispering as it slid down her body and settled against her skin in a soft caress. Anne slipped her drawers on next, again of fine lawn edged with Brussels lace.

"Which corset would you like, Mrs. Sherwood?" Jane asked, her fingers moving softly through Anne's selection of scarlet, peach, sky-blue, ivory, and white.

Anne considered. The pristine white corset possessed not a single bow and was quite safe . . . but it wouldn't match. No one would see her underclothes, of course. Still, her long association with color and her pride in her ability to combine colors in a way pleasing to the eye made her loath to wear anything that clashed. "The ivory silk one. With the rosettes along the bodice."

Jane pulled the corset from the drawer and fastened it around Anne. When Jane began to yank on the strings and tighten up the corset, she did so with such vigor that Anne had to grab the bedpost for balance.

Not for the first time Anne wished her figure was a bit slimmer. She could hardly breathe in a tightened corset, and it always seemed to push her breasts into a fantastic display of cleavage, a display she would do much to avoid. She hid her underclothes but she couldn't hide the curves of her body.

Jane assessed her and nodded approvingly. "Very figuresome."

"Let's get on with it," Anne grumbled.

Her face a study of seriousness, Jane selected a hoop petticoat and an ivory overpetticoat and fastened both around Anne's waist. At last, she dropped the green gown over Anne's head and began to arrange it around her.

As the lady's maid fastened the hooks down Anne's back and pulled the cap sleeves off her shoulders, Anne realized the bodice fit much tighter than it had before, no doubt due to Jane's sewing. Her breasts, already overflowing the corset, now swelled against the silk. When Jane began to pull the lace from her chemise out to cover the edge of her gown, she revealed even more of Anne's cleavage.

Anne felt more than a bit overheated after all these preparations. She was out of breath and very exposed, as well. Paying little attention to Jane's satisfied smile as she fussed one last time with the lace, Anne moved to stand before a looking glass. Full hips, small waist, ample breasts . . . by God, she looked like a whore, not a scholar. A feeling of panic came over her. She couldn't go to Lord Connock's party dressed like this.

"Jane, I'm afraid we're going to have to find another gown. This one isn't right for me."

"Why, Mrs. Sherwood, 'tis nigh onto six-thirty. We haven't the time to press another gown. In fact, I'll have barely enough time to fix your hair."

As though underscoring Jane's sentiment, the sound of carriage wheels coming up the drive drifted into Anne's bedchamber.

Jane's eyes grew wider. "Lord Connock's guests have already begun to arrive." She raced over to Anne's wardrobe and began to pull gowns out, one by one, making tsk-ing noises as she did so. Anne had to agree with her. Her gowns looked horrible. Wrinkles from her journey to Ireland marred many of them from bodice to hem.

"Mrs. Sherwood, you must forgive me for not pressing all of your gowns sooner," Jane said once they'd finished their review of Anne's wardrobe. Her voice low, her shoulders slumped, the lady's maid was the very picture of dejection. "Our washerwoman has been ill, and I've been helping out in the scullery—"

"Nonsense." Anne dismissed Jane's apology with a shake of her head. "You picked out a gown for me and had it all pressed and mended for this evening. That's all I can ask."

"Thank you, ma'am. Your kindness is uncommon. Still . . ." Jane shook her head. "You can't mean to wear one of these."

"How long would you require to iron one of them?"

"At least an hour and a half. You'd miss dinner."

Anne shook her head. She couldn't miss her opportunity to become acquainted with Connock's scholarly associates.

"Tell me why the gown isn't right for you," Jane said, "and we'll see what we can do."

"I'm afraid too much attention will be directed toward my, ah, bosom."

Her gaze critical, the lady's maid assessed her. "I've seen women show much more than you. Even so, let's drag these sleeves back onto your shoulders." Her movements brisk, she pulled the sleeves of Anne's gown up and fluffed the lace around the bodice a bit. "How about now?"

Anne stared despairingly at her image. She didn't see much difference. But she didn't have much choice, either. "I suppose that will have to do."

"Do you have any jewelry you'd like to wear?"

"None."

"Let's fix your hair, then."

In the remaining fifteen minutes, the lady's maid twisted Anne's hair into a severe chignon at the back of her neck and wove a few green silk ribbons through the coif. She brought out a pot of red powder, but faced with strenuous objection, settled on patting some color into Anne's cheeks. Once she'd finished, she stood back to assess Anne and nodded. "You're a fine sight, Mrs. Sherwood."

"Thank you very much, Jane."

Anne's insides rolled with anxiety. She looked lush, ripe, and far too feminine. Somehow, the austerity of the gown and her hairstyle only served to emphasize her softness, her curves. To her dismay, she realized that her inner turmoil had even put a pink bloom in her cheeks and at the tops of her breasts.

What would the scholars Lord Connock had arranged for her to meet think of her?

What would Michael think of her?

A slow warmth spread through her at the thought of him.

"Should I call on Carlyle to show you the way to the drawing room, Mrs. Sherwood?" Jane asked from the doorway.

"No, I'll find it myself. Good evening, Jane."

Her back straight, Anne left the security of her bed-chamber and descended the stairs to utter disaster.

Michael sat in the drawing room of Glendale Hall and observed the very brightest of scholars that England, Scotland, and Ireland had to offer. Fading sunlight drifted through the large mullioned windows that presided over the drawing room, casting a lurid gleam across their animated faces. Quite appropriate, Michael thought, given the sensitive nature of their conversation.

"How outrageous, to suggest no species ever becomes extinct." Thomas Huxley, only five years older than Michael, thrust his chin forward. Professor at Ireland's Royal College of Surgeons, Huxley was Darwin's strongest advocate. "Why, only those organisms best adapted to their environment will survive. Those who are weak, die." His brown Dundreary whiskers nearly quivering, he nodded once to confirm his point.

But Mr. Chambers was having none of it. By far the oldest gent in the room, he also looked the most vigorous. His close-clipped white beard still contained streaks of black and a ruddy flush colored his cheeks. "Organisms develop certain characteristics in response to their environment. Through time, they become more perfect and evolve into new forms. There is no such thing as extinction!"

Professor Huxley clenched his fists. "You speak drivel, sir. Clearly that *Vestiges* book has influenced you. I implore you to consider the evidence Mr. Darwin has so painstakingly assembled—"

"Gentlemen, gentlemen," Sir Charles Lyell interrupted. His nearly bald pate had a shine to it. *Sweat*, Michael thought. "We've no need to come to blows.

Surely there's enough room in Ireland for both view-points to exist."

In the corner of the drawing room, near the fireplace which remained dark and empty in deference to the un-expectedly mild temperature, Lord Connock stood con-versing with Charles Darwin. Darwin, older than Lord Connock by several years, twiddled with his flowing white beard. Just the previous year he had published *On the Origin of Species.*

Michael knew the pope in all his holy glory consid-ered Darwin a revolutionary in league with Satan him-self, determined to shake the very foundations of the church. After reading Darwin's treatise, however, Michael found the theory of natural selection highly plausible. If he hadn't stopped going to confession years before, Darwin's theory would have stopped him, be-cause in his own mind he'd dismissed the Garden of Eden for natural selection. He wouldn't lie to God and pretend to believe in divine creation, nor would he apologize for his beliefs.

Given the way he converted the faithful, Michael mused, maybe Darwin *was* in league with Satan.

Lord Connock and Darwin began to drift back toward the knot of men. Michael grew impatient for Anne to join them. Her fine figure would offer welcome relief from the dry talk and stiff black suits. He'd never had much of an opinion on the nature of worms; and yet, tonight he'd learned a glut of facts about them that he'd rather not have known. And truth to tell, he was interested to see how she'd interact with the scholars Connock had invited to Glendale Hall.

Friends, they were, these five, and nary a wife among them. They'd left the women home. Connock's invita-tion was not social but professional. Michael wondered how the men were going to react when they discovered Connock had invited a woman to join their exclusive little club. He sighed. Perhaps they wouldn't react at all. Anne had a habit of disguising her curves behind ugly, matronly gowns.

Almost five minutes later, after a rousing discussion on the methods worms use to mate, silence descended upon the group. Michael, somewhat bored, immediately focused upon them to see what had robbed them of speech.

All five of them had their attention on the doorway.

Anne stood upon the threshold, her chin lifted high.

Michael blinked once to make sure he was seeing properly.

He'd expected a high-necked gown of gray or black or brown, made of serge or linen or something equally unattractive. Instead, she'd garbed herself in green silk that clung to her breasts and waist before billowing outward around her hips. Delicate ivory lace framed her breasts and throat. In contrast, her skin looked creamy white, other than the slight pink flush covering the tops of her breasts. Her hair fell in soft blond waves about her face and her eyes sparkled a militant gray in the candlelight.

"Good evening, gentlemen," she said in a strong voice, and sailed into the room. If not for that pink flush on her breasts, he would have thought her completely at ease and in command.

Lord Connock strode forward and took her hand. Michael watched the older man gaze at Anne's breasts for one split second before returning to her face. He could tell by Connock's widened eyes that Anne's femininity had startled him.

"Mrs. Sherwood," Connock murmured. He took her

arm and steered her toward Charles Darwin. "I'm so glad you have joined us. Come and meet my colleagues. Do you know Mr. Darwin?"

Anne's throat worked. The pink flush widened to encompass her cheeks. "No, we haven't been introduced."

"Well then, allow me to introduce Mr. Charles Darwin, country gentleman and naturalist, lately of Kent—"

Lord Connock rambled on, listing Darwin's accomplishments. When he'd finished, Darwin observed Anne with a kindly eye and asked her when she and Lord Connock planned to marry.

"Oh no, sir, you have the wrong idea," Anne said, her color becoming a bit higher. "I am Lord Connock's illustrator, not his fiancée."

The Irish nobleman hastened to agree. "She is the one I've been telling you about, Charles. The one who captures the essence of a plant on vellum better than any other I've seen."

Stroking his beard, Darwin ran an assessing eye over Anne's figure. "My pardon, ma'am. I had expected you to appear differently."

A hint of a flush colored Connock's cheeks. Michael watched with interest. Rarely did he see his mentor flustered.

Anne smiled, but it was a sickly one. "And what of your wife, Mr. Darwin? Has she come to Glendale Hall with you?"

"Of course not. This isn't a social gathering, Mrs. Sherwood, but a scientific one." Darwin had assumed the pedantic tones of a scholar. "I assume you'll be contributing to our discussion."

Now Darwin bent a chiding glance on Lord Connock, as if to ask him what he'd been thinking, bringing a woman to their sacred meeting.

"I'll do my best, sir." Anne looked to Lord Connock for help. Michael noticed the little beads of sweat along her temples just before she dabbed them away. Sympathy stirred inside him. These men were going to give her one hell of a time.

Lord Connock pulled Anne rather hastily toward Sir Charles Lyell, the Scotsman who had made geology his life's work. He had comments similar to Darwin's, only he assumed Anne was Connock's niece, not his fiancée. Connock explained the need for Anne's presence, but judging by the way Lyell's brow wrinkled, he remained unconvinced. Anne's flush became a distinct red as the interview with Lyell wore on.

Robert Chambers gave Anne no more than a passing glance and a nod when Lord Connock introduced them; he was still arguing with Professor Huxley about the mechanisms of evolution.

Professor Huxley, when he finally broke off his diatribe, focused on Anne with a good deal of attention. God may have gifted the man with brains, but hadn't given him any common sense when it came to women. Huxley stared at Anne's breasts and lips with such a lack of subtlety that Michael wanted to race to her side and shield her from Huxley's dark, prying eyes.

Anne gave the man polite replies; still, Michael could see her strain in the way she pressed her lips together and clenched her hands. Her eyes had gained a despairing look and with a start Michael realized exactly how much she'd been counting on their acceptance of her value as a scholar.

That brought up a question that had begun to nag at him. Why was she so damned set on becoming a scholar?

She'd nearly denied everything that made her human in the attempt. Didn't she realize these men would see only soft curves and full lips and the promise of pleasure? She was a *woman*, for God's sake. To men like Huxley, women didn't think. They kept house and reared children and shuddered delicately at talk of evolution.

At last Lord Connock brought Anne to Michael's side. He marked her suffering in the whiteness around the corners of her mouth and wanted to enfold her in his arms. He knew what it felt like to live on the outside, always looking in at the cozy glow of companionship and wishing with all his heart for someone to put a friendly hand on his shoulder.

Not that he'd deprived himself of physical touch. When he thought of all the women he'd had, he wondered why God hadn't reached down and punished him. Lovers who had worshiped every square inch of his body, geishas who gave new meaning to the word *intimacy*, concubines who asked three times, "What do you desire?" before allowing themselves to fall asleep—the list was long and varied. And yet, despite their touch, he always awoke lonely.

If he made love to Anne, would he awake lonely?

He mustered some volume to his voice and faced her squarely. "Tell me, Mrs. Sherwood, what sort of methods do you use at Kew Gardens to cultivate epiphytic orchids, such as *Stanhopea insignis?*"

The academic tone he'd used, coupled with his loudness, stopped all conversation. She looked at him, her brows drawn together, and answered slowly. "Why, we plant them in a loose, turfy soil interspersed with small portions of stems of trees. They receive a constant supply of water, an even temperature, and shortly, humidity as well."

Her voice grew stronger. "We've had the most success with *zygopetalum maxillare*, found in Borneo and brought back to London within two months. The original plant proved a valuable source for new orchid cuttings and, unlike our other orchids, grows happily in English soil. 'Tis the original English orchid."

Darwin's eyebrows climbed at her answer before he gave an approving nod. She caught that nod and visibly relaxed. When she turned back toward Michael, she flashed him a smile so brilliant she nearly melted his insides.

Michael sent her a wink only she could see, then drew her aside so they might talk more normally. He thought about mentioning the trip to India he and Lord Connock were planning, set to sail within a month. Indeed, preparations for the trip had consumed them both to the point where they hadn't yet had an in-depth discussion of the peculiar little tree, other than to agree to keep quiet about it. Instinct, however, told him that Anne wouldn't welcome the news of his proposed defection, not when surrounded by the enemy. So he settled on small talk instead.

"Quite a group, aren't they?"

She sighed. "Oh Michael, I wish I were the ugliest hag within ten miles. They don't see my intelligence. They can only think of my potential for having babies."

His gaze flickered across her breasts before returning to her face. Silently he decided he liked the soft, baby-making woman better than the intelligent hag, but he wasn't idiotic enough to tell her that. Instead he simply shrugged. "Then I would say that for all their powers of scientific observation, they're short-sighted."

"You're very sweet. And a terrible liar, too."

"Lie, do I? As sure as I'm an Irishman does my tongue tell the truth."

"What do you know of my scholarly accomplishments?"

"Nothing," he admitted.

"Have you seen any of my drawings?"

"No."

"Have we ever held a conversation on a scholarly subject?"

"No." He grinned. He couldn't help it. If he had his way, the only talking they'd ever do would be of the lip-to-lip variety.

She raised one eyebrow triumphantly. "Case proven. You, dear sir, are a liar."

"Your case isn't proven yet." He took her arm and edged her closer, so that he might drink in the fragrant rose scent of her hair. "You've neglected one important detail. Lord Connock has hired you and speaks highly of your abilities. That, my sweet scholar, is good enough for me."

She gently disengaged her hand from his. "Even though you praise my scholarly attributes, I cannot help but think your true thoughts lie in a different direction, one at cross purposes with my goal tonight."

"What *is* your goal?"

"To force these men to see me as a scholar, not a woman."

"And why are you so hell-bent on being a scholar?"

"Being a *woman* simply isn't enough for me."

He shook his head. She hadn't answered his question, not really, and he could see by the tight set to her lips that she didn't plan on elaborating.

"You've set yourself a hard task, Anne. Not because

of your nature, but because of ours." He'd often thought that if women knew the true depths of the lust an average man held in his heart, they'd faint dead away.

"We shall see." With a fetching swish of her skirts, she left his side and joined the scholars.

8

*A*nne's subtle victory over her gender, won with her knowledgeable discussion on orchids, gave way far too soon for comfort. Professor Huxley, an ardent skirt chaser, proved the center of all her difficulties. He began his antics as soon as Lord Connock had assembled them for their brief walk to the dining room.

"Michael," Lord Connock said, his expression grave, "will you escort Mrs. Sherwood into the dining room?"

Anne jumped guiltily, wondering if Lord Connock had already guessed at the passion budding between her and Michael. She hoped he was simply grouping his two hired employees together as etiquette dictated.

Michael moved to her side. Connock quickly lined the other men up according to rank, privilege, and accomplishment and directed them into the dining room. Before they began their promenade, however, Professor Huxley, who stood in front of Michael and Anne, turned around and regarded Anne with a hungry gaze.

"I say, Mr. McEvoy, won't you exchange places with

me? 'Tis ages since I've had the pleasure of such a pretty lady's company."

Michael slanted a glance toward Anne. She shook her head imperceptibly. The last thing she wanted was to sit next to Mr. Huxley for an entire evening.

"You mustn't be selfish, Mr. McEvoy," Huxley prodded. "You work with her every day. I will only see her this evening before we all depart for the Royal College of Surgeons."

Michael shrugged. "How can I refuse?"

The two men traded places. Huxley took her arm in an ironlike grip and pulled her far too close. She edged away as they promenaded through the hall and into the dining room, but the subtle movement was lost on him. He continued to grip her with the same determination of a fisherman reeling in a prize catch.

They passed by Lord Connock and into the dining room. Huxley maneuvered himself next to her, forcing Michael to take a chair across the table. Anne noticed the nobleman's raised eyebrow as he assessed the change in the seating arrangements. Anger flared within her. She hadn't brought the foolish man's attentions on. Huxley simply didn't know how to function properly in polite society. *Too long in the laboratory*, she mused.

Huxley sat on her right; Sir Charles Lyell took the seat on her left. Lord Connock presided at the head of the table, while Michael lounged across from her. The other men filled in the empty chairs.

Lord Connock's staff had outdone themselves preparing the dining room. Fit for royalty, the walnut burl table that dominated the center of the room sparkled beneath a weight of gold silverware and crystal and fine porcelain. A silver epergne sat in the center of the table, sporting numerous candlesticks, flowers, and an artfully arranged tumble of fruit. Carlyle remained in the room with them, his two footmen standing behind him, reminding Anne of soldiers readied for battle.

One of the footmen began to circulate around the table, pouring claret. As soon as all their glasses had been filled, Huxley raised his in her direction, silently asking her to take wine with him. She did so, feeling ridiculous yet trapped by a need to remain polite. The custom of taking wine had fizzled decades before.

Huxley toasted her and sipped his wine. Anne followed suit, noting how the gesture had created an intimacy between them that Huxley would no doubt try to deepen. She smothered a groan and prayed for the patience to endure him.

"Well, Mrs. Sherwood," Huxley said, "I understand you've been employed at Kew Gardens for two years now. That's a long time for a lady to have to support herself."

"My husband died two years ago," she admitted. "I could have returned to my mother and father, but chose to work for myself."

His eyebrows drew together. "Well, I suppose we are all the better for it. Otherwise I wouldn't be enjoying your lovely presence tonight, would I?"

"And I would be short an excellent illustrator," Lord Connock added from the head of the table.

Anne smiled and said nothing as a footman ladled a portion of soup into her bowl. She intercepted a speaking glance Darwin directed toward Lord Connock and guessed that Darwin had already labeled her a disruptive force who'd made Professor Huxley, his foremost supporter, forget about evolution.

Huxley was going to ruin her, damn the man.

From her left, Lyell remarked, "My poor wife was never able to keep up with the theory behind my work. Couldn't even understand the basics."

"Never met a woman who could," Chambers added from across the table, his mouth full of pork floating in the soup. "Excepting those present at this table, of course."

Anne stiffened. Despite his attempt to smooth over the jibe, Chambers had just stated what every critic who'd examined her work had claimed: women are more primitive than men, suitable for creating a haven for men and rearing their children but nothing else. Ideally they're expected to be transparent, sincere, and trusting, unlike men, who needed to deal with the hard world outside the home.

Huxley paused in slurping to pat her arm. "I understand how difficult life can be for a woman who loses her husband. Too often there is no one who can help. I'm sure you would have preferred to remain Baron Sherwood's helpmate rather than entering the scientific world and securing a post."

"I relished the opportunity to enter the scientific world," Anne said, earning a confused gaze from him.

Chambers shook his head. "Women belong in the home. Excepting the present company, of course."

The footmen brought another dish around. Anne found her appetite dwindling.

Huxley made a laughing noise. "I cannot recall the number of times I heard my mother tell my sister to disguise her intelligence, wear appropriately feminine attire, and smile often if she wished to strike a man favorably." He lowered his voice and leaned close to Anne. "May I say, Mrs. Sherwood, that you strike me most favorably."

Anne sank a little lower in her seat. "Gentlemen, I implore you to discuss a topic other than myself. As flattered as I am by the attention, I would much rather debate something else. Evolution, perhaps," she offered, grasping at straws.

The men looked at one another. A few tense seconds passed before Lyell sighed noisily. "What do you know of evolution, Mrs. Sherwood?"

"Only what I have read in Mr. Darwin's *On the Origin of Species*. I find the idea of natural selection fascinating."

"Natural selection, bah!" Chambers boomed, echoing his earlier argument. "Species do not become extinct. They perfect themselves. I challenge you to explain your proof to the contrary, Mr. Darwin."

The man with the flowing white beard pondered a moment before eyeing the portly Mr. Chambers with a piercing stare.

"Have you read Locke's *Essay Concerning Human Understanding*?"

"Who has not?"

"Then we must all agree that there is only one true way to understand the world around us: through experience. And what is the medium for experience? Scientific observation and experimentation, of course."

Lyell, in the middle of lifting a slice of beef to his lips, raised an eyebrow. "Ah, but observation has its perils, does it not?"

Shrugging, Darwin spread his hands open. "In what way?"

"When we observe, we apply all sorts of subjective viewpoints. For example, when a comet crosses the sky, I see a meteorite nearing the Earth's surface. I ascribe no supernatural significance to the occurrence. But a religious man might label that comet an omen. Who is correct?"

Chambers nodded belligerently.

"Furthermore," Lyell added, "the observed sometimes goes to great length to disguise and diminish the pain of the truth. Certain types of moths have developed wings with spots similar to large eyes. The eyes make them look like owls, but in truth, the moths are small and defenseless."

Anne looked around the table at the animated faces and realized they'd forgotten she existed. The need to say something rational and intelligent after having been dismissed as inferior nearly crushed her with its urgency. A thought was forming in her head, a sensible if provocative way to join the debate. She just needed the right moment . . .

The footmen suddenly began serving a Turkey poult, interrupting their discussion. Disappointment sliced through her. She nearly cursed aloud.

Huxley chose that moment to lean close and whisper, "Mankind, in particular, goes to great lengths to disguise the pain of the truth." He looked toward Michael McEvoy. "The Irish naturalist is a prime example."

Anne involuntarily followed his gaze and found herself looking at Michael who, by his mere presence, somehow dominated the others. "Whatever do you mean?"

"Mr. McEvoy seems civilized, does he not?"

"Of course." She tightened her lips, wondering what Huxley hoped to accomplish with this questionable piece of intelligence.

"I assure you, he is far from civilized. He hides the pain of his origins behind a well-tailored coat. Has Lord

Connock told you where he originally found Mr. McEvoy?"

"No, he hasn't. Mr. McEvoy mentioned that he met Lord Connock somewhere north of Dublin eleven years ago, and has been with him ever since."

"Lord Connock did not *meet* Mr. McEvoy. He used food to coax Mr. McEvoy out of the wilderness, as one might entice any feral animal from its home."

"Professor Huxley, I have no idea what you speak of."

"Oh, so you haven't heard the story of the Green Man?"

"I assure you I have not."

"Well, the Green Man is part of an old Irish legend. 'Green Man' is another name for the Oak King, who rules the warm half of the year and joins with the May Queen, consummating the fertility of summer. The Oak King is wounded at summer solstice by his nemesis, the Holly King, and survives for a time until darkness triumphs. The Holly King then rules until the Oak King destroys him in springtime, and the cycle begins again."

"What does this have to do with Michael McEvoy?"

"Mr. McEvoy," he said with relish, "became an orphan early in his life. He ran away from a workhouse in Dublin when he turned fourteen and lived alone in the woods for the next five years. He became skeletally thin, ragged, wild, unable even to speak, a madman the local townspeople believed a demon spirit. The locals used to scare their children with tales of the Green Man, the dead Oak King who searched the woods for little children to sustain him, until he fought the Holly King and regained his throne."

Anne felt her eyes widen. Surprise left her bereft of words. Even though she'd heard Michael's story of the starving child held at sword point, she still had trouble reconciling the powerful man across the table with a vulnerable little boy. "I had no idea," she eventually managed.

"It took Lord Connock the better part of six months to draw the beast from his lair in the woods, and another two years to reeducate him in the ways of society. He may look civilized now, but no man can erase the stain of experience. I'd wager that fine veneer hides a savage."

As Huxley fell silent, Anne felt her mood plummet toward sadness. Given the tale Michael had told her, she could only imagine what had driven him to hide out in the wilderness. And yet, she understood him better now, and her estimation of him rose proportionately. He had suffered, he had struggled, and in the end, he'd triumphed.

The gaze she directed toward Michael was considerably warmer than it had been a few minutes ago. As though he felt her scrutiny, he looked up at her and gave her a private little wink.

The footmen, having finished serving the turkey, picked up a bottle of Madeira and began to pour a round for all. Likewise, Darwin picked up the thread of their previous conversation.

"Quite correct, Sir Charles. Already our effort to observe without prejudice seems doomed to failure. But let us assume that we learn to observe without applying subjective values," Darwin said with a sly glance toward Sir Charles. "One might be more willing to admit the similarity between man and ape is a result of natural selection rather than a divine act of creation."

Charles Lyell, without a response, sipped Madeira from his wine glass.

"Men are apes, not angels, eh Darwin?" Lord Connock prodded.

The gaze Darwin bent upon each one of them in turn was intense. "I've spent years observing animals. Dogs, apes, horses, monkeys. Their faces express pain, pleasure, rage, fear, and jealousy; they feel as we do. I would not call this coincidence or a psychological curiosity. Rather, 'tis evidence of a true relationship among all higher creatures."

Throughout their conversation, the need to speak her own mind had built again within Anne, coiling through her insides and tightening until she felt flushed from it. She disagreed on a very basic level with Charles Darwin's theory, that pure observation led to truth. Even though his arguments made great sense, her special gift for sensing plants' emotions persuaded her otherwise. Darwin might examine a healthy-looking orchid rooted in moist soil and pronounce it thriving, while she could see how it sank toward death. They'd both observed, and yet, time would prove the truth in her observation, not his.

As the seconds passed and Darwin's statement hung on the air, she felt a sense of a moment being lost, one she might never have again. Her heart thumped with an uncomfortable extra beat. Moisture dotted her temples.

Michael, who had been watching them all with a languid air, abruptly joined in the conversation. "You've observed without emotion, and in doing so distanced yourself from the object of study. You see and understand but do not feel."

Darwin nodded slowly. "If you care about the subject of study, then you cannot observe purely. Selflessness protects the observer from the consequences of his discovery."

"Don't you worry about losing your compassion, the very quality that makes you human, when you practice such selfless observation?"

" 'Tis a small price to pay when one considers the knowledge gained," Lord Connock answered quickly, overriding any rebuttal Charles Darwin might have made.

"I call it selling your soul." A slight smile played upon Michael's lips, as though he enjoyed being a subversive influence.

Anne's heart began thumping double-time. Heat invaded her face. The time had come. She either spoke now and spoke intelligently or forever relegated herself to the ranks of inferior females. "Mr. Darwin," she blurted.

Six men abruptly focused their attention on her. Anne's mind went blank under the weight of all those stares. She couldn't seem to formulate her thoughts in a logical manner or think of a way to support them with adequate verbal proof. Recklessly she plunged ahead.

"We have five senses to observe with," she began, her throat so tight that she sounded hoarse. "From those senses, we derive understanding. And yet, what if there are other aspects that we, as humans, are not equipped to sense?"

Mr. Chambers harrumphed. "Not equipped to sense? Whatever do you mean?"

"I suspect there are types of light our eyes are not sharp enough to see, and types of odors our noses can't smell. One need only observe a bat and a dog, respectively, to come to that conclusion. It follows that there are other things we are not equipped to observe."

"So?"

"If we cannot observe everything, then there is no

such thing as 'pure' observation. Consequently, our understanding of the world will always be incomplete, even incorrect."

"My dear, you are reaching," Sir Charles Lyell said in gentle tones.

Anne refused to be dissuaded. "Consider orchids. You can describe their form and perfume. You can talk about the conditions they grow in and how they respond to certain stimuli. But you can't understand their *thoughts.*"

Lord Connock watched her with a riveted gaze, she noticed. Michael, too, had sat up a little straighter in his chair. Given all the clues she had inadvertently dropped in the past, she knew they were probably starting to figure out that she had some sort of special sense concerning plants. At any other time the notion would have given her pause, but right now, she needed to win this argument and would use any means at her disposal.

"Thoughts? Orchids?" Mr. Chambers exchanged a smile with the other men. "Plants don't have thoughts."

"Humans have thoughts," she countered. "You can't see or observe them, but you know they exist because you experience them yourself. Another species, observing us, would not necessarily know we have thoughts."

"So you're proposing plants have thoughts." Sir Charles's gentle tone gave way to a patronizing smile.

"What I'm saying is that simple observation will not always paint a clear picture of a thing. Sometimes intuition must come into play, too; feelings cannot be rejected out of hand. For it's only our intuition that allows us to sense other aspects of those things that we cannot hear, see, feel, touch, or taste."

"I reject out of hand that any other sense than those we possess—including intuition—exists." Chambers eyed her with a jutting chin.

"And I say there are many realities in this world other than the one we live in." Anne's voice had a defiant ring. "We are not equipped to sense them because they would prove too discordant with human needs to withstand. They would overwhelm us. 'If we had a keen vision and feeling of all ordinary human life, it would be like hearing the grass grow and the squirrel's heart beat, and we should die of that roar which lies on the other side of silence.' "

"George Eliot, *Middlemarch*," Michael softly quoted.

Anne glanced at him, eyes wide, before turning toward the five other men. From his previous attitude, she'd guessed Michael and books had little in common. "I see a certain arrogance in the assumption that man is capable of pure observation. I simply suggest that all knowledge should remain open to question."

Mr. Darwin eyed her thoughtfully.

"You, my dear, propose chaos." Sir Charles shook his head. "What sort of a world would we live in, if every natural law were placed into question?"

"I suggest, Mrs. Sherwood, that chaos is *all* women are capable of." Mr. Chambers nodded his head once, for emphasis. This time, he didn't add *excepting the present company*.

Lord Connock opened placating hands. "Gentlemen, gentlemen, may I remind you that Mrs. Sherwood is in my employ as a botanical illustrator? I assure you, she has a fair talent at illustration and is worthy of respect, not poor manners."

Mr. Chambers had the grace to blush.

Sir Charles shrugged. "Mrs. Sherwood clearly wishes

to make a foray into a gentlemen's world. I entertained
her for your sake, Owain. I won't apologize for dealing
with her faulty conjecture as we might have any man's.
I suggest that if she is incapable of withstanding criti-
cism as a man might, she stop playing at one."

"A fine womanly pursuit, is botanical illustration,"
Huxley announced in almost pleading tones. "Most
women of my acquaintance practice painting or water-
color in some form. 'Tis a harmless pastime, not a foray
into a gentlemen's world. Let us not be too harsh with
her."

Anne sat a little straighter in her chair. She fairly
burned with indignation. Unable to reject her argument logically, they'd resorted to a cliché to dismiss
her. Well, she wouldn't stand for it. Throwing caution
to the winds, she first bent a heated gaze on the portly
Mr. Chambers, then on Sir Charles, the two biggest
offenders. "The size of my brain, so much smaller
than a man's, limits my intelligence, no? I can't develop the inventive powers, the forethought, the daring, and the persistence that a true scholar needs,
correct?"

Five men gaped at her. Michael merely frowned.

She stood up abruptly. "Of course you are going to
dismiss my arguments. If I'm right and you're wrong,
and I'm the weaker of the species, that would make you
even weaker than I."

Etiquette required them to stand when she did. To a
man they jumped to their feet, annoying her even further.

Sir Charles scowled. "Mrs. Sherwood! You are entering the realm of moral insanity."

Lord Connock waved his hands in a pacifying gesture. "Gentlemen, please—"

"I must plead a headache, Lord Connock," Anne cut in. "If you'll excuse me . . ." Without waiting for his reply, she spun around and walked toward the door.

"I'll go after her," she heard Michael say, just as she passed through the threshold. Once she'd walked beyond their line of sight, she broke into a run, her skirts billowing and rustling like a gamecock caught in a net. She dashed through the great hall and to the front door.

"Anne, wait," Michael called.

She yanked the door open and raced into the night beyond Glendale Hall. Her heart beat with great, bruised thumps; her eyes burned and her throat felt so tight she could barely breathe. Air whistled in and out of her mouth.

"Anne!"

She ran blindly, startling an owl from its perch in a tree, hardly noticing the moon which cast a pale glow over the glasshouses several hundred feet in the distance. She heard Michael's quick footsteps as he hurried to catch up with her but she didn't want to see him, couldn't bear to be in his presence after he'd witnessed her utter defeat, her complete shaming at the hands of Lord Connock's associates.

A stitch was growing in her side. Every step became increasingly difficult. Sobs crowded her throat. She tried to hold them back. The last thing she wanted to do was confirm everything the men had said about her by surrendering to tears, a symptom of feminine vulnerability and weakness. She had rage rather than sadness in her, and yet, tears seemed to be the only way she could express it.

"Anne, stop. Please."

Michael had drawn close to her. His arm slipped around her waist even as he tangled himself in her skirts. They both tripped simultaneously and tumbled to the ground. He hit the grass first. Anne fell on top of him, her legs twisted in fabric. Wheezing, she drew in great gasps of air. She felt as if someone had slipped a noose around her throat and was pulling it taut.

He tried to draw her close but she wanted none of him or any man. She twisted and pushed as much as her tangled skirts would allow, dealing him a glancing blow against the ear. He grunted and swung his body on top of hers.

"Anne, stop, hush, please, it'll be all right, stop . . ."

"Let me go," she rasped. Panic drew her limbs tight. His body was so heavy, she couldn't move and by God no man would hold her still. Tears pressed remorselessly against the backs of her eyes. Her head felt near to exploding from the pressure. She thrashed beneath him.

He kept his weight on her, his arms gentle yet uncompromising as he held her against his powerful form. She felt his warm breath against her ear, murmuring to her, trying to calm her, and without quite knowing at what point they started, the tears began to flow. They washed away her need to fight. She felt so damned tired. Still breathing heavily, she fell against him.

"From the start, I knew they weren't going to give you a chance, Anne," he whispered. "They said those things because they resented Lord Connock introducing a woman into their gentlemen's club. It didn't matter how smart you were or how well you debated with them. They wouldn't accept you. Lord Connock was foolish to expect otherwise. Damn the man for putting you in this position."

He peered at her through the blackness, and evidently sensing her quiescence, rolled to his side. Still he held her against him. His body was all hard angles but safe, somehow. The tension began to leak from her, leaving her limbs shaking. She rested her ear against his chest and listened to the beat of his heart.

"I'm sorry, Anne." His voice was very gentle. "Don't let what they said shake your confidence. They treated you abominably."

She choked back a sob. Eyes closed, she pressed her face against his chest. Images of Sir Charles Lyell and Robert Chambers and Professor Huxley filled her mind, making her temples throb.

"Anne?"

"I'm hurt."

"Physically?"

"No."

He drew a long, shuddering breath and fit her more securely against his body. "Let me hold you." His lips brushed her temples, their pressure soft and accepting.

His sympathy was her undoing. She began to cry in earnest, gut-wrenching sobs that came up from deep inside her. She rubbed her face into his shirt and drank in the smell of him and wet the linen with her tears.

Michael held her patiently, and when her sobs softened into little hiccups, he kissed the top of her head. Cradled within his arms, she looked up into the sky. Black clouds had come in and masked all but the brightest of stars. They even muted the moon's glow.

She sighed, long and deep. The wound Lord Connock's associates had dealt her no longer felt like a killing blow. It merely stung. She became aware of other things—like the way Michael smelled. Musky, spicy, exotic, she wasn't certain what word fit.

"What sort of soap do you use?" she asked.

A lopsided grin curled his lips. "Why? Don't I use enough of it?"

"I don't think I've ever smelled such a fragrance before."

" 'Tis vetiver, an East Indian grass used for making perfumes."

"I like it."

"Good."

She pressed lightly against him, aware of the impropriety of her behavior as she did so. Still, he'd seen her shamed, he'd held her as she cried and soothed her broken pride; what difference would it make if she rested against him, particularly when he'd helped ease her embarrassment? At the moment, Michael was her source of warmth, of light. If she moved away, coldness might envelop her again.

He entwined his fingers in her hair, which had fallen loose from its chignon in her wild flight, and dragged them gently through the knots. The soft pulling and smoothing motions made her feel even more languorous. She sighed again. "You'll never get all of the knots out, but don't stop trying."

"Why? Does it feel good?"

"Yes." Her skin tingled with every stroke of his hand. Suddenly she felt shaky all over again.

"You deserve to feel good. You're made for it."

His attention, she noted, had drifted down to her breasts. Just knowing he stared at them was enough to make her nipples tighten with awareness. Heat seeped through her, pooling between her thighs.

What are you doing? a small voice inside her despaired. She thought of Charles Darwin, and her botanical illustrations, and the strange sapling. They'd all brought her here. They'd provided an opportunity that others would sacrifice much for. And yet, this evening, they'd brought her nothing but anger and grief.

Michael, on the other hand, brought emotions far more pleasurable. She snuggled closer, rubbing her cheek on his chest, her heart beating so loudly she heard it in her own ears.

"Ah, lass, you'd better stop doing that." Still toying with her hair, he shifted against the grass. "I'll take you back inside."

But he made no effort to move.

Neither did she.

Time passed, seconds in which the tension grew between them. She felt the hard, hot swelling of him near her stomach, and a lazy heat curled through her. The heavens were a velvety black, filling the land with shadows; but the moon tinged Michael's hair with pale silver glow, and suddenly Anne saw the light amidst the dark, the soothing quality of pleasure especially when surrounded by pain. In that moment she made a decision.

Tonight, she would live, and love.

Tomorrow she'd deal with the consequences.

She kissed his chest through his shirt, and felt him grow still. She knew he was wondering what she'd meant by that soft little kiss. Her touch gentle, she trailed her fingers along his jaw, then into his hair. A soft moan broke the silence and she realized it had come from her. She needed his touch, his mouth, his humanity . . . she needed all of him.

He stared into her eyes and his arms tightened around her. A moment later he rolled on top of her, his weight a comfortable reminder of his maleness. He was so much bigger, so much stronger, he could have done anything he wished with her, but she knew he would never hurt her or act without her consent. He would only pleasure her, and the knowledge that she could call this powerful yet gentle man her own, at least for the moment, was almost as exciting as the molten fire running through her veins.

Slowly he lowered his head and kissed her, their lips locking together as though fused as one, his tongue mingling with hers, their noses pressed together. She smelled his musky scent and felt the roughness of his stubbled chin against hers and moaned, shocked at the depths of her own longing. When he released her, her lips throbbed in an erotic way she'd never felt before. Breathing hard, she opened her eyes.

He was staring at her, the contact so intense that she forced her lashes to flutter downward. A knowing chuckle rumbling in his chest, he began to kiss her again, his mouth leaving her lips to move lower, to her breasts. Her neckline quickly proved a barrier. He rolled behind her and worked at the buttons on her gown.

She knew a moment of fear. Would he think her un-pleasantly plump? Hesitantly she allowed him to draw the gown from her. Her two petticoats went next, leaving her in her underclothes. Clothed only in a chemise and pantaloons, she lay there and waited for some muffled exclamation of disapproval. His gasp of delight when he rocked back on his heels to look at her told her she'd worried for no reason at all.

"Did I mention how much I'm liking your under-clothes?" he breathed, playing with the delicate Brussels lace that tumbled from the chemise's neckline.

Unable to reply, she drew in a long, shuddering breath. Smiling, he loosened the ties on her chemise, baring her breasts. Shyly she watched him take one pink nipple into his mouth, then threw her head back, unprepared for the sudden tremors that shot through her, making her body tighten with need. Just when she thought she could withstand it no longer, he lavished attention on her other nipple until she cried out, enveloped in pleasure.

She felt nothing but him. She smelled him, she tasted him; he'd flooded every one of her senses until there was only Michael and this great, overwhelming desire for him to fill the emptiness inside her. She wanted him naked, to see that perfect body, to touch the muscles on his back, to run her fingers down his arms and through the mat of hair on his chest.

Her fingers trembling, she slipped her hands beneath his lapels and pushed the coat off his shoulders. Shooting her a look filled with passion, he yanked his evening coat off, popped a button on his waistcoat while removing it, and at last rid himself of his shirt.

Exploring every exposed inch of him with her hands, she became far bolder than she'd ever dreamed she could be, caressing his chest and pressing little kisses along his jaw and rubbing the heated fabric between his legs. She had never experienced anything quite as exciting or as wonderful before, and in a faint way she felt as though she were selling her soul to this man. How could she know such pleasure and not want it repeatedly?

Tomorrow, she thought. She'd mull it over tomorrow.

Her breath came in quick little pants. She wanted him inside her now. Trembling, she pulled off her chemise and untied her pantaloons. When he saw her fumbling at the strings, he helped her undo the knots and slipped the last of her clothing off. Cool night air brushed against her thighs. She was naked now. Vulnerable. And unbearably exposed. She pulled him against her, concealing her body with his. Her throat tightened, this time with fear. Abruptly, she realized how completely she'd lost control again. She no longer knew herself.

He seemed to understand the impulses racing around inside her. Murmuring reassurances, he gathered her gently in his arms until she relaxed against him. Then, with a wickedly soft touch, he brushed the thatch of curls between her legs with his thumb and stroked the hard little nub of pleasure that cried out for release. She stiffened in surprise. It nearly tickled. As her pleasure mounted, though, she grew very relaxed indeed, parting her legs wide for him and pressing her face against the grass to cool the heat in her cheeks.

Groaning softly, he slipped his thumb inside her, easily, slicking her thighs with moisture. His breathing grew even more shallow and he paused to loosen his trousers. Anticipation filled her like a live thing. Unwilling to wait, she pushed his trousers down around his hips before he'd fully loosened them.

His erection was more than she'd expected . . . so much more than Henry had ever managed. She stared at him, thinking that she'd never seen anything as potent or thrilling. Swallowing at the thought of him inside her, she wrapped her fingers around him and drew him where she needed him the most.

She knew there likely were ways to prolong the pleasure, but that didn't matter now. There would be time for that later. His muffled gasps and soft groans of encouragement told her he wanted her just as much. Holding her breath, she nuzzled him against the place that ached the most. He required no more encouragement and thrust forward triumphantly.

"Michael," she whispered, lower lip quivering. She had never felt as close to anyone as she did to him. Tears leaked from her eyes. She couldn't stop them. It was as though she'd been waiting all her life for this moment, for this joining with him.

"My beautiful lass." His gold earring brushed against her cheek as he lowered himself to her and buried himself to the hilt, covering her with just the right amount of weight. There was nothing but the raw feel of him.

Then he began to thrust. Slowly at first, hot silk against hot silk, hard moistness, the humid smell of sex lingering between them, the sense of building pleasure, of coming delight, of release and satisfaction so complete she thought she might die of it. The feeling couldn't be denied . . . it brought almost physical pain as it grew stronger, swelling, until finally she felt him shudder deep inside her and she hurtled over the edge too, her body awash in warm waves of pleasure.

Breathing hard, he collapsed to his side, bringing her with him. The ground slowly became cool beneath her, while Michael's body blazed warmth. Shivering, she fitted her limbs closer to his, an inexpressible sadness mingling with the delight his lovemaking had wrought. While she had no regrets, she understood that she'd never forget this night or the feel of him inside her. She pressed her cheek against the grass. A muffled sob she couldn't quite control escaped her.

"Shh, lass," he crooned, his body wrapped around hers. "Don't cry."

The tears kept on leaking out. Tomorrow, it seemed, had come *now*. She began to consider the consequences. Despite the risk to herself and her position, she'd made love to him. Now she had to convince

Michael that it needed to end here, before Lord Connock caught wind of her indiscretion and returned her
posthaste to London, in disgrace.

What alarmed her the most, however, were the tender feelings she had toward him, feelings that told her
to draw him into her arms and brush his hair back from
his face and tell him how much he meant to her.

"I'm sorry," he said, his voice thick. "I took advantage of you. You were in a delicate state—"

She reached around and pressed a finger against his
lips. "I'll never forget this night, Michael. I loved being
with you and haven't any regrets about what we did. It's
tomorrow that I regret."

He sighed. "I know. I'm thinking about your position, and I know you are too."

"This can't happen again." Anne turned until she
faced him, his arms still snug around her. "Someone
will see something, the servants will start putting two
and two together, and I'll lose Lord Connock's respect.
I'll be ruined."

"I'd never do anything to hurt you," he whispered,
and held her quietly until both of their hearts had
slowed to a normal rhythm.

After a time he kissed her on the lips—chastely, as if
they had never been more than friends—and helped
her sit up. When they separated, cold air swirled around
her naked limbs and she felt very alone. She dressed in
her underclothes quickly, all the joy gone out of her.
Once Michael finished putting his clothes on, he laced
her into her corset, slipped the gown over her head, and
fastened her buttons.

Both fully dressed, they turned to stare at each other.

"Thank you for tonight, Michael," she whispered,
feeling tears start again.

Ducking his head so she couldn't read the expression in his eyes, he slipped an arm around her shoulders and pulled her close. "Anne . . ." He trailed off, whatever he'd planned to say lost in the darkness.

She floundered as well, wanting to tell him how deeply he'd touched her, but sensing that such a confession would only add to the misery. Instead, she pressed her face against his arm and made an unintelligible sound.

Loud male voices, hushed by distance, cut through the night. Michael grew very still. "I'd better return you to Glendale Hall, before someone finds us."

He took her hand just as several shadowy figures started across the lawn. Two of the figures held lanterns, illuminating enough of their dress to identify them.

Connock and his scholarly friends.

Michael began leading her away from the scientists, in a large circle that would eventually bring them to Glendale Hall's front door. Her hand warm in his, Anne deliberately dragged her feet. She wondered what had drawn Lord Connock and his guests into the night. Were they looking for her? The occasional laugh drifting from their direction and their leisurely pace suggested otherwise.

As the moments passed, she realized they were heading toward the glasshouses. Not just any glasshouse, but the companion to the composting center. She'd pay a dear sum to see what Connock had in those locked gardens of his.

"Michael," she said, her voice low, "you mentioned you had explored several of Lord Connock's glasshouses. Has he ever allowed you into the one he's bringing his associates into now?"

Michael squinted and stared through the darkness toward the two glowing lanterns. Connock and his guests had stopped outside the glasshouse. A moment later the door swung wide and the men entered with their lanterns. The last man through shut the door behind him.

"No," he admitted. "Lord Connock conducts his most sensitive experiments in there. From what I understand, the tiniest slip might ruin a month's worth of his work: exposure to light at the wrong moment, a bumped flask, even the accidental deposit of pollen on a flower."

"But he's taking his friends into that glasshouse."

"So?"

"He told me to say nothing of the sapling, and yet he's bringing his associates inside."

"Maybe the plants in that glasshouse aren't as valuable as the sapling."

She swallowed. "I want to see what's in there."

"Now?"

"Well, we don't necessarily have to announce our presence."

"You want to *spy* on them?"

She nodded guiltily.

With a slight hesitation, he detoured toward the glasshouse. At first they walked quickly, without paying attention to where they stepped. As they drew close, however, Michael became more secretive, sticking to the shadows and choosing the place he walked with care.

"Why are you so curious about that glasshouse?" he asked, his voice a whisper.

"Don't you want to know more about his experiments?"

"If he wanted me to know, he'd tell me."

"I guess my curiosity has gotten the better of me,"

she admitted. "I don't want to tour the glasshouse . . . I just want a little peek. So I can sleep at night."

He snorted. "You act as though Connock's up to no good. While he's eccentric, he isn't the kind of man to bring evil down upon us."

"Then why lock the glasshouse?"

"He could have many reasons. Perhaps he locks it to keep others safe. I know that some of the compounds he uses are volatile. Even so, we'll spy upon him, if only to prove to you that he's innocent of wrongdoing."

Anne said nothing more as they sidled up to the glasshouse in question. While lanterns lit up the front half of its interior, the back half remained dark and shrouded and the frosted glass still blocked her view. Slowly they circled around its four walls, looking for a chink in its blurry armor. The glasshouse effortlessly resisted their attempt.

Anne heard Professor Huxley speaking in scientific terms. She understood little of his talk, only that he discussed galvanization. When they reached the front door again, Anne paused to listen. Sir Charles Lyell was murmuring about cross-pollination.

"I don't think we're going to see anything," Anne whispered.

Michael nodded in agreement. "Let's take it as a sign that you should never seek a commission as a spy." He started off.

Anne noticed a white object near the ground. It glinted in an errant ray of moonlight. She pulled from Michael's grasp to move closer. A *flower*, she thought. Growing so close to the glasshouse wall that the main portion of the plant likely grew inside. This one single stem had sought and found natural sunlight.

A sweet, pungent fragrance almost like jasmine drifted from the trumpet-shaped flower. A *moonflower*, she clarified, touching its silken surface. Just like the other plants around Glendale Hall, distress emanated from the plant, but this time the red haze that formed in her mind was brighter, hotter, more painful.

She yanked her hand back.

Michael leaned close. "What's wrong?"

"The flower's wrong."

"In what way?"

"I don't know."

"Trust me, Anne. Tell me what you're feeling," he urged.

Reluctantly she shook her head.

He frowned. "You've got to trust in someone."

"I trust you. It's simply a feeling, nothing more," she lied. The part of her that had wanted to make love to him wanted to confide in him about her unusual ability, too. But she knew the folly of that action. Even if he believed in her ability to feel plants' emotions, Michael had defended Lord Connock at every opportunity, as well as Ireland, his homeland, and wouldn't take kindly to her innuendoes of lurking corruption.

"I don't think we're going to discover anything here tonight," she whispered. "Perhaps we should return to Glendale Hall."

Sighing, he took her hand in his. "When you keep too many secrets, Anne, they begin to eat at you. Before you know it, you'll be moping around like a broody hen and seeing nothing but rain on the sunniest of days."

She had no answer for him, and silently, they crept across the lawn and returned to Glendale Hall, with no one the wiser.

She paused to look at him once she'd climbed the steps to the front door, her footsteps light as she passed the sleeping footman slouched near the door. "Good night, Michael," she mouthed.

He paused to stare at her for a moment, his expression unreadable. Then he turned away, and Anne felt as if he took her heart with him, leaving her empty and alone.

9

The following morning Anne donned a plain dress of stout brown Holland, had a quick cup of tea and a scone, and was making her way through the great hall before the tallcase clock had chimed seven. Last night's lovemaking, while exquisite, had left her vulnerable. Silently she vowed to produce the most scientifically accurate, yet exquisite illustrations Connock had ever laid eyes on, if only to cement her position as his illustrator.

She swallowed. Dismissing the memory of Michael's mouth on hers wouldn't be nearly as easy.

The footman dozed by the front entrance. Rather than wake him, she eased out the door. The blue skies she'd become so accustomed to during her short stay in Ireland had given way to mist so fine it scarcely seemed to fall. When the sun shone in this fine land, she thought, the hillocks blazed an emerald green, the birds chirped with good humor, and the water tumbled over pebbles glittering on the riverbed. But when clouds descended, the unlit glens became as gloomy as a dungeon, their trees and bushes so heavy with dew they appeared to be weeping.

Today, a sense of abandonment swelled beneath the gray skies, as if every blade of grass silently protested the loss of the sun and its warmth. Anne, too, felt the sun's loss. Relieved she'd had the foresight to bring a crocheted shawl, she wrapped it around herself and started across the lawn, sketch case in hand.

She hadn't gone far before she smelled it again—that horrible odor, like honey spread atop spoiled meat. Her steps slowed, and she slanted a glance toward the glasshouses. They all sat innocently beneath the sun, as white as an angel's cassock and decorated with wrought-iron flowers.

Except, of course, for the composting glasshouse. It had the smell of corruption, not innocence. Even from a distance she could see the flies swarming all over the windows in creeping black masses, spotting the walls like pox. Without quite realizing it, she turned and began to wander in its direction.

A soft buzzing noise soon greeted her ears. Nose wrinkled, she walked right up to the glasshouse's front door and suppressed a shudder. Up close, the flies looked even more disgusting, massed together like that and crawling over one another's bodies with a stuttering eagerness. There were more flies, she thought, than when she'd first arrived at Glendale Hall. Many more. And the smell was worse, too.

She shifted her attention to the door. Tiny black bodies scuttled back and forth on the iron knob, examining and reexamining its surface, as if they suspected that this was the instrument that would allow them into the inner sanctum of dead meat and honey. A few flies plunged into the keyhole and came back out again. Acting on a hunch, she hunkered down and squinted through the keyhole. Blackness greeted her vision. Someone had plugged the keyhole with a tiny bit of clay, not enough to stop the key from turning but more than enough to keep the flies out.

Grimacing, she shooed the flies away, grasped the doorknob, and turned. Nothing happened. The door remained locked. Disappointment roiled through her, and she chided herself for it. She'd known the door would be locked. Still, a part of her had hoped that Lord Connock had made one small, forgetful mistake.

Flies began crawling on her hand. She shook them off and began to walk along the glasshouse walls. As she rounded the far corner, she paused, a very faint noise catching her attention. Eyes narrowed, she turned and looked at the glasshouse wall. She could barely hear the odd sound, which had a hiss to it, like a whip snaking through the air.

Something was in there.

Something *alive*.

She pressed one hand against the glasshouse wall, in a place where the flies had thinned out. She was amazed, and a little uneasy, at how warm the glass felt, considering the gray clouds and drizzle. Seconds later, a gray shadow formed around her hand, as if someone, or something, was pressing against the glass directly opposite her hand. Her throat tightened and dread swept through her. She yanked her hand back and rubbed it compulsively against her skirt.

Mist settled upon her skin like spider webs. Bewildered, she continued to walk around the glasshouse, aware that no one knew where she had gone. At this hour, the servants were all likely in the kitchen, and wouldn't notice if anything happened to her, and she wasn't supposed to be lingering around the composting glasshouse anyway. If she had an ounce of sense, she'd return to Glendale Hall and wait for someone to escort her into the woods.

And yet, that gray shadow . . . what was it?

Eyebrows drawn together, she skirted the corner and started up the other side. On her left, Glendale Hall huddled on its patch of lawn, its stones a dismal gray, like the pallor of a corpse. A large, smooth stone lay halfway down the length of the glasshouse. She picked it up and hefted it in her hand, wondering all the while what she planned to do with it—break the glass, for God's sake? She had to admit the idea had a wicked appeal. Even so she knew she hadn't picked it up for the sake of mischief but, rather, to defend herself.

From what?

The question echoed in her head. She couldn't answer it. She didn't know from what. She only understood that something was very wrong here, something that would very much like to hold her hand, and probably more.

In the distance, a door slammed. She jerked her head around and saw Griswold's frowning countenance as he exited Glendale Hall through the servants' door. He set off at a determined pace toward her and the composting glasshouse. Evidently he'd seen her.

She dropped the rock and set off for the woods. The last thing she wanted was a confrontation with the old gardener. Just as she reached the edge of the lawn, she turned around and glanced at him. He stood near the rock she'd dropped, staring first at it, and then at her. Judging by the way he placed his hands on his hips, he'd seen her drop it. No doubt he thought she'd planned to bash the glass in. She waited for him to shake his fist at her. Instead, he turned his back on her and began to walk along the glasshouse perimeter, perhaps inspecting it for damage.

Her breathing quick and hollow, she walked into Glendale Forest. A strange sort of quiet permeated the woods; she supposed the mist blanketed the sounds of animals foraging and birds flying from tree to tree. Still, the forest seemed to ooze hopelessness, drawing her thoughts back to Lord Connock and his strange sapling.

She was growing tired of touching plants that emitted only despair. What in God's name was wrong with these plants? She could no longer dismiss the thought that Lord Connock lay at the root of the plant troubles in this little corner of Ireland. The need to confront him about it was becoming stronger in her, and she knew if she gave that urge free rein it would be the end of her position as his botanical illustrator. It would also likely spell the end of her hopes for achieving scholarly recognition. And yet, how long could she possibly endure the suffering all around her?

She found the sapling after only two wrong turns. Mist had turned the small glen that sheltered it into a peaty bog that squelched beneath her shoes and released the rich aroma of decaying leaves. The larger trees that surrounded the sapling seemed to press forward in the gloom, as if trying to smother the abnormality that had taken root in the forest floor.

Nose wrinkled in distaste, Anne stopped by the little tree and touched it. At the moment of contact, a hazy red formed in her mind. Nothing had changed. The sapling still suffered a low-key despair, not as strong as the moonflower by the glasshouse but noticeable nevertheless.

She watched its leaves move in an errant breeze. They rustled in the same way the gray shadow had moved in the glasshouse. Obviously she'd seen leaves blowing in the wind, and her overworked imagination had ascribed more significance to it. No other explanation made sense.

Frowning, she rummaged through her sketch case and brought out a piece of string she'd marked off in inches. Today she would approach the tree in a more scientific manner, and see if that helped her sketching effort. Carefully she measured the trunk, limbs, and leaves of the sapling to become better acquainted with its overall proportions. After making a few notations on a piece of paper, she returned the string to her sketch case and withdrew a small hand lens, not unlike a monocle. With the hand lens she studied the bark, the tracery on the leaves, and every other complex detail that made up the sapling. It was tedious work, but as time went on Anne began to feel more comfortable with the sapling. She decided her scientific approach was a good one.

Close to an hour had passed before she felt ready to draw another preliminary sketch. Her feet starting to ache, she sat down on a boulder and assessed the sapling without the hand lens. Not a particularly pretty specimen, she thought, but a unique one, certainly. She reconsidered her arrangement of the sapling on paper. There were so many angles to cover, so many unique features to capture—she would need a multitude of small drawings next to the larger one of the sapling, to convey a true sense of the sapling's anatomy.

She also wanted to create a beautiful sketch. Therein lay the danger of focusing too much on the science of illustration. At what point would her pursuit of scientific accuracy have to give way to the needs of the picture? Color principles, choices in composition and layout, the challenge of creating a dynamic and unified painting— all of these things, rather than overwhelm her with their complexity, suddenly left her eager to begin.

She snapped open her sketch case and pulled out her sketchbook. Her pencil had a pleasingly hard lead, one that wouldn't smudge. She held it loosely and drew some lines in the sketchbook, keeping the tree's proportions in mind. Although she tried to keep the weight of her lines uniform, one line was fine in the beginning and broader toward the end, presenting a false anatomical view of the sapling's trunk. She turned the page and started again, this time twirling the pencil as she drew the line to keep the wear on the pencil tip uniform.

A soft mewl of pain stopped her mid-line. She froze, her pencil point still on the paper, and looked in the direction the sound had come from. There, in the brush about ninety feet distant, something thrashed in a thicket of raspberries. She saw little flying hooves and a suggestion of a white tail.

A *deer,* she thought. Young, likely hurt. What had it stepped into? A leghold trap? Or had it stumbled into the wrong end of a badger?

Anne just had to find out. She'd help the fawn if she could. She put her sketchpad down, placed her pencil on top of it, and waded off into the thicket. Its thrashing and mewling drew her along more quickly than her gown would easily allow. Her skirts caught in thorns and ripped, while branches whipped at her hair, pulling it down from the neat twist she'd fastened it into. She had to lean forward and barge on through, otherwise become hopelessly tangled.

Only about twenty feet away from the struggling deer, she heard a slithering noise. She looked down at her feet but saw nothing out of the ordinary, just a few pieces of that odd ivy native to Glendale Forest. A queer chill stole through her nevertheless. The decayed-honey odor she had noticed at the glasshouse now floated on the air around her, as though the thing in the glasshouse had followed her out into the forest . . .

Jaw set, she marched the last few feet to the deer and stopped short. Its eyes were very dark and its ears too large for its body. She quickly realized the deer had tangled itself in a piece of that damnable ivy. Vines coiled around its legs, and one trailed upward across its torso. Still, the ivy wasn't its only problem. Blood trailed from the deer's mouth and ears, and some marked its legs. It mewled again and thrashed more wildly when it saw her.

Pity filled her. The poor thing was just a baby. At least its legs seemed intact. Obviously it hadn't stepped in a leghold trap. She wondered why it bled. Would she find an arrow jutting from its side or discover a bullet hole? Whispering nonsense syllables meant to reassure, she reached down and began to pull the ivy from its body. Soon she had freed the deer to the point where it could stand. It did so, on four very shaky and spindly legs.

"Poor thing," she murmured, studying its sides and neck for signs of injury. She found nothing. A sticky substance clung to her hands. Nose wrinkled, she wiped them on her skirt and sat back to see if the deer could survive on its own.

The deer stumbled and fell, then struggled to its feet once again. In a drunken manner it wove its way further into the forest, falling at regular intervals. At last, Anne could watch no more. She would gather the fawn into her arms and take it to Michael. He would know how to heal it. Drawing her skirts tight against her, she walked further into the forest.

The deer seemed to gain a little strength. Its course became more steady, its step more spry. Anne found she had to walk faster to stay within range. Now that she had decided upon a course of action, she was determined to catch that deer. If she didn't bring it to Michael, it wouldn't last the night.

Anticipating the feel of its warm body against hers, she left the sapling far behind, walking through stands of pines and around peaty marsh. Always the deer stayed one step ahead. They walked through another stand of pines that appeared similar to the first set. She couldn't help wondering if they'd circled around. Suddenly aware that she hadn't the slightest idea where the deer had led her to, she paused and looked around. The deer sprawled in a thicket about twenty feet further on.

It began mewling again. This time the mewling had a desperate quality to it. Her breath stopped in a gasp. Her heart gave one mighty thump, then seemed to contract to a cold, hard stone. She'd been right all along. Something had followed her from the glasshouse, and now it was here with her, to feast on the deer, and then on her. Something that liked warmth and made a soft whipping noise. Like a snake. A big one.

The deer let out one final, ululating cry. Anne heard the stealthy rustling of leaves. Coming closer. A cry built on her lips. She slapped a hand across her mouth just in time. It came out muffled. She didn't want to alert the thing that had hurt the deer, God no, but then again, it already knew she was here, didn't it?

She spun on her heel and raced through the trees, back the way she thought she'd come, only then she was running through pines again, the same pines, and she realized she was hopelessly lost. The thing would have her soon, because it knew these woods better than she, and it had a purpose, a goal to feed on her delectable flesh, and nothing motivated anyone better than a goal, God she knew that didn't she—

Without warning, she bumped into a very solid, very male form. She looked into Michael's eyes and fell against him.

"Anne!" He grasped her arms and held her upright. "Mother of God, you're white as a sheet. What's happened? What are you doing out here?"

She wrapped her arms around his torso and held on for dear life. He became motionless for a moment, and then his arms went around her. He held her tightly, but not tightly enough. She didn't think she'd ever feel safe again.

"What's wrong?" he repeated.

"There's something in these woods," she said, her voice husky, her eyes wide. "It killed a deer right before my eyes. It could even be coming for us now." She tensed, ready to bolt, but he held her too firmly for that.

"What's coming for us?"

"I don't know. The ivy, maybe. It likes blood, I know that much. The poor deer was bleeding everywhere. I found ivy wrapped around its legs, its torso. Lord, I've never seen the like."

His eyes flickered. With recognition, she thought.

"Let's start from the beginning," he said, his voice taut. "While you talk, we'll make our way back to the sapling."

"How did you find me in the first place?"

"I saw your sketchbook, abandoned, and followed your trail. I'm also very familiar with these woods. Remind me to tell you about it sometime. But first, explain this ivy to me."

Still shaking, but calmer, Anne allowed him to lead her through the pines, past the peaty bog, and into the oaks. "I left Glendale Hall early this morning to sketch, and I stopped by the composting glasshouse."

"You have to stop meddling around Lord Connock's glasshouses," he said. "You aren't going to find anything worth all this effort."

"There's something in there, Michael, I don't care what you say," she blurted. "The honeyed-decaying smell coming from the glasshouse had gotten worse, and more flies were clustering on the windows. I heard this strange noise, very faint, coming from inside the glasshouse. When I touched the glass, it felt very warm, and a gray shadow formed around my hand, as though something had touched me back from the inside."

He said nothing.

In the silence that blossomed between them, she realized she sounded like a hysterical female. She tried for a more even tone. "Griswold approached the composting glasshouse. When I saw him, I walked quickly into the forest and found the sapling. I had almost finished my measurements and preliminary sketches when I heard the deer."

"Heard? What do you mean?"

"It was mewling in pain. I saw it thrashing in the bushes some fifty feet away. Naturally I tried to help it. As I said, ivy had tangled around its legs and torso, and it bled freely. Once I removed the ivy, it stumbled off into the woods, but it looked so weak that I knew it wouldn't survive the night. I decided to bring it to you, and followed it deeper into the forest."

"Do me a favor," he said. "Don't go wandering off into the forest anymore. You have a way of getting lost."

"You needn't worry about that after today," she assured him, then recounted the final moments. "I followed the deer for quite a while before I realized I had become disoriented. A moment later, the deer fell for the last time into the bushes. I heard all sorts of mewling, and then, nothing. Seconds later, the rustling started toward me. I ran, and bumped into you."

He stopped. "As you must know, there are any number of explanations for what you saw. The deer could have had some sort of disease, a wood mouse could have been scurrying along the ivy—"

"I realize that, Michael. And yet, how could a deer become that entangled with ivy? You should have seen it. The ivy coiled around its legs like some kind of leafy bracelet."

Without warning, he turned around. "Let's go back."

"Go back? Where?"

"To the deer." He held her arm and steered her back toward the stand of pines.

"But why?"

"If we don't find that deer and a rational explanation, it'll haunt your nights for weeks."

Appreciating his logic, she went along with him, if a bit slowly. When they arrived in the stand of pines, she directed him to a thicket about twenty feet away, where the deer had thrashed for the last time. His steps assured, he left her side, walked right over to the thicket, and pushed the brambles aside with his boot. "There's nothing here."

"What?" She joined him near the bushes. As he'd

said, the ground and leaves looked untouched. "It died here, I'm certain of it. I *watched* it die."

"Sometimes, on days like these, when the clouds are low and rain is drizzling down, we're more susceptible to dismal imaginings—"

"Oh, stop it," she barked. "Don't try to tell me I imagined it."

"Where's the deer, then?"

"I don't know."

He shrugged and took her arm. They started back to the sapling. As they walked, Anne caught a whiff of that honeyed-decaying smell. Her steps slowed and finally stopped. "It's here. Somewhere close by."

"What's here?"

"The thing that killed the deer."

"How do you know?"

"I can smell it."

He sniffed the air. "You're referring to that sweet yet rotten smell?"

"I am indeed." She left the path and pushed her way into another thicket, following the smell, and soon she came upon it. A young deer. Only it didn't look much like a deer anymore. A pile of fur and bones, it seemed to have had the life sucked out of it. Even its eyeballs were gone. A thin film covered its eye sockets and blood crusted its mouth and ears.

Hand pressed to her lips, she turned away.

Michael swore softly. He knelt down at the deer's side and prodded the corpse with a stick. "This deer does smell rotten. Look at the state of decomposition. It's been dead for at least a month," he pronounced. "This can't be the same deer you tried to help."

"But it is," she insisted, knowing somewhere deep inside that this very deer had just been within her grasp.

"How did it get this way, then?"

"I don't know. Perhaps if we found the ivy and collected a specimen, we'd have some answers."

He nodded, his face shadowed, his eyes dark. "We'll look on our way back to the sapling."

They retraced their path, Anne keeping a close eye on the ground for anything that even faintly resembled ivy. Michael left the trail often to thrash around in the underbrush. He found nothing either. When they returned to the clearing, it looked just as Anne had left it, untouched by any bogeys hiding out in the woods. Still, she hadn't the slightest enthusiasm for drawing.

Anne caught Michael's glance and held it. She stated what she knew weighed on both their minds. "The ivy disappeared."

"Ivy doesn't belong in old woods," he said. "It doesn't like all of that mulch, preferring the bare patches of a newer forest. I don't think it disappeared. Rather, it was never there in the first place."

"But we both saw ivy the other day. It twined around your ankle."

"There may be one or two plants struggling to live in Glendale Forest. Still, I've no doubt they're rare. We just haven't run across any again. When we find an ivy plant, though, we'll take a specimen to Lord Connock and have him examine it."

She sighed, knowing she'd have to content herself with that. "It isn't normal, that ivy. It has pulpy leaves with serrated edges and it leaves a sticky substance on your skin. I handled a piece my first night in Ireland."

"The same night you had that scare, after your long and tiring journey?"

"Are you saying I'm imagining things?"

"No, I'm just reminding you that there could be many explanations—"

"I know, I know." She sighed again, noisily and with great feeling. "I don't think I can sketch anymore today."

"I'll bring you back to Glendale Hall," he offered.

"Please do," she agreed. "Why don't we return tomorrow? I'll try to finish my illustration of the sapling then."

10

A basket on his arm, Michael fetched her on the following day and returned her to the sapling. The sun had almost climbed to its zenith and banished all but the most persistent shadows in the underbrush. Anne had to admit that the clearing, at least for the moment, appeared quite harmless. She settled onto a boulder and placed her sketch case in her lap.

He fixed a considering gaze on her. Seconds later, a smile began to play about his mouth. "Why don't we eat before you start sketching?"

She nodded, aware they had both deliberately avoided mentioning the ivy. In truth, she didn't want to mention it. Talk about the ivy had the habit of spoiling a perfectly wonderful day. She needed a break from dire thoughts. "All right. What did Cook pack us?"

He stood, swept the basket off the ground, and lifted the lace covering to peer at its contents. "Cold tarragon chicken, rabbit pâté, oatmeal bread, raw carrots and celery, *port salut* cheese, apple *gateaux*, and a nice Beaujolais." His smile widening, he allowed the lace to drop from his fingers and settle back over the top of the basket.

Her stomach fluttered, more from Michael's proximity than hunger pangs. Abruptly she noticed the long, lithe legs encased in gray trousers and the fine lawn shirt that hugged his shoulders, emphasizing their broadness and strength. His stance, she thought, was casual, and yet he filled the woods with his presence, as though he had conquered them in his time and now ruled them with knowledge born of experience. She remembered Huxley's garbled tale about the young Oak King and the May Queen consummating the ritual of fertility, and her heart quickened. "Sounds wonderful."

"Very good." He gestured toward her with a flourish and affected a courtly English accent. "Please forgive me, madam, but you must stand, for your boulder is the only one flat enough to use as a table."

"Are you sure you haven't some English blood in you?" she teased, knowing he was doing his level best to dispel any poor mood that might encroach upon them. She stood a few paces back from her former seat. "You sound remarkably like an aristocrat."

"If there's a God, I'm pure Irish." He spread the lace over the boulder and began to withdraw earthenware pots and linen-wrapped packages tied with brown cord. After arranging them on the boulder, he brought out a bottle of Beaujolais and popped its cork. He set the bottle, silverware, goblets and plates on the boulder and then dragged a fallen log over for her to use as a seat. "Sit down, and I'll pour your wine."

With only the slightest hesitation she swept her somewhat tattered skirts to the side and slid onto the fallen log, her legs folded up in front of her.

Michael sat opposite her and splashed some of the Beaujolais into her goblet. A clear, gentle red, it begged to be sipped. His smile a satisfied one, he began to serve her a little bit of everything. Anne nibbled. Tarragon, parsley, thyme, shallots . . . the smells of the chicken and pâté combined to create a truly mouth-watering fragrance, while the cheese and oatmeal bread proved a delicious complement to the heartier portions of their picnic. She sighed in contentment.

"Rather delicious, hmmm?" he asked.

"My compliments to Cook."

"And what do you think of the wine?"

She sipped the red liquid and her eyes widened in surprise. It hadn't any bite at all; instead, it slipped smoothly past her tongue after delighting her taste buds with a fruity flavor. "Sublime."

" 'Tis from the village of Villefranche, in the Bas-Beaujolais, France. I collected wildflowers from the region about five years ago." He, too, sipped his wine, savoring it against his tongue before swallowing. "While I was there, a man ran naked through the streets. A few hours later, a woman ran naked through the streets, just like the man. Crowds had gathered to watch both events. I discovered later that the pair had been caught in an adulterous union."

"Running naked through the streets is punishment for adultery in France?"

"Not in all of France, but at least in Villefranche."

Anne swallowed another mouthful of wine, then speared a piece of cold tarragon chicken with her fork. She lifted it to her lips and munched on it, aware of his gaze ever upon her. "Running naked through the streets. What a notion! I can't imagine being naked anywhere outside a tub for bathing."

"Take off your gown," he murmured, "and discover what it feels like to have the mist caress your bare skin."

She choked, then recovered, her eyes wide. "Pardon me?"

"I'm simply suggesting that you experience rather than imagine."

"I think some experiences are better left to the imagination."

He smiled. "How do you like the chicken?"

"Very good." A strange sort of disappointment surged through her, that he hadn't tried harder to press his point of experience over imagination. "All of these questions concerning the food lead me to believe you've cooked it yourself. Did you?"

"No. I simply want you to taste."

Her eyebrows drew together. "Of course I'll taste. I have a tongue, don't I?"

"You do have a tongue, but that doesn't mean you'll taste. We often have so little time that we no longer bother to truly savor what we eat."

"All right, let me try." She spread rabbit pâté on a piece of oatmeal bread and bit into the bread. A sharp flavor filled her mouth, along with the sweeter taste of shallots, and something quite pungent, besides. She rolled it around her tongue before swallowing. "The rabbit has a bitter edge to it, which mingles quite nicely with the more mellow-tasting bread. A slice of cheese, I think, would complete the flavor."

Michael obediently cut off a piece of the *port salut*. Rather than hand it to her, he bypassed her outstretched palm and held it up to her lips. "You're careful to note what pleases you. Well done, Anne."

Even as her cheeks grew warm at his praise, she became still at the thought of his fingers, so near her mouth. Silently he waited for her to part her lips and take what he offered. A second passed, then two. She felt as though he'd offered her more than food, though she couldn't explain why; the simple act of opening her mouth for him felt unbearably intimate.

Warmth began to build deep inside her, concentrating between her legs before fanning outward, engulfing her in lazy desire. She wondered if she looked beautiful to him, if he wanted to kiss her and caress her. Slowly she opened her mouth, her gaze locked with his.

He placed the *port salut* on her tongue, his fingers brushing against her lips before he dropped his hand to his side. She chewed and swallowed, but didn't really taste anything. The dark Irishman with the devastating smile had left her unable to savor anything but the thought of his powerful body pressed against hers.

"Do you like it?" he whispered, his full lower lip becoming more pronounced.

She dragged her gaze away from his and stared at the ground, aware she was fighting a losing battle against Michael and his sensuality. Sunlight lit up the glen, creating a shadow of his profile near her feet. She took such pleasure in looking at that profile that she knew she teetered on the brink of utter profligacy.

Michael picked up his wine and drank deeply before returning his goblet to the boulder. "Isn't it more enjoyable to taste fully?"

She nodded, mute.

"The body is full of sensation. 'Tis designed for stimulation," he murmured. "I've made a study of the senses. I'd like to share with you what I've learned."

"I can't learn, Michael. You'll ruin me."

"I'm not talking about making love. Rather, I would teach you how to pay attention to your senses."

Anne thought back to his lovemaking and knew it had changed her forever. Now she resented her scholarly goals for forcing her to turn her back on what could have been between them. His lessons only seemed to make her long for things she couldn't have. "I don't know if I want to learn."

"Why wouldn't you want to learn? Tell me why you've shut yourself away from the world," he urged. "Who hurt you?"

"No one hurt me." She bristled a little and spoke too harshly.

"I can't believe that. You try too hard to be aloof and unfeminine. I promise you, you'll never succeed in either attempt."

"I'm unfeminine because I haven't a choice. You saw how Lord Connock's associates reacted to me at dinner. The more womanly I look, the less credibility I have as a scholar."

"Yes, but for what reason? Why are you so hell-bent on gaining recognition as a scholar?"

The sunlight brought a sheen of promise and hope to the leaves and trees. She felt it shining on her head, warming her hair and the tip of her nose. As she watched the blue highlights in Michael's black hair sparkle beneath its gentle touch, a feeling of well-being enveloped her. Perhaps the wine was working on her, or maybe the warm interest in Michael's clear gaze had affected her. Whatever the case, she decided to trust him with the particulars of her past.

"My parents and I didn't really suit," she admitted. "They own a horse farm in Cambridge, where I was brought up. It consumed all of their time. I didn't share their interest in horses, preferring the woods and fields to barns. They couldn't understand why I would rather sit and sketch than ride to the hounds. As the years passed we, well, grew disinterested in each other."

Michael began to pack their lunch back into the basket as he listened, and somehow, the diversion of his attention made it easier for her to talk about the past.

"When Henry, Baron Sherwood, began to pay his addresses to me, my mother thought us a superior match," she continued. "You see, Henry and I shared the same interest: botany. I had already become quite adept at sketching, although neither my mother nor my father appreciated my talent. The first time Henry visited Kilbourne Farm in Cambridge, he raved about my illustrations. My father decided then and there that I would marry Henry."

Michael shook out the lace and draped it atop the basket. "And you? Did you want to marry him?"

"I suppose so. I saw him as a way to escape Kilbourne Farm and the relentless smell of horses. He seemed to appreciate me as no other man had."

"Your marriage seemed to have the makings of a very good one," Michael remarked, settling himself against the boulder again.

She sat next to him. "I thought so too, right up until the day we married. The wedding night"—she paused, her voice growing tight—"left much to be desired."

"He hurt you?"

"No, not exactly. I was a virgin, of course, and the initial thrust—" She broke off again and lowered her lashes.

Michael placed his hand on hers, the contact sending shivers throughout her body. Pleasant shivers. "He took you rather than give you pleasure."

"Yes, that's it exactly. Henry *took* me. Once or twice

a year. It didn't hurt my body, nor did it touch my mind."

He rubbed the top of her hand with his large thumb. "I think he did hurt you."

Lips pressed together, she looked away at the sunlight playing upon the rough bark of the trees and turning each blade of grass to a brilliant emerald. A soft breeze curled past her cheek and teased a few curls against her temples.

"How long were you married?" he asked.

"Five years." She took a deep breath, tried to speak more naturally. "Outside the marriage bed, my time with Henry wasn't all that unpleasant. Together we worked on the *Encyclopedia of Flowering Plants*. I acted as his secretary, copyist, scribe, and illustrator. Never have I worked as diligently as I did with my late husband."

She struggled to keep her train of thought, for Michael was tracing lazy circles on the back of her hand, his touch sublimely pleasing. "At last, about two years ago, our encyclopedia was published."

Anne turned to look Michael full in the face. For the first time in front of anyone, she allowed her anger to show. "Henry gave me no credit for anything in that book, not even the illustrations I had drawn. He became the toast of every scientific circle in London and made the most of it. While he made merry with the finest of aristocrats, I remained home, in my cold little salon. I realized then that Henry had used me utterly."

Michael shifted his focus to the ground, the lines around his mouth tightening. When he returned his attention to her his eyes were dark. "I'm sorry, Anne."

"No more so than I. After he died, I swore I would

gain recognition for my work in the same scientific circles that had shunned me. But that isn't the worst of it."

He stopped teasing her with his fingers and wrapped his hand around hers instead, comforting her with his touch.

"All of that carousing loosened something in Henry's brain, and he died soon after *Encyclopedia of Flowering Plants* was published. At Henry's funeral, I met his mistress."

Michael showed not the least amount of surprise.

A shudder went through her. "The woman was coarse, blowsy, her countenance as foul as her speech. Henry had discussed me with her at great length. But that's enough about me," she insisted, the memories finally becoming too painful to bear. "You mentioned yesterday in the woods that you had a rather long story to tell about yourself."

He rubbed his chin. "I did?"

"You did, and don't try to convince me otherwise. Perhaps I can get you started. Professor Huxley explained to me the particulars of your youth."

"Told you about the Green Man, did he?"

"Ad nauseam. I found his prurient interest in your affairs most distasteful."

"But it didn't stop you from listening."

"I'll listen to anyone who can offer insight into your character, Michael. I'll admit to finding you a puzzle." She glanced at the treetops as if there she might find a gentle way to tell him what she needed to say. "I've seen your cottage and noticed all the domestic touches you've made to it, and yet, you say your cottage is a port, not a home. In short, if you'll pardon my bluntness, your words do not agree with your actions."

"Now you're the observant one," he murmured. He

stood and pulled her to her feet. "I'll take you back to Glendale Hall."

"But I'm not ready to go." She resisted him when he tried to urge her toward the path. "Keep your promise, Mr. McEvoy, and tell me about yourself. Why do you call your cottage a port, not a home?"

"Because it doesn't feel like home."

At his bald statement, she relented and allowed him to lead her through the woods. She realized she'd touched a nerve and didn't want to press him any further. For a time they walked rather quickly, but then a change seemed to come over him. His pace slowed and his brows drew together in a thoughtful manner, until finally, he stopped walking altogether and turned to face her. Hands in his pockets, he slouched as though this were the most casual conversation he'd ever had. Still, darkness muted the blue of his eyes, and she understood that what he planned to say was anything but casual.

"I was born in Connaught to a poor couple who did everything but bleed upon the soil to make the crops grow. It was a hard life, and a good one. I thank my father and mother every day for teaching me how to work the earth."

"You enjoyed common labor? Such as hoeing, digging?"

He startled her with a smile, his teeth a quick flash of white in the cool shadows of the forest. She didn't see much humor in it. "I'm not surprised you find that difficult to believe."

"Most gentlemen of my acquaintance go to great lengths to avoid any sort of labor, common or otherwise. What attracted you to the fields?"

"When I was young, and awoke in the morning, the

day was full of potential. Working a farm, while difficult, brought me great satisfaction, for at the end of the
day I saw that potential realized. The field was plowed,
the seeds had sprouted, the vegetables were harvested.
On rainy days, I cursed the clouds for keeping me from
a day of work."

She nodded, thinking of the moment when she
completed a sketch to the best of her ability. "Were you
very young when your parents died?"

"I'd just turned ten years old. My father had rented our
farm, and upon his and my mother's death, the landowner
reclaimed the farm and turned me over to the parish authorities. They placed me in a workhouse in Dublin."

She was unable to suppress a shudder at the word
workhouse. Several years before, a story had circulated
about the dead of a London workhouse being used to
fertilize nearby fields, to save the expense of coffins.

Michael slanted her a sideways glance. "I survived
the workhouse, Anne. It didn't kill me. It made me
stronger."

"I cannot imagine . . ." She shook her head. "How
did your parents die?"

"In the famine. They made sure I had enough food
so I might live, and in doing so, they starved."

She swallowed. "I'm sorry."

"No need to be. I was their child. They wished me to
live." He stood a bit straighter. "The workhouse was a
hellish place, an ugly pile of stones and bars matched
on the inside by hard, cold guardians. My daily rations
barely kept me from starving as my parents had. After
four years, I'd had enough. First I ran, and then I walked
for three days without stopping, afraid they might pursue me. Finally I collapsed into a burrow and slept.
When I awoke, I crawled into the woods to make my-

self a home, and told myself that someday I'd dance on the guardians' graves."

The thought of a child tormented and alone left a sick feeling in the pit of her stomach. She clasped his hand in her own and squeezed.

His eyes remained unmoved. Clearly he wanted none of her sympathy.

She released his hand. "How long did you remain in the wilderness?"

"Almost five years. At first I did nothing but rove through the woods, searching for food, hating everyone I'd ever met and being afraid of dying. Eventually, though, I settled down into a routine. I began to understand the world of the forest rather than fear it; I watched the animals and copied them."

"You became the Green Man."

He nodded. "Occasionally during a hard winter, I'd trek to a local village at night. I'd break into the more prosperous houses and steal from their larders. I didn't care that most people would consider me a criminal. I had no faith in the society that had raised me.

"Several times the villagers saw me. Once I was almost caught. They came looking for me in the woods, but I easily eluded them. I was a creature of the forest by then. I had learned what the deer and fox know."

"These skills never left you," she guessed. "That's why you're such an accomplished naturalist. You're uniquely qualified to hunt down a plant in the forest. You know how to find a path, to sense the approach of a storm, to find fresh water."

He smiled. "I've put those five years in the wild to good use."

"That's also why you place such value on sensuality." Her voice gained the intensity that comes with understanding. "Living in the wild as you did, you had to rely on your senses . . . or die." Silently she speculated that his suffering in the workhouse and subsequent years in the wild had also taught him to insulate himself from any deep emotional ties.

His manner was offhand, as though he wished her to believe he'd remained unaffected by it all. "Maybe you're right. In any case, the villagers created a legend around me. They called me a boggart and told their children I would come from the forests to claim them. This legend eventually reached Lord Connock and sent him in pursuit of me."

"Lord Connock coaxed you from the wild," she said, paraphrasing what Professor Huxley had told her earlier. "He helped you reenter society. In return, you put your special skills to use for him and began collecting rare plants."

"I enjoy traveling. I've been to many places, Anne, each more exotic than the last." He frowned. "But nothing compares to Connaught, the prettiest piece of land I've ever known. Even my cottage in Glendale Forest seems lacking."

She eyed him with curiosity. "Why don't you return to Connaught, Michael, and find a farm to live on?"

"I've returned to Connaught many times. Even that doesn't feel like home anymore, so I don't stay."

"I thought you were a man who didn't care about having a home. One who travels from port to port."

"I am." He shoved his hands into his trouser pockets and fell silent. Suddenly he seemed reluctant to say more.

"Then why are you looking for a place that feels like home?"

He looked away.

"Michael?"

"There's Glendale Hall," he said, directing his attention toward the glimmer of gray stone between the trees.

"Michael, you haven't answered my question. Why must you find a place that feels like home?"

"Damn it, you know how to push," he growled. "All right, I'll tell you the whole, unvarnished truth. On that little farm that my parents owned, I was *home*. It felt *right*. I felt *good*. Since then I've moved from place to place, searching for that same feeling of rightness, of goodness. I've explored all of Ireland. I've searched the territories around the China Seas, the Americas, everywhere. I still haven't found what I'm looking for."

"Perhaps you're not looking for a *place*," she hesitantly offered. "There's more to a home than a house."

"You think I need a woman?" Lips set, he regarded her closely. "I've had so many women I've lost count. Geishas, prostitutes, a nobleman's wife . . . sometimes I even had two in my bed at once. None of them did anything more than slake my lust. Companionship is not the answer."

Her cheeks grew warm. "I think you need to take some time to find out what will really make you happy."

"As do you," he charged, his voice harsh. "You are hell-bent on gaining recognition in scientific circles. But at what cost to yourself? You've become colorless, Anne. You live in a colorless world. You have no more desire for a husband than I have for a wife. Am I correct?"

Unwillingly she nodded. "I'm determined to pursue my scholarly goals. Many might think me morally corrupt, but marriage and children do not figure into my future."

"Well then, they don't figure into my future either. It seems we're quite a pair." Still frowning, he gestured toward the path that led out of the woods. "Ladies first."

She began walking with a rather stiff gait. His assessment of her, as always, was so correct it stung. She'd walked no more than five paces, however, when she realized he'd remained behind. She swung around to see what had delayed him and found his attention fixed upon the bushes. Something about his stillness set her instinct on edge.

"Michael? What's wrong?"

"There." He nodded toward a thicket.

Eyebrows drawn together, she walked back to rejoin him, then studied the thicket that had captured his attention. Green pointed leaves, fuzzy stems, hard green berries that would ripen into raspberries within a month or so . . . she detected nothing untoward, other than a slight wilt to the younger stems and leaves. "That's a raspberry bush. I see nothing strange about it."

"Look below the bush."

She dropped her gaze lower and examined the thick, mulchy leaves around the base of the plant. She saw the flower almost immediately. It snuggled against the base of the raspberry bush's canes. The lower part of the flower disappeared into the mulch. "It looks like a large wild snapdragon."

"I don't think so." Michael pushed away some of the mulch to reveal the entire stem. A large tuberous bulb with spiderlike roots stretched to the left and right, but didn't penetrate deeply enough into the mulch to reach soil. The stem sprang up from this bulb.

Anne crouched down to examine it more closely. "Lord, that's ugly," she couldn't resist saying. Gray and gelatinous, the bulb looked like a slug's underbelly.

He slipped his fingers behind the flower stem and tried to pull the flower away from the raspberries. It resisted the movement. Anne saw little suckerlike projections from the stem attached to the raspberry bush canes.

" 'Tis a parasite," she breathed. "It's attached itself to the raspberry canes. Do you see how the raspberry bush is wilting? The flower must be sucking the raspberry plant's juices."

Michael pulled harder and with soft snapping sounds the flower separated from the raspberry bush. He held it up between two fingers with a look of disgust. "Have you ever studied a flower such as this?"

Anne felt her heart quicken. "It looks similar to *Antirrhinum majus*. Still, the differences are significant. Did you notice how it gives off a strange scent, something very spicy? The true snapdragon is virtually odorless. Have you ever seen the like?"

He shook his head.

"It could be a new species," she offered. "Glendale Hall seems full of new species." All of the suspicions she'd harbored against Lord Connock abruptly resurfaced to nag at her.

Michael threw the flower onto the mulch. His countenance became shuttered, revealing nothing of his thoughts. "I'll mention it to Lord Connock when I see him next."

Without waiting for her answer, he returned to the path. When she didn't follow, he gestured toward Glendale Hall. "Are you coming?"

"Just a moment." She espied another thicket, this one of gooseberries. The edges of the gooseberry bush's leaves appeared brown and had begun to curl up; indeed, this plant was in worse shape than the raspberry.

She walked to the gooseberry and pushed aside the leaves near the bottom. Two parasitic snapdragons nestled against its base.

Anne made a moue of distaste with her lips. "There are more over here, Michael. And these are bigger. I'd say the bush has suffered proportionately."

He made no move to join her. "I said I'll speak to Lord Connock about it."

Something in his attitude convinced her that he hadn't the slightest intention of talking to Lord Connock about the flower. For reasons of his own, he seemed to be protecting the nobleman. Was Michael somehow involved in Lord Connock's schemes? The thought stabbed at her with startling intensity. Her mood instantly plummeted.

Steeling herself, she reached down and placed her fingers around the stem of one of the bigger snapdragons. The dull red haze of distress immediately assaulted her mind. But in this case, peculiar veins of black permeated the red, giving it a marblelike appearance. A cold knot of sickness gathered in her stomach at the impressions this flower left with her. Suffering. Madness. Voracious hunger.

Lips pressed tight together, she detached the flower from the gooseberry canes and eased its bulbous roots out of the mulch. With care she slipped the flower into an empty compartment in her sketch case and returned to Michael's side. "We'll both talk to Lord Connock. I'll bring this flower as evidence."

He shrugged. "As you wish, lass."

11

$\mathcal{A}$nne located the butler, Carlyle, and discovered that Lord Connock had holed up in the library. With Michael by her side, his tanned, handsome face utterly closed to her, she found the library and knocked on the door.

"Who is it?" Lord Connock's cultured tones echoed from within.

"Mrs. Sherwood." She glanced at Michael. "And Mr. McEvoy. We've made an interesting discovery, one we'd like to share with you."

The door opened almost immediately. Lord Connock greeted them with an urbane smile. Dressed casually in navy-blue trousers and embroidered waistcoat, his brown hair neatly brushed back from his forehead, he seemed completely at ease. Nevertheless, Anne thought she detected caution in his blue eyes. "Come in."

She entered first. Michael followed behind her and immediately went over to a side table near the windows. Lord Connock had pulled the heavy drapes back, flooding the room with light, sparkling on brandy decanters that sat on the side table. Michael poured himself a few fingers of brandy and took a healthy swallow from his snifter.

"Please, sit," Lord Connock directed, his generous wave encompassing every chair in the room.

Anne placed her sketch case on the floor and sat on a nearby settee.

"Anyone else want a drink?" Michael asked.

Anne shook her head no. Lord Connock spared him a glance before focusing on Anne.

"Tell me about this discovery you and Michael"— Lord Connock cast another curious look toward the Irishman—"have made."

"Yesterday," she began, aware that Michael remained still and silent, "I returned to the sapling to begin my sketches."

"And how are you doing?" the nobleman asked.

"Passably well. I usually do several practice sketches in preparation for the final, 'good' sketch. I'd say I need a few more days of practicing. I am, however, becoming very familiar with the sapling."

"Very good." Connock moved to the side table, selected a decanter, and poured amber liquid into a glass. After taking a sip, he turned back to her. "During your sketching, you made a discovery."

"An unpleasant one," she admitted. "I found an injured deer, which seemed to be the victim of a new species of ivy—"

Lord Connock stiffened. His eyebrows nearly touched his hairline. "What? Explain this to me, please."

"There isn't much to explain," Michael cut in. "Anne found a deer bleeding in the woods. The deer had tangled itself in ivy. The scene was apparently very peculiar, and Anne thought for a moment that the ivy had somehow strangled the deer."

As Michael finished his explanation, which sounded outrageous even to her ears, Anne realized she'd spoken far too hastily about the ivy. No one would ever believe her unless she gathered a specimen and figured out where the ivy kept disappearing to. She smiled and shrugged. "Mr. McEvoy is correct. The scene was very peculiar. I may have jumped to an erroneous conclusion. In any case, I plan to investigate more thoroughly as time permits."

Lord Connock took a handkerchief out of his pocket and dabbed at moisture which had gathered along his brow.

"The deer wasn't our only unpleasant discovery," she said, her voice stronger. This time she had a specimen. "Today, we found a flower that has much in common with *Antirrhinum majus*. The irregular shape of the flower itself, the location of its anthers, like little teeth . . . its similarity to the snapdragon is nearly complete but for a few odd details." Noting Lord Connock's quick frown, she went on to describe the flower's bulbous roots and the proboscises it had attached to the raspberry and gooseberry canes.

Lord Connock listened to her description with his head bent, in the manner of a man concentrating fully. When she'd finished, he focused on Michael. His face betrayed nothing. "Was this another peculiar 'scene,' or do you have a specimen?"

Anne opened her sketch case and withdrew the flower.

Connock walked to her side and lifted his hand toward her. "Let me see."

She stood and gently dropped the flower into Connock's outstretched palm. "Rather ugly, no?" she murmured.

Connock gazed at it, an abrupt frown creating deep lines near the corners of his mouth. His lips tightened. She'd expected him to show some curiosity, or even disgust . . . but he simply seemed angry.

Without warning the nobleman closed his hand around the flower, making a fist, crushing its fragile petals.

Anne tried to stifle her gasp. It came out like a hiccup.

" 'Tis flawed," Connock said, his voice detached. Paying Anne no attention, he dropped the flower onto the carpet and crushed it beneath one highly polished black boot. It left a moist gray smear on the Aubusson carpet.

Anne stared at Connock. Obviously he knew more about the snapdragon than she and Michael, and judging by his reaction, the snapdragon had displeased him.

Tension gathered in the air. Michael stiffened beside her.

The Irish nobleman walked to the window and stared out at the grounds, his back to them, as if he needed a moment to compose himself.

Anne studied Connock in the same way she'd studied his strange sapling. What had happened to the cool, logical scholar, the botanical visionary? His gesture seemed so childish. She found something quite frightening about a grown man displaying a childish temper while speaking in such a controlled tone.

Abruptly he swung around and faced them. A pained smile curved his lips. "I beg your forgiveness, both of you. I forgot myself."

Michael took a step toward him. "Lord Connock?"

The older man reclaimed his glass and took a healthy swallow of amber liquid. Then he waved at Michael in a shooing gesture. "I'm fine, Michael. Please, give me a moment, and I'll explain." Then he turned to Anne and took her hand. "Mrs. Sherwood, can you forgive me for that unsightly display?"

His grasp, dry the few times in the past he'd taken her hand, now felt clammy. Wishing she could withdraw her hand without appearing to reject his apology, she nodded. Indeed, she eagerly awaited his account. Finally, she would discover the reason behind the red haze of distress most of the plants near Glendale Hall suffered. What wild experiment would he reveal to them?

Lord Connock released her hand at last and gestured toward three chairs clustered near the fireplace. "Please, return to your seat."

Anne fought the urge to wipe her palm on her skirt and sat. Michael and Lord Connock followed suit. Once they'd all settled themselves in, Anne focused on the nobleman, and noticed Michael did the same.

"I suppose you're wondering why I reacted so oddly when I saw that snapdragon. 'Tis rather simple. I had been planning to auction the species of snapdragon you found in the woods. I've already had several lucrative offers for it and, recognizing its rarity and value, kept it locked up in one of my glasshouses." Connock shook his head. "If it is growing in the forest, then the security of my glasshouses has been compromised. Someone stole either the flower itself or some of its seeds and dropped a few of those seeds in the forest as he or she escaped."

Anne watched Connock carefully during his explanation. His gaze never wavered as he spoke and his voice held not the slightest tremble or nuance. After he'd finished she decided he'd been telling the truth. The notion left her deflated. She'd been hoping for some scientific revelations.

At the same time, some of the tension left Michael's posture. He slouched back against the chair. Anne marked how the news of a burglary eased rather than dismayed him. Had Michael, too, been harboring some concerns about Lord Connock and his plants?

"Do you have any idea who the culprit might be?" Michael asked.

"None at all. I trust all of my gardeners implicitly. Few would dare to incur Griswold's wrath," Lord Connock said, referring to the old, grizzled gardener he employed.

"Are you certain a thief took only *Antirrhinum majus* seeds?" Anne asked. "We also encountered another odd flower. A plant very similar to a moonflower, but with some marked differences, is growing just outside one of your locked glasshouses. Michael and I noticed it last night. After dinner."

Lord Connock raised an eyebrow. "Outside my glasshouse, you say?"

"Yes, the one next to your composting glasshouse. It grows right next to the glass, as if it burrowed beneath the wall to emerge outside."

"I don't remember planting that one. I'm not even certain which flower you're talking about. A moonflower, you say?"

"Something much like it," Anne confirmed.

Lord Connock shook his head. "I'll look into it. I'd hate to think that more of my rare flowers have been stolen. They'll be worth half of what I'd originally thought. The money would have gone a long way in keeping the duns satisfied."

"What about the ivy?" she asked.

"I know nothing about any ivy." Rubbing his temples, he fixed on Anne with a bleak gaze. "I need your assistance, Mrs. Sherwood. I need you to document these rare species for me once you have finished with the sapling. Perhaps if we document these flowers, and I register them with the Royal Botanic Society before they are stolen, I might have a chance of prosecuting the thief when they appear for auction. Will you do that for me, Mrs. Sherwood? Michael will assist you."

She looked from Lord Connock to Michael and back again, uncomfortable. She hadn't imagined staying at Glendale Hall for any length of time, and what the nobleman had proposed could take months. Months where she'd be thrust into close quarters with Michael, months where she'd question the lack of emotion in her life and wonder if Michael could ease her loneliness. Months of temptation.

Before she could answer, Lord Connock turned to Michael and put a hand on his shoulder. "I'll need you to cancel that trip you'd planned to India, at least until Mrs. Sherwood has finished documenting my rarer species."

"How would I assist her?" Michael asked.

"I'd like the two of you to check the grounds near my glasshouses to see if any other of my flowers have taken root in the wild. You, Michael, will find them, and Mrs. Sherwood will study and illustrate them. When you've finished, I'll examine both your notes to see if the flowers have mutated."

Michael looked at her, then out the window. A muscle in his jaw flexed. "I've already bought the provisions for that trip to India."

"Finding and documenting the species I already have is more important to me than bringing new ones in," Lord Connock insisted. "Give the provisions that will spoil to the villagers. I'm sure they'll appreciate it."

Anne had heard the resistance in Michael's voice. She supposed she could expect no less, after she'd prodded him so remorselessly about why he wanted a home. She felt some resistance, too. Every day she spent with him made her want him more. And yet, what could they offer each other? He was looking for a special farm in Connaught, while she wanted scholarly recognition, requiring her to move in the appropriate scholarly circles in London.

They didn't suit at all.

Anne frowned.

"Mrs. Sherwood?" Lord Connock prodded. "Will you do it? I assure you, your illustrations will bring you the highest regard in the scientific world—I'll see to it myself."

Her attention drifted toward Michael. Would her passion for him lure her into forgetting her goals and ruining her chances to gain recognition for her work?

At her continued silence, Lord Connock moved to her side and touched her arm. "Don't worry, I *do* wield my share of power with the Royal Botanic Society. You will never again have to experience a dinner party like the one I had a few nights ago. Indeed, I offer you my humble apologies for having to entertain that half-wit Huxley."

" 'Tis no matter. Please, think no more on it." She

waved his apology aside. Again, Lord Connock had offered her an opportunity no one else could match. She would stay and sketch these new species, even at the risk of her heart.

"Yes, Lord Connock," she said, "I'd be happy to document your rare plants for you. I'm grateful for your confidence in me."

Lord Connock beamed at her. "Confidence that is rightly placed. Michael?"

"If you wish it," Michael finally agreed.

"Good. I suggest you begin tomorrow morning."

The next week passed slowly for Michael, slowly because he had to spend hours each day with Anne, his sight filled with visions of her blond hair whipping around her face and the breeze molding her clothes to lush curves. Her laughter when she discovered something new or unexpected delighted his ears, and his fingers burned where he touched her arm to guide her from one place to another. She smelled good, always, clean and soapy. The only sense she hadn't filled was that of taste, and he remembered all too clearly how she'd tasted. Thinking about how she'd tasted kept him up at night.

Now, as he went to collect her for their field trip, he set his jaw, aware that a new day of torture awaited him. He would spend his day being charmed by Anne Sherwood and wishing he had her in his bed, silky underclothes and all. Christ, he'd never had such a fascination for any woman.

Early-morning sunlight washed the lawn with a pink glow. It sparkled on the dew that had gathered on each blade of grass. Michael strode through the grass toward Glendale Hall, its crenellated towers and ramparts an inscrutable gray in that weak light, its windows opaque, revealing nothing of its interior.

Likewise, Anne's gray eyes had become inscrutable. Opaque. He could no longer tell what she thought of him. He'd also noticed that she'd begun to move away when he reached for her hand. Evidently she'd put those damned goals of hers ahead of life and love. Still, who could blame her? They hadn't a prayer of having a future together. She wanted to move in those stuffy scientific circles, while he wanted a place where he could let the earth run through his fingers.

Truth to tell, even he'd felt a little reluctance when Lord Connock had asked him to postpone his trip to India. If he'd learned anything in this world, he'd learned that emotional ties didn't last. Those he'd loved—his mother, his father, his dog—had died. The guardians he'd trusted in the workhouse had betrayed him. He now harbored doubts about Lord Connock, the man he regarded as a surrogate father. Given his dubious luck concerning affairs of the heart, how foolish was he to have tender thoughts toward Anne?

Michael exited the forest near the carriageway and began to walk across the gravel to the front entrance. One of Carlyle's footmen sat on his stool at the top of the steps, his chin pressed against his chest, evidently sleeping. Good. That meant Anne hadn't left the hall for the tree without him, as she had once or twice this week when he'd shown up a few minutes late.

That woman was prompt.

Michael found himself shaking his head. Why couldn't he have become fascinated with one of the several women who'd come to him more than willingly? What made her so different?

Usually he didn't know too much about his women, other than the curves of their bodies. He didn't want to know. They always thought about dresses or the cake they'd put in the oven or the baby they'd like to have. God knew romance disappeared with the first flap of a baby's blanket.

And yet, for some reason, Anne Sherwood eased that loneliness that had become an indelible part of his soul. He had this sense that she truly understood him. His mother had once told him the Celtic legend of the *anam cara*: for every man, only one woman existed with whom he could share his innermost thoughts and intimacies. Maybe their shared gift for nature created the connection between him and Anne, or maybe she was his *anam cara*, his soul friend, the only one in the world who would ever fulfill him.

Michael curled his hands into fists. Unfortunately, Anne preferred to study nature rather than immerse herself in it. A fire burned within her, one he saw in her eyes when she mentioned her illustrations, one that didn't include him. His gut insisted she was the star he'd never touch, but his heart said something entirely different and for the first time in his life Michael felt truly frightened.

"Good morning, Michael." The soft voice invaded his thoughts. He looked up and stared into eyes as rich as gray velvet.

Gladness filled him at the mere sight of her. Furiously he tamped it back down. Jesus, he was acting like a young pup experiencing his first love. "Did you sleep well?" he asked, noticing a slight bluish shadow beneath her eyes.

"Very well." Her gaze flickering away from him, she nodded toward the woods. "Ready?"

"As always." He took her sketch case from her and together they started off into the trees. He slanted a sideways glance toward her. As always, her skin looked like cream with a swirl of pink in it, on her cheeks. Her gown was an old muslin peppered with violets. Dirt had stained the hemline brown.

Oddly enough, he'd come to like her old gowns more than the fancy satin ones he'd seen once or twice. Not only did her cleavage often press against the neckline, washed and sewn many times as it was, but the dirty hem placed her on par with the village girls. Dressed this way, he could almost pretend she was attainable. And sometimes, he even caught a glimpse of lace along the edge of her bodice. Lord help him, he spent far too much time imagining what silken scrap she'd chosen to wear against her skin.

They exchanged small talk as they tramped into the woods, Anne a few paces away. Oak boughs rustled above them and weak sunlight filtered down through the canopy to splash the undergrowth with yellow. Michael breathed in the smell of thick forest loam and scanned the undergrowth for peculiarities.

Over the past five days, they'd explored nearly two square miles of forest. While they hadn't discovered any more ivy or desiccated corpses, they had found three mutated flowers worth studying. With each find, Michael became more uneasy. He didn't like to think Connock responsible, but what other explanation remained? He'd seen enough of this forest and others like it to know these plants existed nowhere else.

If Lord Connock hadn't been trying to pass these specimens off as "natural" species, most likely in an effort to boost their value at auction, he might have persuaded himself to mind his own business. After all, he damned near owed the Irish nobleman his life. Without Lord Connock's patronage, he might still be living in the wild outside Dublin, a hermit, a madman. He might even be dead. And yet, his sense of fairness, honed from years of being treated unfairly, demanded that he take action. He nearly felt physically ill at the idea of betraying Connock.

Anne apparently felt a sense of unease this morning too, judging by her stiff posture and air of distraction.

"Is something wrong?" he finally asked.

"Tell me what you're thinking about the odd occurrences in the forest," she blurted. "We haven't talked about it at all this week, and I'm near to bursting with a need to discuss it."

He sighed. This was just about the last subject he wanted to talk about. Nevertheless, he spoke frankly. Anne deserved no less. "I'm thinking that nature didn't intend these flowers to exist."

"Then where did they come from?

"I don't know. But I plan to find out."

"What about the ivy and the deer?"

"We haven't found any more corpses or run across any ivy this whole week," he pointed out.

"Then we're not looking in the right places. We can't ignore it, Michael."

"I'm not planning on ignoring it, lass. I need to do some more investigating."

"So you think there's some connection between the ivy and the deer?"

"I'm not willing to agree to anything until we've gathered some proof. We'll follow our initial plan and gather a specimen of this ivy . . . if we can find it. In fact, I'd really like to find the mother plant, from which the vines grow. That'll tell us a lot more about it."

"Why don't we look specifically in the areas where we last saw the ivy?" she asked.

"I've already done that," he admitted. "Didn't find a damned thing."

"Well, then, where would we most likely find ivy?"

"As I said, ivy doesn't like old forests. We shouldn't find it anywhere. Even so, let's make an outrageous assumption. We'll imagine Glendale Forest harbors ivy that's cultivated a taste for deer flesh. To find the ivy that prefers venison for dinner, we should look where the deer gather."

A frown gathered on her lips. "And where is that?"

"Near water. We'll work our way down to the Balkilly Falls, then, and see what we can find."

She nodded her acquiescence. Shaking his head at the idea of carnivorous ivy, Michael continued to lead her into the forest. After they'd walked for a few minutes, he cast a glance toward the horizon. Good weather had made their task easy so far, but judging by the darker clouds that had begun to gather in the west, their luck was about to run out.

They came to a fork in the path. He turned left, onto an overgrown animal trail. Anne had already proven to him several times that despite her abundant skirts, she could manage the most debris-cluttered path, sidling around the brambles without catching herself on the thorns.

Early May tulips pushed up through the undergrowth to brighten the forest floor with splashes of pink and yellow. Fir trees, their bottoms free of branches, flanked them on both sides, creating a bower above them. Michael had the notion they were walking through a green tunnel. Pine cones, covered with sap, littered the ground and spiced the air with a clean odor. Not for the first time, he noticed the ground remained oddly free of animal tracks and droppings. Nor had the tender leaves on the bushes been chewed off. He remembered the corpses of the rabbit and the deer. The ivy again? No. Plants couldn't move. It had to be something else, some chance disease creeping through the forest, infecting the animals that came in contact with it.

"Michael, I think I've found something," Anne suddenly announced, her voice tight.

Startled, he realized he'd been so involved in his thoughts that he hadn't noticed her leave the trail. She crouched some ten feet back, her attention directed toward a group of smallish tulips. He retraced his steps and hunkered down at her side, expecting to see ivy or another dead animal. Instead he discovered weird-looking mushrooms.

She parted the tulip stems with her fingers. "Did you ever see anything like this before?"

Opalescent white balls—perfect spheres—snuggled at the base of the tulips. They almost looked like big pearls. Tiny bumps studded their surfaces.

Eyes narrowed, he touched one with his finger. It felt warm. Beneath its surface, dry to the touch, something seemed to move . . .

He pulled his finger back. Frowning, fascinated despite his revulsion, he touched it again. This time he felt it clearly, a crawling sensation. " 'Tis like a mushroom. There's something strange about it, though—"

The white ball suddenly exploded. Tiny spores puffed outward in a cloud of white smoke. Michael smelled something indescribably bad, sulfurous, the way hell was supposed to smell.

Anne began to cough. Michael quickly pulled her backward. The spores settled on the leaves of the adjacent bushes. A wave of dizziness assaulted him. He steadied himself with one hand on the ground.

She fell heavily against him. "By God, that stinks."

"I'd say it more than stinks. We'd better move away from them, before another explodes." He helped her shuffle back toward the path, noting how her eyes were watering. His watered, too. He wiped them with the back of his hand.

"That had to be one of the most unpleasant mushrooms I've ever encountered." She pulled a small linen handkerchief from her pocket and wiped the tears away.

Michael continued to support her with one arm. "I've seen mushrooms that send out spores before. There's one in the Americas that reacts to water, spurting a yellow cloud whenever it rains. But these . . . these give off some sort of toxic mist. Jesus."

"Other than the ivy, we've never encountered anything dangerous," she whispered, her eyes wide.

"Until now." A chill settling into his bones, he knew he had to act. He could tolerate the flowers, because in the end, they weren't hurting anyone. The ivy he wouldn't act upon until he found evidence of its carnivorous nature. But these . . . these threatened the well-being of anyone who found them. He was going to have to confront Lord Connock.

He hoped, for Anne's sake, that Connock had an acceptable explanation. Otherwise, if Anne published her illustrations as those of new species, and the critics discovered they weren't new species at all but manmade creations, she'd be ruined forever in the scholarly circles she so fervently courted.

"I'm returning you to Glendale Hall," he said, his throat tight with dismay. "I want you to go directly to your bedchamber. I'll speak to Lord Connock. By the end of the day we'll know the truth behind his experimentation."

12

%

*T*hey spoke little on their return to Glendale Hall. Roiling gray clouds had gathered above them and darkened the forest. The odd, storm-induced twilight reminded Michael of an eclipse of the sun. He could feel the forces gathering around them, in the cold wind that stirred the trees and the faint vibrations in the ground, signaling far-off thunder.

They emerged from a stand of pines and hurried across the lawn, Anne's hand in his for the first time in days. He gripped her palm tightly as they fled the approaching storm, thinking that an even worse storm was about to break inside Glendale Hall. Their pace slowed as they reached the stone steps leading to the front entrance. The footman, noting their approach, opened the door for them. Anne preceded Michael into the hall and stopped once inside.

When he paused next to her, Anne placed a slender hand on his arm. "I'd like to go with you. I want to hear Lord Connock's explanation."

"No, Anne. Go to your bedchamber. I don't want you confronting Lord Connock."

Her brows drew together. "Why? Are you afraid of him?"

"No, of course not. But I'm very likely going to put his nose out of joint. I don't want him angry at you, too."

"You shouldn't have to bear the brunt—"

"Enough, lass," he cut in, steering her toward the stairs. "Go to your bedchamber as I've asked, and wait for me to send for you."

When he saw her trail off toward the stairs, pausing for frequent backward glances, he said a little prayer of thanksgiving that she'd obeyed him this once. He waited long enough to watch her disappear up the stairs before turning and striding toward the library.

A quick glance into the book-filled room convinced him Lord Connock was spending his day elsewhere. Michael fervently hoped the nobleman hadn't decided on a journey to Dublin this morning. He wanted . . . no, he *needed* to confront Lord Connock now and put it behind them. He left the library and made for the kitchen, where he found Carlyle standing primly at Cook's side. Both were examining a piece of paper. A *menu*, Michael realized, *for this evening's dinner.*

Carlyle's frown pulled his face downward, giving him the look of a basset hound, while Cook's cheeks were bright red and her eyebrows drawn low over furious eyes. They were so far into their argument, Michael realized, that they'd stopped talking to each other. Normally the observation would have amused him. At the moment, he simply wanted to find Lord Connock.

"Carlyle, have you seen Lord Connock?"

His nose in the air, Carlyle swiveled to examine him. "No, Mr. McEvoy, I haven't."

"He's in his glasshouse with that gnome Griswold," Cook barked. "You'll find him there, although they probably won't let you in. They don't let *me* in, not unless I'm bringing them a plate of animal entrails."

Diverted, Michael lifted an eyebrow. "Animal entrails?"

"Uncooked," she confirmed. "And fresh from the slaughtered beast. If more than ten minutes pass between the time the beast dies and the time I deliver the entrails, Lord Connock won't use 'em."

Michael grimaced. "Which glasshouse are they in now?"

"The big one."

He thanked both of them and left them to their argument. The big one, he thought, must be the glasshouse nearest the composting glasshouse, the same one Lord Connock had brought his dinner guests into the previous week. Silently he wondered about Connock's curious need for fresh animal entrails. Surely it wouldn't matter how fresh they were if he simply planned to throw them on a composting pile.

He left Glendale Hall through the servants' door and started out across the lawn. The clouds had become darker and pressed more heavily against the earth. Thunder had become audible and echoed among the mountains to the south. Rain was only a few moments away.

To the left of him, Glendale Hall sprawled toward the river, which flowed high against its banks. A movement on the castle's second floor caught his attention. He looked upward, scanning the windows that looked out over the glasshouses. He saw it again, a flash of white.

A woman. Anne.

She moved out of sight, but not quickly enough. He'd already seen her. *Please, God*, he thought, *let her stay in her bedchamber.*

Three minutes later he had reached the glasshouse in question. He paused, nostrils flared. The cloying, honeyed scent he'd noticed several days ago in the forest curled around his body before vanishing on a violent gust of wind. Seconds later, another breeze brought to him the smell of decaying vegetable matter. He glanced at the composting glasshouse, about fifty feet away. Hordes of flies clung to its windows.

Male voices, muffled behind glass, diverted him. He identified Lord Connock's smooth, cultured tones inside the glasshouse he stood near, mingling with Griswold's rasp. He put a hand on the glass, noting how warm it felt. As always, the frosted glass prevented him from making sense of anything on the inside. He walked to the glasshouse's wooden door and tried the knob.

Locked.

Michael rapped on the wood.

"Go away," Griswold threatened. "We aren't wanting tea yet."

" 'Tis Michael, not Cook," Michael said.

"Michael?" Lord Connock asked. Before Michael could reply, the glasshouse door opened just enough for the nobleman to peer outward, while blocking Michael's view of the interior with his body. "Why are you here? Can't it wait?"

"We found a mushroom in the woods," Michael said. "It sprayed us with some sort of cloud—"

"You'll be fine," Lord Connock assured him, impatience written in every line of his body. "Have Mrs.

Sherwood sketch it, and bring the sketch to me later, in the library." He began to close the door.

Michael stuck his boot into the opening.

Lord Connock's eyes widened. He allowed the door to swing back open a few inches. "What's the matter, Michael?" His voice had gained an edge to it, reminding Michael of a tinker guarding a pot of gold.

"I'm sorry, Lord Connock. You know how much I admire and respect you. By God, you've treated me like a son and I've appreciated every gesture. But I can't ignore these mutations anymore." He took a deep breath and somehow found the strength to say what had to be said. "Mrs. Sherwood and I have discovered the truth. I insist you confess the origins of that sapling you have Mrs. Sherwood sketching."

His chest felt tight when he'd finished, and his stomach felt a little sick at the sight of Lord Connock's grimace, quickly hidden behind a calm but very pale countenance.

"Come inside." Lord Connock allowed the door to swing open all the way.

His gut fluttered the way it had a couple of times in the jungle, when one of the big cats or snakes lurked nearby but hadn't been spotted yet. Logic told him that the reaction was completely out of proportion. He wasn't walking in the jungle, he was entering a glasshouse, for Christ's sake. Setting his jaw, he stepped inside.

They stopped in some sort of antechamber about twenty feet square. Another door, this one made of frosted glass, led into the glasshouse proper. The interior door was closed and the glass separating the antechamber from the rest of the building was also frosted, so Michael still couldn't see what sort of plants Lord Connock had grown.

"How do you like my laboratory, Michael?" Lord Connock asked solemnly. "It's supposed to be a shed, for storing the glasshouse's tools and supplies, but it makes a comfortable laboratory too."

Michael scanned the rows of shelves filled with jars of strange-looking objects, some of them similar to pickled roots in appearance. A large marble worktable with iron legs dominated one side of the room. Peculiar instruments were lined up in a neat row along the back of the table, coiled copper tubing connecting one to the next. Apothecary pots filled with God knew what covered one wall from floor to ceiling, and a selection of surgeon's instruments gleamed on a wheeled cart.

He focused in on the plant spread out in the middle of the table. A faint sense of disgust slithered through him. It looked as though Lord Connock had been dissecting the plant. Thick yellow sap oozed from its stem. The plant's roots were attached to metal pincers that in turn connected to an instrument whose purpose he couldn't even guess at. He didn't recognize the leaves themselves or the berries the plant produced.

Griswold was scowling at him from another corner of the room, where a great vat squatted above hot coals. A reddish-brown syrup bubbled indolently in the vat. Flecks of that same reddish-brown peppered the gardener's dirty white beard. The vat gave off the smell of ether which almost, but not quite, covered a musky scent reminding him of . . . blood.

" 'Tis grand, make no mistake," Michael finally said. "I'm sure it serves your purposes."

Outside, thunder growled, much closer than before. A few drops of rain pelted the glass roof.

"It does indeed," Connock agreed. "Apparently I'm going to have to tell you exactly what my purposes are."

"We found mushrooms in the forest," Michael reminded him. "They gave off some sort of dangerous mist. I can't ignore your strange hybrids anymore, not with Anne's and my own safety in question."

A faint smile touched Connock's lips. "Do you think I'm acting criminally, Michael? Are you worrying I'll release another *pestilence?*"

"I don't know. That's what I came here to find out. We have other things to talk about, too. Things like fraud."

Lord Connock raised one eyebrow. "Fraud?"

"The sapling in the woods is not natural." Michael took a deep breath and plunged ahead. "There is no sense of harmony between its delicate limbs and the rough, leathery leaves that terminate them. The sharp thorns on its branches ward off man and beast, and yet it bears no real fruit worth protecting, just a substance insects favor. In short, the tree looks pieced together."

Lord Connock's other eyebrow lifted until they both formed a line of surprise high across his forehead.

"Your sapling doesn't seem to me like a new species at all," Michael continued, his tone blunt. "Rather, it seems a manmade invention. Are you pretending the tree—and all the other mutations on the estate—have natural origins to raise their value and bring in funding for new research? After all, a new species is worth more than a manmade one, just as a natural pearl is prized above its cultured cousin."

A beat of stillness passed between them. Without warning, Lord Connock began to chuckle. The chuckle expanded into a hearty laugh. Moments later Griswold had joined in, his laughter sounding more like a bark than anything else.

Michael frowned.

"Oh, Michael." His eyes twinkling, Connock patted Michael on the back. "You are priceless. When you said you and Mrs. Sherwood had discovered the truth—"

A tinkling smash, that of glass breaking into a hundred pieces, silenced him. Michael and the other two men spun around and stared at the doorway.

Anne stood amid the broken glass, her eyes two gray pools in a face without a trace of color. Simultaneously, the storm broke with a deafening crash of thunder, and rain poured down from the skies as if seeking to drown them all.

Her heart pounding madly in her chest, Anne regarded Griswold, Lord Connock, and Michael. The three of them stared back, frozen. They appeared shocked at her presence. No one, however, could have been more shocked than she. She hadn't meant for them to discover her, she'd just wanted to listen to Lord Connock's explanation.

But when she'd felt something tickle her ankle, she'd jerked her leg aside only to find the stray ends of a rope had teased her skin. By then it was too late. The glass jar, set precariously on the shelf, had already begun tumbling to the floor. It broke with an explosive sound so loud they'd probably heard it in the village.

Scowling, Griswold took a step toward her. Michael and Lord Connock simultaneously put a hand on his arm. "No, Griswold," the nobleman said.

The old man harrumphed and retreated a pace. Lord Connock moved to her side, an easy smile on his lips. He appeared in complete command of the situation. "Mrs. Sherwood, I see you've decided to join us."

Outside, thunder rolled across the land, making the glass walls around them vibrate.

"I'm sorry about the jar," she managed. "I didn't mean—"

"Think no more on it. We have plenty of jars." He took her arm. "I assume you've come here to discover what you can about the sapling."

Guilt sliced through her. She'd come here to witness Michael accuse him. She slanted a quick glance at Michael and saw his bewilderment in the way he stood, his hands in his pockets, his eyes slightly widened, his eyebrows drawn low. Whatever schemes Connock had embarked on, he had obviously not informed Michael about them.

Her own face no doubt reflected puzzlement too. She examined the little room they stood in, wondering what possible use Lord Connock had for all that equipment. The gauges and coiled copper tubing and little bubbling glass vials reminded her of a brew house. And those apothecary jars . . . what did they contain? Why, the apothecary shop she'd visited in London hadn't half of Connock's selection. Nose wrinkled, she looked at the vat of red fluid that Griswold tended. It smelled positively revolting. What was he cooking up?

Lord Connock took her arm and drew her over to Michael. "So, you'd both like to understand the origins of the sapling. I would have preferred to avoid telling you, for fear of biasing your study of the sapling, but I see I must. You are both quite correct when you say the tree hasn't natural origins. I did, indeed, create it."

She stifled a gasp. His claim defied understanding. How could he have created a tree?

The nobleman patted her arm, as if sensing her confusion. "At the Royal College of Surgeons in Dublin, I learned the latest techniques for repairing facial injuries and deformities. The war for independence from the

British, even though undeclared, supplied us with a limitless number of patients who'd lost a nose, a finger, an ear; I sewed them back on and made certain they didn't become gangrenous.

"After the famine, I studied every aspect of chemistry and botany until my proficiency astounded my masters and eventually surpassed theirs. I began to experiment with cross-pollination methods, in an effort to prevent future starvation. Eventually I hit upon the idea of combining both grafting and pollination techniques. The sapling in the woods is one of my greatest successes."

"You took specimens from several different trees," Michael said, a muscle in his jaw flexing, "and combined them to create the sapling."

"The method is a bit more complicated than that, but in essence, yes, I created it."

"And the forest is there for you to use in whatever way you see fit," Michael prodded.

"I am a religious man." Lord Connock released Anne's arm and stood between Anne and Michael. "If God hadn't intended for mankind to experiment, he wouldn't have given us curiosity and intelligence."

"And what of the results of your experiments? This sapling, for example. Is it left to grow in pain?"

"Plants don't feel pain," Connock chided.

Michael nodded. "I think I understand. All great scientists must learn to deny their compassion if they wish to pursue the greater scientific good."

"But plants *do* feel pain," Anne broke in. She clenched her hands, then buried them in her skirts.

"How do you know?" Connock nodded encouragingly. "You can tell me, Anne."

Griswold's face perked up. For the first time he

showed some curiosity about the conversation. Michael's countenance, on the other hand, remained shuttered. Even so, Anne felt a mounting desire to confess all about her gift, to tell them that from the moment she'd learned to walk, she'd seen colors around plants, and that colors were the way plants talked.

In the end, though, she simply hadn't the nerve, not around men who required proof of any theory. "I have no evidence. I just have a feeling."

The nobleman shook his head. He seemed overly disappointed in her answer. "Unlike animals, plants haven't nerves running through the leaves and stems. They do not react to painful stimuli. I'm afraid your supposition is a fanciful one, Mrs. Sherwood."

"And yet a plant's roots will automatically gravitate toward water. If a plant cannot react to stimuli, such as moisture, why do the roots reach out for water?"

"A point well made," Connock said. "Nevertheless, I still do not believe they react to *painful* stimuli. For years I've tried to prove otherwise and have had not the slightest success. So if you're worrying about me torturing the plants, Michael, your fears are unfounded."

Anne thought Michael's fears very well founded, but couldn't prove it. How could she quantify the red haze of distress that filled her mind every time she touched one of Connock's plants?

Michael shook his head, evidently unconvinced. "Why are you so determined to keep your successes quiet?"

"You should know the answer to your question." Lord Connock's gaze became piercing. "Do you remember 'Connock's Pestilence'? Do you recall how they drummed me out of Dublin? When the details of my experiments became known, almost every one of my friends and associates deserted me. Only Darwin and his cronies remained by my side, because they too had suffered ostracism. The public wasn't ready to understand my goals and still isn't. I won't fall out of favor again. I need the meager funding I've been able to secure."

The nobleman turned to Anne. "As Sir Richard's niece, you should well understand my other reason. How many valuable species have been stolen from Kew Gardens? How much money have Sir Richard and the Kew Gardens trust lost? You must know what would happen if someone stole my methods and took credit for my work. I would end up bankrupt and unable to pursue any further experimentation."

Anne loosened her fists and nodded, albeit unwillingly. She knew very well what happened when someone else took credit for a person's work. Not only did it lead to physical penury, but a penury of the soul as well. After all, she'd experienced it firsthand with Henry. She recalled the years of recriminations, the years of feeling like a dupe for allowing Henry to use her so, and knew a spurt of sympathy for the nobleman. Still, he *was* committing fraud by trying to pass off his creations as new species.

She touched Lord Connock's arm. "Lord Connock, I'm sorry we had to come to you with these accusations. Michael and I simply didn't understand. Nevertheless, you are misleading the public about your plants and that bothers me."

The nobleman spread his hands in a placating gesture. "Remember, Mrs. Sherwood, that several new varieties of roses are bred and sold every year. It isn't a crime to crossbreed plants."

"But it *is* a crime to pretend they're natural species."

"I beg your forgiveness, both of you, for misleading you for so long. I didn't know if I could trust you, Mrs. Sherwood; and Michael, I . . . feared your disapproval. Rightly so in the second case, I'm afraid."

Arms crossed over his chest, Michael lifted one dark brow.

"However, if you understood the nature and importance of my work, you might be willing to overlook such transgressions in the interest of science."

"I doubt it," Michael muttered.

"Perhaps there is a way I can change your mind. Come into my glasshouse with me, and I'll show you what I've accomplished." Lord Connock reclaimed Anne's arm. "Griswold, open the door."

His face still creased with a scowl, the crusty old gardener balanced his wooden stick on the edge of the vat and shuffled forward with a key. He fit the key into a lock on the inner door and swung it open wide.

Eyes alight, his sorrow of a moment before vanished, Connock guided her through the door. "Behold my Eden."

13

Anne gasped aloud. She pulled from Connock's grasp and walked a few paces down the gravel path. Red light spilled down from the tinted glass roof to color a jungle of plants with crimson. Her eyes took a few moments to adjust to the weird gloom.

Most glasshouses she'd worked in had been flooded with light. This one was murky. The frosted walls filtered the sunlight and washed everything with a lambent glow, leaving shadows between the plants that sprawled with lush abandon.

A feeling of wonderment built inside her as her gaze flitted from plant to plant. Some of them she recognized, and some of them she didn't, but they were all so green, so large, so fertile that she could scarcely credit what she saw. Apple trees whose branches had bent with the weight of too much fruit, vines overflowing with firm, green cucumbers, lilies sporting white flowers that had grown impossibly large; they overwhelmed her with their perfection.

In the background, she heard the sound of water flowing over rocks, like a waterfall. A low hum that reminded her of a beehive drifted from a far corner of the glasshouse. She spun around in a circle, trying to take it all in.

Michael drew up to her side and paused. He, too, scanned the room with wide eyes.

"I cannot believe it," she whispered.

He nodded. "Eden it is."

"Go, explore," Lord Connock urged. "I want you to understand what's at stake."

Her lips parted, Anne trailed down a side path that led through a group of palm trees. Plants hung from pots attached to metal girders in the ceiling. Their fronds brushed against her face and they released a pungent floral fragrance as she passed. She breathed them in and paused by a wire fence.

A vine with light green, fan-shaped leaves and heavy pink flowers clung to the fence. Moisture was dripping from the center of the flowers. Anne touched the dewdrop and rubbed it between her fingers. It had the consistency of aloe, and a bit of a tingle besides. Her hand trembling, she touched the fan-shaped leaves and watched the colors form in her mind.

Red, marbled with black.

The plant was distressed. Black made her think it teetered on the edge of madness. Only the very worst of the city plants she'd encountered in London had looked this way, those that grew in a sewage ditch or along the edge of the Thames, near the factories.

Uneasiness crept through her, leaving her chilled despite the humidity. She moved past the vines, to a bed of vegetables. Asparagus stalks stretched at least eight feet toward the ceiling, love apples crowded thick, pulpy stems, and carrot fronds reached waist-high, promising abnormally large carrots. Silk bags covered corn-stalk tassels that towered over her.

Lord Connock nodded toward the corn. "We've fertilized the corn with special pollen and bagged the tassels to prevent foreign pollen from interfering with our experiment. We've also snipped the corn's anthers to remove even the slightest threat of self-pollination. This is just one of the ongoing experiments Griswold and I are conducting."

"What changes to the corn are you hoping for?"

"We want to produce plants that are inhospitable to the corn borer. So far, we've had a fair bit of success."

She lifted an eyebrow. "How so?"

"We've managed to breed some of the properties of the *Chrysanthemum coccineum*, or the pyrethrum daisy, into the corn. As you know, corn borers and many other insects become paralyzed when exposed to a concentration of pyrethrins, and eventually starve or are eaten by birds and other predators."

His back hunched, Connock assumed measured tones. "Usually, different species of plants cannot be interbred. Their ecological isolation, flowering times, physical fertilization incompatibilities, and weak or sterile offspring create a barrier that is overcome with only the most unusual methods. We've found, however, that some parent populations are more cross-compatible than others. Indeed, special emasculation and pollination techniques allow a transfer of properties that nature wouldn't normally approve of, while the application of growth regulators promotes pollen tube growth—"

"Emasculation techniques?"

"Yes, we remove the anthers before pollen is shed.

Emasculation can be tedious work! We snip the anthers with scissors, forceps, needle, pencil, stick, scalpel, whatever is appropriate for that plant. In certain cases, we immerse the flower's reproductive organs in alcohol or hot water, or grow the plant at a high temperature to induce male sterility, or at high humidity to prevent anther dehiscence . . ."

Lord Connock droned on, his description becoming so steeped in scientific terminology that she could no longer follow along. Instead, she gazed about her with wide eyes, and when he'd finished, she smiled. "Fascinating."

The older man preened. "The harvests of all these plants have doubled, as has the size of each vegetable. Many of our plants are resistant to drought and blight, and can even withstand several frosts. Think of it, Mrs. Sherwood. Think of all Ireland covered with these plants. No one would ever go hungry again."

Sighing, she imagined every Irish table laden with a bountiful harvest. Lord Connock, she thought, was a genius. He had done great good for the people of Ireland. "I'm truly impressed. Tell me, though, why you've tinted the glass on the roof red."

"Griswold and I have observed the effects of various colors of the light spectrum on plants. Red light has the effect of boosting upward growth, enhancing individual plant survival. I've also noticed that plants fill up gaps better and prevent the thinning of vegetation when exposed to red light. I believe"—he paused and narrowed his eyes for emphasis—"that plants use red light to determine the location of their neighbors even before they begin to encroach on the actual available light."

"Do they not suffer from a lack of other colors of light?"

"We change the roof panels regularly to ensure an even distribution of color." The nobleman picked a green pod from a nest of vines and cracked it open. Twenty perfect, pearl-sized peas tumbled into his palm. "Try one," he urged, and dropped a pea into her hand.

She stared at the pea for a second before lifting it to her lips. With Connock's smile encouraging her onward, she placed it on her tongue and chewed. It tasted delicious, crisp, exactly as a pea should taste, but somehow better.

"Wonderful," she said, its sweetness chasing her uneasiness away. She began to wonder how much the red haze of distress coming from the plants really mattered. Despite the mother plant's aura, the pea had a perfectly delightful flavor. A wild hope began to grow within her. Lord Connock's experiments, she thought, really *could* lead to the eradication of starvation.

"We've sweetened our peas by slowing the conversion of sugar to starch," Lord Connock informed her. "You can see that our cross-breeding techniques haven't had any detrimental effect on the final product. High-starch potatoes, high-oil flax, all are possible, even probable, given enough funding and the right type of experimentation."

She turned toward the sound of flowing water.

"Let me show you my water garden," he said, and led her over to a large, square pool in the middle of the glasshouse. As they walked, she looked for Michael. Was he as shocked, awed, and absolutely delighted with Lord Connock's experiments as she? Did he see the potential?

Indeed, where *was* he?

They stopped in front of the pool. Parsley, celery, lettuce, and other types of leafy green vegetables floated upon its surface, their roots suspended in a metal cage that hung beneath the water. A porcelain pipe thrust up from the ground at one end of the pool and spilled water over an artfully arranged pile of rocks, creating a waterfall. Another pipe at the opposite end allowed a small stream to flow from the pool, keeping the water fresh.

Lips parted, Anne stared at the plants. She'd never heard of celery or any other vegetable growing in water.

"As you know, these plants normally root in soil," Lord Connock said, evidently reading her surprise. "We've substituted water containing special nutrients for earth. I believe we've finally discovered the perfect combination of nutrients to support vegetables that usually prefer land to water. Think of the use we could put our loughs to, if I perfect my water-growing techniques."

"Nothing goes to waste," Anne said.

The nobleman's eyes gleamed with enthusiasm. "Nothing at all."

She took a deep breath and allowed her gaze to drift from one end of the glasshouse to the other. "I scarce know what to say. I can't find the right words . . ."

As she trailed off, she began to think that his sin of deceiving the botanical community was a small one, perhaps even an acceptable one, when compared to the benefits his research could bring to mankind.

"Do you understand my position now, Mrs. Sherwood?" Connock asked.

She turned to face him, her hands lightly clenched. "I believe I do. Still, is there no other way to gain funds for research?"

He shook his head. "I have a black mark next to my name. 'Connock's Pestilence' haunts me still. For many years I pleaded with and begged anyone who had funded other scientists' botanical research to support mine. Other than Charles Darwin and his associates, who contributed what they could, I've received very little funding, certainly not enough to support my endeavors. And so I've sold a few little plants that I've created for great sums and continue with my research." He paused to examine her with a solemn frown. "Are you going to reveal my deception, Mrs. Sherwood?"

She hesitated. Several images passed in quick succession through her mind. That of a starving boy, held in a room beneath a broomstick for stealing an apple; of a wife grown thin with starvation until death claimed her; and then of the impossibly large vegetables that would prevent a famine from ever occurring in Ireland again. Wasn't that worth keeping quiet about a little deception?

She simply wasn't certain. The notion that she was compromising her principles for the sake of scientific achievement nagged at her. How worthwhile could such an achievement be, if it came at the cost of her self-respect?

Still, the benefits to humanity . . .

The ends, in such a case, must surely justify the means.

"I'll keep your secret," she reluctantly admitted. "But I won't allow my sketches to be used in any manner relating to a fraudulent auction."

Lord Connock visibly brightened, his ruddy face lifting as he smiled. "Thank you, Mrs. Sherwood. Will you stay on? I still wish you to sketch for me. When I'm ready to inform the world of my achievements, 'tis your sketches that will chronicle my work and support my claims. I promise to use them in no other way."

Slowly she nodded. Connock had offered her an opportunity that surpassed even that of publishing with Charles Darwin. She would assist in what might possibly be the most influential scientific discoveries of the nineteenth century. And all she had to do was keep quiet about a harmless little lie. "I'll stay."

His smile became a full-fledged grin. "May I call you Anne?"

A return smile curved her lips. "Yes, of course."

"You must call me Owain, then."

"As you wish."

They exchanged glances, Lord Connock clearly delighted. Anne couldn't dredge up quite the same enthusiasm.

"I'm so pleased you've decided to support me, Anne," Lord Connock said. "Now, let's find Michael and see if we can persuade him to do the same."

He steered Anne away from the pool, and they began to stroll through the glasshouse, pausing by various beds to examine and speak about the plants they contained. Anne noticed a patch of moonflowers and recognized the species as identical to the flower that had grown beneath the wall and found freedom.

Bravo, little plant, she thought, and moved on.

In particular she appreciated the small collection of orchids Connock maintained in the corner of one room. He admitted to having failed in his efforts to improve the flower and pointed out the small humidors that emitted a warm mist to coat the orchids with dew. After their dinner discussion a few weeks before, he'd installed the humidors and observed an immediate improvement in the orchids' appearance.

Thinking that there was so much she could learn here, so much she could pass on to the gardeners at Kew

Gardens, she espied Michael's dark head about ten feet across from them. A thick patch of bamboo and a screen of vines hid his body completely from sight.

"There's Michael," she said to Lord Connock, and started off. Rather than remain at her side, the nobleman lagged behind.

Anne brushed past a group of plants with palm-shaped leaves that slapped at her, as though chastising her for leaving Connock's side. A red haze formed in her mind, one she quickly dismissed. As she drew closer to Michael, she noticed that the low hum pervading the glasshouse had become an insistent buzz. Slipping between two potted palms, she rounded the bamboo patch and stopped short.

The vines and bamboo acted like walls, creating a small clearing filled with cages, glass tanks, and a large worktable. One glass tank contained a selection of snakes; another, snails. White mice filled the cages, their eyes very black in the dim light. The cages and tanks seemed in immaculate condition. In the corner, a large hive encased in glass crawled with bees. A hole in the glasshouse wall allowed the bees access to the outside.

She switched her attention to the worktable, the one Michael was examining in a fixed manner. When she saw what it contained, she recoiled.

Upon its surface, a black snake more than two feet long lay stretched out. Leather straps kept its body from moving. The snake's head was fixed in a leather bridle of sorts, and its fangs were pressed into a rubbery-looking sheath. Milky fluid dripped from its fangs and collected in a little glass tube. As she watched, revolted, the snake's fangs stopped dripping.

Venom, she thought. *Connock is using venom in his experiments.*

Griswold abruptly stepped from a shadowed niche of plants. Anne let out a little yelp. Grinning at her, the old gardener held the snake's head in one hand and removed its fangs from the rubber sheath. The snake stiffened and began to coil, clearly expressing its outrage. With his free hand Griswold loosened the bridle and leather straps. Once he'd released the snake, he put it back into a glass tank, with several more of a similar variety.

"That's a black adder," Michael said, turning to Anne and Lord Connock, who had stopped behind them. He still looked unsettled, his brows drawn together at a slight angle, his eyes dark, his jaw set, and his lips tight.

Connock lifted his eyebrows.

"Isn't that a copperhead?" Michael asked, pointing to a large snake with a diamond-shaped head, kept in a different glass tank. Reddish-brown crossbands decorated its light brown body.

"Indeed. I use their venom in various experiments."

"For what purpose?"

"Venom has the same properties as pyrethrins, only it works more quickly and produces a stronger effect. As you know, pyrethrins paralyze insects. We've had some success introducing a low level of pyrethrins into certain plants and are now trying to repeat our success with certain types of venom."

Michael leaned close to Anne. "Have you heard the story of Saint Patrick and the snakes?"

Anne could almost feel the tension radiating off him. "In general, yes."

" 'Tis said he came to Ireland in the year three hundred, stood upon a hill, and used a wooden staff to drive the serpents into the sea, banishing them forever from

Ireland's green hills." Frowning, Michael stared at the glass tank containing the snakes. "One old serpent resisted, but Saint Paddy produced a box and invited the snake to enter. The snake said the box was too small and refused, and they argued back and forth until the snake entered the box to prove he was right. Saint Paddy promptly slammed the box shut and threw it into the sea. To this day, snakes do not live naturally on this island."

Connock shrugged and looked at Anne. "A splendid tale, is it not?"

"Ireland is full of splendid tales," she agreed.

The nobleman turned his attention to Michael. "Are you afraid I'll release my copperheads and adders and finally create the pestilence I've been accused of? Am I Satan, releasing the serpent into the Garden of Eden?"

Michael looked away. He seemed to ponder for a moment. When he finally refocused on Lord Connock, the furrow in his brow still hadn't cleared. "I've found many odd plants in the forest, and they aren't beneficial to mankind. Why have you planted them in the wild?"

"You must understand, Michael, that I need to understand what effects the Irish environment will have on both my vegetables and the other plants I use for cross-breeding purposes. 'Tis also interesting to see natural selection at work." Lord Connock paused and rubbed his chin. "By the way, those 'toxic' mushrooms you found don't contain toxins but rather an irritant. You and Anne are quite safe, I assure you. The mushrooms are important because of their quick-release mechanism, which mimics movement."

"And the mice in those cages? What are they for?"

"Griswold feeds them to the snakes."

Michael looked away, his gaze unfocused. When he returned his attention to Connock, he nodded, albeit unwillingly. "My own parents died of starvation. I'll never forget their last days. For that reason, I can't fail to appreciate the nature of your work or your successes. You have my congratulations."

Connock nodded like a king accepting his due. "Thank you, Michael. You cannot know how much your blessing means to me. Will you also stay on and assist me in my research?"

Michael shot a quick glance toward Anne. "I'll help Mrs. Sherwood document your plants, but when she's done, I'll return to traveling. I'm not meant for closed walls and secrets. I prefer to live out in the open. Still, I won't interfere with your . . . deception."

The older man put a hand on Michael's shoulder. "I can ask no more from you, Michael. Today you've acted like a true son, and I thank you." He slipped his arm through Anne's and steered them both toward the glasshouse door. "Let's return to the library and celebrate our pact with a glass of brandy."

Michael made his way through the forest and back to his cottage, haunted by rustling sounds in brush as he did so. God knew he had a few brandies in him—he'd drunk them down to steady himself—but not enough to make him hear things that weren't there. Things like snakes. Or ivy that had a habit of winding around a person's foot. So what was making that rustling noise that seemed to follow him down the path and stop every time he paused to listen more closely?

His brain quickly cooked up a logical explanation. The rain, which had come down furiously before stopping a short while ago, had probably flooded mice holes and sent the creatures scurrying. Even so, the explanation just didn't feel right.

Rustle-rustle.

There it was again, behind him. Michael spun around on his heel and stared hard at the underbrush. He thought he saw something moving. Green, flat, it looked like . . . ivy. Yes. Yes. Ivy indeed. He could see the little points on the leaves. They *did* look leathery, as Anne had said. He crept closer, his gaze locked on the vine. It didn't move at all as he watched it.

Of course it didn't, the logical part of him chided. What did he expect it to do, a jig?

Nonetheless he moved slowly, as if he might startle it and send it scurrying, aware the brandies had left him slightly befuddled. His reactions weren't nearly quick enough. It could easily get away if it wanted to. But it didn't seem to want to. It was . . . waiting for him.

Michael brought his arm up an inch at a time and hooked his fingers, so he could scoop the ivy up and hold on. He moved a couple of steps closer. The ivy lay innocently along the ground, its leaves motionless. He was within five feet of it now, then four, then three. Finally he moved into position to make a solid catch, and coiled the muscles in his arms tight. Absurdly he thought of his days in the wild. He used to catch fish this way. His logical side reminded him he wasn't catching fish, but a plain old piece of ivy.

"Idiot," he whispered softly.

The ivy rustled right before his eyes.

Mice, he thought, and brought his hand down in a lightning-quick motion. His fingers curled around the ivy. Triumph shot through him. He had it! He took a moment to examine its features, noticing the odd qualities that Anne had already mentioned: sticky, leathery leaves, serrated edges. Then he began coiling it in his hands, bringing up the slack and following along the vine as he might follow a rope. The mother plant couldn't be far away.

He hadn't gone more than two feet, however, when the vine began running through his fingers, as if someone were pulling it from the other end. His grip tightened. The vine kept running through his hand. Leaves and sap stained his fingers. His palm began to smart. He realized the damned thing was giving him a rope burn. Eyes wide with disbelief, he let it go, and stared into the bushes, looking in the general direction of the disappearing vine. Leaves stirred in its wake. Suddenly the end of it disappeared into a hole.

Open-mouthed, Michael raced over to the hole, stumbling over an exposed root as he did so. Dirt collapsed around the hole's entrance. Further away, the earth thrust upward in a tiny channel similar to a mole's. The mole tunnel led away from him. The ivy, he thought, was escaping beneath the ground.

Michael shook his head. He simply couldn't believe his eyes. Nevertheless he chased after the tunnel, crushing it as he ran. If he didn't catch the ivy, no one would ever believe him. Even *he* wouldn't believe him.

Jesus. Ivy that dug holes and retracted like a damned coil. What would he find next?

The tunnel led him into an older part of the forest, where the tree roots were black with age and skeletal. One tree had fallen over, its roots thrusting at the sky rather than the earth, evidence of some cataclysmic upheaval. He raced around the tree and nearly ran into a gaunt human form.

"McEvoy!" the gruff voice chided.

Michael stopped abruptly. "Griswold. What are you doing out here?"

"I'm seeing to Connock's ongoing experiments." The old man thrust his bearded chin forward. "What about you?"

"I saw a vine."

"A vine? What kind of vine?"

"One that—" Michael broke off abruptly, about to say *moved.* He didn't want to sound crazy, not without evidence. He scanned the underbrush behind Griswold's shoulder. The leaves were so thick here he couldn't see the tunnel anymore.

"One that what?"

"One that had some rather odd features."

"You mean like this?" Griswold dug into a little pack around his shoulder and pulled out a piece of coiled vine.

Michael tensed. "That's it exactly."

"I've been out here collecting it for Lord Connock," the old man revealed. "Pulling it off the dirt, coiling it up . . ."

Eyes narrowed, Michael studied the older man. Although Griswold had neatly explained the ivy's odd movement, the explanation sounded rehearsed. "How long ago?"

"Just a few minutes ago."

"Would you mind if I took a piece of it?"

"Lord Connock told me exactly how much to get." Griswold's gaze shifted away from Michael's. "I haven't any to spare. You'll have to find some on your own."

His impression that the old man was lying strengthened. "Thanks anyway."

Griswold shrugged and went about his business.

His gut still throbbing with a premonition of danger,

Michael headed back to his cottage. He just couldn't dismiss the notion that Griswold had been lying. Covering up.

He emerged from the woods to pause in his gardens, listening. Nothing moved. Nothing made the slightest noise. The hairs on his arms standing on end, he studied the darkness around him. He identified stalks of bee balm near his front door and buds on the roses that had begun to unfurl with robust determination. The gardens he'd thought dead had sprung to glorious life, just as Anne had predicted. How in *hell* had she known?

Grimacing, Michael closed the final yards to his cottage and let himself in the front door. The darkness in his kitchen seemed full of secrets. Quickly he lit a few lanterns and started a fire in the hearth, replacing the dark with shadows. Normally shadows wouldn't bother him, but tonight, everything bothered him. He shrugged out of his jacket, slung it on the back of a chair, and made a hasty check of the cottage's three rooms.

Nothing appeared out of place.

Of course not, he told himself. Why expect otherwise?

And yet he did expect otherwise, some primitive impulse within him setting off alarms he couldn't ignore. Listening to those alarms, he bolted the door and made sure the windows remained locked. Once he felt secure enough to relax, he grabbed his box of cigars off the mantel shelf and selected a Montecristo. He cut the end of the cigar, lit it with a piece of kindling, and slouched into a hard-backed chair.

Fragrant white smoke curled around his head, teasing him with its mellow perfection. He lifted the cigar to his lips and puffed a few times, aware that he was damned near committing sacrilege, smoking a Montecristo in this sort of mood. Montecristos were designed for those moments when a person felt very mellow and satisfied. Lovemaking, eating a stupendous meal . . . those were the times that called for a decent cigar. Still, tonight he felt in need of a little indulgence, especially after his tour through Connock's glasshouse.

Not a little. A lot.

He glanced out the window. Was it possible that Griswold had tried to hide the ivy's true nature? For what purpose? He shook his head, confounded. Nothing made sense anymore.

Puffing on the cigar, he began to wonder what other curiosities the forest hid. The ones he'd discovered with Anne over the last week were bad enough, but today, walking through that glasshouse and seeing those plants, he'd learned the true meaning of the word *oddity*.

The plants had looked healthy, he'd admit that much. He also had to admit that the vegetable plants produced with such vigor that he could almost imagine an Ireland forever free of starvation. Overall, a man with a less discerning eye might have thought the results of Connock's experiments a godsend, and the man himself pure brilliance.

But Michael had trained himself to look beneath the surface. He'd learned to see beyond the leaves of a gorse bush to the peahen that hid among its branches. And when he'd investigated between the branches of Connock's plants he'd seen roots ten times their normal size, rapacious roots that appeared capable of sucking the very life out of the earth. He'd smelled flowers with such a potent fragrance that it had lingered in his nose for minutes. He'd pricked his finger on a thorn from a pint-sized loganberry tree and watched his fingertip swell up almost immediately, before settling into an uncomfortable itch.

An image of a black adder formed in his mind.

Connock might consider these plants experiments that still needed additional research to perfect them, but on some primal level Michael thought them abominations of nature. It didn't matter to him that they might prevent another famine from ever occurring again in Ireland. Nature hadn't meant for Connock's plants to exist and Michael felt certain the nobleman would upset the land's delicate balance by releasing them into the wild.

And yet, even as these thoughts occurred to him, he realized his own special connection with nature might be prejudicing him against Connock's experimentation. Maybe he was being unreasonable. Anne, who shared his connection with nature, hadn't voiced any doubts over Connock's research. Her eyes had reflected awe and delight, not suspicion. And he couldn't deny the benefits Lord Connock's research might eventually bring to society, given his own experiences with starvation.

Michael growled a few choice oaths and stubbed out his cigar. He hadn't felt so torn, so unsure of himself since that day in the workhouse when he'd first contemplated running away. The brandies in the library and the excited conversation between Anne and Lord Connock hadn't clarified anything for him. He'd simply come away hating himself for questioning the man who once rescued him from perpetual loneliness.

He had only one choice, as far as he could see. He would remain at Glendale Hall, and watch, and evaluate, and hope that Lord Connock's research hadn't led them all into something they couldn't control. The locals north of Dublin had once called him the Green Man, and by God, the Green Man he would become, protecting the forests around Glendale Hall with all the devotion of Ireland's fey folk. He'd run from his problems once before, but this time, he was staying. For Anne.

Of course, the Green Man was also known for his fertility. Michael silently admitted he'd been feeling a mighty strong need to exercise that particular aspect of the Green Man's personality. Anne had been on his mind far too often, leaving him with an ache that damned near drove him crazy. He was in the mood to see some underclothes. And he had an idea she was in the mood to show them off.

14

Pencil held loosely in her fingers, Anne drew a final few lines on the piece of vellum spread upon her lap.

There, she thought. *Finished.*

She glanced first at the golden-limbed sapling, then at Michael. Arms folded across his chest, the dark Irishman had propped himself up against a boulder and promptly fallen asleep while she'd sketched, giving her a few secret moments to draw his likeness. She glanced at the sun's position on the horizon, judged the time near four in the afternoon, and considered waking him. Instead she decided to savor the moment by herself, just for a minute or so.

For the last two weeks, she and Michael had wandered across the estate, documenting the species Connock had created and then released into the wild. They hadn't found any ivy but did discover a few corpses, which lent a grim aspect to their work. To his credit, Michael managed to make light of the situation. While she'd sketched several peculiar flowers, he'd told her tales of the Tuatha De Danann, the very first Irish people whose special abilities put them on par with the gods, and Cu Chulainn, Hound of Ulster and perhaps Ireland's greatest warrior.

A smile curved her lips. She held the vellum away from her and assessed her drawing of the sapling with a critical eye. *Fresh, hopeful, spontaneous . . .* these were the words that came to mind when she viewed it.

Her drawing style had changed since she'd left Kew Gardens. Gone was the schematic representation that had become her forte, the flat though exacting manner in which she portrayed her subjects. Her recent sketches had a boldness of color, a painterlike feel which left her shaking her head. These new drawings would be of little use in the analysis of plant structure. While they pleased the artist in her, they worried her greatly. What would Lord Connock say when he saw her striking, yet nearly useless illustrations of his plants?

She rolled the vellum up and shoved it into her sketch case. "Michael," she murmured. "I'm finished for the day."

At the sound of her voice, he opened his eyes and smiled lazily. "May I see it?"

"You're forever asking to see my drawings. You know the answer," she reminded him tartly.

His smile widened, as it always did when she used that tone on him. "I've already seen some of your sketches, the ones you did for Kew Gardens. You needn't be so shy with me."

"I'm not being shy. I never show anyone—"

"—my illustrations until they are completed," he

finished for her. "When do you expect to finish with the sapling?"

"Actually, I'm finished."

"Then you have to show me."

"I'm afraid you're not going to think it a very good sketch," she admitted.

"Show it to me, Anne." Studying her with devastating blue-gray eyes, he rose to his feet and rested his hands on his thighs.

Her heart beat a tiny bit faster as she stared up at him. He had dressed in tall black boots that reached nearly to his knees, fawn-colored trousers that molded themselves to his hips, and a cotton shirt that bagged at the wrists. The clothes only emphasized the powerful, trim lines of his body. His golden hoop glinted in the sunlight and his firm chin, shadowed by a day of stubble, begged to be kissed.

She forced her gaze downward, to her sketch case, and took a deep breath. "All right, I'll show you."

Her hands trembling, she pulled the vellum from her case and unrolled it slowly. She hoped he couldn't tell how nervous she felt; she didn't want him to murmur false compliments or platitudes out of pity for her.

He took the vellum from her and held it open. She watched him closely, almost dreading his reaction.

A smile curled his lips. His eyebrows crept upward.

"Hmm," he said, but she could tell he liked what he saw.

Elation filled her. She tamped it down, still nervous, still uncertain. "It's not up to my usual standard," she informed him quickly. "It isn't detailed enough. I'm not sure Lord Connock will have any use for it at all. Perhaps I'll find myself shortly unemployed—"

"Hush," he said, and walked into a patch of sunlight, where he might see it even more clearly. He looked from the sapling to the illustration and back again. Finally he gave her his full attention. His eyes, she saw, were filled with admiration. " 'Tis beautiful."

"Well, thank you, but beauty isn't the ultimate goal of a botanical illustrator—"

"Spontaneity, childlike passivity . . . only a master can evoke emotions with an illustration, as you have."

His praise was a double-edged sword. "Emotions don't matter here, Michael. I care only for scientific accuracy, as does Lord Connock."

"You may tell me that emotions don't matter, but I'm not believing you anymore, Anne. You have something entirely different in your heart."

"Nonsense." She took the vellum from him, rolled it up, and hid it in her sketch case. "I've simply lost my touch. I had better find it again, and quickly. I don't want to disappoint Lord Connock."

"You won't. No one could find fault with your illustration. In fact, I think that you've finally drawn for *you.*" He slipped his arm through hers and, before she could question him on his enigmatic assessment of her, adroitly changed the subject. "If our work for the day is done, why don't we play?"

She swallowed. "Play?"

A soft laugh escaped him. "You don't have to be a child to play."

Play what?

She searched his face for answers. In the hazy light filtering through the forest canopy his features were harsh, lean, and so very vulnerable that her chest tightened and she wanted to stay with him, to protect him, to share in his laughter, to cry in his arms and draw strength from him.

She looked away. Staring at Michael was far too dangerous an occupation. "How do you propose we . . . play?"

"Why not walk with me to the waterfalls of Balkilly? They're a pretty sight, I promise you."

"That's all we'll do? Look at the waterfalls?"

"If you want." He grasped her hand in his own and brought it to his lips. His breath was warm as it blew across her skin a second before he touched her with his lips, the contact between them so thrilling that she nearly closed her eyes to enjoy it better. "Come with me."

Helplessly she left her sketch case behind and allowed him to lead her deeper into the forest. She couldn't remember a time when she'd enjoyed herself more. Michael's deep love of nature, vast knowledge of the plant world, and sensual view of all things had touched her deeply these past weeks. When she was with him, she could hardly recall her goals of scientific achievement and recognition. She forgot she had no place for a husband or children in her life. As they passed a fence sagging beneath the weight of honeysuckle, the sun a pale silver disk in a cloudless blue sky and the pine boughs above them stirring in a soft breeze, she knew today would prove no different.

"Today I'm going to tell you about Etain and Midir," Michael said as they maneuvered between two gray boulders festooned with moss. "They lived in Tir-na-n-Og, the Land of Youth, a golden place invisible to most human eyes. Etain was the most beautiful and kind-hearted woman in all the land. She fell deeply in love with Midir, a warrior who was handsome, clever, and fiercely devoted to her."

Delight filled her at the sound of his compelling tones. He had a gift for storytelling. When he wove his magic around her, she knew nothing but the man at her side and the excitement he evoked within her.

Michael tightened his grip on her hand. "Not all in Tir-na-n-Og were happy with Etain's and Midir's love for each other. Midir's first wife grew sick with jealousy. A powerful witch, she changed Etain into a magnificent golden fly. Still, Midir recognized her even in her new form and spent all of his time with her.

"The witch, seeing that she'd failed in her attempt to split the lovers, conjured a fierce wind and drove Etain out to sea, where the salt spray lashed her and drenched her wings. Cold and lonely after several years above the ocean, she nearly came to an end in its gray depths."

Anne strained closer to him, to better hear his story, for he walked ahead of her as he led her to the falls. In the distance, she heard the dim roar of water splashing over rocks.

Michael helped her around a thicket of brambles. When the path became more navigable, he didn't immediately resume his story.

"And? What happened?" she finally asked.

A grin played about his lips. "Just wanted to make sure you were listening."

She poked him on the arm. "I'm listening."

Clearly pleased with himself, he resumed his tale. "By chance, Etain came to land on the roof of a house filled with people feasting. The warmth and merry laughter drew her inside. She flew closer and closer to the man and his wife, longing for companionship. Her desperation drew her too close, though, and she fell into a goblet of wine. The wife drank her; and on the next day, she conceived a daughter."

"The daughter was Etain," Anne guessed.

"Don't jump ahead, you're ruining my story," he told her in stern tones.

Anne giggled. She couldn't help herself.

With a mock frown, he continued. "Etain was reborn into Ireland. She found a husband, and while her life was happy, she couldn't dismiss the feeling that she had forgotten something.

"One day, a heavy mist obscured the woods she was walking in. A man came up to her and begged her for a kiss. Normally, she'd refuse such a request, but something about the man compelled her to agree. As soon as his lips touched hers, she recognized Midir. She'd been sleeping, but he had awoken her. With great sadness she left her second husband for her first love, the only one who had ever truly brought her to life."

Her silly mood disappeared. She wondered if Michael was her Midir, the only lover who would ever truly bring her to life.

She closed her eyes.

She felt as if she were drowning.

Only it wasn't so unpleasant a feeling at all.

He suddenly stopped. An afternoon breeze ruffled his raven-black hair.

As if awakening from a dream, she felt the mist on her face, heard the muted roar of the water, saw the gushing stream spilling over a rocky gorge to collect in a pool below them.

For some odd reason she wanted to cry.

She turned away from him.

Michael didn't say anything. He stepped behind her and slipped his arms around her waist and held her. A great weight seemed to be pressing in on her. Sighing, she relaxed against his strong form. The weight disappeared.

He leaned into her from behind until they touched from thigh to shoulder. She almost knew what was coming before he kissed her, but the shock of his warm lips against the nape of her neck still left her breathless. When he lifted his head, she saw the question in his eyes. He wanted more. They both wanted more. But at what cost?

Shaking her head, she pulled away, and he let her go. He seemed content to wait. They watched the waterfall, the minutes passing quietly between them. Anne felt herself weakening. Her entire body yearned for him. Still, she couldn't make love to him and fall in love with him and turn her back on all she'd worked so hard for.

"Are you afraid, Anne?" he asked.

Hands knitted together, she swung around to face him. "We have no future, Michael. We're too different. You want a farm and a brood of children. I want to move in the same scientific circles frequented by Darwin. How could I keep abreast of developments and attend the social functions so necessary to advancement if I lived on a farm in Connaught?"

"We aren't living in the future. We're living now."

"My heart has been broken once. I don't want to chance it again."

"I'd never hurt you."

"Not on purpose." She gathered her skirts up in one hand and began to descend toward the pool at the bottom of the waterfall, trying to escape from the one man who insisted she *feel* rather than study and theorize.

"You mean so much to me, Anne. You've become more to me than just an associate, or a woman, or even a friend. Please don't shut me out, not now."

He spoke in such a simple, truthful way that she shot him a glance over her shoulder. Craggy, imperfect, his face ruddy and his nose slightly off-kilter, his black hair gleaming with blue highlights, he was harsh, he was vulnerable, he had changed her forever.

The need to believe that she meant more to him, too, gnawed at her insides. She had never really belonged, not with her parents, not with Henry, not even with Sir Richard and Eliza. And yet here she was, out walking in the woods with a man many might judge uncivilized, and for the first time in her life she felt truly understood.

"Take my hand," he said, when the embankment became too steep. She obeyed, slipping her palm against his. He gripped her far tighter than necessary and let go with only the greatest of reluctance when they reached the pool.

They stood side by side, quietly, admiring the beauty of the water-filled gorge which sprayed them with a fine mist. When Anne looked upward, she saw a clear sky filled with sunshine; and where that sunshine met the mist, she discovered a rainbow, made of colors so beautiful they didn't look real. Trees climbed up the slope on either side of the gorge, their trunks wet with spray and their leaves green and full. Mountain laurels dotted the brush beneath them with delicate white flowers.

She looked at Michael and realized he'd been watching her, not the gorge.

Tell him to bring you home, she thought.

You know you must.

Now, before you give up everything for him and resent him always.

She opened her mouth, then shut it again, the words just not coming. He remained quiet, solemn, not saying anything, evidently sensing her inner struggle and unwilling to interfere anymore.

The decision would be hers, and hers alone.

Silence grew between them.

"How deep is the pool?" she asked when the quiet became too much, not really giving a fig for his answer, but delaying the decision. Delaying, delaying.

"About six feet." He hunkered down, picked up a rock, and skipped it across the pool's surface. The rock popped up three times before settling beneath the water. "Ever try skipping stones?"

"No, I haven't."

He searched the ground, selected a flat rock about the size of a small egg, and handed it to her. "Try this one."

She hefted the rock in her palm. "How do I throw it?"

"Try to aim the rock so that it skims the water, and flick your wrist as you release it."

"All right." She did as he'd instructed and released the rock on what she hoped was a course even with the water's surface, but the rock plunged into the pool without skipping once.

"Try again," he said, and handed her another rock.

This time when she threw it, it skipped three times before disappearing beneath the surface. Anne turned to him and smiled. "It's not so hard after all."

His eyebrows drew together. "Are you sure you aren't hustling me, lass? You did far too well for the second throw of your life. 'Tis a good thing I didn't put money down on it."

She chuckled.

He laughed, too. "Did you ever wade in a stream like this one, when you were young?"

Anne thought back to the years she'd spent on the farm in Cambridge, remembering dusty old barns and meadows and the ruins of a long-forgotten church. "My parents had a farm, but from what I remember, we hadn't a stream on the property."

"Would you like to now?"

"What?"

"That's right, lass, I'm asking you if you'd like to wade in this stream."

"Bare-footed?"

"What other way is there?"

Anne shook her head. He had his share of strange notions. Still, a smile had already begun to form on her lips. She'd been around Michael long enough to realize that his ideas were part of his charm. Indeed, those strange notions had stirred up all sorts of new influences in her.

"That isn't a very proper suggestion, Michael."

"And it isn't very proper for you to be walking the woods alone with me. And yet, we've walked alone very successfully over the past month, without a complaint from anyone."

"But to strip off my shoes and stockings—"

"And what do you expect to happen, when your pretty feet touch the air? Will lightning rend us in two? Will the earth open up and swallow you whole?"

She snorted at his silliness. "No, of course not."

"Well, then?" he prodded.

Eyeing him narrowly, she glanced at his tall black boots. "Will you go barefoot, too?"

"If I can get my boots off."

"Don't expect me to pull them off for you."

Rather than answer, he slipped his hands around his right boot and yanked it off, revealing a foot encased in a cotton stocking. A rather dirty cotton stocking.

She lifted an eyebrow.

"So, let's see yours," he challenged.

Her nose in the air with mock disdain, she shuffled her skirts aside, yanked her shoe from her foot, and wagged her foot at him. Her silk stocking was nearly white.

His gaze widened as he took in her foot. Suddenly she realized that he could probably see the edge of her pink-striped pantaloons, too, one of her loudest pairs. She quickly dropped her toes back to the ground.

"That's quite a foot you have there," he murmured.

"Perhaps this isn't such a good idea."

He promptly reached down, dragged his other boot off, and threw the pair into a stand of ferns. His cotton socks soon followed. While she watched, her breath caught in her throat at the sight of his very masculine, very naked feet, he rolled up the bottoms of his trouser legs.

"Where's your courage, Mrs. Sherwood?" he called out as he walked to the edge of the pool.

Her heart beating faster, she removed her other slipper and pulled her silk stockings off. Her feet as bare as his, she stood up and scrunched up her toes. The grass felt cool beneath her feet, and spongy, and tickled her in a peculiar way.

She smiled. And in that moment, she felt very free. Gathering up her skirts, she joined Michael near the water's edge.

"A lass after my own heart," he said when he espied her bare feet. "I knew you weren't half as stuffy as you pretended to be."

"You're very full of talk," she pointed out, "but you've yet to do any wading."

"I've been waiting for you."

"Since you suggested it, you have a go at it first."

He stepped into the pool and sucked in a breath. "By God, that's cold."

Following behind him, she dipped her toes into the water and let out a yelp. He had a knack for understatement. That water was cold. But it felt good, too. She took a few steps deeper into the pool. The water caressed her as it flowed across her skin and the tiny pebbles at the bottom eased away her aches from too much walking.

"If we follow the stream for a while, we'll come upon a meadow as sweet as any to be found in Ireland, full of daisies and sweet clover and goldenrod," he said. "Want to explore it with me?"

She shrugged. "Sounds delightful."

Smiling his pleasure, he went back to fetch his boots and her shoes. His fingers lingered over her silk stockings before he shoved them, along with her shoes, into his boots and bundled them beneath his arm.

Seconds later he returned to her side. Slowly, they picked their way down the stream, Anne stopping occasionally to admire a piece of quartz rubbed smooth and milky by the flowing water, or watching the little gray and black fish that darted just beneath the surface. As they walked, Michael filled her ears with lore, telling her about the spiritual nature of water, and how the wells in Ireland lead to the soul of the earth, and must be protected.

His deep voice curled around her, velvety and smooth. The cold water trickled across her toes, and sunshine warmed her head, and she realized she had never felt more alive. How lonely it would be, she mused, to stand at the bedside of someone who was dying with regrets, someone who had never learned how to live fully and now awaited the dubious comfort of a grave.

Michael stopped and fell quiet, his attention directed toward the left.

Anne followed his gaze with her own and stifled a gasp of delight. A meadow of daisies and goldenrod and pink clover, all newly unfurled, stretched back to the horizon. The sheer size of the meadow, and its magnificent balance of color and delicacy, excited the artist within her. She wished she had her pencil and sketchbook.

They held hands as they strolled into the meadow, a few bees and dragonflies flitting around them. Once he'd led her to the center, he released her hand. "Look around. Tell me what you see."

Lips parted, she spun in a loose circle. "I see flowers everywhere. *Everywhere*. I see a blue sky. Puffy white clouds. Oh, Michael, 'tis beautiful. Thank you for showing me."

She reached down and caressed the petals of a daisy before plucking it. A brilliant white aura formed in her mind, that of a normal plant. At the absence of the red haze she'd become accustomed to, her mood soared. "How far away are we from Glendale Hall?"

"Three miles at least. Why?"

"That explains it," she said. "We're beyond Glendale Hall's influence."

He shook his head slowly. "You have a penchant for speaking in riddles. Are you going to tell me what you mean by influence, or are you going to torture me some more?"

"Torture you some more," she admitted with an impish grin.

Without warning, he slipped one arm behind her knees, the other around her back, and scooped her up into his arms. His shirt, slightly moist from their walk, clung to him and smelled faintly of lye soap. "Tell me, or I'll drop you on your arse."

She punched him lightly on the arm. In spite of their light banter, an ache mounted inside her. He held her far too tightly and his head dipped close to hers, revealing eyes dark with the same need.

"Put me down or I'll never tell you," she threatened.

"Wicked lass." He set her back on the ground, his form fitting against hers for a few delicious seconds before he moved away and sprawled against the grass.

"Sit down with me. Let the flowers hide you." He grinned and patted the grass next to him. "Perhaps you'll see the fairies that tend them."

She plopped down, her skirts billowing around her and slipping up over her ankles. Tiny airborne seeds swirled in the breeze above them; Michael caught one in his hand and told her to make a wish.

She closed her eyes and silently wished for him to kiss her.

Laughing softly, he let the seed go. It fluttered upward on a current and floated out of sight.

Anne sighed, at peace with herself. Here in the meadow, time seemed to move backward. The past had mixed with the present, leaving her feeling like a girl again, only seventeen, dreaming of love. The pain of her life with Henry had disappeared beneath the warmth of Michael's regard, and at some point during the last hour, she realized she'd made her decision. She would let Michael love her, despite the risk to her heart and her scientific goals.

Yes, that path was likely fraught with hurt and disillusionment, for she and Michael had no future. He wanted his farm, and she wanted scholarly recognition. And yet, as Michael had said, living without fully experiencing life was living in a colorless world. For a few months she would become a fulfilled woman, and after she and Michael had parted, she'd always know that she'd followed her heart despite the likelihood of pain and abandonment. She would have no regrets.

Michael reclined on one elbow, curling his body around hers. After a moment's pause, she buried her fingers in his hair and ruffled them backward, the feel of the silken strands against her fingertips tantalizing her. She'd never caressed him like this before and the thrill of it left her breathless.

At her touch, Michael became still. His smile disappeared.

She gazed at him, savoring the sudden realization in his eyes, the quick joy that glowed in their depths. He angled upward and kissed her gently on the lips, holding her loosely, and when he pulled back she saw such tenderness in his face that it suddenly didn't matter what might happen between them in the future. They had this perfect moment, and they had each other, and that would be enough to see her through even the worst times ahead.

15

*A*nne fell back against the grass and ran her hand along the curve of his jaw before trailing it downward to her breasts. She sprawled against the flowers, enjoying the anticipation that had been building between them since they'd first made love. Theirs was a need too deep for instant gratification, and she knew Michael well enough to realize he would take her slowly this time, allowing himself satisfaction only after he had left her weak-kneed with pleasure.

Her entire body burned at the mere thought of it.

The sunlight shone behind him, surrounding him in a corona of pale yellow. "I'm going to make you forget Henry," he said. His husky voice seemed to ache with longing.

"I've already forgotten him."

He let out a low moan and kissed the hollow of her throat, while she stroked the hard muscles along his back, then slipped her fingers downward, to his trousers. She rubbed her palms across his buttocks before slipping her hands beneath his waistband to touch him more intimately.

Michael pulled her close to him until she lay on her side, her body fitting into his. He pressed tiny kisses on her forehead, her cheeks, her eyes, her mouth, before moving lower, trailing his lips along her skin, tickling her.

She threw her head back and surrendered to the exquisite delight of his lovemaking. Her skin felt hot beneath the glare of the sun and silky-smooth, while her breasts lay full and tempting against his arm. She kissed the strong line of his jaw, catching his mouth with her own before allowing him to return to her breasts, still covered by her clothing. He buried his face in her cleavage, his hair very dark against her white skin, his beard scratching her lightly, the sensation thrilling.

She held on to him, her breath coming quickly as he kissed her breasts and left a hot, wet trail downward toward her nipples. Her clothes remained a barrier between them, and abruptly he shifted behind her, his sharp impatience to free her breasts evident in the hurried way he unbuttoned her gown and pulled it from her.

Her petticoat quickly followed in a heap of bright red cotton. With her gown and petticoats went the restrictions she placed on herself every day, leaving her free, uninhibited. She stretched sinuously and fit herself even more closely to him, the hard bulge of his arousal pressing into her stomach.

For a moment, she had a sense of unreality that she, Anne, could be making love to this man who had driven out nearly all other thought, that within a month she would have discarded her prim, careful attitude for that of a wanton. *But it's happening*, she told herself. Michael was kissing her tenderly yet urgently, devouring her with his lips, and he was warm and strong and he smelled very masculine and this was no dream that she would wake up from.

Oak leaves rustled from afar and a warm breeze blew across her skin, the luxurious feel of it an indulgence she wouldn't likely experience without Michael. Treasuring every moment, she ran her hand along his jaw. He pulled back to gaze at her, and when she trailed her thumb along his lips he bit it, gently, before releasing it.

Urgency made his eyes gleam. "You know how to tempt a man, Anne Sherwood."

She realized he was looking at her underclothes, studying them, perhaps even committing them to memory. She'd worn her pink-striped pantaloons and a matching pink corset, the corset shot with silver thread and purchased from a milliner's shop on the edge of respectable London. She felt beautiful in it and it gave her a new measure of confidence.

He slipped a hand into her bodice and cupped her breast, pushing it upward until her nipple peeked over the lace edging her corset. The sensation of the lace brushing against her nipple was like a delicate caress and she trembled against him. He leaned down to lick and tease her through the lace until her nipple hardened into a little peak, then took it into his mouth and sucked, the sensation so elusive yet so exciting her breathing became involuntary little pants.

Her breasts began to throb. Sensation built inside her, mounting and mounting, forcing a moan from her, then another. Her senses overloaded, she wound her fingers through his hair and pulled his head away, but he merely shifted his position and kissed her, his tongue thrusting against hers, the weight of his body crushing her gently.

After he'd silenced her moans with his mouth, he lavished the same loving care on her other breast as he'd done with the first. Again, the yearning sensation swamped her, made her cling to him. His erection was hot and hard beneath his fawn-colored trousers, trousers that stood between her and ultimate deliverance.

"Help me take the corset off," she murmured. At the same time, she fumbled with the buttons at the front of his trousers, needing to see him, to feel him, to possess every square inch of him.

His face tightening, Michael yanked off his shirt and unfastened the buttons that her own trembling fingers couldn't manage. She dipped her hand into his pants and wrapped her palm around him and pulled until his erection sprang free.

She sucked in a breath, thinking of him inside her. And yet, despite the hard, silken heat of him in her hand, she knew she could manage all of him, just as she had before. That only all of him, in fact, would be enough to soothe the need he'd roused in her.

Eyes closed, he growled low in his throat as she ran her fingers up and down his erection, exploring, squeezing, handling him in the manner that Henry had taught her and that until now had left her vaguely revolted.

"You feel very fine, Michael McEvoy," she whispered.

He stayed her stroking motions. "Stop, lass, you're moving too fast. I want this to last."

She saw the strain on his face, the lines on either side of his mouth and the dark pleasure in his eyes, and smiled, the knowledge of how much he desired her making her feel incredibly feminine and provocative. Deliberately she taunted him further with another languorous stroke.

"Anne, please," he muttered.

She laughed, low in her throat. The knowledge that she could take this man, a man who freely admitted to considerable experience in the art of lovemaking, and reduce him to begging only intensified her desire. She felt powerful in a way she'd never felt with Henry, and that made her bold.

Michael grabbed her around the waist to hold her still and pressed a hard, punishing kiss against her lips. Then he flipped her over and untied her corset and pulled it off her, strain deepening the lines in his face. Her pantaloons followed, and then her stockings, his fingers warm as they slid up her thighs, pausing to brush the silken curls between her legs before slipping beneath the top of her stockings and pulling them down. She jumped at that feather-light touch and grasped his erection, marveling again at the size of him, aching for him to fill the emptiness inside her.

She moaned, her need becoming too much to bear.

A quick smile formed on his lips at the sound. "We've hardly begun, lass. Let's get your chemise off, and then we'll make love properly."

He pulled the chemise over her head and then rocked back on his heels, his attention resting first on the light brown curls between her legs, then traveling upward to her breasts. Her nipples grew hard beneath his gaze, and when he saw this he swore softly. He yanked off his trousers and shirt, revealing the hard, muscled body she'd always imagined, and a few thin scars along his ribcage and down his lower back that she hadn't. His erection thrust up proudly beneath her gaze and his blue-gray eyes blazed with challenge.

Without a word he plucked a daisy. "Lay back, lass."

Trembling, she obeyed him.

Completely naked, his form a dark silhouette against a pale blue sky, he leaned down and kissed her swiftly on the lips. "Relax. Let me see you. *All* of you."

Her heart beating a swift tattoo in her chest, she allowed her legs to fall apart slightly. His gaze briefly rested on the curls between her thighs, the curve of his lower lip full, taut, expectant.

"Good," he murmured. "Now close your eyes and *feel*."

Hesitating only a second, she closed her eyes tightly. At first she felt nothing. She imagined him looking at her and felt her most secret parts burn in response. Her nipples tightened and a flush of shame heated her cheeks, that her body would be so responsive to the mere thought of his gaze.

Unexpectedly, a soft tickling sensation traced across her stomach. Her skin jumped. Her eyes snapped open. She stared at him.

He had the daisy in hand, his gaze very warm. He was smiling a devilish grin and his erection thrust at her, betraying his own enjoyment of their game. "Close your eyes," he chided. "That's part of the delight."

Swallowing, she did as he'd requested and soon the tickling began again, circling around her nipples, grazing the tops of her thighs, even fluttering along the soles of her feet. She felt as though he were trailing a path of fire across her, scorching her with a simple flower and the knowledge that he would do as he wished, without a single complaint from her.

"Open for me a little more." The daisy teased the place between her thighs.

Trembling now, trying not to writhe, she spread her legs apart for him a bit further. Another blush of shame heated her cheeks. Still, the need in her was stronger than the embarrassment. When the daisy began to brush against the curls between her legs and the more sensitive skin below she lost control of herself and whimpered.

"That's it," he whispered. "Feel it, Anne. Feel the desire it arouses in you."

The place between her thighs was afire with scorching need. She had stopped thinking. She could only feel. Writhing now, she reached down and bared her most secret place to his hungry gaze and the flower's delicious torment.

She heard his swift indrawn breath, but she kept her eyes closed and felt the daisy tickle her there, the tickle quickly swelling, swelling into a wonderful sensation that threatened to flood her with pleasure.

She cried out, urgently now.

He immediately stopped. "Open your eyes, lass."

"Michael, please . . ."

"No, not yet." He kissed her on the lips, his kiss more gentle now. "Breathe deeply. Don't let the pleasure overwhelm you. We're not nearly finished."

"You're tormenting me—"

"Shh. I'm teaching you about pleasure. Be patient."

Sighing shakily, she opened her eyes. He was right above her, his face sharp with suppressed need. Moisture beaded his brow.

Almost reverently he trailed his fingers down from her neck to her breasts, pausing to rub and stroke her nipples before slipping one finger down between her curls and teasing the place that burned for fulfillment. She gasped and thrust her hips against his hand.

"That's right, show me how much you want me," he encouraged, and she opened her legs wider, giving him full access.

"Tease me no longer, Michael," she begged. "Kiss me. Fill me. End it now."

He laughed softly and positioned himself between her legs.

"What are you doing?"

"Kissing you," he informed her, his voice rough, raw. "Filling you."

Without further warning he dipped his head downward and ran his tongue between her brown curls, circling around the center of her pleasure, licking it gently, making her cry out. She bucked wildly against his mouth. Wrapping his arms around her legs to hold her still, he continued tormenting her, his attention divided between her secret parts and her face. She closed her eyes and moved her head from side to side, the grass doing little to cool her inflamed cheeks.

His tongue thrust into her moist recesses, then withdrew, then thrust again. She thought of his erection and how large and hard and hot he'd felt, and just as she'd decided his tongue was a poor second, his teeth pressed into her, lightly, the feeling a sharp contrast to his tongue and therefore all the more exquisite.

Drenched in a surge of pleasure, she felt his lips encircle the hard little nub that remained the source of all her current difficulties. To her shock and utter delight he began to suck her there, gently, just as he'd tormented her nipples. She wanted to writhe and thrust against his mouth but forced herself to remain utterly still, savoring the sensation, feeling the waves of ecstasy that surged between her legs in an indescribable torrent. Moisture slicked her thighs and the part of her that he worshiped clenched and a low groan built in her throat.

Without warning, he pulled away.

"Michael, please," she begged, nearly sobbing.

"Turn over," he ordered, his voice harsh.

She quickly turned onto her stomach. He positioned himself behind her and raised her hips until she rested on her knees, and teased her with the tip of his erection. She felt him spreading her, looking at her, testing her with one finger.

One finger wasn't nearly enough.

"Michael," she began to say again, but before she could finish his name he filled her, slowly, slowly. He was so large and hot that her flesh seemed to tear, and she knew a moment's pain. Within seconds the pain had disappeared, replaced by the sensation of being completely possessed. Her terrible need eased for a second, then began to build into something wholly new and even more demanding.

He buried himself deep inside her and held there for a moment, then slowly withdrew only to plunge in again, holding, then withdrawing and filling her with hot, velvety strength. Writhing against him, she met each of his thrusts with one of her own, and soon they had achieved a perfect rhythm. Faster and faster he rode her, his low groans revealing that he, too, had finally lost control, but he couldn't ride her fast enough, for she was climbing to the edge of sweet, sweet oblivion, an ecstasy enhanced a hundredfold by Michael's expert tutelage.

Her senses soaring, she moved her hips faster, forcing him to move more quickly to meet her thrusts, drawing a tortured gasp from him. He held her hips and claimed her as fully as any man had ever claimed a woman and at last Anne felt a tidal wave of delight crest within her, mind-shattering pleasure that washed away even her sense of self. She cried out his name, loudly, and then collapsed into the flowers, gasping for air.

Michael had paused when she'd cried out, and on some primitive level she understood he'd wanted to feel and enjoy her moment of ultimate bliss. Still pressed tightly against her, he began to drive into her again, and she rocked her hips against him, pleasurable sensations washing over her. After five quick thrusts he, too, cried out and stiffened, his erection pressing deep. He poured himself into her and then covered her with his body.

Seconds passed, blissful moments in which the pleasure slowly ebbed away. Too soon, he rolled to his side, drew her into his arms and kissed the top of her head. She snuggled against him, the sunlight turning his skin a burnished gold. How long they lay like that, locked together from head to toe, she couldn't tell. At some point she felt the perspiration slicking both their bodies and so, apparently, did he.

"Can you stand?" he asked, laughter dancing in his gaze.

"I think so. Do we have to move, though?"

"I was going to suggest a dip in the stream."

She thought of that cool mountain water running across her body and shivered with delicious anticipation. "That sounds wonderful." She began to gather up her chemise.

He pulled the chemise from her and grasped her hand. "We don't need clothes, Anne. We've only a ten-foot walk to the stream."

"You mean you want to leave our clothes behind?"

"Why not?"

"What if someone sees us?"

"Who will see us? The trees? A few birds?" He gazed at her, a ruddy flush invading his cheeks. "We won't be disturbed."

A shy smile tilted her lips upward. Without saying a word, he helped her to her feet and led her through the meadow, flowers brushing against her tender skin. She felt terribly naughty but also very, very sensual at the knowledge that someone, indeed, could be watching. Heat building within her all over again, she focused on Michael's powerful form and watched his buttocks flex with every step he took.

At length they reached the stream. Michael led her to a spot where boulders had dammed the water up, creating a pool similar to the one at the bottom of the Balkilly Falls. Taking a quick breath, he waded into the pool, turned around, and rested his arms against a fallen log near the edge of pool. Water covered him from his chest downward.

"Come on in," he encouraged her, smiling.

She dipped one toe into the water and yelped. "I forgot how cold it is."

"Where's your courage?"

She shot him a disgruntled look that drew a laugh from him. "You may be used to bathing in cold Irish streams, Michael McEvoy, but I prefer warm English tubs. Give me a moment."

Over the next several minutes she inched her way into the pool, and when the water finally covered her up to her breasts, she admitted that it felt wonderful. She waded over to him and settled against his lap.

He sighed deeply and brushed her hair back from her

face. "Ah, lass, you felt good. I made the right decision when I canceled my trip to India. I'm thinking I'm going to be postponing a few more."

Anne stilled, her heart quickening. The contentment and tenderness in his voice frightened her. When she'd allowed him into her life, she'd known that their eventual parting would be difficult. Still, she'd always assumed Michael would want to return to his traveling. She'd assumed that they both understood their relationship couldn't last. He was wild, he was untamed, he couldn't possibly want to tie himself down with a woman. And yet, suppose he didn't want her to leave. Would she have the strength to insist they part?

"Michael, you mustn't postpone any more trips on my account."

He stiffened and shot her a quick glance before relaxing again. A soft laugh erupted from him. "So that's the way it's to be, hmm? You'll entertain yourself on me while you sketch, and then, once you've gained the scholarly recognition you crave, you'll move on?"

Shamed, she knotted her hands around his neck and pressed her cheek against his chest.

"Shh, lass, it's all right. I'll give you pleasure, if that's what you want." He wrapped his arms around her and enfolded her in a gentle embrace. "You're right to question whether or not I can give you anything more."

Anne felt her throat close up. Words hovered on her lips, emotional words telling him how much she'd come to rely on him, how much she trusted and respected him, how much she . . .

No, you don't love him, she told herself furiously.

Deliberately she conjured thoughts of Charles Darwin and Professor Huxley and all of the men who saw her as a woman, nothing more. She thought of the members of the Royal Botanic Society who had accused her of plagiarizing her late husband's work. Their contemptuous faces kept the emotional words from spilling out.

"God knows my years in the workhouse have left me unwilling to surround myself with people and follow their senseless rules," he continued. "You prefer a town house in London, but to me, a town house would be naught but a gilded cage."

She swallowed past the sudden lump in her throat, understanding very well what he was saying: that he would never go to London with her and move in the scientific circles she needed to court. Theirs was a love ill fated from the very beginning and even though she'd already realized as much, the knowledge still hurt terribly. Her head told her to enjoy him while she could, and then concentrate on her sketches, but her heart kept insisting she trade in her sketchbook for an Irish farmer.

Something prodded her bare legs. Anne lifted her head. She tried for a playful tone. "You, dear sir, are far too eager."

His chest rumbled. "And you, my sweet scholar, are far too tempting."

She flicked some water onto his face. "Perhaps you need to cool down even more."

Shifting her so she sat directly on his growing erection, he spoke softly into her ear. "I'm needing your legs wrapped around my waist."

"You had better learn some manners, Michael McEvoy." Before he could respond, she slipped from his grasp and swam away from him, kicking water on him as she did so.

A provocative grin curled his lips. He swam after her

and caught her around the waist. She managed to escape again, splashing him until he caught her and dunked her under the surface. That started a playful game that left them gasping for air and laughing at the same time. When they finally settled down, Anne noticed that the tension had melted into something more companionable.

"I'm growing cold, and I can see you're shivering. We'd better get dressed, as much as I hate the thought." He took her hand and drew her from the stream.

Reluctant to surrender this magical time between them to more practical thought, Anne moved slowly. She gazed at his dark hair, now wet and sleek against his head, and watched his single golden earring sparkle in the sunlight. In the aftermath of their lovemaking, she felt as though she knew him intimately, at the same time realizing she knew him not at all.

Michael dressed quickly and then turned to help her. Anne shoved her arms through her chemise, pulled her pantaloons over her pleasantly aching body, and allowed him to fasten her into the corset. As he pulled on the strings, his admiring gaze on her bosom, which surged ever higher the harder he pulled, she decided to dig a little into his past.

"Michael, when did you pierce your ear?" she asked, noticing his earring sparkling in the sunlight once again.

"About ten years ago." He paused to kiss her breasts, one after the other, before tying her scarlet petticoats around her waist. That done, he picked up her gown and shook it out.

"Did you pierce it yourself?"

"No." A half-smile curved his lips as he settled the gown over her head. His skill at dressing her made her think he'd had a lot of practice putting the clothes back on women he'd just undressed. A surge of jealousy tightened her throat.

"I was sailing as a passenger on a tea clipper in the South China Sea," he said. "We were heading for the British colonies in Australia. A monsoon wrecked the ship. By some miracle, I washed up on land."

Her eyes grew round. "Thank God for that."

He helped her put her arms through the sleeves, then shook the gown out from the hem. "I learned I'd washed up on the China coast. I found a small town and bribed a local fisherman with a few bolts of silk I'd found in a trunk, which had also survived the monsoon. Soon I was headed for the British colonies in Australia."

He assumed a wry grin. "The fishermen were drinking local whiskey that had the kick of poteen. I swilled my share and passed out in a coil of rope. When I awoke a day later, my ear was pierced."

"The fishermen pierced your ear?"

"That they did."

"Why?"

" 'Tis a custom among sailors to pierce a fellow sailor's ear when that fellow crosses the equator for the first time. When we passed from the Northern to the Southern Hemisphere, one of the fishermen took a pin and put a hole in my ear. They thought they'd done me a great service. I agree with them."

"How so?"

"It makes me different and reminds me what I've accomplished."

He began to button the back of her dress.

"You don't like being the same as everyone else, do you, Michael?" she said over her shoulder.

"If we were all the same, life would be very boring. I'm a firm believer in differences. You're a bit different too, aren't you?"

"In what way?"

"You know plants better than anyone I've ever met. Better than myself, in fact, and I've made a determined study of them. I might even say your ability to sense their needs is . . . uncanny."

About to slip her shoe onto her foot, Anne stilled.

Seemingly unconcerned, he tucked his shirt into his waistband and pulled on his boots.

Swallowing, she finished putting her shoes on. Then, completely dressed, she wrapped her arms across her breasts and walked a few paces away from him. "You're correct. I have one rather large difference from most people. But I'm afraid to tell you. If I do, you'll think me mad."

A beat of silence passed between them, in which he measured her with one short gaze. "Tell me and we'll see."

16

Michael had a very good idea about the nature of her difference, and the realization that she was about to answer all his questions elated him. Even so, he forced himself to keep quiet and be patient. He didn't want to frighten her with too much enthusiasm.

Anne slanted him a quick glance before focusing on a large oak tree that jutted into the meadow. She refused to look his way, and that told him better than words how uncomfortable she was, sharing this little nugget with him. "My difference is a complicated thing to explain."

"We have hours before sunset," he urged. "And I'm a very good listener."

"All right, I'll try." She took a deep sigh and knitted her hands together. "We both have a strange connection to nature. Do you agree?"

He nodded, not daring to speak.

Hands buried in her skirts, she focused on the flowers beneath her feet, flowers they'd crushed while mak-

ing love. Michael also stared at the flowers, memories
of her soft body beneath his stirring up a new tightness
in his loins. How many times had he imagined his first
time with her? He'd planned it all out in his head,
thinking of the masterful way in which he'd seduce her.
In the end, though, he hadn't been masterful and he
hadn't seduced her. Instead, he'd felt as though he'd
stepped into a whole new world.

He lifted his head to gaze at her delicate profile,
then at the soft blond curls that teased her cheeks and
at her hair, which hung in a heavy mass to her waist.
When he'd first met Anne, he'd thought of nothing but
talking her into parading around in those underclothes
of hers. Sometime over the last several weeks, however,
she'd become more than just a beautiful woman he'd
wanted to possess. She was his brave Anne, surrounded
by men who thought her worthless, yet determined to
succeed; his courageous Anne who fought back, full of
vinegar, when she felt the heel of a manly boot coming
down upon her.

"Your connection to nature," she continued, drawing him away from his thoughts, "is a physical one,
learned through years of living in the wild. Mine is
more . . . spiritual."

"Spiritual? In what way?"

"When I touch a plant, I see colors. Not with my
eyes. With my mind."

Confused, he shook his head.

She let out an impatient sigh. "You may be a man
who knows his senses, but you're also trapped by them.
It *is* possible to see without using your eyes."

Jesus, this wasn't at all what he'd expected. "What
exactly do you see?"

"A haze of sorts. It's deep in my mind. White haze

usually indicates a healthy plant. A tinge of yellow suggests the plant needs more compost around its base, or perhaps has too much compost, while blue could mean the soil isn't draining properly." She bit her lip and continued after a moment, "Plants that lack water develop a brown or rust-brown color—"

She broke off suddenly and spun away from him. "Oh, it's no use! You're never going to believe me. When I listen to myself talking like this, even *I* think I sound mad."

God's truth, she did sound crazy. Even so, he wasn't about to agree with her aloud. She was hugging her breasts and trembling and so agitated that he knew she needed a dose of reassurance. Maybe after she'd calmed down enough to talk sensibly he'd get to the root of things.

He stepped behind her, wrapped his arms around her waist, and pulled her against him. "I'm listening, lass," he soothed. "And I'm not passing judgment on you. I just want to hear whatever you're willing to tell."

"You surprise me, Michael McEvoy," she said in a tart voice. She hadn't relaxed against him in the slightest. "You, who believe in fairies and Tir-na-n-Og, dare to look askance at me when I try to explain my ability with plants."

"I'm not looking askance—"

"Yes, you are. I can hear it in your voice, see it in your eyes. And you're frowning. If you don't believe me, say so, but for God's sake, don't lie to me." She moved out of his arms.

"I'm not lying—"

"You are."

"Will you give me a chance?"

Nose in the air, she looked past him.

His patience snapped. If that was the way she wanted it, then fine by him. With an abrupt nod he began walking toward the stream, listening all the while to see if she would follow. She trailed behind him at first, but by the time he'd reached the stream she followed right on his heels.

The silence lengthening between them, they walked until they reached the bottom of Balkilly Falls. When they stopped to rest at the pool, Anne had begun to look uncomfortable. She shot him little glances beneath her lashes and chewed her lower lip and appeared so damned contrite that he wanted to kiss her full on the mouth.

They had a steep climb ahead of them, to the top of Balkilly Falls. He offered her a hand. "May I help you to the top?"

"Yes, please," she said in soft voice, and he knew she would listen to him now.

He grasped her warm palm in his own and together they picked their way up the embankment. Upon reaching the top they each took a deep breath.

Michael wiped his brow. "Let's sit down and rest for a moment before we move on," he suggested.

Anne moved over to a boulder and settled herself on it. Michael chose a fallen log across from her and sat as well. They faced each other. Neither spoke. The moment stretched out between them, full of strain. Michael wondered who would speak first. Quickly he realized she had no intention of opening her mouth unless forced to do so.

"First of all," he said, using the plain and sensible tone that had talked him out of trouble in the past, "I'll admit that your 'seeing colors' sounds far-fetched. Still, I'm from Ireland, and we Irish are known for our fairies and our open minds. I'm wanting you to tell me more about this gift of yours. Maybe we can figure it out together."

She kept her gaze on the forest floor. When she spoke, her voice was husky, the words obviously coming with great difficulty. "I don't need to figure it out, Michael. I already understand it. It's you who needs to think it through."

She was as stubborn as a tinker's mule.

Michael cast his gaze to the sky, praying for his patience to hold out. "Let me repeat what you've already told me. When you touch plants, you see colors. White reflects a healthy, balanced plant, while too much of any other color suggests illness of some sort."

"That's right. Have you ever directed white light through a crystal? Crystals split white light into all the colors of the rainbow. I believe white light represents a healthy plant because it also represents an even distribution of all the colors."

"And you've had this unusual ability all of your life?"

She lifted her chin. "I have."

"When did you first notice it?"

"I can't recall the first time. I suspect I must have been very young." Her brow furrowed, as though she were sorting through her memories. "I believe I had turned eight years old before I realized everyone couldn't see the colors. My father was rubbing his hands together over a field of hay, anticipating a bountiful harvest. I insisted that the hay was yellow and sickly, but he didn't understand. He saw only green stems. We argued, and eventually he punished me. That season we reaped the worst crop of hay in a decade."

A subtle throb of emotion in her voice told him

she'd suffered dearly over that crop. "He punished you, did he?"

"Sometimes I think he even blamed me for the crop's failure. Needless to say, I didn't speak of the colors after that."

She paused. Around them, water gurgled over rocks before crashing into the pool, and the oak trees shivered in a breeze.

"So you learned to keep it all inside," he said, striving for a neutral tone. He could well imagine the confused young girl she'd been and knew a spurt of anger at her parents, who'd dismissed her tale so quickly. A second later he realized he had just done the same thing. He, who had lived in the wild to escape society's restraints, had just thrown in his lot with conventional thinking and cast a rigid eye on Anne.

"So you began to illustrate flowers," he said, sitting up a little straighter and leaning toward her.

"I sketched because I had no other way to express what I saw in my mind," she said, her voice gaining strength. "Over the years, I learned to translate the colors into needs and emotions and discovered a deeper layer to plants, one beyond the physical. When I illustrated them, I discovered I could imbue them with the qualities I sensed rather than saw, using nearly imperceptible color shading. This hidden level makes my illustrations appear more accurate. More real. It's an optical illusion, really, but it's effective."

She met his gaze for the first time since they'd sat down. "You know the rest. Henry saw my illustrations and married me. He took credit for them. And now I wish to prove myself to all the scholars who looked down their noses at me and accused me of copying his work after he died."

He saw it all then: the child who had a secret she'd been forced to keep, neglected by her parents because she was different, married off to a man who'd used her. Sympathy for the little girl who'd held a piece of lead in her hand rather than a butterfly filled him, sympathy he kept carefully hidden.

"I believe you, Anne," he said, his voice as gentle as lamb's wool.

She didn't appear to have heard him. "I wish I had some proof to offer you."

"I don't need proof."

"Do you remember when we first met, and I predicted the oak outside the Balkilly Arms would fall upon its roof?"

"I remember now."

"You asked how I knew about the carpenter ants eating away at its trunk. Well, the tree told me. It had a greenish black color that I've come to associate with ants and termites."

"I'd wondered about that for a long time. Your explanation makes sense."

"We also talked about orchids during our first dinner," she said, her eyes beginning to gleam like gray satin. "I explained that they were dying from lack of water, even though their soil was moist. You hit upon the solution of misting them and providing them with humidity. But you didn't understand how I knew they were dying."

"They told you."

A hesitant smile curved her lips. "I guess I do have proof of sorts."

The pieces fell into place for him. He thought back to their dinner with Charles Darwin. "Do you recall your discussion with Charles Darwin about pure observation? You said that human beings aren't capable of pure observation, because they aren't equipped to sense every aspect of nature."

She shook her head ruefully. "I would rather forget that evening."

"You were referring to your ability to see plants' emotions, weren't you?"

"Yes, and foolishly so, for I hadn't an ounce of proof to support my conjecture."

He grabbed her hand, stood, and pulled her to her feet. She must trust him very much, he mused, to reveal her deepest secrets to him. "I believe you, Anne."

"What?"

"I believe you."

Her eyes wide, she stared at him. "You do?"

"I do."

Eyes suddenly narrowing, she assessed him, and after a moment her face smoothed out. She wrapped her arms around his neck, drew his face down to hers, and gave him the biggest, juiciest kiss he'd ever had the privilege of receiving.

"Thank you, Michael."

He suddenly felt so giddy he thought he might laugh aloud. An idea occurred to him. "Come on." He pulled her arm, leading her toward the golden sapling.

"Where are we going?"

"I want you to touch the sapling and tell me what you see."

Her steps began to lag. Her smile disappeared.

He slowed down, some of his enthusiasm dissipating. "What's wrong?"

"There's something I haven't told you."

He didn't like the sound of her voice—scared and worried and far too careful. He stopped altogether. She maneuvered in front of him and continued down the path. "Not here. I'll tell you when we reach the sapling."

Suddenly she stopped and stared off into the heavy undergrowth on the left. "Did you see that?"

He followed the direction of her gaze. "What?"

"Something was moving in those thickets."

"Like a squirrel?"

"No, much bigger."

"A deer?"

"A person."

Michael paused, motionless. He studied the undergrowth for signs of movement and colors that didn't fit in. Nostrils flaring, he sniffed the air for any traces of cologne or perspiration. His senses insisted they remained alone. "Did you actually see someone or just a shadow?"

"Someone was there, Michael," she insisted.

"Well, I'll go flush him out, then." Half expecting a deer to fly out of the thicket, or ivy to twine around his ankle, he strode into the prickly branches. A gray squirrel skittered up a tree, but nothing else moved. He searched for footprints and any other evidence that would suggest they'd been spied upon.

Nothing.

He returned to Anne's side. "I couldn't find anything."

She frowned and began striding toward the sapling. With the sense that something was *off* in the forest returning to nag at him mercilessly, he followed behind her. An odd thought occurred to him as they walked. Lord Connock had created some very helpful plants. In the process of creating them, had the nobleman made a few mistakes? Mistakes like ivy that had a taste for flesh?

When the golden limbs of the little sapling came into view he grasped her arm and pulled her around gently, to face him. "What's wrong with it?"

"The same thing that's wrong with all of Connock's plants."

"Which is?"

"They're suffering terribly."

"Tell me about the sapling's emotions."

She edged away from him, and he released her arm. Lips pursed, she began to walk a wide circle around the sapling, her attention fixed on its hoof-shaped leaves. Chewing on her lower lip, she touched one of the leaves with her finger and then withdrew, clearly perplexed. "I see a red haze. I know the haze represents great distress."

She shook her head and walked another circle around the tree. "A few of Connock's flowers project red marbled with veins of black. Plants growing in sewage or near the factories in London often give off that kind of aura. They're usually physically distressed on the outside, too: warped stems, odd protuberances, blight, and the like. I only see black if I touch a dead plant."

"What about the plants in Lord Connock's glasshouse? Are they red, too?"

"Overwhelmingly."

"Could the glasshouse's red roof be affecting the plants?"

"I wondered the same and asked Lord Connock about his roof. He insisted that he changes the roof tiles regularly to expose the plants to different colors. I don't think the two are related."

He pondered for a moment. "Maybe your gift for sensing plants' emotions works differently for Connock's plants, since his are manmade rather than natural."

"I've wondered as much. How can a distressed plant grow so verdantly and produce such abundant fruit?"

They looked at each other. Michael saw the worry in her eyes and knew his own eyes reflected the same.

"There's something else," she said, her voice dropping a notch. "The night I arrived in Balkilly, I touched the ivy we've been looking for. It projects only black, the aura of a dead plant. As you know, it's very much alive."

"Are you certain about its aura?"

She nodded.

At her calm certainty, uneasiness slithered through his veins. "What do you think it means?"

"I don't know. It doesn't seem logical. We need to gather a specimen. Perhaps we could ask around the village and see if anyone else knows of a place where this ivy grows."

Michael nodded slowly. "I've heard Paddy O'Shanley had a run-in with some sort of demon in the woods. He might have encountered our ivy. In fact, there's going to be a wake in the village tonight, for old Paddy's father, who's gone to join his maker. We'll both attend, pay our respects, and ask Paddy a few questions."

"Is a wake an appropriate place to be asking questions?"

A wry smile fought its way to his lips. "Have you ever been to an Irish wake?"

"Never."

"In that case, you're in for a treat."

"Whatever do you mean?"

"Irish wakes aren't the solemn affairs you English are

used to. They're a night of turf throwing and frivolity, and far merrier than a wedding."

"That sounds disrespectful," she murmured.

"Not at all. The wake is a party with one guest of honor, the deceased, and the guests are simply giving him a royal send-off, in a way the deceased would have wanted. By making merry, the relatives of the dead man are partly celebrating his life and partly thumbing their noses at death, healing the wound that death leaves behind."

Anne placed her hand in his. "I'm intrigued."

"Somehow, I knew you would be."

Together they began to walk toward Glendale Hall. Michael thought of dancing and making merry with her and heat invaded his limbs. Her sketchbook tucked under his arm, he told himself if he had the slightest bit of sense, he'd stay away from Anne Sherwood. In fact, he'd hightail it to India without a backward glance. She was becoming as necessary to him as the air he breathed, and she'd already informed him that a farm and a husband did not figure into her future. What the hell would he do once she'd gone?

Michael came to collect Anne at precisely eight o'clock that evening. She'd just finished her dinner with Lord Connock and had retired with him to the salon. When Michael joined them, his eyes dancing with blue-gray devilment, the drab evening suddenly became unbearably exciting.

"Good evening, Anne. Are you ready to pay your respects to Paddy's father?" Michael asked. Dressed in black trousers and a black evening coat, his cravat tied expertly at his throat and very white against his tanned skin, he might have been asking her if she wished to join him for an evening at the opera.

Her heart fluttering, Anne schooled her features into solemnity and stood. Inside, however, anticipation coursed through her, and with it, guilt that she could take such pleasure in a wake, of all things. "Yes, and to Paddy as well. 'Tis a sad thing to lose a loved one."

A smile twitching his lips, Michael raised an eyebrow. Clearly, her grave tone had amused rather than deceived him. "Will you be joining us, Owain?"

Lord Connock cleared his throat. "Not tonight. I have an experiment under way that I must attend to. Give the O'Shanleys my sincerest regards and heartfelt sympathy." He patted his waistcoat with a forgetful air and then walked toward a side table and picked up a slim mahogany box. "Oh, here they are. Please give these to Paddy for me."

Michael flipped open the top and whistled, long and low. "Imported Havana beauties, from Vuelta Abajo, with Partidos wrappers and made by the Spanish hand method." He lifted one to his nose and sniffed. "Well conditioned, too."

"Make certain Paddy shares them," Lord Connock said in gruff tones.

Eyebrow raised, Anne studied her employer. The pouches beneath his bright blue eyes had darkened since he'd shown them his Eden. Judging by the servants' chatter, he now spent all of his free time in one of his laboratories. And within the last few days, a new side of him had emerged, a cranky and quick-tempered personality she didn't recognize. He seemed almost, well, desperate, and a desperate man took chances a rational one would not. The perception didn't comfort her, not in the slightest.

Michael tucked the cigar box beneath his evening coat. After bowing briefly in Lord Connock's direction, he slipped his arm through hers. "Come with me, Mrs. Sherwood, and we'll go mourn one of Balkilly's oldest and most venerated citizens."

Together, they made their way through the central hall and out onto the carriageway. A high-sprung gig awaited them, its single horse pawing nervously at the ground. One footman held the horse's bridle, while another waited near the carriage door, ready to open it for them.

Smiling, Anne piled into the gig with the footman's help. Michael climbed in after her and took the reins. With a soft jingle of the harnesses they were off, trotting down the moonlit carriageway, heading for the village of Balkilly. The trees on either side of the lane were silhouettes of gray against a velvety dark sky, while stars twinkled among a smattering of clouds. The clouds closest to the moon glowed as though lit from within, their edges silvery with pale light. Overall, the lane had a magical feel to it and Anne sighed as a warm spring breeze, untouched by the night's cold, brushed across her face.

On such an evening, she had a hard time believing that ivy roamed the woods, looking for victims. It opposed everything she'd ever learned about plants and, given her gift, she knew more than most. Nevertheless, she couldn't look at Lord Connock without thinking of a mysterious something hiding out in Glendale Forest. A hungry something. He stirred nothing but revulsion in her anymore.

She'd even begun to question her goal of gaining scholarly recognition by illustrating Connock's new species. At first, she'd thought the nobleman's research

justified a noble goal, but now she wondered if the price
had soared too high. His tampering with nature suddenly seemed like arrogance rather than genius. Confusion had become the order of the day, and with it, a
sinking feeling that her hopes of gaining scholarly
recognition were unraveling.

She slanted a look toward Michael. He was concentrating on the road, the two lanterns mounted on either
side of the carriage doing little to light the way. Memories of him naked and surrounded by a corona of sunlight abruptly filled her head. He'd loved her
thoroughly and she'd treasured every minute of it. In
fact, he'd become the only bright spot in her days. The
need to tell him so grabbed hold of her.

"Michael, about this afternoon . . ."

He threw her a quick glance. "Hmm?"

"I just want you to know how much I, ah, enjoyed
our lovemaking." She shifted on the leather-covered
bench, thinking her statement hadn't come out the way
she'd meant it.

"Good, lass. Glad to be of service."

"I mean, I . . . you . . . Henry never did that to me."
Silently, she cursed herself. She simply couldn't seem to
tell him what she needed him to hear. She wasn't even
certain what she needed him to hear.

Silence bloomed between them. Anne shifted some
more.

At last, Michael spoke, his voice noncommittal.
"I'm hoping I would show better than Henry."

"That's not what I meant at all."

"What did you mean?"

"I don't know. I suppose I wish our situation were
different."

"In what way? You wish I was a scholar like yourself,

so I might throw in with your schemes to gain recognition? You wish I would come to live with you in London?"

The word *yes* hovered on her lips. She bit it back, realizing that wasn't what she wished at all. A scholarly Michael, living in London, wouldn't be *her* Michael. She'd fallen in love with the Green Man, the Oak King, the one who preferred the rules of the wild to those of civilization.

She stilled, her own words echoing in her head.

She'd fallen in love with him . . .

No, it couldn't be. How could she be in love with a man so antithetical to everything she wanted from life?

She muffled a gasp.

No, no, no!

Yes.

That little voice had returned.

And this time, it spoke the truth.

"Don't worry, Anne," he said, evidently misinterpreting her gasp as one of panic. "I have no intention of moving to London to remain near you. I've lived long enough to understand that emotional ties between people such as you and I never last."

Her stomach clenched. Tears started in her eyes. "Oh, Michael, I didn't mean to imply that I tolerate you simply because I enjoy your lovemaking. We've so much more between us than that. You're a fine man, a very fine man, and over the past few weeks I've come to feel . . . quite deeply for you."

"I'm touched," he said, an edge to his voice. "Do you feel deeply enough to forgo your London parties for a farm in Ireland?"

A long moment of quiet settled between them, quiet in which Anne considered his question and realized she didn't have an answer. Perhaps she did love him. What difference would that make? Love didn't change anything between them; it only added a new complication. If love forced her into giving up her goals of scholarly recognition to be with him, she'd likely end up resenting him for the rest of her life.

Unless, of course, she didn't really want scholarly recognition but something else, something deeper . . .

She just didn't know anymore.

"If you came to live in London, you wouldn't be Michael anymore," she offered hesitantly. It was the only answer she could come up with. "Likewise, if I came to live in Ireland, I wouldn't be Anne."

His grip on the reins tightened. "So we're agreed, then, to savor these moments while they last?"

"Agreed," she said, and wiped away a stray tear that had rolled down her cheek.

They finished the rest of the trip in silence.

Feeling wretched, Anne sat at stiff attention as the gig rolled through the village proper and stopped before a long thatched cottage. Men lounged around the cottage's front porch—some on the ground, others on stools, and one on a bale of hay—and smoked pipes with owlish expressions on their faces. Recognizing a few of them from her earlier visit to the Balkilly Arms, she could tell they already had three sheets to the wind.

Michael jumped out of the gig and handed the reins to an Irish lad. His lids drooping low over his eyes, masking their expression, he helped her out of the gig and steered her toward the cottage's front door. The pipe smokers called out greetings to Michael as they passed by. A few gentlemanly souls even nodded their heads in deference to Anne.

Perfectly miserable, Anne smiled and nodded back.

Now she had the proper attitude for a wake.

They climbed the steps to the front door and paused in a hall. The rooms to the right and left, their beds and tables suggesting a bedchamber and a salon, remained dark and closed off. All of the light gleamed from a single large room at the end of the hall. Michael drew her down the hall and stopped just inside the kitchen.

Stools, a butter churn, a spinning wheel, and other similar items were pushed back to make room. Earthenware jugs, cobalt-blue glasses, copper pots and iron tools filled shelves which hung on the timber-and-plaster walls. Tobacco smoke gathered in gray clouds near the thatched ceiling, while the smell of whiskey and poteen wafted through the room, making Anne's nose tingle.

People crowded everywhere. Conversation included both Irish and English and seemed to be focused on the day's events. Most of the villagers had dressed in black, their clothes simple and of a coarse fabric. She and Michael stood out in their clothes, which were of a noticeably finer cut, and drew the attention of many in the room.

Michael pushed his way through the crowd, toward a fire which only added to the heat and closeness in the kitchen. Near the open-hearth fireplace, a grizzled old man lay inside a coffin. Someone had given Paddy's father a fresh shave and had dressed him in a white habit, placed a crucifix on his breast, and entwined his fingers in rosary beads.

Paddy, his gray hair neatly combed, sat near the head of the coffin. The strange growth that Anne had marked upon first meeting him had become a dull red. For the sake of politeness, she tried to keep her gaze focused elsewhere, but her scientific curiosity was nagging at her. Looking around, she saw that the older people in the room, those with graying hair, had similar growths near the ear or along the jaw. The younger set appeared free of deformity.

Michael approached Paddy with Anne in tow. He stopped before the bereaved Irishman and murmured, "I'm terribly sorry for your troubles." At the same time, he withdrew the mahogany box from his evening coat.

His attention glued to the box, Paddy's rheumy eyes widened.

"Lord Connock sends his heartfelt sympathies, to you and Moira," Michael continued, and handed Paddy the box.

Paddy took it and lifted the lid. He selected a cigar and sniffed it reverently. "Ah, our Lord Connock is a generous man. Please be thanking him for me, Mr. McEvoy."

Michael nodded and moved toward a white-haired woman stationed at the other end of the coffin, leaving Anne in front of Paddy.

Anne touched his hand. "I'm so sorry, Mr. O'Shanley. If there is anything I can do . . ."

"Have a whiskey for me, lass, and brighten up your face," he replied. "You look sadder than me, and that's not good. Hey, Sean," he shouted, "bring the lass a swallow of poteen."

Anne took a step backward. "I prefer wine or ratafia."

"Have you ever tried poteen?"

"Well . . . no."

" 'Tis as fine a drink as exists in Ireland," he told her. "Try some."

A sweaty-faced youth with bright red hair appeared at her side. He pressed a cup into her hand. With

Paddy's nod encouraging her onward, she took a timid sip. Liquid fire traced down her throat, into her lungs, and backed up into her nose. She began to cough, violently. Her eyes watered. When she managed to get control of herself she discovered several mourners were watching her.

She smiled weakly and waved at them. "Very good."

Boisterous laughter filled the room. Someone slapped her on the back.

"My wife Moira's bringing more food over. When she returns, I'll introduce you," Paddy offered, amusement lifting his gray brows.

"I look forward to meeting her."

Smiling, Michael returned to her side, grasped her elbow and propelled her toward the white-haired woman. "Mrs. O'Shanley, I'd like you to meet Anne Sherwood. Anne, this is Paddy's mother."

"I'm so sorry for your loss," Anne repeated to her.

Her craggy face wreathed in a sudden smile, Paddy's mother patted her arm. "I'm glad you've come to meet him, lassie, even if you're meeting him in death. He would have liked that. Go say hello to him."

A sense of unreality setting in, Anne turned and approached the corpse. Michael and Paddy's mother accompanied her. Anne looked at the graying face in the coffin and said, "Nice to meet you, Mr. O'Shanley. I do hope your trip to heaven is an uneventful one."

Michael, who hadn't heard Mrs. O'Shanley's request, stared at her with wide eyes, then threw back his head and roared with laughter. Paddy's mother laughed too. Anne looked askance at them both. She had a faint sense that somehow, Mrs. O'Shanley had made a fool of her.

Once he'd gotten his laughter under control,

Michael steered her to a corner of the kitchen. The men standing there made room for them and bent warm smiles on her. Anne turned around to contemplate the rest of the folk in the kitchen.

She stuck her elbow into Michael's ribs to get his attention. "I normally don't make a habit of chatting with corpses. I spoke to this corpse because Mrs. O'Shanley asked me to, and I'm unfamiliar with your traditions. For all I knew, you Irish whirl around the room with your dead before you bury them. Why did Mrs. O'Shanley deliberately set out to make a fool of me?"

"Don't take it personally, lass," he murmured. "Insults are an art form here in Ireland, and scogging is one of the favorite pastimes practiced at a wake."

"Scogging?"

"Certain persons are made the butt of jokes, to entertain the others present. As an Englishwoman you were bound to serve as the butt to at least one taunt."

"She certainly enjoyed scogging me," Anne murmured.

He shrugged. "Resentment of the jibe only makes matters worse. The better you put up with it, the sooner it's over. I'd say you handled yourself beautifully. Look, they've already moved on to someone else."

A titter of laughter from the corner of the room caught her attention. Two large, bearded men were discussing a hapless young lad named George who stood barefoot, his long hair unkempt. Evidently it was George's turn to be scogged.

Shaking her head, Anne looked elsewhere.

Several women with plates of beef, bread, potatoes, and cheese were circulating among the attendees, offering nourishment. Anne thought the potatoes looked remarkably plump and golden. Another woman pressed glasses of amber-colored liquid into their hands. Poteen, Anne guessed, vowing to avoid the fiery stuff in the future.

Michael took two glasses from the poteen-serving woman and handed one to Anne. She took it and sipped, thinking, *What the hell.* She'd broken every other vow she'd made over the past two months. Why not this one?

A fit of coughing overcame her and passed quickly. The world suddenly became much warmer, and Michael's eyes darker, full of liquid promise. Her mood began to improve rather quickly.

She moved closer to Michael, earning a quick glance from him. "When should we talk to Paddy? Now?"

"Not yet. The mood isn't right."

"When will it be right?"

"Soon. Until then, we enjoy ourselves."

17

❧❧

*B*y eleven o'clock that evening, the wake had become quite lively. Clay pipes were making the rounds and guests who tried to carry on a conversation had to speak loudly to hear themselves over the laughter. Anne felt heat in her cheeks and knew the poteen had gotten into her blood. She sat on a stool while Michael stood near her side, protecting her from the stray rowdy who careened in their direction.

Several young men jostled one another over the few remaining stools, each trying to claim one. Clearly drunk, a red-haired youth fell clumsily onto a sack. The sack burst open, spilling potatoes in every direction. Grinning, he picked a potato up and tossed it at Paddy, hitting him squarely on the buttocks.

Paddy spun around, eyes narrowed and fixed on the youths. "Who threw that?"

They all shrugged innocently.

Paddy casually picked up a potato and shoved it into his pocket. As soon as the youths became occupied with another game of push-and-shove, Paddy threw his potato at a youth whose chin sported a scraggly brown beard. The vegetable bounced off brown-beard's head and landed harmlessly on the kitchen floor. Brown-beard wheeled around and scowled at Paddy, who stood in earnest conversation with an elderly man.

The other youths shouted with laughter.

Thus began a free-for-all where everyone was throwing potatoes, but in a sneaky way, all but the clumsiest culprits remaining undetected. Potatoes weren't the only objects sailing through the air, either. People who had their backs turned were squirted with water. Someone found a basket of turnips, and soon they too joined the melee. Horseplay became the order of the night.

Michael caught a stray potato flying through the air and handed it to Anne. "Ammunition," he whispered.

"You don't really expect me to throw this." A smile crept onto her lips. The whole scene was very silly but amusing, too.

"Keep it as a memento," he suggested, and abruptly she wanted to throw it at *him*. She hefted it her hand, almost giving in to the impulse. The potato's soft golden skin stopped her.

She ran a curious finger along the vegetable's curves. "This is a very fine potato."

Michael leaned closer. "Pardon?"

"I said, this is a very fine potato."

Both of his eyebrows climbed upward. "Oh?"

"Don't you think it's remarkably large and blemish-free?" she insisted, feeling slightly idiotic.

He took the potato from her and examined it closely. "Now that you mention it, it *is* a fine specimen."

"It reminds me of the vegetables in Connock's Eden. Is that possible?"

Michael nodded. "More than possible. Lord Connock regularly supplies the village with produce from his glasshouses."

She jerked backward, her hand fluttering to her throat. An image of a black adder formed in her mind, twined around a piece of ivy. "I had no idea."

"Do you object to the notion?"

Her attention fell first on Paddy and the odd growth behind his ear, then shifted to others in the room who displayed similar deformities. Her heart quickened. "Indeed I do. Lord Connock's research is still in the experimental stage. His vegetables may look and taste fine, but who knows what sorts of effect they will have on people?"

"The villagers have been eating Connock's produce for many, many years. Believe me, they're the strongest, healthiest people within fifty miles."

"Look at Paddy, Michael. He's got some sort of deformity behind his ear. So do many of the other people in this room."

"The older people, you mean."

"I don't see why their age is an issue."

"If Lord Connock's vegetables were poison of some sort, wouldn't everyone who ate them show symptoms? The youngest and the oldest share from the same plate; and yet, only the old ones have deformities. I think the deformities are a result of the famine."

Anne remained unconvinced. "Perhaps the effects of the vegetables are cumulative. Only those who have eaten them for a certain number of years show symptoms. Or maybe the vegetables only affect the weakest."

"We can come up with several theories, all of them equally plausible, no?"

"I suppose you're right." A horrible thought occurred

to her. She gripped Michael's arm far too tightly. "Do you eat the produce from Lord Connock's glasshouses?"

"No, I purchase from local farms, to support the villagers. Lord Connock does the same."

"How convenient."

Michael's eyes narrowed. "Indeed. You've whetted my curiosity. I think it's time to ask some questions."

Anne stood, relinquishing her stool, and followed Michael through masses of people who jostled and pressed against her good-naturedly. The room had become very close indeed and moisture formed on her brow. She brushed it away and bumped into Michael's backside.

He had stopped to converse with a pretty red-haired woman, whose tresses flowed down her back in a luscious unpinned mass. Self-consciously Anne touched her own tightly coiled chignon and wondered if she looked as frumpy as she suddenly felt. Working her way around to his side, Anne wished she'd taken a bit more time with her appearance this evening.

"Mrs. Sherwood, I'd like to introduce you to Moira O'Shanley, Paddy's wife," Michael said.

"A pleasure to meet you, Mrs. O'Shanley." Anne touched the other woman's arm. "I'm sorry we had to meet under such troublesome circumstances. You have my deepest sympathies."

"We'll miss Mr. O'Shanley, there's no doubt about that," the redhead admitted. "Thank you for coming, Mrs. Sherwood."

Paddy's wife began to talk of village matters. While Michael joined in the conversation, Anne could only follow politely, knowing little about Balkilly. She studied the woman for deformities as they spoke, but saw nothing other than a slight rounding of the woman's belly.

Apparently old Paddy was young at heart.

"I returned from the China Seas a month ago," Michael drawled on. "Saw Paddy at the Balkilly Arms my first night home. Heard some interesting tales, too, from Sean O'Sullivan."

"Interesting tales?" Moira asked, her attention divided between Michael and her mother-in-law, who had begun to keen softly at the foot of the coffin. "Sean O'Sullivan ought to stick to managing that inn rather than telling Paddy's tales."

Anne focused fully on their conversation.

"So you know that Paddy's been having some odd experiences in the forest," Michael said.

"I know about them." Moira nodded her head for emphasis. "And I'm believing him, unlike Mr. O'Sullivan, who thinks my Paddy dips into the poteen overmuch."

"When I spoke to Mr. O'Sullivan," Michael hastened to reassure her, "that laddie had fear in his eyes. I'd say he's believing Paddy. What happened to your husband, Moira?"

"One night, about four months ago, he was coming home from the Arms and took a shortcut through the woods." Moira leaned closer to Anne and Michael and lowered her voice. "He said he heard a rustling in the bushes but dismissed it as nothing . . . at first. Then he began to smell it. Paddy said that in all his days, he'd never smelled anything as putrid—like something had died, but sugary too. The rustling, which at first had a secretiveness to it, suddenly became bold, and Paddy felt something snake around his ankle."

Anne nodded, the other woman's tale striking chords of recognition within her.

"Go on," Michael encouraged.

"Well, the thing in the woods grabbed my Paddy and brought him down. Paddy felt it wrapping around his leg and creeping upward toward his . . . unmentionables. At the same time, something tried to get into his mouth. Paddy managed to pull out the little knife he carries around in his pocket, and he cut the thing off his mouth, then off his leg." Color suffused Moira's face.

Michael put a steadying hand on Moira's arm. "Did he ever see what attacked him?"

"When my poor Paddy came home, his mouth was bleeding, and he had a rope burn around his ankle. He brought me a piece of the thing that got him to prove his story."

The sudden sharpening of Michael's features betrayed his excitement. "Did you keep it?"

"I did, though it brings me nightmares."

"Moira, you must show it to us."

"All right. You can even take it with you. I'd rather have it out of my house. Come this way."

Frowning, the red-haired woman led them back through the kitchen to a well-kept scullery piled high with jars, sacks and earthenware dishes. She selected a jar with a wide mouth from a shelf, then yanked its cork top off. "Here it is, though I have to say it looks a wee bit different from how it did when Paddy brought it home."

Her frown becoming a grimace of distaste, Moira turned the jar over and poured it into the sink. Anne craned her neck forward to see its contents.

A dried piece of a plant lay listlessly against the porcelain. The plant's general appearance had a lot in common with normal ivy. Still, Anne noticed differences, too. Jubilation filled her. They finally had their specimen.

"Ivy," Anne breathed.

"That isn't ivy," the other woman declared, her chin set. "When Paddy brought it home, it was all plump-like and had leaves with the texture of sandpaper. Pick it up and look at it. You'll see."

Gingerly Michael grasped the ivy between two fingers and examined it from all angles.

Anne leaned close to study it, too. "This ivy hasn't the smooth margin of a normal leaf," she murmured. "Its edge is serrated, like a saw or a knife. And the texture is all wrong, as Mrs. O'Shanley said."

"I have to return to the kitchen," Moira announced. "You two look all you want at it, and then throw it out. Now that I've shared the story with someone else, I'm done with it." The redhead turned with a swirl of her skirts and left the scullery.

"Now we can say for sure that it isn't a species native to Ireland," Anne whispered. "It almost has a tropical jungle look to it."

"Lord Connock must have created it," Michael agreed.

"He said he was creating vegetable plants. This isn't a vegetable. Even worse, it's escaped the glasshouse. Why would Lord Connock allow it to roam free? The thing is a danger to us all."

Michael's voice dropped to a whisper. "Only by examining the mother plant will we understand exactly what we're up against. We have to find it."

"How? We've looked for almost a month now and discovered nothing at all."

"Maybe we need some bait to attract it, like blood."

"You mean you want to set a trap?"

"Why not? I'll act as the bait, and when it comes for me, I'll follow the vine back to the mother plant. At least then we'll know its location."

Anne stared at him, wide-eyed. "Michael, I don't want you to risk yourself."

Frowning, Michael dropped the ivy back into the jar and capped it. "I don't see that we have a choice."

"Once you find the mother plant, what will you do?"

"Destroy it, of course."

They exchanged glances. Wide-eyed, she took in his scowl and knew he would find that mother plant at any cost. While she admired his determination, the thought of him tangling with the ivy made her stomach turn sour flips.

She slipped her arm around his waist. Abruptly she wanted to forget the ivy, to forget Lord Connock and everything that had gone wrong in Glendale Forest. "We've spent enough time worrying for one night. Let's return to the kitchen and try to relax."

He nodded, his big body leaning against her in an altogether pleasant manner. This time she led him through the people milling about, and found an open space near the coffin. Michael set the jar on a shelf. His arm went around her until their bodies were locked together, side by side. She knew their close embrace would cause speculation but she didn't care, not tonight, not on the evening when she'd discovered she loved him, not when she knew how limited their time together was.

A few old men sat nearby, a crate set up between them. They each held a hand of cards. Her eyes widening, Anne noticed that the corpse also held a hand of cards. "Michael, look . . . they're playing cards with the dead Mr. O'Shanley."

"Card playing was one of O'Shanley's favorite pastimes," Michael informed her, unconcerned. "He used to sit until all hours of the night at the Balkilly

Arms, playing *macham*. They're honoring his memory."

A low-pitched murmuring caught her attention. The elder Mrs. O'Shanley was sitting near her husband's head, speaking into his dead ears, her voice throbbing with anguish: *"Ce dheanfaidh gno an mharga? Ce raghaidh go Cnoc an Aifrinn, a's tusa sinte feasta? Och, ochon!"*

"Is Mrs. O'Shanley all right?" Anne asked.

"She's doing what she needs to do."

"What is she saying?"

"She's asking him who will go to the market and to Mass with her, now that he's dead."

Conversation languished beneath Mrs. O'Shanley's grief, which grew stronger by the moment. The mood in the room went from high-spirited to worried.

"For hours, she's been laughing and carrying on," Anne whispered to Michael. "I wonder why she's at last surrendered to her grief."

"I suspect she's finally comfortable that her husband's soul has left his body. Folklore tells us that the devil's dogs try to snatch souls as they leave their bodies. Premature keening of the dead might wake the dogs before the soul has had enough time to escape."

Two old women moved to the widow's side, put arms around her, and led her from the coffin. Paddy watched his mother leave, then sent a gray-haired man in a tattered frieze coat a fierce look. The gray-haired man promptly yanked a battered fiddle case from beneath his chair and opened it, revealing a woebegone-looking instrument. He lifted that old fiddle into his arms and began to play a lively reel.

Conversation resumed. The mood swayed toward merriment once again. Those in the center of the kitchen cleared out, pressing Anne and Michael against the wall.

Anne shook her head. "I can hardly keep up with the quick shifts of emotion. First we laugh, then we cry, then we play cards and dance."

"To the Irish, death and life are but two sides of the same coin." Michael pulled her against him, until her buttocks pressed into his thighs. He rested his chin on her head. "We embrace both, and in doing so, fear neither."

The fiddle wailed, as though demanding that people start dancing. Four couples moved into position and began to step through the reel. Before long, they were stomping their feet so hard that the floor shook beneath them. Anne clapped as they finished the reel, and went on to a hornpipe, then a jig.

Everyone perspired freely and whiskey flowed with copious abandon. The music's simple beat worked its way into her veins, and suddenly she wanted to dance too. She hadn't the least idea how to perform the steps for a hornpipe or a jig, but the reel was another matter entirely. The local parties she'd attended in Cambridge as a girl had often featured the reel, and it had become one of the few dances she truly enjoyed.

Paddy wandered in their direction. He still had a few of Lord Connock's cigars and now he offered one to Michael. "Have a smoke, McEvoy."

Smiling his thanks, Michael accepted it. Paddy pulled a wooden stick from his pocket and lit the end in a lantern's flame, then held it to the cigar's tip while Michael puffed. In no time the tip of the cigar glowed a dull red. Michael thanked Paddy again; the gray-haired Irishman nodded and wandered to a man standing a few feet away, another cigar outstretched in his hand.

Anne tried to keep a straight face but ended up coughing as smoke wound its way into her lungs.

"Is the cigar bothering you?" Michael asked.

"No," she lied.

"It's impossible for me to enjoy a cigar if I know I'm offending someone," he said. "I'll give it away."

"Here, give it to me," she said, and took it from his fingers.

Eyebrows raised, he stared at her.

Head cocked at a jaunty angle, she lifted the cigar to her lips and puffed. Heat seared into her lungs, bringing on another coughing fit that left tears in her eyes.

Chuckling, he took the cigar from her and handed it to an elderly man. "I don't think you're ready for a cigar just yet, Mrs. Sherwood."

A sudden ruckus near the coffin drew everyone's attention. Anne stared in that direction and blanched. The corpse was sitting straight up in his eternal bed! She knew that the delayed release of gases occasionally had that effect on the dead, but she'd never witnessed it before herself, and she had to admit, the sight was damned gruesome.

The elder Mrs. O'Shanley rushed over to her dead husband and slapped him sharply across the face. "Speak to me, damn ye. Speak to me!"

All conversation ceased. The fiddler stopped fiddling.

Paddy ran to her side. "There, there," he soothed, the words having little effect on his mother. "You know he's gone."

"Fionn O'Shanley, you speak to me now." Glowering at the corpse, she drew back her hand, ready to slap him again. The same two old women who had first drawn Mrs. O'Shanley away from her husband hurried to reclaim their prisoner, tugging her from the coffin and to a healthy shot of poteen.

Disquieted, Anne looked away.

The fiddler started playing a hornpipe so quick and complicated that it bordered on hysteria. Evidently more used to such happenings than Anne, the crowd threw themselves into laughing and smoking and dancing once again. Paddy began wrestling with the corpse, trying to make it lie back down.

"Want to dance, Mr. McEvoy?" she asked some five minutes later, when the fiddler ended another jig and began sawing a boisterous reel on his instrument. With difficulty, she'd managed to erase from her mind the sight of Mr. O'Shanley sitting up, and said a silent prayer of thanksgiving that his widow hadn't insisted the dead man dance with her.

Michael assessed her features with a quick glance and smiled, evidently liking what he saw. "I'd be delighted, Mrs. Sherwood."

Shouts of encouragement nearly drowned out the fiddle's spirited melody. Women clapped and men stomped their feet, the impromptu drumbeat adding to the feeling of merriment. Tobacco gathered in even thicker clouds as Paddy passed his prized cigars around to whoever wished to puff.

Michael placed one hand on Anne's shoulder and another around her waist, and swept her into the middle of the kitchen. Three other couples lined up behind them. His smile becoming a wicked grin, he galloped her down the middle of the line of couples and back again. Lightheaded, she split from him and skipped down the outside of the set, only to meet with him again at the end.

The second couple wove their way through the

other dancers. Anne stayed in place, tapping her foot to the music, trying to catch her breath. She stole a glance at Michael and realized he was watching her, his lower lip full and sensual, his eyes as dark as his hair. Her body responded to his stare, knowing well what he wanted.

The other dancers daisy-chained, and soon Anne found herself moving back and forth in a dizzying pattern before landing in Michael's arms again. They split into two sets of four and created a right-hand star, then a left-hand star, before lining up again.

Their turn to go down the middle of the set had arrived again. Michael swept her up into his arms and twirled her around in place before setting her on the ground and galloping her through the other couples. Giddy, she threw back her head and laughed aloud. Moments later he swooped down to kiss her full on the mouth before relinquishing her.

Shouts and laughter bubbled around her like champagne, heating her blood and making her bold. Feeling far too warm, she fanned herself with her hand. A few tendrils of hair tickled her neck. Her hair, she discovered, had come loose; their wild dancing must have dislodged the pins. Aware of Michael's gaze upon her, she slowly removed the rest of the pins and ran her fingers through her hair. It flowed freely down her shoulders, just like Mrs. O'Shanley's.

She peeked at him from beneath her lashes. He continued looking at her, wanting her—she could tell by the soft intensity in his eyes and in the way his lower lip protruded. Indeed, he had that look honed to perfection, and even as she wondered how many women he'd used it on, she wet her lips in anticipation. Some little imp of the devil encouraged her to tease him more. She

wondered how far she could go before he lost control
and took matters into his own hands.

He remained polite, and kept her at the proper distance, but his nostrils flared in a primitive manner, as
though he were scenting her. Recklessly she pulled the
fichu from her neckline and tossed it at him. The scrap
of lace landed on his shoulder. He lifted it with two
long fingers and shoved it into a trouser pocket. His
gaze fastened on her breasts and he licked his lower
lip—purposefully, she thought.

Her insides coiled tight. Dangerous, that sparkle in
his eye. Instinct told her that their lovemaking this eve
would go beyond the ordinary, the everyday, to new
realms she hadn't even dreamed of.

When their turn came along again, Michael swept
her into his arms and galloped her down the middle of
the set, but he didn't let her go once they'd reached the
end. Instead, he galloped her right through the crowd,
down the hallway, and outside, much to the amusement
of the onlookers.

Shouts and laughter accompanied them into the
night. His movements urgent, he swung her up into his
arms and gave the Irish lad a coin. Less than a minute
later the lad steered their gig up to the front door.
Michael bundled her into the gig, and not saying anything, drove at a quick pace through the village. Anne
also remained silent, unable to talk for nervous excitement, imagining what he planned to do. She had a
sense that precious time between them was dwindling,
and she wanted to make the most of whatever moments
they had left. She guessed he did too.

At some point the path became too narrow to drive
on any further. Michael lifted her out of the gig and,
holding her in his arms, began a fast walk to his cottage,

leaving the horse and gig behind. He put her down on the porch steps long enough to open the door and then picked her up again, betraying not the slightest strain. He strode inside, navigated around furniture, and then climbed the worn stone risers before entering his bedchamber.

Clinging to him, she tried to identify objects in the room. A small window filled with moonlight helped somewhat. Lanterns, a bureau, a beaten old sea chest, a washstand with porcelain basin and pitcher, and a very large bed dominated the room. The bed, she discovered when he set her down, was soft, the mattress likely filled with goosedown.

She had little time to luxuriate in the softness. Michael turned her around, popped the buttons on the back of her gown, and drew it over her head. The corset came next, along with her slippers and petticoats, leaving her dressed in stockings, a chemise, and pantaloons.

Then, inexplicably, he sat back on his heels. "That's a very pretty chemise," he said, his voice tight. "Take it off for me."

Trembling, she grasped the hem of her chemise and lifted it over her head, aware that his hot gaze never left her. Once she'd exposed her breasts to the night air he swooped down and kissed each nipple, as though he couldn't help himself. "Now the pantaloons."

Her body and her face growing flushed, she untied the drawstring at her waist and slipped the pantaloons down her legs. Naked except for her stockings, she allowed her legs to fall apart slightly. His swiftly indrawn breath told her how much he'd enjoyed the gesture.

"God, you're beautiful," he said, his voice rough, raw. He bent down to kiss her, but she stopped him with an open palm.

"You're still dressed, Michael," she said, climbing onto her knees in front of him to grasp his lapels. "It's a situation I'd like to remedy."

While he stood stock-still, she pulled his evening coat over his shoulders and downward. Once she'd drawn it as low as his elbows, she tightened it around him, imprisoning his arms gently against his sides. Smiling, she stretched upward to kiss his lips, her nipples scratching lightly against his waistcoat. Liking the feel of it, she rubbed her breasts lightly across the embroidered fabric until her nipples hardened, kissing him all the while.

He groaned, low in his throat.

Finally relenting, she allowed his evening coat to fall to the floor. Next she worked on the buttons of his waistcoat, her breasts still rubbing lightly against him, teasing him. She could feel the tension in his arms and torso and wondered how much longer he'd allow her to continue before surrendering to more primal urges.

She pulled his waistcoat off, then started on his shirt buttons. Those were not only numerous but difficult to unfasten. She managed to free most of them but a few defied her every attempt. Impatience built in her. She gripped the fabric on either side of the buttons in her hands and stretched upward for another kiss. This time, however, she bit his lip softly just as she ripped his shirt apart, the few remaining buttons popping onto the floor.

He groaned again and pushed her backward on the bed. She dragged his shirt from his body on their way down. They tangled together, Anne working quickly to unfasten his trousers, then telling him in a throaty voice to take them off. A moment later, his trousers fell into a heap of black superfine at the foot of his bed.

He rolled on top of her, his naked body a glorious weight on hers. His erection pressed against her stomach, hot and velvety smooth and demanding. As Anne took him into her hand, she decided that tonight she would explore his body as thoroughly as he'd explored hers. As soon as the thought formed in her head, she rolled him onto his back and slid down between his legs.

Breathless, she took him into her mouth, but wasn't sure what to do next. Inspiration struck and she began to worship him with her tongue in the same way he'd teased her nipples. His low groans told her she'd picked the right course and soon he was shuddering, his body taut, his eyes squeezed shut.

"Anne, stop," he suddenly growled. Wasting little movement, he pulled her up on top of him, and holding her hips, settled her on his erection. She marveled at the newness of their position and the choices it gave her. Slowly she began to ride him, at first driving him deep into her, then only part of the way in. While she lifted herself up and down, he rubbed her most sensitive part with his thumb, circling and caressing, filling her with mindless pleasure and a deep, relentless ache.

Forgetting herself in pursuit of that ultimate delight, she threw her head back, her hair streaming down behind her to brush his thighs. Now she was thrusting him all the way into her, as far as she could take him, and riding him quickly, her breasts bouncing, wave after wave of bliss mounting inside her. His hands squeezed into her thighs, and his lips parted, his gaze narrowed and he suddenly cried out, trembling all over. She, too, began to shudder as the wave finally crashed against her, swamping her in delight. Exhausted, she fell across his chest.

Murmuring endearments, he rolled her onto her back without ever withdrawing from her, and held her close. Anne snuggled into his embrace and began to wonder how she could continue to let him love her, and still have the strength to leave him when the time came.

18

She woke him up.

"Michael, 'tis almost dawn," she murmured in his ear, her fingers trailing across his chest.

He opened one bleary eye. Her wheat-colored hair spread out across the pillow, she gazed at him with sleepy gray eyes. A flush colored her skin, but Michael was even more aware of the way her limbs fit perfectly with his. *Viking woman,* he thought. All light and softness on the outside, but as stubborn as a tinker's mule and twice as strong on the inside.

"What of it?" he muttered. "The room's still dark. Be quiet, lass, and we'll keep each other warm for another hour or so."

She stretched like a cat, yawned, and then snuggled more tightly into his side. "I have to return to Glendale Hall."

"Let me hold you for a few more minutes, and I'll make you a quick breakfast before we leave."

"All right." She closed her eyes, her lashes brushing

against his skin and tickling him as they fluttered downward.

Counting himself damned lucky to have her in his bed, he gathered her into his arms and looked around his little room. He liked the way her clothes draped over his bureau, across the sea chest, on the floor. They made the place seem different, somehow. Friendlier. Homier. Certainly messier, he thought. Or maybe the clothes hadn't made the difference. Maybe it was Anne who had suddenly made his Irish port-of-call feel like a home.

Michael stopped breathing for a moment.

Had he finally found what he'd been seeking for so long?

The first rays of dawn crept into the bedchamber. He sat straight up. "Stay here, lass; I'll call you when breakfast's ready."

He slipped into a pair of trousers and a shirt, made his way into the kitchen, and started a fire in the hearth. In a matter of minutes he had a pot of oatmeal frothing over the fire, and a teapot full of water ready to boil. As he poured them both tea and began setting out bowls, he considered the notion that home existed only with Anne.

God Almighty, wouldn't that be a fine kettle of fish? The irony of it made him chuckle aloud, a dark chuckle full of dismay. All adult life he'd been searching for a home. He'd finally discovered that elusive sense of belonging, only to realize he stood to lose it again, forever. Was there another woman out there who might fill Anne's shoes someday, and make him love again?

He didn't think so. No one understood him like Anne.

Stirring the pot of oatmeal, he swore softly.

Jesus. He loved her. He hadn't thawed her cold heart. She'd thawed his. At the realization, a flush of heat washed through him, followed quickly by a chill. He swore softly, chills raising bumps on his arms.

He *loved* her.

And on the heels of that thought, another, more insidious one: *Emotional ties don't last.*

A moment later she appeared at the bottom of the stairs, wrapped in his quilt. She walked to his side, kissed him, then covered her mouth to hide a yawn. "I thought you wanted to sleep."

"I changed my mind. Did you sleep well?"

"Not at all, you rogue." She slid down onto the deacon's bench and gathered the quilt around her.

"Did I mention how much better my cottage looks, with you in it?"

"Thanks for the compliment, but I know what I look like in the morning."

He stirred the oatmeal a bit faster. "I don't suppose you'll ever be willing to leave that smoky city of yours and become a permanent fixture here in my cottage."

"Like a bed, or a table?"

"No. Like my wife."

Anne sat up straight, as though someone had poked her. Lips parted she stared at him; then her hand fluttered to her throat and she looked away.

"Never mind," he said quickly, already knowing her answer. "Have a seat. We'll eat, and I'll have you back in Glendale Hall with no one the wiser."

She gathered the quilt more tightly around herself, walked to his side and placed a gentle hand on his arm. "Michael, I—"

Furious pounding on the door interrupted her. Eyes

wide, she scooted over to the stairs and hid in the shadows.

Michael jumped. Only bad news came at this hour. He strode over to the door and opened it a crack.

Paddy's anxious gray face stared in at him. "McEvoy, open the door. Please. 'Tis an emergency."

"What's happened?" Michael let the door swing wide open.

The other man charged inside. "My wife, Moira, she's miscarrying the baby. The doctor's in Dublin visiting family until two days from now. Can you bring Lord Connock to us?"

"I'll get your boots, Michael," Anne said from her position near the door.

He nodded, wincing as Paddy looked in her direction. The old man's eyes widened when he saw Anne. "Mrs. Sherwood!"

"Good morning, Mr. O'Shanley." Her voice steady, she nodded to him.

"I know I can count on your discretion, Paddy."

"Of course you can," the old Irishman agreed.

Michael dragged his jacket on and stuffed his shirttails into his waistband. Still wrapped in a quilt, Anne hurried to his bedchamber, fetched his boots, and returned to the kitchen. With a murmured thanks, he took them from her and shoved his feet into them.

"Why did you bother to come all the way out here to my cottage?" Michael asked Paddy. "You could have run straight to Glendale Hall from the village and saved precious time."

"I've already sent someone to Glendale Hall. Carlyle has no idea where Lord Connock has gotten to."

"Has he checked all the glasshouses?"

"That he has, and no Lord Connock, or Griswold,

either. Carlyle thinks he may have gone into the woods to study some strange tree and suggested you might know where the tree is."

"Yes, I do." Michael headed toward the door. Then, as an afterthought, he turned around and kissed Anne on the nose. "Can you dress and return to Glendale Hall on your own?"

"I'll find a way."

"I'm sorry, Anne."

"We'll talk later," she murmured, her cheeks pinkening. "When we're alone."

Michael kissed her again, then raced out the door with Paddy. "Go back to Moira. I'll find Lord Connock."

"Thanks, McEvoy." Paddy disappeared into the woods.

Michael started off in the opposite direction, toward the sapling. On most days he loved to watch the sun come up in the woods, filtering through the leaves and pine needles with a soft pink glow. This morning, however, shadows abounded and the brush rustled in its threatening way and Michael found himself scanning the forest floor for snakes. Or ivy.

He heard their voices before he saw them. Just as Carlyle had predicted, Lord Connock and Griswold were standing around the golden sapling, talking in low tones. Judging by the way they peered at its leaves and manipulated its trunk, they were evaluating it, in the same way a potential buyer evaluated a horse up for auction.

"Owain," he called out.

Griswold started in surprise. Lord Connock swiveled around to stare at him. The pouches beneath his eyes had turned purple. Gravy spotted his cravat and wrinkles creased his coat and trousers. "Michael? Is something wrong?"

Michael hesitated, shocked at the change in the nobleman's condition. After a second or two he found his voice. "Moira O'Shanley's miscarrying her child. The doctor's in Dublin. Will you help her?"

Connock stiffened, clearly startled by the news. Then he looked at the forest floor, his eyebrows knitted together. "Damn, I thought—"

Griswold quickly put a hand on Connock's arm, his touch silencing the nobleman.

Michael stared at them, perplexed. He wished he had the time to ask Connock to finish his sentence. But he didn't. A woman was losing her baby.

"Are you coming, Owain?" Michael pressed.

"Of course. Griswold, you must fetch my medical bag and bring it to Paddy O'Shanley's house. You know which bag I'm speaking of, Griswold?"

"I'll have it to you right away." Griswold shambled off toward Glendale Hall.

Connock promptly turned to Michael. "Would you lead the way? You know this bloody forest better than I."

"I'll get us there as fast as I can."

Left alone in Michael's cottage, Anne didn't even bother with her corset; in any case, she had no one to lace her in. She wrapped it up in her two petticoats, which she'd also disregarded, and stepped into her gown. Buttoning it proved extremely difficult, particularly when her fingers shook so. She was, in fact, trembling all over.

He had asked her to marry him.

But why? Did he love her?

She could hardly credit it. He didn't *act* as if he loved her. He hadn't *said* that he loved her. Nevertheless, fierce joy bubbled inside her at the knowledge that the man she had grown to love treasured her enough to spend the rest of his life with her.

A life that he'd already told her didn't include London.

She frowned, her joy subsiding.

And what about her? Was she willing to surrender her scholarly aspirations to stay at his side? Perhaps, she mused, she wouldn't have to surrender all that much. If she went to live with him on a farm, she would still be able to sketch and illustrate.

Still, unless she moved in the very best scholarly circles, she'd have a damned hard time publishing her illustrations. She was just a woman, after all. And once she married and gained the monikers *wife* and *mother*, her credibility would spiral downward to nothing.

A hard knot of tension formed in her stomach. She didn't know which to choose. Achievement or marriage? Science or nature? A lifetime of loneliness or Michael's warm smile? Indecision nearly making her ill, she wrapped her shawl around her shoulders, to hide the buttons she couldn't fasten, and left Michael's cottage for the woods.

Sunlight streamed through the treetops, indicating the day had truly begun. Glendale Hall's entire staff, she thought, would be up by now. When she returned this morning, they'd all know she hadn't spent the night within its gray walls. Anne felt quite certain Paddy would supply the missing details, such as where she'd slept and with whom. By the time the day was out, she might not even have a choice between Michael and her scholarly goals. Lord Connock may have discovered her torrid affair with his naturalist and let her go by then.

Moving more quickly, she followed the path through the trees, and after only two wrong turns, entered the clearing that contained the sapling. Throwing the little tree a harassed look, she passed it by and finished the walk to Glendale Hall. Carlyle greeted her as soon as she entered the great hall.

"Good morning, Mrs. Sherwood," he said, his eyes taking in every detail of her appearance. "Will you be repairing to your bedchamber?"

"Ah, yes, Carlyle. Send Jane to me."

"At once, madam." Bowing, he turned on his heel.

"Oh, Carlyle?"

He swung back to face her.

"Any word on Mrs. O'Shanley?"

"None at all."

"Please let me know when you discover anything."

"If you wish." Inclining his head this time, he left the hall.

Anne hurried up the steps to the second floor and her bedchamber. Once she'd entered its depths she shut the door and leaned against it. She needed some time by herself. To think.

A knock on the door promptly dashed that plan.

"Who is it?" Anne called out.

"Jane, ma'am. I'm having water brought up for a bath."

Anne opened the door, her mood lifting somewhat. A bath would be perfect.

The lady's maid bustled in, her cheeks bright, evidently with a need to gossip. "So I'm assuming you've heard about poor Moira O'Shanley."

"I've only heard the basics: that she was miscarrying her baby. Is there any news?"

"Fiona Mor, the charwoman, arrived but a short while ago from the village. She says that Lord Connock wasn't able to save Moira's baby."

"Lord, she must be devastated."

Jane nodded. " 'Tis a terrible thing to lose a child, especially for the third time."

"The *third* time?"

"In five years."

Anne tried to make sense of such horrible luck. "Poor Mrs. O'Shanley. She looked so healthy last night, at the wake."

"I heard you went to the O'Shanleys' to pay your respects, with a certain Mr. McEvoy, and did more than your share of dancing." Jane shook out a fresh gown for Anne to wear.

"Yes, I did, and I feel guilty for it. Somehow, it just isn't proper to enjoy oneself at a wake."

"And you say Moira looked well?"

"Roses bloomed in her cheeks," Anne insisted. "She was the prettiest woman there."

The lady's maid frowned. "Poor Moira. She ended up just like the rest."

"Like the rest? Whatever do you mean?"

Two footmen appeared at the door, a large porcelain tub in their hands. Jane broke off their conversation as she directed the footmen to place the tub near the fireplace, then the lady's maids to fill the tub. When the bath was ready, the room cleared out but for Anne and Jane.

Anne disrobed and stepped into the tub. The water rose and ebbed over her skin, drawing a long, heartfelt sigh from her. Still, she couldn't relax, not with Jane's last statement hanging unexplained between them.

"Tell me what you meant by saying that Moira ended up just like the rest," Anne said.

"Haven't you noticed that there aren't many children romping in the streets of Balkilly?"

Lathering rose-scented soap in her hair, Anne thought back to the few times she'd been in the village. "I've only visited the village at night, when most children would have been abed."

"Take my word for it, ma'am. There are very few children in Balkilly. Through the years, many of the women in Balkilly have miscarried. No one knows why. Of those few babies that survive, many die a few months later, from illness."

Anne froze, her hands still buried in her soap-filled hair. Just the previous evening, she and Michael had discussed the possibility that Connock's vegetables were causing the villagers' defects. Michael had dismissed the idea, pointing out that only older people showed deformities. Now she learned that children were hard to come by in Balkilly. If the vegetables affected the weakest, that would include the very old . . . *and the very young.*

Anne finished lathering, moving more slowly now. Coldness grew in the pit of her stomach. Something in her rebelled at the thought of Connock's vegetables creating miscarriages. If so, why hadn't Connock noticed the effects before now, and why hadn't he stopped sending his vegetables down to the villagers? Perhaps he felt miscarriages were a regrettable, yet unavoidable side effect of his experimentation.

Jane moved close to rinse Anne's hair with a bucket of warm water. Anne gripped her arm. "You mustn't eat Lord Connock's vegetables."

The maid's eyes widened. "That's an odd suggestion. Why shouldn't I?"

Hesitating, Anne released the girl. She didn't dare accuse Lord Connock of such a heinous crime without adequate proof. Suddenly the mere thought of the nobleman made her stomach turn. How could she continue to work for him, feeling this way?

She couldn't.

Her shoulders caved inward. All of her hopes, her plans, her efforts here in Glendale Hall had been for naught. Her scholarly recognition would have to come from elsewhere. If not for Michael, she might have just curled up in a ball and cried.

Jane frowned. "Are you all right, Mrs. Sherwood? You seem . . . unhappy."

"I'm just in a mood, Jane," Anne said.

Even though she'd decided she could no longer remain in Ireland and sketch for Connock, the load on her shoulders felt ten times heavier. She couldn't leave Balkilly knowing what she did. Somehow, she'd have to find a way to prove that Connock's vegetables were wreaking havoc with the villagers.

"So, why aren't you wanting me to eat Lord Connock's vegetables?" the girl asked.

"I simply meant you must have a balanced diet, including meat and bread. You can't just eat vegetables," Anne invented, wincing at how lame she sounded. She couldn't give her real reason. Not yet.

Her brow scrunched up, Jane tilted her head and stared at Anne. "I eat in the kitchen, with the servants. We all eat rather well."

Anne patted her hand. "Good, Jane. I'm relieved to hear it."

Shaking her head, Jane held a towel open for her. Anne stepped out of the tub, and the maid quickly wrapped the towel around her. Anne dried off, then slipped into a linen wrapper. "Have either Lord Connock or Michael . . . er, Mr. McEvoy—returned from the village?"

"Lord Connock arrived a little while ago and went straight to his glasshouse with Griswold. I don't know if he'll come out. The master's schedule has become so odd that he eats breakfast at midnight and drinks port at nine in the morning. No one's seen Mr. McEvoy."

Frowning, Anne digested this news. She had to talk to Michael, but she wanted to do so with a clear head. Sleep would help. "I believe I'll take a little nap. Wake me for dinner, Jane."

"Of course, ma'am. Sleep well."

Anne lay down on her big four-poster bed. Images of stillborn children and leathery ivy that moved like snakes filled her head. Even so, she drifted off to sleep. When she awoke, she had a nagging sense of having suffered bad dreams. Bleary-eyed, she squinted at the clock on the mantel and discovered she'd slept through the afternoon. And no wonder, considering how long Michael had kept her awake last night with his mischief.

Jane came in soon afterward and announced that no one would be joining her at dinner that evening. Lord Connock had closeted himself in his laboratory and Michael hadn't been seen all day. Rather than sit all alone in that imposing dining room, Anne opted to have a tray brought to her room and spent the rest of the evening pacing. Just when she needed to see him, Michael disappeared. Where had he gone? Should she go and try to find him?

Good God, what a coil! Her life had turned upside-down. Instead of inching closer to the scholarly recognition she so craved, she found herself in love with a man many would judge uncivilized, and faced with the odious task of gathering proof against a scientist who'd run riot. The notion brought a wild chuckle to her lips. Who would have guessed?

More important, where was Michael?

She thought again about searching the forest and village, but her lack of knowledge of the two convinced her she'd be better off waiting for him. He would come for her, if not tonight, then in the morning, to collect her for their daily field trip.

At half past five, her tray arrived, stacked high with cold chicken and vegetables. She eyed it with dismay. Even though she knew Connock's kitchen staff purchased their food in the village, she couldn't help but think of Moira's miscarriage. Her appetite quickly deserted her and she pushed the tray aside.

The rest of the evening in her bedchamber passed slowly. She tried a few books she'd brought earlier to the room, then worked on her illustrations a bit. Her room began to feel stuffy, so she drew back her drapes and opened the window. After staring out at Glendale Forest for a while, she began to flip through her many sketches of Michael, completed over the last three weeks.

The sun had long since set when she at last settled herself into her bed with her nightgown on. By all rights she should have been tired, after weighing her options a hundred times. Nevertheless, she found herself rolling from one side of the bed to the other, then positioning the pillow between her knees, then rolling onto her back . . . nothing seemed to work.

She lay there wide-eyed.

Looked out the window.

Watched the moon make its slow trek across the sky.

Tried to will sleep onto herself.

Cursed with great imagination.

And finally felt herself dozing off.

Screeeech!

Anne sat straight up in bed, her heart pounding. Her mind felt foggy. Half wrapped in a dream. An unpleasant one.

What in God's name . . .

She threw the covers back and stood on shaky legs.

Another screech suddenly pierced the room, this one softer, yet equally disturbing. She fixed her gaze on the window. She'd heard dying rabbits before. They sounded like very small children crying for help. The screech had sounded remarkably like a rabbit caught in a wolf's jaw.

She walked over to the window and peered outside. The moon had disappeared beneath the horizon, leaving the manicured lawns cloaked in blackness. A few stars glittered, but they weren't enough to dispel the gloom that turned the glasshouses into hulking shadows.

An abrupt flash of bluish light caught her attention.

Lightning?

She leaned out the window a bit to better view the property to the left and right. Another blue flash split the darkness, followed by a quick squeal. She focused in the direction it had come from and her gaze settled directly on the composting glasshouse. The one with the flies.

A very faint blue light glowed deep within the composting glasshouse. Elongated shadows moved behind its frosted glass walls. Anne stared, trying to make sense of what she saw. The shadows moved in a sinuous manner, and were long and thin, just like a handful of snakes. The only problem was, snakes didn't usually grow to that size. These seemed more like . . . tentacles.

She squinted at the glasshouse, wishing she had more light. At the same time, she tried to reason it out. How could those squiggly things possibly be tentacles? Lord Connock and Griswold must be in there, doing something with ropes.

That little voice inside her suddenly spoke. It dripped contempt.

Ropes, hah.

Maybe they're dancing, too.

Another burst of light caught her attention. She stared and stared, her eyes hurting with the effort. Then it flashed again, and this time, she noticed something very interesting indeed.

The door to the composting glasshouse was ajar. Not much, perhaps ten inches at most, but enough for someone to get a really good peek at its interior. A breeze blew into the bedchamber. Anne shivered and drew back from the window, her curiosity like poison ivy—an itch she wasn't supposed to scratch. The clock on the mantel read three in the morning, the darkest and loneliest time of night.

Curiosity killed the cat . . .

The voice again.

Anne frowned. She didn't really want to go down there investigating. Not now. Not when anything at all could happen, and no one would hear her scream, because Carlyle snored loudly enough to wake the dead and the footmen always dozed when they were supposed to be alert and no one would hear her.

Absently she stroked the curtains, thinking, *Be sensible. What could possibly happen?* One might think Satan himself lived down in that glasshouse, the way she was carrying on. At three in the morning, after hours of bad dreams, emotions rode close to the surface. Her logic had surrendered to primitive instinct. Lord Connock or Griswold was probably stirring the compost.

At three in the morning?

She reminded herself that the nobleman no longer kept a normal schedule. He ate breakfast at midnight and drank port at nine in the morning. Perhaps he now stirred his compost at three.

Still, those shadows . . .

Her gaze flitting from the glasshouse to her wardrobe, she edged over to wardrobe and opened it. Her old flannel robe and leather slippers hung innocently on a peg. Easy to reach, warm, comfortable, they nearly begged her to wear them. She grabbed them and slipped them on before she'd really known what she was going to do.

Now that she had dressed, she needed a candle. For what? An expedition, of course. An expedition into the night and the composting glasshouse that probably contained some smelly old rotting food but might conceal something large and tentacled, something that looked a lot like ivy and had an appetite for flesh. She wasn't going to gather any evidence against Connock by sitting in her bedchamber. She had to go down there.

Lips pressed together, Anne lit a candle and fixed it in a porcelain candle holder with a loop to hook her thumb in. She picked the candle up and watched its puny flame tremble violently. She held her shaking hand still with her free one and the flame evened out.

Gripping the candleholder with both hands, she edged into the hallway. Thin shadows stretched upward at odd angles, like fingers clutching at the cold night air. She began to hum, very softly, one of the songs that had received several plays at Mr. O'Shanley's wake: *Deal on, deal on, my merry men all, deal on your cakes and your wine; for whatever is dealt at his funeral today shall be dealt to-morrow at mine.* For some reason, she didn't feel so lonely when she hummed.

She crept through the hall and down the staircase, pausing in the great hall to gain her bearings. Her humming trailed off. Just as she'd suspected, the two footmen charged to remain at the front door—awake— snored softly. Otherwise, the house had the silence of a tomb. To avoid waking the footmen, Anne sneaked into the kitchen, passed embers that glowed a dull red in the open-hearth fireplace, and slipped out through the servants' entrance.

In the past, she'd always used the front door rather than the kitchen door. Now she regretted it. She hadn't the slightest idea how to find the composting glasshouse from the servants' entrance and didn't relish the idea of stumbling around in the dark.

Grimacing, she picked her way down the steps and paused on the flagstone landing. She'd entered some sort of kitchen garden, a veritable maze of herbs, early vegetables, and berry bushes that formed a prickly wall, hiding the glasshouses beyond.

Where would she find the gate leading out?

She looked for a break in the berry-bush hedge, her candle flickering dangerously in the breeze. The hedge seemed impenetrable. Taking a deep breath, she walked along its perimeter and found nothing. Her shoulders drooped. Was she finished before she'd even started?

She began searching again. *Deal on, deal on, my*

merry men all . . . Chives, basil, lemon balm, sweet peas, lavender—

Something made her pause. Not sure why, she scented the breeze, her eyes as wide as she could make them, and studied the kitchen garden. After a minute or so she saw it. A pile of gardener's tools, the kind she'd lived with most of her life. A rake, a hoe, a crooked wheelbarrow, and a pile of rope.

Rope. Coiled around and around, in a neat little circle. Just like a sleeping snake.

In the meager light it had a soft gray color.

Dark leaves partially hid its coils.

It was too dark to tell if the leaves were normal ones or had more in common with the ivy that had tried to creep into Paddy's mouth and his unmentionables . . . if one believed the tale of a man who liked his poteen far too much. Anne wrinkled her nose. Why in *hell* would Paddy claim the ivy had attacked his unmentionables?

Whatever the reason, she didn't like the way that rope was just lying there, all innocent-looking. Instinct told her it was far from innocent. Indeed, she had an urge to stay as far away from it as humanly possible. Watching the rope-snake carefully and feeling foolish for doing so, she lifted her candle high and backed away from its coils. As she moved, she glanced behind it and saw a rusted iron gate.

Damn, damn, damn.

She would have to step over the thing, or remain trapped in the kitchen garden. Candle lifted about waist-high, she studied the leaves around the rope. They weren't moving. They hadn't moved during the entire time she'd crept around in the kitchen garden. Perhaps they were leaves from some other vine, like the honeysuckle or trumpet flower.

She examined the rope next. A large knot in the rope formed its head. It had frayed beyond the knot, like a forked tongue. All it had to do was hiss and she'd run screaming. Her eyes aching, she searched its soft gray coils for movement. Several minutes passed in this manner. Should she, shouldn't she, should she, shouldn't she . . .

Another faint burst of bluish light from behind the berry hedge finally convinced her. If she wanted to see inside that composting glasshouse, she would have to face the rope-snake. Shaking her head at her own absurdity, she gathered up her nightgown and wrapper in one hand and moved forward. Carefully. One step at a time. Humming all the while, the sound of her voice loud in the stillness of the night. *Deal on, deal on, my merry men . . .*

When she had drawn about eight feet away from it, the rope quivered. Anne stopped short, her heart slamming in her chest. Had she really seen it move, or had her overworked imagination invented the movement? She stared at its knot-head, thinking it had mesmerized her as surely as a cobra mesmerizes its evening meal. Crickets ticked off the seconds with each chirp. The rope remained quiescent, the leaves immobile.

Anne frowned. It had quivered, all right, but that didn't mean it planned to bite her. That didn't mean it planned to slither into her mouth or unmentionables, and it didn't even suggest the rope was alive. A mouse must have been hiding in its coils. The mouse had made it twitch. And when she drew closer, the mouse would make it twitch even more. Mice didn't like people and this one would likely burrow for cover. When she saw the rope twitching as she stepped over it, she would remain calm and think of the tiny mouse that felt even more frightened than she.

She tried to take a step toward the rope-snake. Her feet seemed attached to the ground, as though they'd taken root. They refused to move forward. She took one deep, hitching breath.

Nothing's going to happen, she told herself. *Go.*

Go, go, go!

With a little moan she started toward the rope-snake. A breeze blew through the garden and made the leaves covering its coils rustle. Or had they rustled because it knew she was coming? Swallowing, she took larger steps until she came close enough to jump it. It hadn't moved, but a scream formed in her throat nevertheless. Tightening her throat so the scream wouldn't escape, she jumped over the rope-snake with more aplomb than Jack-Be-Nimble, her nightgown and wrapper billowing around her.

Breathing hard, she raced to the gate and fumbled at its hasp with fingers that shook. Behind her, she heard a stealthy slithering in the herbs. It was coming after her. Whimpering now, she smacked the hasp with her palm in frustration, then pulled at it, silently begging. Praying.

Come on, come on . . .

The hasp suddenly clicked upward, too far, past the latch, pinching her fingers. She yelped, thinking, *Almost there. Hold steady.*

Something slithered in the herbs again. To her left. Bigger this time. Nearly crying, she rattled the hasp, coaxed it, threatened it, and with a suddenness that nearly overwhelmed her it slipped into the latch. The gate swung open. Anne pelted through, certain the rope-snake was hot on her heels.

She threw a glance over her shoulder and stopped short.

The rope still lay innocently coiled exactly where she'd seen it first. She turned around fully, her body still throbbing with panic, and studied the rope. The damned thing had never moved.

A relieved laugh burst from her.

Move over, village idiot, and make room for Anne Sherwood.

Shaking her head at her own folly, she turned away and started down the path.

Something tickled her ankle.

She froze. Slowly she pivoted on her heel and stared into the kitchen garden.

The rope was gone.

A tendril wrapped around her leg, then crept upward. Exploring. Prospecting. She only had a nightgown on, with nothing underneath, no barriers. She yanked her hem upward and clawed at it, nausea turning her stomach over and over. The tendril came off her with a dry crackle.

Around her feet, the rope-snake lay coiled, its knothead lifting upward like some foul serpent. She realized it wasn't a rope at all but a thick gray vine, one that wanted to explore her unmentionables just as it had tried to explore Paddy's. Some primitive, hysterical part of her whispered *I told you so*.

Groaning, she staggered away. Her feet moved faster and faster until she was running, top speed, down the path, away from the vine. She ran at least one hundred yards before feeling safe enough to slow down. Still, she didn't see the large, smooth rock in the middle of the path until the last second. She stumbled over it and fell down on the grass.

Her candle smothered among the dew-soaked blades. Pain lanced through her ankle and for one agonizing moment she thought she'd either broken it or the ivy had gotten her. She scrabbled at her foot and discovered that she'd simply twisted it, and not all that badly. The pain was already fading.

Anger took its place, surprising her with its white-hot intensity. Had any scientist more irresponsible than Connock ever lived? He'd released some sort of pestilent ivy into the woods, and now it preyed on innocent passersby. Twice it had tripped her and nearly frightened her into her grave. Silently she vowed it wouldn't have a third chance.

She hoisted herself to her feet and hobbled down the path, more determined than ever to discover what Connock had concealed in that composting glasshouse.

19

*A*nne had almost reached the composting glasshouse when she realized she'd left the candle behind. For a moment she considered returning to retrieve it, but then decided it would do her little good snuffed. She'd retrieve it on her way back to her bedchamber.

Instead, she stared at the soft glow deep within the glasshouse, some twenty-five feet away. Her nose twitched at a honeylike odor, sweetness covering decomposition, which wafted through the air stronger than ever. The shadows in its interior leaped and moved in long, sinewy dances, their meaning beyond her. At least the squealing had stopped.

Another burst of light caught her attention. It illuminated the partially open door. The glasshouse, she mused, kept drawing her forward with its flashes. She felt like a foolhardy sailor who watched a lighthouse beacon and misread it as an invitation to sail ashore, rather than beware the rocky shoals. Nevertheless, she closed the remaining twenty-five feet to the glasshouse and paused next to the door. She stared at the darkness inside with a horrible fascination, then touched the door with one finger. It felt dry and smooth and slightly warm.

Come on in.

She jerked, the thought coming from nowhere. Her heartbeat quickened. She felt sick, her throat tight, nearly insane with bravado. Of course, she was going inside. She had to see what sort of tentacled pest kept trying to slip into her pantaloons.

Smothering a wild giggle with her hand, she pressed her ear against the glass wall. Very faintly, voices echoed from within: Lord Connock's and Griswold's. The sound bolstered her courage. Clearly the two men had whatever-it-was under enough control to prevent themselves from being attacked, so it would be safe for her, too.

She slipped around to the other side of the door and, with her back pressed against the wall, peered around the corner. Shapes at a crazy angle filled her vision. Squinting, she waited for her vision to adjust to the even deeper blackness inside the glasshouse. Eventually the shapes came into better focus and she discovered that she'd stumbled upon some sort of tool shed. A large, flat-headed shovel, perfect for shoveling manure or compost, lay against the wall, along with a host of other gardening equipment.

Without warning, bluish light began to flicker from behind another door inside the tool shed, this one wooden. Remembering the construction of the other glasshouse she'd visited—Connock's Eden—she understood that this room was an antechamber that led into the glasshouse proper. Beyond the door, she heard Griswold murmuring in his raspy voice.

She crept up to the wooden door, pressed her ear against it, and listened.

"I want to be done with this, Owain," the old gardener complained. "I'm a-tired of smelling it."

"Blood and bone are the finest nutrients nature has to offer," Lord Connock said in patient tones. "We should finish in another few moments, and then we'll see how well the new grafts take."

A soft whirring noise accompanied their conversation.

Her touch gentle, she put her hand on the door latch. They had it in there, whatever it was. Coldness seeped through her body, and she thought: *I'm not really going to open this door. I'm going to mind my own business and return to my bedchamber.* Clearly of another opinion, her fingers lifted the latch and allowed the door to swing inward an inch or so.

She fitted her eye to the crack and stared.

Lord Connock huddled around a table fitted with the same apparatus as in the Eden glasshouse—copper tubing, some coiled and some straight, a collection of surgical instruments, vats of fluid, apothecary jars, and the like. In the center of the table, a rabbit lay spread-eagled on its back, in the most ignominious position imaginable, all its furry little parts visible. Thrust forward for examination, in fact. Leather straps held it in place.

Evidently the squeals had been the sounds of its struggle, but it wouldn't struggle anymore. Its eyeballs protruded from their sockets like huge, glassy marbles. Unblinking, they had the sheen of death to them. Partially vivisected, its entrails hanging out at neat, surgical angles, the rabbit dripped blood into a metal basin.

Anne shifted her attention to Griswold, who sat partially in the shadows, his legs pumping up and down at a frenzied pace. He was sitting on a peculiar contraption and wheezing with the effort. The whirring noise came from the contraption.

"Faster, Griswold, faster," Lord Connock urged, and then clamped four metal pincers to various points on an ivy vine she hadn't noticed before. Similar to the one she'd seen in the kitchen garden, the vine coiled behind the table before disappearing into the dirt.

Wires connected the metal pincers to a black box. Griswold seemed to be powering the black box with his effort; sparks began to shoot out from a vent on the top. As she watched, blue arcs of lightning shot along the wires, concentrated in the metal pincers, and administered shocks to the vine.

The vine reacted by smoking a bit. Lord Connock wiped fluid on the contact point and the smoke dissipated. The ivy leaves began to rustle as if caught in a light breeze. As the seconds passed, their rustling became more noticeable until finally the vine itself began to creep along the laboratory table. With perverted eagerness it immersed itself in the blood that had collected in the metal basin. A minute later, the ivy leaves had sucked the blood up like a sponge, leaving nothing behind.

Her gorge rising until she felt certain she'd throw up, Anne covered her mouth with her hand. Lord Connock, she thought, had stepped over the line between good and evil. Such freakish specimens couldn't possibly have any positive effect on society. Looking at him now, with his oily hair, dirty clothes, and eyes dark and narrowed, she could easily believe him capable of feeding poisoned vegetables to the villagers.

Sweat running down his forehead, Griswold climbed off his seat. "Are you pleased, Owain?"

Busy with a machine squatting on the laboratory table, Lord Connock nodded. "Tolerably. I had expected a higher absorption rate. We'll have to fiddle with the graft a bit."

"You're going to be wanting me on that damned contraption again?"

"I'll have you on that damned contraption every night if I need to, Griswold," Connock snapped. "Don't forget your place."

"And you'd better not be threatening *me*. I'd only have to say one word in the right ear and you'd be finished."

The nobleman shifted his gaze to a pitch-black portion of the glasshouse several yards behind the gardener. "You're becoming a liability, Griswold."

Griswold jerked his head around to stare at the same place. "When are you going to let me burn that thing? It's escaped from the glasshouse to root in the forest, and I'm tired of covering up its messes."

"I see no need to burn it."

"It's hungry, and it's feeding. The villagers have begun to notice, Owain. Soon they'll be up here with pitchforks and torches to burn the place and string us up."

"That *thing* is my creation. I feel for it as you might feel for a son or daughter. I can't burn it. What parent kills a child for misbehaving?"

"It'll come to no good, mark my words," Griswold said in dire tones.

Lord Connock shrugged off the old gardener's prediction and continued to work on the machine.

Her internal temperature plummeting, Anne

squinted at the blackness deep within the glasshouse. She couldn't see a thing. Even so, she had a pretty good idea what Griswold objected to.

The black box that had produced the shocks for Lord Connock's experiments suddenly belched a flash of bluish-white light, illuminating even into the far reaches of the glasshouse. In that brief glimpse she saw something rooted in the dirt, something very big and gray, with many branches and leaves—only the branches moved like snakes and the leaves trembled with a gentle susurration.

Anne cried out, but the sound never left her lips. Shock had frozen her vocal cords, bottling the sound up inside her until she shook with the force of it. She blundered backward, knocking into the tools and scattering them.

Lord Connock and Griswold froze.

Her heart flapping wildly in her chest, she spun on her heel and charged out of the glasshouse. My God, she thought, what was it, where had it come from, why had he made it, *why, why, why?* Her temples pounding, she half ran, half staggered back to Glendale Hall and crept inside the front door, taking care not to wake the footmen who still snored peacefully.

An image of the thing formed in her mind as she crossed the hall. Her stomach rolled with nausea. Quickly she banished the image. A few moments later it returned. It wouldn't leave her alone. When she finally skittered into her bedchamber and shut the door, she felt as though she'd fought in a war. She ached everywhere. A vise of pain tightened around her head.

Grimacing, she locked the door, placed the key near her bedside, and collapsed onto the bed. She could spend all week trying to answer what and why. The true question was, had she escaped detection? Lord Connock knew someone had been spying on him, but he didn't know *who*.

And if he found out, then what? He would probably consider her a threat, someone who might expose him. How far would he go to ensure that his experiments continued? Murder?

Cold to the bone, Anne grabbed the key off the nightstand and clutched it in her palm. She huddled under the covers.

With such a secret, why would he even invite her to Glendale Hall to study his plants? Little by little he'd revealed his experiments to her. He must have realized she would eventually stumble upon the whole truth. Were her illustrations so wonderful that they compensated for the risk he was taking?

No. They weren't.

He'd brought her here for another reason.

She shivered as certain things became clearer in her mind.

There was only one thing that made her special besides her illustrations: her gift for sensing plants' emotions. Growing even colder, she thought back to all the times she had betrayed her unusual skill and had immediately gained Connock's undivided attention. She hadn't told him flat-out about her ability, but she'd certainly dropped enough hints.

Somehow, he wanted to use her gift. Perhaps he wouldn't murder her in her bed. Indeed, Connock couldn't even be sure she was the one who'd spied upon him. She'd run away so quickly into the shadows that he couldn't have possibly seen her. She also felt reasonably certain no one had observed her creeping around the house and lawn, so the servants wouldn't give her away.

What about the candlestick?

Anne sucked in a breath. The candlestick! She'd forgotten it in the grass. Lord Connock would find it, she had no doubt about that. But would he know the candlestick had come from her room? Of course not. How could he know?

Unsettled, Anne snuggled deeper into the covers, key still clutched tightly in her palm. *Michael,* she thought. She had to warn him. He would know what to do next. Still haunted by images of the thing in the glasshouse, she called up all the pleasant memories she had of their times together, and only by doing so could she fall asleep.

A forceful knock on the door snapped her out of another bad dream, this one full of leafy tentacles. Anne sat straight up in bed and blinked, totally disoriented. Sunlight shone through the windows. The walnut burl furniture gleamed with a recent coat of polish. Something warm and hard bit into her palm. She uncurled her hand. *A key.*

Suddenly she remembered it all.

"Mrs. Sherwood? Are you awake yet?" Jane called through the door. "I've brought your breakfast. Mr. McEvoy is here and he's ready to begin another one of your treks into the woods."

Michael. He would know what to do, for God help her, she didn't.

Anne rushed over to the door, slipped the key into the lock, and opened it. She pulled the door open for Jane, who edged the tray inside, then stopped short.

"Are you ill, ma'am?" the lady's maid asked, her eyes wide.

Anne returned to the bed and climbed atop the mattress. "Why? Do I look so terrible?"

"You look . . . very pale, but beautiful as always."

Anne's attention dropped to the tray. A pot of tea, a scone, some jam, *the candlestick*. Her stomach plummeted. She forced a smile to her lips. "Am I to eat breakfast by candlelight?"

"Oh, no. I put the candlestick there so I would remember to deliver it to your room. Lord Connock found it this morning, but he didn't say where. 'Tis of no consequence, in any case."

"How do you know the candlestick belongs in my room?"

"By the pattern on the porcelain. Only this bedchamber contains pieces of this type."

Swallowing, Anne quickly scanned the bedchamber, seeing the same pattern on the clock, washbasin and pitcher. "Place the tray on the mattress, Jane," she said, her voice terse. "While I'm eating, please tell Mr. McEvoy that I'll be down in a minute. Under no circumstances is he to leave without me."

Eyebrows climbing, the maid nodded. "Of course, ma'am. I'll return in a moment." Her step hesitant, she left the room.

As soon as the door closed behind Jane, Anne was dressing herself. She chose only the plainest of underclothes, neglecting a corset and all but one petticoat, and even managed to draw a gown over her head. Partially unbuttoned, she sipped tea and nibbled at the scone and waited for Jane to return.

The maid did so in a gratifyingly short period of time, stepping slowly into the room to survey Anne's appearance. "Why, you're already dressed. Let me finish the buttons for you."

Jane busied herself at the back of Anne's gown. Once she'd finished, she began to fuss with Anne's hair.

"That won't be necessary today," Anne told her, taking the brush from Jane's hand.

"But Mrs. Sherwood, do you actually mean to go through the day with your hair unfastened?"

"No, I'll knot it into a loose bun." Anne tied her hair in the most primitive of fashions, without using a single hair pin. She smoothed down her skirts, grabbed her sketch case, and marched toward the door.

"Ma'am, you didn't eat your breakfast," Jane wailed behind her.

"Don't worry, I promise I'll eat a very good lunch."

She hurried out of the room, through the hall and down the steps. A brief detour at the landing brought her to Connock's library. Eyes narrowed, she searched row after row of scientific tomes, and even paged through a few of them until she found what she wanted: a treatise on electricity by the English scholar Michael Faraday. She opened the book and read for a few minutes, until she felt she understood at least the basics of Connock's strange black box that emitted bluish arcs of lightning.

The knowledge stored in her head, she returned the book to the shelf and joined Michael in the great hall.

He stood as soon as he saw her, a warm smile on his face, his hand outstretched. "Anne." His smile faded as he studied her. "You look like you've seen the Dullahan again."

"I've seen something much worse," she muttered. "I must speak to you privately. Where can we go?"

He took her sketch case from her and tucked it under his arm. "My cottage?"

"Is it safe?"

"From what?" He looked even more closely at her, then took her arm. "You're frightening me. Why wouldn't my cottage be safe?"

"I don't want anyone to overhear us."

"Our privacy is assured in my cottage."

"Let's go, then."

He took her arm, led her out of Glendale Hall, and hurried her into the forest. More than once he asked for an explanation. Anne stubbornly remained silent, afraid that Griswold could be hiding anywhere, listening for signs of rebellion.

After many backward glances on Anne's part, they reached Michael's cottage and went inside. A few embers still burned in the hearth, giving the room a warm feeling. She turned to face him and crossed her arms over her breasts.

"All right, we're in my cottage," he said, his mouth drawn tight. "Tell me what's sent you up into the boughs."

She looked at his strong chin, shaded by stubble, at his mussed hair and the simple linen shirt that encased his muscular form and went to him. "Oh Michael," she cried as his strong arms went around her, "where were you yesterday? I needed you."

A grimace tightened his face. "I was in the forest, dripping calf blood around, hoping to catch the ivy. I didn't want you with me. I don't want you endangered, Anne."

"Did you find it?"

"Unfortunately, no."

"I did."

He stiffened. *"What?"*

"Last night, I couldn't sleep." She spoke quickly, the words just tumbling out of her. "At about three in the morning, I heard this horrible squealing noise, so I went to the window. A strange bluish light was flickering inside the composting glasshouse."

"Tell me you went back to bed, closed your eyes, and fell asleep."

"I didn't. I investigated. The glasshouse door stood partially open, and I couldn't resist."

Michael swore softly. "Damn it, Anne, haven't you an ounce of sense? We both know something odd is going on. You should have waited and told me."

"I'm telling you now," she pointed out.

"All right, what did you see?"

"I went down to the composting glasshouse and peeked inside. 'Tis built in a way similar to Connock's Eden. The outside door leads into an antechamber filled with gardening tools. Another wooden door inside the glasshouse leads into the glasshouse proper."

She closed her eyes briefly, remembering the blood-drinking plant. "I opened the wooden door an inch and saw a laboratory. Connock had eviscerated a rabbit and collected its blood in a metal basin. With Griswold's help, he was administering shocks to a piece of that strange ivy."

"Administering *shocks?* What sort of shocks?"

"Electrical ones. Griswold was sitting atop a strange machine and pumping his legs." Her brows knitted for a moment. "Have you heard of a scientist named Michael Faraday?"

Michael shook his head no.

"Faraday was an Englishman who discovered that magnetism and motion produce electricity. He created a dynamo by placing a magnet inside a coil of copper wire. I think Lord Connock's machine works on the same principles as Faraday's dynamo." She sucked in a breath. "The electrical shocks it produced somehow gave the ivy the power of movement. God help us all, that ivy began to slither toward the metal basin. It immersed itself in the blood and absorbed it like a sponge."

Michael shook his head, his face a mask of disgust. "How is that possible?"

"I don't know. Connock spoke about grafts, but I didn't understand him. I only know it happened. That's not the worst of it, though."

He ran a hand through his hair. "Don't tell me they saw you."

Swallowing, Anne fixed her gaze on his shirt buttons. "Lord Connock's machine—his dynamo—gave off infrequent bursts of light. During one of the bursts, I saw something far back in the glasshouse, something very big. It looked almost like a tree, with a very short trunk, and its branches . . . well, they moved."

"Moved?"

"Sinuously. Like the tentacles on a sea serpent. And its leaves were similar to the ones Mrs. O'Shanley had collected from Paddy. I think we've found the mother plant."

He swore softly.

Clutching his arm, she looked him directly in the eye. "After I saw it, Lord Connock and Griswold saw me. Or, I should say, heard me."

"Mother of God." He groaned.

"I knocked some tools over, attracting their attention. Even though they didn't see me, I'm pretty sure Lord Connock knows I'm the spy. In my haste to escape undetected, I lost the candlestick I'd brought from my room. Lord Connock found it, and Jane returned it to my bedchamber this morning. Evidently the pattern on the candlestick marked it as mine."

"What a shoddy piece of luck." Michael tightened his arms around her. "I can't believe Lord Connock capable of such wickedness. Are you sure about what you saw?"

"Absolutely. I no longer have a hard time believing Connock capable of wickedness, either. Jane, my lady's maid, mentioned to me yesterday that there are very few children in Balkilly. The women keep miscarrying." She looked him squarely in the eye. "Connock's vegetables must be affecting the weakest in the village— the very old and the very young—and I'm certain he knows it. How could he not know?"

Michael closed his eyes. A muscle in his jaw tightened. "You're right. There are too many coincidences to ignore. I'm aware that the birth rate in Balkilly is poor. I've seen the deformities on the older villagers. Why didn't I put it all together before now?"

"I feel the same way. We should have discovered it sooner. Last night, when I heard the squealing, I had already made the connection between Connock and the miscarriages. I knew I had to investigate, if only to gather evidence against him and expose the corruption in Balkilly."

A deep sigh rumbled out of his chest. He opened his eyes and released her. "Let's think about what to do next. Has Lord Connock threatened you at all?"

"I don't think he will. He needs me yet." Wasting little words, she explained her theory about Lord Connock wanting to use her special ability in some manner.

Michael nodded when she'd finished. "That makes sense. Perhaps that gift of yours has bought us at least one more night."

"For what?"

"To gather that proof you spoke of and expose him, as painful as it will be."

"In the manner of 'Connock's Pestilence'?"

His blue-gray eyes dark, he frowned. "The very same. First we'll collect evidence from the composting glasshouse, and then we'll approach the *London Evening Star*."

Anne's throat grew tight at betraying Lord Connock, despite all that had happened. She was a scholar, too, and knew exactly what such exposure would do to him. "When do you want to collect the evidence?"

"Tonight. I'll go alone."

"No you won't, Michael McEvoy," she told him, her eyes narrowed. "You can't carry the whole glasshouse to London, nor will I allow you to snip a piece of that . . . thing. I'll come along and make creditable illustrations of whatever we find."

He thought it over for a moment, then nodded slowly. "As much as I dislike the thought, you're going to have to sketch."

Quietly, they planned out the details of their escapade, agreeing to meet on the grounds at around two in the morning, and then wait for the opportunity to enter the glasshouse. Anne hoped Lord Connock wouldn't remain within the glasshouse all night, foiling their attempts to sneak inside and collect evidence.

After laying everything out, Michael gathered her into his arms again. His touch was so very gentle and loving that she melted against him and soon his mouth was against hers. Sighing, Anne surrendered to his lovemaking, knowing in the back of her mind that they had some very important things to talk about, things that had nothing to do with Lord Connock and his glasshouses. Still, she just couldn't bring herself to discuss their future when the next twenty-four hours were uncertain. They would finish this business with Lord Connock, and then she would broach a subject much closer to her heart.

Michael took her clothes off, and pressed tiny kisses along her neck. Silently, she prayed that in twenty-four hours, they'd both be around to talk.

20

After he'd returned Anne to Glendale Hall, Michael spent the rest of the night sitting on the deacon's bench in his little cottage, smoking one cigar after another. He kept asking himself how he could have been so blind. The forest had gone to hell, the villagers were being poisoned, and his surrogate father had shown a malignant side Michael hadn't even guessed at.

Michael stubbed out one of his best Cubans and promptly lit another. He was going to deplete his entire supply within the hour and God damn it, he didn't care. This little patch of Ireland, second only to Connaught in beauty, had become fouled and he, the so-called Green Man, a man at one with the forests, hadn't noticed. Mother of God, he'd brought back the plants Connock was perverting, so didn't that make him partially responsible for the corruption?

Scowling, he watched his little mahogany clock tick past midnight, then past one in the morning. Outside, the night pressed in, a special kind of darkness only found in a forest, where starlight never penetrated and moonlight only rarely. He stared out at the shadows and silently vowed to collect that evidence and get the hell out of the glasshouse as quickly as possible. While their plan had merit, he knew if anything ever happened to Anne, he'd never forgive himself. He'd just lie down and die. For the next several minutes, he reviewed every possible scenario that might occur in the glasshouse and planned contingencies for each.

At a quarter to two, he couldn't sit still anymore. While he didn't need fifteen minutes to put a few things together and walk to Glendale Hall, he stood anyway and packed a leather satchel. Glass jars topped with corks, a few sacks, a blanket, a brick, a small lantern, and—God forbid—a knife with a thick, eight-inch blade. What else would he need? His gaze drifted across a coil of thin rope. When in the jungle, he'd never traveled without it. Rope had a thousand uses, and though he couldn't think of a single use for it this night, he packed it anyway.

That done, he set off for Glendale Hall and arrived a full ten minutes early. He sat near a tree and waited for Anne's pale face to appear in the blackness. He heard a hundred menacing sounds and saw an equal number of dangerous shadows. Time passed so slowly for him that one minute seemed to equal ten and, long before the appointed meeting time, his shoulders had locked up with tension and his jaw ached from clenching it.

Gaze fixed on the front door, he silently willed Anne to exit. Even from this distance he could see the footmen sleeping with their mouths open. Other than a few random lights that the servants had left on, Glendale Hall appeared dark and quiet, a behemoth slumbering beneath purplish heavens. She would have no trouble remaining undetected when she left the hall.

"Michael."

The whisper came from somewhere behind him. He twitched and spun around, heat flooding his limbs and leaving them shaky.

"Jesus, lass, you scared the hell out of me."

She'd tucked her long blond hair beneath a kerchief. Her sketch case dangled from one hand. "At the last minute I changed my mind and crept out the servants' entrance. Didn't want to wake those footmen. I'm sorry I frightened you."

He could tell by the sparkle in her eyes that she wasn't really sorry, though. Frowning, he decided that she'd enjoyed putting him off-balance. She'd made an art of it, in fact. The notion made him sound more gruff than he intended. "We're not larking about, lass. We're here to do a job and a dangerous one it is, at that. Now is not the time to go sneaking up on people."

"I said I'm sorry."

He snorted. "Let's find that glasshouse, before I change my mind and insist you return to my cottage."

"You're not my keeper, Michael McEvoy, to tell me what I may and may not do."

Defiance gave her voice a lilt. Michael worked very hard to suppress an urge to kiss that mouth of hers shut. Carefully they made their way across the lawn, the complete lack of moonlight effectively masking their passage. Within five minutes they'd twisted through trees and cut a wide path around the other glasshouses to arrive at the composting glasshouse.

Darkness reigned within its frosted glass walls. Michael couldn't even hear a whisper of movement from inside. But he more than smelled the honeyed-decay odor he'd come to associate with the composting glasshouse. The stink nearly assaulted his nose.

Anne grabbed his jacket and pulled him aside. "Lord Connock and Griswold aren't here. Otherwise we'd see some light, perhaps hear their voices."

"I know," he whispered.

"Don't you think it odd that for the first time in several nights, Lord Connock is elsewhere?"

"He could be working in another laboratory, maybe one within Glendale Hall itself. He has several, you know," Michael rationalized, but his gut was turning in slow, uncomfortable circles. "We'll sit for a while in the shadows, and see what happens. Do you think you can stand that smell?"

"I'll try."

Anne followed him to a dark niche. They both sat on the ground. She fitted her form to his, bringing some heat to his cold body. Eyes wide, he searched the lawn and glasshouses for anything that moved, listened carefully, and sniffed the air for stray odors that might suggest they had company. Other than that disgusting smell, which grew more tolerable with time, the night seemed normal. Nevertheless, his midsection continued to churn, sensing danger that his eyes and ears couldn't verify.

They waited in the niche for almost an hour. Nothing changed. His muscles cramping, Michael stretched and climbed to his feet. "The night's quiet, lass. We'd best investigate the glasshouse now before the horizon starts lightening."

He held out a hand to her, which she took, and pulled her to her feet. Very cautiously they crept to the door. Standing to the left of the door, Michael opened the sack, removed the brick, and wrapped a small blanket around it.

"The blanket will muffle the worst of the noise," he whispered. "As soon as I've broken the glass, I'll reach in and throw the latch. You open the door, and we'll slip inside. The whole operation shouldn't take more than a few seconds. Remember, the quicker we're in, the better."

"All right. Let me try something first." Without further warning she sidled up to the doorknob.

"Don't bother," he murmured, understanding what she planned to do. "Lord Connock always locks this glasshouse. You're wasting precious seconds—"

She turned the knob. The door swung open silently, invitingly, as if on greased wheels.

Her eyes wide, she stared at the door, then at him. "Why did he leave it open? Is he expecting us?"

Michael ran a hand through his hair. His heart began to beat a little faster. "Connock's made it clear he doesn't want us in this glasshouse. If he were expecting us, don't you think he would have double-locked it and put a guard nearby?"

"Yes . . . unless he wants us in the glasshouse."

"If he wanted us in the glasshouse, why not invite us to tour it with him, in the full light of day, as he invited us to tour his Eden?"

She nodded. "You're right. He must have forgotten to lock it. It's a piece of happy luck, no more. Should I go first?"

"Are you sure I can't persuade you to return to my cottage?"

"You've no chance, McEvoy."

"All right then, we both go inside. Tonight, gentlemen always precede ladies."

Michael stepped through the portal and waited a few seconds, to let his eyes adjust to the deeper gloom. Silhouettes of rakes and hoes hung on a pegboard and a black square bisected an inner wall. The decaying smell gained overtones of damp earth. As Anne had explained, he stood in a tool shed. The black square, he realized, was a wooden door that led to the glasshouse proper. He circled the shed, then waved her in when he'd assured himself of their safety.

She squeezed through the doorway, her figure momentarily blotting out what little light filtered in from the outside. Inexplicably, his stomach tightened and he looked over his shoulder, certain something was creeping up to wrap its soft tendrils around his leg—

Anne pressed herself against him, as quiet as a wraith, and put her hand in his. Her fingers trembled.

Berating himself for his foolishness, he squeezed her hand once, then let her go. "I'll light the lantern. We'll keep it low, so anyone who chances a look at this glasshouse sees only darkness and shadows."

His movements spare, he managed to draw a spark from a piece of flint and soon, the lantern cast a sickly glow around the tool shed. He lifted the lantern high and looked around before nodding once. "There's nothing here worth investigating. Let's move on."

Anne hung back and didn't say anything, adding to his feeling of discomfort. Sack in one hand, lantern in the other, he walked to the inner door and turned the knob. This one remained unlocked, too. Remembering Anne's description of the plant that writhed near the back of the glasshouse, he felt the skin on the back of his neck tighten as he took a step into the glasshouse proper.

Eyes straining, he stared into the darkness. The

lantern illuminated shapes of leaves and vines, but nothing became absolutely clear. The honeyed smell, however, remained more than clear; it hit him in waves.

"What do you see?" Anne whispered, her voice urgent.

"It's hard to see anything."

She pressed against his back, her sketch case banging into his thighs, and coughed delicately. "Move aside, so I might enter too."

"I don't yet know that it's safe—"

Cutting him off, she elbowed her way into the room and paused at his side. "I need to see what I'm sketching, Michael."

"Foolhardy lass," he hissed, but secretly felt glad for her company.

Silently, they both assessed the gloom around them, one so complete they might have been standing in a cave. Casting a circle of dim light only about five feet wide, the lantern proved useless for anything but close-up study. A soft twitching noise drifted toward them on a stray breeze.

Anne lifted a scrap of linen to her nose, presumably to mask the smell. "From what I remember, a laboratory sprawls to the left of us. I didn't notice much on the right. Should we, ah, examine that thing I saw near the back of the glasshouse first?"

He heard the slight quiver in her voice and knew what had caused it: fear. His mouth dry, he stared into the oily blackness where the tentacled plant supposedly rooted, and had the oddest feeling it returned his stare. Should they charge back there and confront it right away? Or would it be wiser to explore the immediate vicinity first? He opted for the second choice, if only to ensure that other equally dangerous plants wouldn't creep up behind them while they gaped at Connock's prize plant.

"We'll work our way back there," Michael said. "But it may be slow going. We haven't enough light to do anything other than explore inch by inch. Which way should we start?"

A shudder went through her. "To the right. I'm not particularly anxious to explore Connock's laboratory."

Michael clasped her hand and together they crept toward the right-hand section of the glasshouse. The lantern's meager glow created shadows in a grouping of poles and leaves. Beanpoles? Squinting, he edged closer to the poles, then reared back in shock.

What were they?

Long, funnel-like tubes—at least two feet wide at the lip—sprouted from vines that hung on bamboo poles. Light green on the outside, they sported pink throats that deepened to red. Their flesh had a leathery look to it. The lantern swaying crazily in his hand, Michael peered down their throats and saw liquid, at least a gallon of it. Within the liquid, dark bits of furry matter floated, along with a multitude of dead flies. His nose told him that an overwhelming stench of decay was coming from these tubes.

Pitcher plants, he thought. From Borneo. Malaysia. Madagascar.

He glanced over his shoulder at Anne. Her gaze caught his and held it. She stood in semidarkness, out of the circle of light cast by the lantern. Suddenly those shadows around her had a very unfriendly feel to them. He grabbed her arm and urged her to his side.

Her attention fell on the pitcher plants. She drew in a forceful breath, then let it out slowly.

Understanding her reaction entirely, he turned the lantern so the light would shine upon them. Anne leaned forward, her lips parted. "*Nepenthes.* Likely from a tropical climate. A naturalist working for Kew Gardens once brought a dried specimen back from an island in the Pacific Ocean. I hadn't realized they grew this large."

"They don't." Michael touched the rim of the plant, then rubbed his two fingers together. A honeylike substance coated his skin. "Connock must have crossbred the plant to produce a larger one, just as he's crossbred the vegetable plants. For what purpose, though, I can't even guess. These plants won't help to eradicate starvation. Besides being poisonous, they're carnivorous."

"They eat insects, you mean?"

"I'd say they eat more than insects. I thought I saw pieces of fur deep inside them."

"Fur?" Her brows drew together. "Any animal caught in a pitcher plant would claw its way through the pitcher within moments."

"The pitcher's flesh looks leathery," he pointed out. "Maybe it's strong enough to withstand claws."

"Or perhaps someone placed a dead animal inside the pitcher."

They stared at each other. Anne visibly shuddered. Wondering if he should have insisted she stay behind, he lifted the lantern and followed the vines twisting through the bamboo poles until he found the pitcher's mother plant, a monstrous tangle of vines in a huge wire basket. Chains suspended the basket from the ceiling. Beneath the basket, a plate of wet clay balls diffused humidity, presumably by evaporation. A few flies crawled around the balls.

Anne stepped forward with parted lips until she

stood next to the mother plant. Trembling, she lifted her hand and touched the vine with one finger. Her eyes widened and she cried out. She didn't break the contact, however.

Michael pulled her hand away. "Are you all right?"

Her face had gone completely white. "Madness. Hunger. Desperation. I've never seen colors or felt those emotions so strongly from a plant before. They nearly overwhelmed me."

"Don't touch any others," he warned.

"I assure you, I won't." She rubbed her hands together, presumably to bring warmth back into them, then opened her sketch case and began to draw with hesitant pencil strokes. "These plants are so perverted, 'tis difficult for me to draw them."

Michael stared at the tangled plant. He'd once brought cuttings of a pitcher plant back from Borneo. The sight of Connock's creation, likely made from those cuttings, sickened him. Inadvertently or not, he'd helped Connock create this thing. He felt as if an icy hand had squeezed his heart.

"Are you going to collect some cuttings?" Anne asked, breaking into his thoughts.

Not trusting himself to speak, he pinched off a few leaves, shoved them into a jar and snapped the lid closed.

She slanted him a quick look, her mouth curved in sympathy, before returning to the sketch. "I know this must be horrible for you to see, Michael. The natural world means so much to you."

"You have no idea."

She sent another glance his way, then began to work more quickly. "Why don't you find another plant for me to sketch, while I finish this one?"

She was trying to keep him busy, he mused. At any other time, he would have agreed with her tactic. By moving around, he'd have less time to think about each plant. But today, action meant finding new, diseased species, every one reminding him of his participation in Connock's misdeeds. "I'll wait by your side. You'll need the lantern's light to sketch by, anyway."

He held the lantern at an angle to give her a better aspect. Her brows drew together and she focused on her work. Grimacing, he watched the sketch of *Nepenthes* emerge on her paper. Compared to this, the golden sapling was the very picture of beauty and innocence.

Without warning, a gurgling noise drifted from one of the pitcher plants. It shivered and contracted. A moment later, drops of fluid flew from its insides. The plant settled down again.

Michael had the strange notion that *Nepenthes* had just burped. The skin at the back of his neck crawled. He wanted to move to the next plant in the worst way. Eons seemed to pass, however, before she finally finished the sketch and indicated that they should press onward.

Michael lifted the lantern high. "Where to next?"

Lip caught between her teeth, she stared into the deepest recesses of the glasshouse, then averted her gaze. "Do you feel it?"

"What?"

"That breeze."

A puff of air whispered past his ear. "I do." Abruptly he understood the significance of her observation. They were in a glasshouse whose windows remained shut. There shouldn't have been a breeze.

"Odd," he offered, unable to think of an explanation.

She pointed at a square of black further into the glasshouse. "I can hear running water. Isn't that wavy glow a pool's reflection of the lantern's light?"

"It is. Let's try that next."

So close they might have been one, they shuffled over to the pool and allowed the light to sweep across its surface. Anne muffled a gasp.

The lantern wobbled. He tightened his grip on the handle. At least fifty snakes were rearing up out of the water, with fangs pointed their way. And not just any snakes. *Cobras*.

Tension flooded his body. His arms told him to pick up Anne, and his legs told him to run. He took a deep breath and swept the surface again with light.

The snakes hadn't moved.

They weren't snakes after all.

Swearing softly, he moved closer to study them. Anne stayed right with him. Each sported a strange pitcher that curved upward, topped by a rounded "head" and two projections coming from the mouth that appeared like fangs.

"*Darlingtonia*," he whispered. "Only found in the Americas. The locals call it the cobra lily. Again, this one is much larger than normal."

"If Connock's other glasshouse is a Garden of Eden, then this one is a Garden of Hell," she observed.

" 'Tis a madman's nightmare."

Silence settled between them.

Anne's attention drifted toward the oily blackness near the back of the glasshouse. Her body grew stiff. He put an arm around her and held her close for a moment, wondering again how he could have missed the signs of Connock's madness. He should have known.

"These cobra lilies, they grow in water?" she asked, diverting him.

"Not exactly. I've seen them growing in moss, near streams. They always have cool water running over their root systems."

"Look at the fangs on it, Michael," she said, her voice hushed. "They almost seem to drip poison."

He examined the white protuberances in its mouth. Indeed, a small drop of clear fluid stood poised on the end of each fang. "The fangs are probably coated with some sort of insect attractant, to draw the insect into the throat. We won't touch it and test my theory, though."

" 'Tis almost beautiful in an unusual way. And so ugly I can hardly bear to look at it." She opened her sketch case. "I suppose I'll have to look my fill."

"And I'll collect a specimen or two."

While Anne sketched, he snipped parts he felt representative of its nature. Soon they'd completed their study of the cobra lily and were ready to move on. Over the next hour, they worked their way into the far reaches of the glasshouse, their subjects full of misshapen stems, fleshy protuberances, oozing leaves, and blight. The farther back they went, the more frequently they felt the peculiar breeze. At length a twitching noise, like the sound of a whip arching through the air, began to accompany the puffs of wind.

Anne's manner became more grim as the minutes wore on, and Michael's own sense of responsibility for the plants in the glasshouse grew steadily until he wanted to put his fist through the wall. At the same time, a sense of urgency had grabbed hold of him, a need to escape the glasshouse before something bad happened. He'd felt this way before, in the jungle, and he'd always listened to his instinct. More than once it had saved his life.

"We need to finish this soon," he said softly.

Anne evidently hadn't heard him. She'd fixed her attention on a raised garden of light pink flowers. Roses. Great purplish tumors sprouted from their stems in every direction. She touched one, then jerked her finger back as if the plant had scorched her. "The blackness from these plants is like wasps in my head," she whispered. "Buzzing, hateful, oily, they only want to hurt me."

Michael groaned, low in his throat. Something inside him snapped. "God help me, I'm partially responsible. I brought the plants back from the jungles and gave them to Lord Connock so he could corrupt them."

She stared at him. "Michael, you couldn't know what Connock intended to do with them. Your intentions were pure, even if his weren't."

"It's not what I did, but what I didn't do." Hands clenched, he turned to face her more fully. "I should have noticed the changes in the forest. I should have realized Connock's vegetables had poisoned the villagers. But I didn't. I was too enamored of my own senses."

"What do you mean, enamored of your senses?" she demanded. "Haven't you just returned from the China Seas? You haven't been here to notice."

She made sense, but not enough for him to absolve himself. He frowned, disgusted by his own gullibility. "Why in hell did I trust Lord Connock? After my years in the workhouse, you'd think I'd have learned something."

Anne put her sketch case down and stood directly in front of him, forcing him to look at her. Her eyes were strangely bright. "Do you remember our dinner with Lord Connock and his scholarly associates? We were discussing the merits of observation without emotion. You told them that they saw and understood but didn't feel, and in doing so had lost the quality that made them human."

He nodded slowly. "I remember."

Her voice gained a pleading note. "When you refuse to trust and to love, you too are losing the quality that makes us human. Not every experience in life will be pleasant, but the pain defines us even more so than the happiness. We need them both to understand who we are."

He didn't respond, instead listening to a secret chord her words had touched inside him, a chord that she had struck once or twice before without result. And yet, this time things were different. Now he understood how much he loved her. That chord which had remained silent for so long vibrated and resounded as if plucked by a crazed fiddler.

A peculiar feeling of freedom washed over him, one that had been in him all the time, waiting to be discovered. Freedom to trust, and to love, and to be hurt and betrayed. It was all part of the human experience. He would embrace it and learn from it.

"As you once said, you'll never understand the beauty of light until you've wandered in darkness," she whispered.

Swallowing, he set the sack and lantern on the ground and caressed her cheek. Life suddenly gained new, fiery color. "I love you, Anne."

Her gray eyes widened. She stared at him, lips parted. A moment later she was in his arms, her cheek pressed against his chest, a few tears leaking from her eyes to dampen his shirt. Nothing, he thought, had ever felt better. He wrapped his arms around her quivering form, kissed her hair and realized that with Anne by his side, he could do anything.

"Oh, Michael, you wouldn't believe what I've been thinking as I've sat here sketching these monstrosities," she said, her voice soft, husky. "When I look at these plants, I see Lord Connock. I see what happens when a person loses his or her humanity in the pursuit of science. Connock has forgotten how to feel and no longer cares about inflicting pain. He's lost the one virtue that places man above other creatures: compassion."

"That he has," Michael admitted, his voice grim.

"God help him, but I believe his soul is equally as perverted as that of his plants. And I might have become just like him if you hadn't entered my life and taught me how to feel." She took a deep, shuddering breath and let it out slowly before continuing. "I love you, Michael. With you I see things hidden to me before. Now, in an ordinary flower, I see the wonder that I had always looked for but never found."

He held her against him and nearly groaned at the irony of discovering something of such high import in a glasshouse filled with corruption. They should have been standing in a field of flowers with the sun shining upon their heads, drinking champagne. But as Anne had pointed out, life rarely worked that way.

"We need to finish quickly," he repeated, his joy evaporating. "Later, we'll . . . discuss this in great depth."

Anne cast a furtive glance toward the last unexplored pocket of darkness. "Why don't we go now? Forget about that plant I mentioned. We don't need to investigate it—"

"Oh, but I think you do," a calm voice said from near the doorway. A gush of light descended on them, momentarily blinding Michael. When his eyes adjusted, he saw Lord Connock and Griswold standing just inside the glasshouse proper, both carrying lanterns.

Lord Connock's hair stuck up at odd angles. The pouches beneath his eyes had become so dark they looked like black paint. In the dim light, his gaze had a reddish sheen. Stains covered his shirt and jacket. He was smiling, his urbane expression at frightening odds with his appearance.

His dirty gray beard brushing against his chest, Griswold began lighting gas lamps inside the laboratory portion of the glasshouse, throwing even more light onto the grotesqueries around them.

Michael stared at Lord Connock, his blood flowing like sluggish ice through his veins. He realized that Connock and Griswold had left the door open purposefully, to entice them in. At night. When no one would see them enter, and no one would question their never leaving. "Owain. Obviously you were expecting us."

The other man inclined his head. "I knew Anne had visited last night and anticipated her restless mind would force her back here. She's a slave to curiosity, that one."

Michael became conscious of Anne near his side. She'd become very stiff and hadn't the slightest interest in Lord Connock. She'd directed her gaze elsewhere. Behind them. He spun around.

Even as he became very still, his mind lurched drunkenly.

He wasn't seeing this, no, not at all, this was a trick.

He would close his eyes, open them again and it would be gone.

He blinked, once, twice. Anne clutched his sleeve.

A massive green stem, easily as wide as a tree trunk, rose out of the dirt floor. The stem split into a network of grayish-brown branches completely denuded of ivy leaves except at their ends. The branches were swaying in the air like the snakes on Medusa's head.

His chest tight with a shout he refused to utter, he studied the more trivial aspects of it, in the way of a man trying to cope with something far too horrifying for comprehension. Knots and whorls and inexplicable protuberances marked the stem. Small drops of liquid had formed on the leaves, giving them a jewel-like appearance. On one of the branches, the leaves curled around a small furry body, trapping it. Michael detected the glisten of bone through the fur.

Some distant part of him silently catalogued the plant's primary features as relating to *Drosera*, the sundew plant. A litany of facts paraded through his mind. The leaves exuded nectar, adhesive compounds, and digestive acids. Insects, attracted by the nectar, landed on the leaves and stimulated them to close around their bodies. The sundew quickly digested the insects.

Only this sundew ate far more than insects.

He knew he was staring at it with a drugged sort of curiosity but he couldn't tear his gaze away. His attention dropped lower. Around the base of the plant, desiccated bodies sprawled in the mulch, evidently meals well digested. As he watched, little puffs of mulch sprayed into the air. Something was moving, molelike, underneath the ground. The sundew's roots, maybe.

He thought of the rustling noises in the forests, the stories of attacking ivy, Mrs. O'Shanley's strange specimen, and knew that the monstrosity's roots stretched far beyond the glasshouse. He felt certain Griswold

hadn't been coiling the ivy up when Michael had found
it a few days previous. No, the old gardener had been
covering for the plant, trying to hide its presence in the
forest. Sudden resolve descended upon him, lighting up
the pockets of fear in his mind. He *would* kill it before
he left this glasshouse.

21

*A*nne clenched her jaw at the sight of *Drosera*'s waving tentacles. She flinched at their little snapping noises as they whipped through the air. Their movement created a foul breeze that brushed against her cheek. Scrubbing at her skin with a clawlike hand, she fought to keep her meager dinner in her stomach. If it wasn't for Michael's presence at her side, she would have run screaming from the glasshouse.

An almost drowsy terror stealing through her veins, she edged away from the plant. She'd never seen the like of it and hadn't the faintest idea where Connock might have gotten it from. One glance at Michael's pursed lips and narrowed eyes, though, told her he knew what it was. She fervently hoped he wasn't blaming himself for its existence.

Lord Connock spoke very closely to her ear, his dulcet tones grating on her nerves. "Beautiful, isn't it? 'Tis my greatest triumph, and my greatest failure."

Michael moved to her side and assessed her with one

quick glance. His face was very pale, and he'd set his lips into a thin line.

She gave him an imperceptible nod.

His features seemed to relax somewhat. "Tell us about it, Owain," he said to the older man, and leaned down to pick up his sack.

"Leave the sack there, Michael," Lord Connock instructed. "Demonstrate your good faith to me, and perhaps we'll all leave this glasshouse alive." He smiled, his cheeks bunching up into two little mounds of cherubic delight. "And I must ask you both to move away a bit. *Drosera's* always hungry, you know."

Michael hesitated, looking first at the sack and then at Lord Connock. His mouth tightening, he abandoned the sack and hustled Anne several paces away from *Drosera.*

Lord Connock nodded approvingly, then tucked his arms behind his back and adopted the pedantic tones of a lecturer. "As you know, I've been working on eradicating starvation by producing bigger, more resistant vegetables. I've had a fair amount of success but also suffered from one persistent problem. My plants deplete the nutrients in the soil before a single growing season is even half over. Perhaps it has something to do with their rapid growth or the large fruit they produce, but they die far too quickly to be of any real use."

Michael's brows drew together, his expression one of calm interest. His tight grip on her hand, however, told her he felt far from calm. "It isn't practical to expect farmers to fertilize their fields in the middle of the growing season."

"No, it isn't." Lord Connock continued his pacing. "One day many years ago, I was studying a specimen of

Drosera I had growing in one of my glasshouses. A bird had flown into the glasshouse a day before, and—if you'll pardon me, Mrs. Sherwood—defecated on *Drosera's* leaves. To my utter amazement, I realized *Drosera* was digesting the matter as it might an insect. I began to examine all carnivorous plants much more closely. Many never even root in the soil, preferring tufts of moss in the treetops to anchor themselves. Some live in places where cool water flushes constantly across their roots. In short, they draw their nutrients primarily from the insects and other matter they catch and digest. They are amazing creatures."

Anne nodded slowly, following his reasoning, however twisted she might judge it privately. "If you were to combine the carnivorous plant's ability to draw nutrients from animal life forms and the vegetable plant's ability to produce food, your problem would be solved."

"Indeed, Mrs. Sherwood." Lord Connock's tone gained an edge of excitement. "Think of it. We could feed this new vegetable hybrid with insects, leftover food waste, even our own excrement, and it would produce a limitless supply of food. A perfect symbiosis, no?"

Anne's stomach did a couple of slow rolls.

"Nothing like a little chamber-pot soup to start your day off properly," Michael muttered.

"Come now," Connock said, shaking his head in the manner of a parent reproaching a child. "Your disgust is misplaced. Why, we eat excrement every day . . . indirectly, of course. Are you forgetting that we plow our fields with manure, then grow vegetables in the nutrient-rich soil?"

"If you're crossing carnivorous plants with vegetables," Michael asked, "why didn't we see any vegetables on the plants in this glasshouse?"

"I haven't been able to perfect the union," the older man admitted. "I've tried everything. Pollination techniques, grafts . . . everything. Nothing takes as I wish it to. As I said, the *Drosera* behind you is my greatest failure."

Anne swallowed. "But it is also your success."

A prideful smile twisted the nobleman's face. "I've given it the power of movement. Although many plants can move, none can do so as quickly as my *Drosera*."

Anne raised an eyebrow. "I'm not familiar with any moving plants."

"Many carnivorous plants move in some way, to capture their prey. Often their movement is triggered through growth or water movement inside the plant. The tentacles of a pure *Drosera* slowly close around an insect, and the *Dionaea* snaps itself shut when the insect tickles its inner hairs. Why, even the *Mimosa* plant folds its leaves and collapses to the ground when touched, and it's not even carnivorous."

"How did you give your *Drosera* such a free range of movement?" Michael asked.

Connock pressed his lips together and looked away, as though considering his next words. When he finally returned his attention to them, his cheeks had become flushed. "Some types of flesh are more flexible than others. Indeed, I've discovered that various digestive tracts in animals have a curious suppleness found nowhere else."

Michael sucked in a quick breath.

"You can't mean . . ." Anne pressed a hand against her throat. Every pore in her body rebelled against the notion her mind had already deduced. She felt hot, feverish all over, and yet very, very cold.

"I'm afraid I do, Mrs. Sherwood. Mice and rabbits are my favorite subjects. I've had some success with pigs and horses, too . . . particularly the newborns." Connock paused, his entire face flushing with color. "Animal flesh allows a network of nerves to develop within the plant, nerves that give it the ability to move."

"And human flesh? Is that useful too?" Anne heard her voice as if from far away.

"I don't know. I haven't attempted to harvest any. Perhaps I ought to pursue that angle if my current branch of research leads nowhere."

"I thought you *were* pursuing it. The women in the village are miscarrying—"

"A regrettable circumstance, but also unavoidable," the older man admitted, his face smooth. "I have to test my vegetables somewhere. I hope to pinpoint the cause soon, as well as to discover why tumors grow on subjects exposed to my vegetables long-term. In any case, it's a small price to pay for the great advances I've made toward eradicating starvation, don't you agree?"

Anne opened her mouth, not even sure what she planned to say, only that it would be loud and vociferous. Michael's quick elbow to the ribs stopped her just in time.

"Of course we agree," Michael said in neutral tones. "Anyone could see the value in what you're doing."

Lord Connock eyed him closely. "I would have expected otherwise from you, Michael. You've certainly complained loudly enough about my vegetable experimentation. Your sudden turnaround seems a bit too easy."

"My own parents died of starvation," Michael pointed out. "How could I feel any different?"

Anne stretched her fingers. Michael was holding her so tightly he'd nearly cut off her circulation. He gradually loosened his grip.

"And you, Anne? What are your thoughts? Are you going to contact the press and tell them you've discovered a new pestilence?" the nobleman asked.

Anne understood from Michael's cues that their best chance of escape stood with lulling Connock into a false sense of security. She swallowed and did her best to sound convincing. "I'm a scholar, Lord Connock. I've worked with plants for too many years and know how difficult they are to propagate and crossbreed. What you've wrought here is truly . . . miraculous and far too important for me to undermine."

Her last sentence ended on a desperate note. She hoped Lord Connock wouldn't notice.

"Ah, but you're not as much a scholar as you'd have me believe, Mrs. Sherwood. I suppose your gift with plants has something to do with it. How can you be objective with colors swirling in your head?"

Anne stiffened. "How did you know?"

"Griswold." Connock shrugged. "He overheard you in the forest."

Her eyes narrowed. Griswold stood to the side, grinning at her. She stared back and thought about the satisfying crack her hand would make if it connected with his smiling cheeks.

"Don't be angry with him, Mrs. Sherwood. He was simply following my orders and gathering information," Lord Connock soothed. "You see, I knew you had an unusual ability concerning plants from the start. Your cousin, Sir Richard, hinted as much. And 'tis obvious no woman could draw as well as you without some secret assistance. You yourself told me inadvertently many times that you sensed more than the average person did concerning plants."

"That's why you brought me here, isn't it?" she murmured.

"I thought you could help me with my research, by telling me why certain plants died and various experiments didn't produce a positive result. I must admit, at first I thought us a perfect pair. You seemed to have the mind of a truly great scientist, one who ignored emotion in the pursuit of pure observation. Naturally, I'd hoped to persuade you to assist me, but I hadn't realized what a sentimental nature you have, your weakness evinced in your love affair with Michael."

A hot blush spread across her face. She felt Michael's tension in his abrupt stillness. Had they any secrets at all from the nobleman? Her hopes sinking, she realized the futility of trying to convince Connock that they'd support his experimentation. The older man knew them both too well.

Lord Connock shrugged. "I think its a fool's errand in any case. I've been trying to modify vegetables with rather startling results; and yet, those results have no real practical use."

He paused to swat at a fly which buzzed in lazy circles around his head. "These damned flies, they'll be the death of me," he complained. "The light must have roused this one; normally they sleep at night. They're constantly finding ways into the glasshouse and fouling the integrity of my experimentation. I suppose the scent from *Drosera* attracts them."

"Your *Drosera* has spread its roots considerably beyond this glasshouse," Michael said carefully. "It's been eating the animals in the forest. Even the villagers have noted its presence, though they don't understand it."

Griswold took a step toward them, his wrinkled face screwed tight with a scowl. "I told him to burn the damned thing before we have that Darwin fellow back on our doorstep, trumpeting our secrets to the world."

The nobleman frowned. "Griswold, you're forever trying to eradicate my most exciting success. You want it dead. I assure you, *Drosera* wants you dead too. You'd make quite a satisfying dinner."

"Did you know that *Drosera* attacked Paddy O'Shanley?" Michael shook his head and focused on Griswold. "One of its roots wrapped around his ankle, took him down, then tried to crawl into his mouth. If it kills someone, you'll both have more than your share of interested parties on your doorstep. The press will be the least of your worries."

"Did you hear that?" Griswold poked Connock in the chest with one gnarled finger, his face gaining a ruddy flush. "We have to burn it, before we're all revealed."

The nobleman swatted his finger away. "I'm growing tired of your ranting. You're a coward, Griswold, do you hear me? A selfish little coward."

"Oh, I am?" Griswold took a step closer to his master. "Who harvests flesh from the animals? Who milks the snakes for their venom? Who feeds that godforsaken beast?" He hooked a thumb and pointed over his shoulder at *Drosera*, then pounded his chest. "I do. You fiddle with your copper coils and your jars, while I'm out there risking my goddamn neck."

One eyebrow raised, Lord Connock studied Griswold with a calm demeanor belied by the color rising in his neck.

At the other man's lack of response, the gardener's voice rose a notch. "I'll tell you why you don't want to burn *Drosera*. You haven't the courage to do so. You aren't sure you'll ever have another success, so you're holding on to this one. You're the coward."

Lips parted, the nobleman stared at Griswold but said nothing.

Griswold growled low in his throat and rushed over to grab a lantern from the laboratory table. Lantern in hand, he strode over to *Drosera* and waved the flame near its trunk.

The color rushed out of Lord Connock's face. His eyes glittered dangerously within pallid skin. Without apparent purpose he strolled to the gardener's side. "You've only made one statement of import, Griswold, and that was when you said you feed *Drosera*."

His movements quick and efficient, he placed two hands on Griswold's chest and shoved him back into *Drosera*.

The gardener screamed and crashed against the stem. Instantly roots broke through the mulch to wrap around his ankles, pinioning him. Branches bent his way, their leafy ends smothering Griswold's face, his nose, creeping up his pants.

Michael started toward the gardener, his face a mask of horror.

The nobleman quickly stepped in front of him. "If you go any closer, *Drosera* will take you, too. Griswold hasn't been feeding it well, so it's very hungry."

Griswold spluttered and moaned but couldn't make much noise because the leaves were inside his mouth.

As they crept down his throat he began to gag and vomit. At the same time, a vinelike shape tunneled upward, traveling to his crotch. His body jiggled and danced.

"Jesus," Michael swore softly. He pulled Anne against him and pressed her face into his chest, so she wouldn't see. But she'd already seen enough to haunt her for a thousand nights. She groaned, wondering if she and Michael were going to die like Griswold.

"Pay attention," Connock scolded. "Don't worry about Griswold. He deserved it. Look, instead, at *Drosera's* feeding mechanisms. They're unique in the entire world. A common *Drosera* will trap its prey with adhesive compounds and then digest it with acid secreted through the leaf. Often the entire leaf curls around the prey."

Anne tried to focus on the sound of Michael's heart beating wildly beneath her ear, but the nobleman's voice kept intruding.

"Now, my *Drosera* has many of the same properties as the common *Drosera*," Connock boasted, "and it digests soft-skinned food in the same manner. Still, animal—and apparently human—skin is too thick for its acid to penetrate, so my *Drosera* has adapted in an unusual way. It sends runner branches into the prey's orifices, seeking softer membranes which it can successfully digest. Thus *Drosera* eats its prey from the inside out. Amazing, isn't it?"

Anne began to shudder. She risked a glance at the nobleman and saw a pleased smile curve his lips. His grinning affability was her undoing. Tension flooded her limbs. She prepared to bolt.

Michael's arm settled heavily onto her shoulders, pinning her to his side. "Easy, lass," he whispered, his gaze never leaving Lord Connock's face. His eyes looked like blue-gray bruises. " 'Tis truly stupendous," he said, his tone conversational. "I don't think I'll ever forget this moment."

The older man beamed. "Ah, *Drosera*, my greatest success." He slanted a curious glance at Anne. "I don't think Mrs. Sherwood approves."

"Oh, she approves." Michael squeezed her around her shoulders. "Don't you, Anne?"

Anne looked into Connock's brown eyes, the dim light giving them a reddish sheen, and saw nothing . . . no compassion, no sorrow, no horror, nothing. For some reason, the observation terrified her even more than if she'd seen homicidal rage in his eyes.

She forced herself to smile. "Yes, of course, *Drosera* is quite lovely, how wonderful of you to make it for us . . ." She trailed off, aware she was babbling like an idiot.

Connock's smile disappeared.

Anne held her breath. Now, she thought, he would push her into *Drosera*.

His grip on her tightening, Michael suddenly began walking her toward the laboratory. "Why don't you show us some of the particulars of your research, Owain? We'd both love to discuss them with you."

"Yes, we would," she managed.

The nobleman shuffled behind them, his smile faltering. "Well, as I said, *Drosera* is my greatest success and my greatest failure. While I've managed to create plants that produce enormous vegetables, they aren't practical on a large scale. My attempts at crossbreeding and grafting vegetable plants onto carnivorous plants have proven futile. Indeed, I began thinking a few weeks ago that I was approaching the problem at the wrong angle."

Michael's glance slid to a coil of rope lying near the door and then settled on an eight-inch knife.

"At the wrong angle? What do you mean?" Anne asked. For the first time, she examined the laboratory behind him. Scalpels glittered with a silver sheen on their pegboard and rows and rows of apothecary jars lined the shelves. At first she'd thought the jars contained fruit, but on closer inspection, she saw hearts and lungs and long gray tubes of flesh . . .

Animal entrails. Preserved in some sort of viscous fluid.

Her stomach swirled with a fresh bout of nausea. Blackness fuzzed the edges of her vision. She fell heavily against Michael. He gripped her elbow tightly and shook her arm. The blackness receded, but the nausea did not. She pressed a hand against her mouth.

"Mrs. Sherwood seems a bit faint," the nobleman remarked, his lips tight.

Michael shook his head. "She's had a couple of shocks tonight. You know women, they can't stand the sight of blood or anything likewise. Don't fret, though. She'll be all right."

Connock's lips loosened into an apologetic smile. His gaze swept past the rows of entrails. " 'Tis a bit difficult to see these things at first, but I assure you, you too will become used to it once you've exposed yourself long enough."

"I'm all right," she weakly confirmed. She heard the thread of vacuous brutality beneath Connock's mellifluous tones and knotted her hands in her skirts.

"I keep entrails on hand because of their suppleness. They blend well with plant cells to form a hybrid serum of cells, each species contributing its best characteristics to the mix. 'Tis my hope that the serum I've been developing will allow me to pursue the other angle of research I mentioned."

Michael lifted one black brow. "What other angle?"

"Considering my failures with the plant world, it occurred to me to change my tactics and modify humans rather than plants, so they require less food and process different food sources. After all, plants draw nourishment from earth, water, and sun. With the proper equipment, humans could too." As he spoke, he took off his evening coat and began rolling up his shirt sleeve.

Michael grew very still. "Have you had any success modifying humans?

"Not yet."

Anne carefully searched Connock's face. His actions were so purposeful and his lips so tight that she knew something momentous was about to happen.

Sighing, Connock tied a rubber band around his upper arm. "Everything's been falling to pieces these last few weeks. I suppose it's *Drosera's* fault mostly, for escaping the glasshouse and alerting the villagers. Perhaps I should have listened to Griswold and burned it."

He shrugged and began to fumble around in his laboratory. "In any case, I knew weeks ago that my research would soon be found out and the public outcry would force me to stop, just as I had to stop a decade ago. So I began work on my most innovative serum."

While he talked, Michael edged Anne toward the door that led to the tool shed. Evidently he too felt the tension building around them.

Connock pulled a rubber tube and a bag off the shelf and filled it with a thick greenish syrup. "The serum is a combination of the best features of several species, both plant and animal. Even *Drosera* has contributed."

Anne gasped and fought the urge to hunch over.

"Come now, Mrs. Sherwood," he said, narrowing his eyes. "Don't you see the beauty in my science? You're far too emotional. You've fallen prey to compassion, which invariably prevents scholarly advancement."

The nobleman attached a needle to a rubber tube which in turn connected to the bag filled with serum.

"Owain, don't," Michael said urgently. He took a step toward Connock. "You've just started working on this serum. You can't know what it will do—"

Connock slipped the needle into his vein. A trickle of blood raced down his arm and dripped onto the floor. "You're quite correct. I don't know what it will do, so stand back."

Without warning, Michael rushed forward and tried to rip the needle from Connock's arm. Connock anticipated the maneuver and shuffled behind the laboratory table, squeezing the bag all the while.

"It's done," the nobleman said.

Michael froze.

Serum rushed down the rubber tube and into Connock's vein.

His vein, flooded with serum, bulged beneath his skin and turned a faint green color.

For almost a minute, nothing happened. They all stared at one another. Then Connock groaned and began to quiver.

Michael took an uncertain step backward.

"By injecting the serum directly into my bloodstream," Connock informed them in a strangely falsetto voice, "I'm expediting the absorption of the serum. When this is over I'll emerge a glorious combination of plant and human. God approves, Michael, don't you worry. He put these ideas into my head because he wants me to help man evolve to a newer, better form—"

His trembling became too much for him to speak. Hands hooked into claws, he let out a high, keening moan. The veins on his hands and face bulged from his skin and took on a light green color. An odor like freshly scythed grass filled the laboratory.

Chill after chill racing through her limbs, Anne watched open-mouthed.

Connock squealed as the trembling degenerated into a convulsion. His eyes rolled up into his head, exposing only greenish-white orbs. Arms contorted, he thrashed about the laboratory, his veins pulsing and flowing with green fluid. A thin, clear serum tainted only slightly with green began to leak from his ears.

Anne pressed a hand against her throat. She wanted to close her eyes. The horrible fascination inside her kept them open.

His grip tight on her arm, Michael backed away until they both bumped into the door.

Moaning, the nobleman fell to the floor, his arms and legs flailing. At the last second Anne saw the lantern sitting on the flagstones near Connock's feet.

"Michael, the lantern—"

Connock kicked and the lantern went flying. Oil spilled on the floor. Flames licked along the oil, catching a coiled rope on fire. The rope was attached to a hoist above the laboratory table. Within seconds flames had climbed the rope and spread onto the table, near several flasks of unidentifiable fluid, many of them uncorked. A piece of charred rope fell onto a shelf of additional flasks and sponges.

Anne looked at those flasks, horror swelling inside

her. At least one or two had to contain flammable liquids. She watched as a pile of twigs atop the table caught fire with a hiss of despair, and she realized the whole glasshouse was going to blow.

Michael rushed forward and stomped on the fire. He tried to rip the rope away from the table, to no avail. The fire was too greedy and had spread too quickly. Breathing heavily, he crouched next to Lord Connock.

The nobleman's skin started swelling. His pants ripped at the thighs and buttons popped on his shirt. Beneath the big green veins, smaller purple veins crossed his body like a spider's web. Michael groaned, his jaw tight and eyes dark. He tried to lift Connock by the shoulders. "Owain. We have to leave."

Connock let out a gurgling noise. Green syrup leaked from the corner of his mouth. His eyelids fluttered. He continued to thrash, but his movements were growing slower, weaker.

Anne flung the door open and stepped into the tool shed. "Michael, come on, the laboratory's going to explode!"

A small pop sounded in the laboratory, then another, and another. The fire flared with each explosion. Stringy matter rained down on Connock. The apothecary jars were blowing up, their burning contents a noxious addition to the smoky air. Another wave of revulsion swept through her. She pulled the kerchief from her head and held it up to her nose, to block the smell.

"There's nothing you can do to save him," she cried. "Come on!"

Michael looked at her, despair written clearly in his face.

Connock's gibberish melted into a tortured scream.

He stiffened and arched his back. Flames started to lick at his clothes.

Michael stumbled away. He fell against the door jamb leading into the tool shed. Anne grabbed his arm and pulled him through. She paused to peer into the glasshouse one last time. Smoke created an acrid haze that enfolded the plants. Most had wilted from the heat. She shifted her attention to *Drosera*. Its gray tentacles writhed and its roots kicked up mulch.

It was dying.

She could almost hear its wasplike scream in her head.

Choking, she put Michael's arm around her shoulders and together, they staggered outside. The first rays of dawn had already lit the eastern horizon, giving the mist that blanketed the land a pink glow. Moisture wafted against her skin, cooling her but doing little to ease her mind. The sizzling and crackling noises coming from the composting glasshouse had increased to a dull roar.

"Run," Michael ordered in a raspy voice. "We have to run before it explodes. The glass . . ."

Anne needed no more encouragement. Arm in arm they shambled across the lawn, toward Glendale Hall. Ahead, the two footmen normally positioned at the front door were running toward them, their eyes wide, their gazes fixed on the conflagration.

"Don't go any closer," Michael yelled. "It's going to explode—"

An inhuman scream split the night. Seconds later, a tremendous explosion rocked the glasshouse. Heat rolled across the lawn in a wave and glass shot outward, knocking Anne and Michael down. They fell into the dewy grass. Anne pressed her face against the blades and closed her eyes, her mind shocked into nothingness.

A few moments later she felt an arm slide beneath her knees and shoulders. Someone picked her up. She forced her eyes open and focused on Michael's concerned features.

"Are you all right, lass?"

She began to cry.

"There, there," he soothed. He began walking with quick steps toward Glendale Hall.

Something inside her twisted at the thought of going inside those gray stone walls. She would feel trapped, surrounded, eaten up if he brought her to her bedchamber. "Take me to your cottage," she pleaded. "I can't bear the thought of entering that place again."

He stopped, still holding her easily in his arms.

Someone approached him. She heard Cook's panicked tones. They conferred for a moment, then Michael began walking again, this time toward the woods. She risked a peek over Michael's shoulder and saw Carlyle, wild-eyed, yelling orders, running to and fro, commanding first a serving maid and then a footman, his visage gray with soot and dismay. A line of people, many still in their nightclothes, stood shoulder to shoulder and passed buckets along to the glasshouse. Tears streamed from their eyes as clouds of smoke rolled over them, their faces grotesque masks beneath the flickering orange flames.

She pressed her face against Michael's chest and listened to the strong beat of his heart. Memories of Lord Connock's final moments rushed into her mind. Whimpering, she pushed them away.

"Shh, Anne, it's done," Michael whispered, his

voice a soft caress against her ear. "The composting glasshouse is leveled. Even Connock's Eden has caught on fire. Looks like the villagers are going to have to grow their own vegetables again."

His words penetrated slowly, bringing with them fresh knowledge that they'd routed the corruption plaguing Glendale Hall. God help him, Lord Connock was dead and his *Drosera* surely burned.

A feeling of peace settled over her.

Minutes later, she was sleeping soundly.

Anne opened her eyes. She felt warm, cuddled, comfortable. Then the horror of the morning returned to her and she sat straight up in bed. A cry built in her throat. She looked wildly around the room.

A small window, a patched quilt, a sea chest—she was in Michael's cottage. Weak light splashed through the window, suggesting the sun had given way to twilight. Michael sprawled on a chair next to the bed. His dark hair gleamed, the ends curled up from a recent washing. Purplish circles under his eyes and little lines around his mouth spoke of exhaustion.

She relaxed. Love for him rushed through her. She remembered how he'd asked her to become a more permanent fixture in his cottage and wondered if the offer still stood. Now more than ever, she understood how much she wanted, no, *needed* to spend her life with him. If not for Michael reminding her how to feel, she might have ended up like Lord Connock . . . or worse.

Shaking her head, she forced the memory of the composting glasshouse from her mind. She knew it would always lurk in her subconscious. Someday, perhaps she'd figure out how to put that memory to good use.

Her sketch case and a trunk of her clothes crowded

a corner in his bedchamber. She climbed out of bed, noting that her skin was clean and she wore a fresh nightgown, and opened her sketch case. Her fingers trembling, she pulled out the sketchbook and began to turn the pages.

First she paged through some illustrations she had completed at Kew Gardens. The scholar in her admitted they were very good—full of detail and anatomically correct. The arrangement of the specimens on the page and the cross-sections and close-ups of their reproductive cycles were not only effective but pleasing to the eye.

Still, the illustrations were missing something.

She kept turning until she found pictures of the golden sapling. They, too, had the mark of a talented illustrator, but as she went along, she saw that they'd begun to lose some of that anatomical detail in favor of change she could scarce define. She only knew that the later illustrations evoked something in her. The sapling looked vulnerable, and the mushroom dangerous.

She continued to leaf through the sketchbook. A smile forming on her lips, she found the pages she'd been looking for, the ones of Michael, the pictures of the fairies, the landscapes that had touched her in a special way. Michael, she thought, had shown her a new form of thinking, one full of passion and spirit. For the first time in her life she was drawing with harmony of mind and heart and she knew these were the best pictures she had ever done. These were the illustrations that truly made her proud. These would bring her recognition, although in some corner of her soul, she realized she no longer really needed recognition. Michael had given her the acceptance she'd craved since she'd been a child.

She closed the sketchbook and slipped it back into her sketch case. Joy welling inside her, she moved to Michael's side and touched his arm. "Michael, wake up at least enough to join me on the bed."

He opened one bleary eye. When he saw her, he opened both eyes, sat up, and studied her closely. "Are you all right, lass?"

Touched that he would forsake his own rest to watch over her while she slept, she climbed back onto the bed and patted the mattress beside her. "Whatever are you doing on that chair? You belong here."

A slow grin spread across his face. "I was hoping you'd say that." He hoisted himself out of the chair and sprawled on the mattress next to her.

Snuggling against him, she sighed. "I see you've had my things brought down from Glendale Hall."

A footman delivered them an hour or so ago."

"What of Lord Connock?"

"Several glasshouses burned entirely, including the composting glasshouse and Lord Connock's Eden." His voice deepened and became more hesitant. "Carlyle and several men from the village couldn't find Lord Connock's body. 'Tis thought it burned to embers. They're holding a service for him later tomorrow."

"Whenever I think about him, I feel sick inside."

He put his arms around her and pulled her tighter against his body. "We aren't ready to talk about him, lass. Let's save it for later, after time has blunted the memory a bit."

"What will happen to Glendale Hall?"

"I suppose it'll fall into Parliament's hands, as Connock has no relatives to place a claim on his inheritance. I've had Carlyle send letters to the Royal Botanic Society and Connock's various scholarly associates, informing them of his death. You'll want to write your cousin at Kew Gardens, of course."

A warm glow stirred inside her, banishing the shadows. "Immediately," she confirmed.

He fixed his gaze on the ceiling. "I've taken the liberty of asking Carlyle to send a carriage for you in the morning. I'll ride with you as far as Dublin and make sure you're able to book passage to Liverpool. I'll miss you, Anne."

"But I'm not going to Liverpool," she informed him, sitting up on one elbow.

He turned to study her carefully. "Oh? Where are you going, then?"

"To Connaught."

"Connaught?" A spark brightened his gaze.

"I've heard it's a place northwest of here, the prettiest little place in all of Ireland, with scarlet fuchsia growing along the coast and mountains whose green peaks nudge the clouds into a soft, misty rain. There's a farm there that I'm trying to find. Would you care to join me?"

He grasped her arms and in one elated movement rolled on top of her. Supporting himself above her, he stared deeply into her eyes. His brow furrowed, as though he couldn't believe what he saw.

A little grin curled her lips. "Is something wrong?"

"I thought you were going to write your cousin, Sir Richard," he breathed.

"I am. I'm going to invite him to our wedding."

Without warning, he planted a hot, exuberant kiss on her lips, then drew back again, brow still furrowed. "But what about your illustrations? And your desire to gain scholarly recognition?"

"Shh, laddie," she murmured, affecting an Irish accent and nearly bubbling over with laughter at the sound of it. "We'll talk about that later. Haven't we more important business to discuss?"

His brow smoothed out and he planted another hot, exuberant kiss on her lips, but this time, he didn't pull away . . . not for a long, long time.

POCKET BOOKS
PROUDLY PRESENTS

Daughter of Destiny

TRACY FOBES

Coming soon in paperback
from Sonnet Books

The following is a preview of
Daughter of Destiny. . . .

WITHOUT FURTHER TALK, Brock took Georgiana's arm and led her toward the door. Behind them, the orchestral ensemble struck up a merry tune, and four couples positioned themselves on the dance floor. Shouts of encouragement and laughter urged them onward.

Georgiana's spirits fell in direct proportion to the laughter. She thought she had never felt more miserable.

Rees intersected their path just as they reached the vestibule. Lips pinched, his skin pale, the younger man stuttered out a greeting to Brock, then fell silent.

Brock studied him with one eyebrow raised. "Well, Rees, it seems you've gotten my wife into a fine kettle of fish this evening. I'll admit I'm wondering where else you've taken her. A whorehouse, perhaps?"

Two spots of color formed high in Rees's cheeks. "My apologies, Brock." He turned a swift, tortured glance on Georgiana. "You must not blame Georgie. It was my idea entirely—"

"Pshaw! I forced Rees to take me here." Georgiana turned to the blond man. "Rees, I know your sense of chivalry demands that you accept blame for our escapades, but I won't allow you to."

Brock's other eyebrow rose to join the first, forming a look of mild scorn. "I'll receive you in the morning, Rees, and we'll discuss, ah, your role in all of this."

The younger man swallowed. "It would be my pleasure."

"Until tomorrow, then." Brock turned away and placed Georgiana's cloak around her shoulders. "I believe you ought to wear this," he said, assessing her costume, "despite the temperature. I don't want to start a riot."

Georgiana allowed her lashes to flutter downward so Brock wouldn't see the sudden shame that filled her eyes. Silently they walked outside and waited for a footman to bring Brock's gig around. When it arrived, Brock handed her in none too gently. He drove very fast, and as Palmer House was situated on Brook Street, their ride home was distressingly short. Throughout the ride Georgiana shivered, wondering what Brock had meant when he'd said he would make her his mistress. Did he actually think she would allow him in her bedchamber?

She hated Brock. She hated what he'd done to her. He'd pretended to love her, taken her away from her family and friends, and then ignored her once he'd gotten what he wanted. She wouldn't make love to him and wouldn't give him an heir. Theirs was a marriage in name only. She lifted her chin, aware that a queer warmth was spreading slowly through her limbs.

They pulled up in front of Palmer House. A footman stationed near the door hurried down the steps to assist them out of the carriage. Georgiana refused the footman's hand, climbing down with no one's assistance and starting toward the triumphal-arched doorway leading into Palmer House.

The house had always intimidated her. Built by William Kent in the previous century, it was solid and massive, heavily festooned with cornices and friezes, every room an individual work of art. Tonight it felt like a prison, too. She imagined she would disappear into its ornate interior, never to emerge.

"Inside, Georgiana," Brock muttered.

Abruptly she realized she'd been lingering on the porch. Drawing her cloak tightly around her body, she slipped past the footman who held the door open for her, hurried through the foyer, and made for the staircase. Within minutes she had navigated the stairs and second floor to her bedchamber. She closed the door behind her and locked it. Nearly crying with relief, she fell onto her bed.

Her bedchamber was her one refuge from her husband and Society. She'd exchanged her cumbersome mahogany bureaus and massive four-poster bed for delicate satinwood pieces decorated with floral marquetry and a gilt tester bed. Lace rather than velvet hung from the tester, and sprigged wallpaper replaced the paneling on the walls. She dragged an ivory satin counterpane around her body and pressed her face into a pillow.

Her cheeks felt so hot she wanted to splash water on them. Tension formed a knot in her stomach as she waited for her husband to knock. What would she tell him? Would he go away if she pleaded a headache? Not likely.

A soft rap on the door made her jump. "Who is it?"

"Nellie, ma'am."

"Nellie." She breathed the name out as if it were a benediction. "One moment. I'll unlock the door."

She walked to the door and opened it for her lady's maid, who entered with a basin of steaming water.

"I thought you'd like to freshen up." Her soft blond hair stuffed into a cap, Nellie began to prepare Georgiana's evening toilette. She poured water into the basin on the washstand, laid out a towel, spread a nightgown on the bed, and then moved behind Georgiana to unbutton her Italian peasant costume. "Did you enjoy your evening, ma'am?"

Georgiana watched Nellie's ministrations, a feeling of calm settling over her at their familiarity. "Not particularly. I'm afraid Watier's Club isn't for me."

Nellie pursed her lips. "I didn't think it would be. God willing the master will never find out."

"He already knows," Georgiana admitted. "I don't know who told him."

"It wasn't me," Nellie said, her eyes wide. "Good Lord, ma'am, what are you going to do now?"

"That will be all, Nellie," a deep male voice announced from behind her.

Georgiana spun around.

Brock stood in the doorway, his body filling the opening.

"Stay, Nellie," Georgiana demanded, realizing she'd forgotten to turn the key behind the lady's maid.

Nellie looked from her to Brock and back to her again. Her shoulders drooped. Giving her a look that pleaded for understanding, the lady's maid slipped out of the room and closed the door behind her.

Georgiana threw her shoulders back, lifted her chin, and assessed the enemy. He still wore his jacket and trousers, but he'd loosened his cravat, giving him a rakish air. His dark brown hair looked mussed, as if he'd run a hand through it several times. Still, it was his eyes that captured her attention, brown eyes that smoldered with fury and something else, something that made her heart race in her chest and her breathing quicken with anticipation.

Damn her body's wayward response to him! It had always been like this, from the first moment they'd met. She remembered an afternoon almost two years ago. They'd been walking through the forest, their horses beside them. Without warning, he'd kissed her with shocking fervor. Her legs had weakened and the oddest feeling had grown in her, a desire to possess and be possessed, something she had never known before.

And yet, after their marriage, he'd changed. He became distracted, and when he looked at her, sadness glittered in his eyes, and guilt, too. He'd visited her bedchamber only twice before she'd found out the truth behind his courtship, and then she'd forbidden him to enter it again.

After that moment, loneliness had become the order of the day. Even the chance kiss she'd exchanged with some laughing nobleman, because the night had been fine and the party exciting, hadn't eased the emptiness in her. Brock had ruined her life, and she had set out to ruin his.

"What possessed you to attend Watier's Club this evening?" he asked while advancing into the room. "Were you addled, or simply drunk?"

"Neither, my lord. I was seeking entertainment."

"Ah, we come so quickly to the crux of the matter. What sort of entertainment were you seeking, Georgiana?" He moved behind her and brushed his fingers across her neck, making her jump.

She took a step away from him. "You prefer to spend your days at Palmer House mired in ledger books, and your nights rehashing old times with your cronies. I desire a livelier existence. Watier's Club proved an unusual diversion, nothing more."

His arm went around her and drew her back to him. He touched the back of her neck again. This time his fingers played with the gold chain around her neck. Her glass pendant fluttered between her breasts. "Are you certain you didn't attend for another reason?"

She swallowed. "I have nothing to hide."

Fingers tightening around the gold chain, he leaned in close until his breath brushed across her skin. "Who gave you this necklace? Your lover?"

Lips pressed together, Georgiana said nothing.

He grasped the chain in both hands, broke it, and threw it in the corner. The pendant bounced against the wooden floor with a muted crack. Then he spun her around to face him. His nostrils flared and his lips thinned. "You will accept presents from no one but me."

"How dare you?" she choked out. "How dare you tell me what I may and may not do? You aren't a husband to me. You're not even a friend. You have no right."

"I have every right," he informed her, his voice tight. "When I married you, I promised your dear father I would take care of you. You're my problem now, Georgiana, and as a result, I must deal with your antics."

"You're making more of this than necessary. My attendance there was marked by no one. Rees and Neddy remained by my side the entire time. No harm was done—"

"Your attendance was marked by *everyone*. Who could fail to identify you, surrounded as you were by Rees and Neddy, your constant companions?"

She shrugged. "Perhaps others guessed my name. What of it? I'm an Incomparable, remember. I have a reputation to uphold."

Brock snorted. "Are you so bored with life that you must act in such an outrageous manner? God's blood, woman, you were dressed as a whore and prancing around in a room full of demi-reps."

He took in a deep breath and let it out slowly. "For

two years now I've looked the other way. I've paid your debts and indulged your every whim because I felt guilty for misrepresenting my feelings when we married. But damnit, Georgiana, I thought you understood. Men and women don't marry for love, they marry for convenience."

"I may have loved you once," she interjected, her voice bitter, "but I assure you, I love you no more. Don't flatter yourself otherwise."

He nodded, then faced her squarely. "Whatever the case, I simply cannot tolerate any more scandalous behavior on your part. If I must punish you into acquiescence, then so be it."

"I dare you to punish me," she hissed, her eyes narrowed. "What will you do—lock me in my room, like some feudal lord?"

A toe-curling grin suddenly curled his lips, setting her hackles up even higher. "I had something a bit more . . . inventive in mind."

"I promise you, if you lock me in, I'll need only send a few missives to my friends explaining the situation, and you'll find your good name more blackened than I could ever make it."

"More likely I'd receive a standing ovation for finally taking my wayward wife in hand. You've gone too far this time, Georgiana. I'm afraid I'm going to have to curtail your activities with Rees and Neddy."

"The hell you will."

He touched her hair, twining one of her curls around his finger. "You are beautiful when you're defiant."

"Get out," she demanded, pulling her hair from his grasp. "Get out before I scream the bloody house down."

He slipped his hand into her bodice and yanked on the delicate fabric, ripping it apart at the seams, exposing her breasts to his hot gaze. Her nipples immediately contracted.

She backed away, her arms crossed over her breasts, concealing them. "Brock, I'm warning you."

"A mouth as luscious as yours shouldn't be issuing threats," he purred, closing the distance between them. "It's been two years since we've made love. Two years is a long time, and I'm of a mind to change things between us."

"I'm *not* of a mind. I don't want to change things between us." Memories of her anguish when she'd first learned Brock had married her for her monetary holdings, not love, surfaced in her mind. Suddenly she wanted to hurt him as badly as he'd hurt her. "I've already accepted another man as a lover. It's his touch that I desire."

His face became rigid. He grabbed her shoulders and shook her slightly. "Who is he? Tell me, damnit."

"And if I tell you, what will you do then? Challenge my lover to a duel? I thought you, of all people, would understand that our marriage is one of convenience only. I received a title, and you gained government securities, and now we must seek our happiness elsewhere."

"You're *my* wife," he snarled.

"In name only."

"You leave me no choice. You are no longer allowed out of this house without me."

"If you dislike me so, Brock, why don't you simply divorce me?" she cried.

His eyes darkened and his mouth twisted. "No."

Something inside her broke, some invisible dam that had kept her rage from boiling over. Her vision grew red and she flew at him, fingers hooked into claws, determined to rake his eyes from his head, to pull that lying tongue from his mouth. A sound rent the bedchamber, and dimly she realized it was her own shriek of rage.

He clapped a hand over her mouth, and together they fell onto the ivory counterpane covering her tester bed. Eyebrows drawn low, eyes dark, he removed his hand and brushed her hair back from her forehead. "Shh, Georgiana—"

"Bastard!" She angled her knee toward his groin and connected with his thigh instead, drawing a gasp from him. Even so, he held her tightly, his arms around her like bands of iron, his weight pinning her down as she twisted against him, hating him, wanting him dead. Her vision narrowed and became a single point of white light, and she thought wildly she was about to swoon. For the first time in her life, she was going to faint, and Brock was at the root of it.

Ornery pride kept the darkness at bay.

He began whispering in her ear, telling her he was sorry, admitting that the fault was mostly his, that he shouldn't have misled her and longed to make it up to her. His endearments and apologies meant little at first but eventually penetrated her consciousness. Inside, she rejected every word he said. Even so, she calmed a bit, and grew tired from struggling against him, for she'd had just about as much effect on him as if she'd tried to level a tree trunk with her fists.

At last she grew quiescent. Sensations began to impinge on her awareness. She could feel the hard length of him pressed against her, the tenderness of his hands as they stroked her hair, the strong beat of his heart beneath her ear. How long had she wished him to notice her? How many times had she awoken from a dream of lying in his arms? She was so tired of fighting. She hadn't anything left in her, no strength, no willpower, no harsh words, nothing. He'd taken her pride and anger away from her and left a void only he could fill.

Lids at half-mast, he kissed her forehead. "By God, Georgiana, I've wanted you for so long. Why do I always act the fool around you? In your company, pompous words fly out of my mouth and my anger swells at your slightest provocation. When I look in the mirror I think, 'Brock, you're ten years older than your wife; she needs a younger man, a carefree companion who hasn't the responsibilities that weigh on your shoulders.' And then I want to put my fist through the wall. Why do I feel this way? Why?"

She shrugged. She had no answer for him. She didn't want to think about the troubles between them. The bed was soft beneath her, the counterpane fluffing up around their bodies, but she didn't notice, so intent was she on that look in his eyes, that sleepy look of concealed desire. Perhaps he thought if he allowed her to see the full force of his desire he would frighten her. But she wasn't frightened. God knew she wanted the same thing, regardless of the way she'd cursed him mere moments before . . .

Look for
Daughter of Destiny
**Wherever Books
Are Sold
Coming Soon
in Paperback from
Sonnet Books**

Return to
a time of romance...

SONNET
BOOKS

Where today's

hottest romance authors

bring you vibrant

and vivid love stories

with a dash of history.

PUBLISHED BY POCKET BOOKS